Circles in Stone

Search for the Jewel of Power

D C Faber

Circles in Stone

Cover design by DC Faber

This book is a work of fiction. Names, characters, places, and incidents either are the product of the author's imagination or are used fictitiously.

This book is written in American English.

Website: dcfaberwrites.com

Facebook: https://www.facebook.com/Dragon7171

ISBN 978-1-7392790-0-4

Circles in Stone

Contents

Circles in Stone

Circles in Stone

Chapter 1

The Break In

The river Thames running through the heart of London was calm tonight. There was a chill in the air but there was also lots of energy. It was a very special night in London. Thousands of people lined the river in anticipation of the show to come. It was, after all, New Year's Eve, and the expected fireworks were, as usual, looked forward to with great anticipation. Like any great event, police and other security were out all around the city, to keep the peace and ensure the safety of all.

The section of river that runs in front of the Tower of London is a very poor place to watch the fireworks so the crowds, as would be expected, are very thin there.

The Tower of London, this night, looked as grand as always with floodlights showing off its gleaming white facade.

The Tower dates to just after the Norman invasion in 1066. Built as a castle, in the motte and bailey style of the Normans, as a palace for Willian the Conqueror. It remained a royal palace for many centuries until the Tudor period. The tower complex has had many uses over the ages, including a prison, an armory, and even a royal mint. Today it is very much a royal museum. Along with the many royal armory displays, it is also where the Royal Crown Jewels are kept. Those jewels represent the Monarchy and the very heart of England and the UK.

King Henry VIII established standard guards to protect the tower. They are known as the Yeoman Warders. Today they are commonly called the Beefeaters and still, guard the tower as they have done since Henry's time. They are overseen by the Resident Governor, who is one charge of everything that takes place in and around the Tower complex.

Among the many rooms within the tower complex, there is a room that is unseen by the public. Updated with the most modern technology, this is a room filled with computers and monitors that display and control the view from the many CCTV cameras located all around the tower grounds, including those that watch the Crown Jewels located in the Jewel House. Of course, the Jewels are always locked inside the huge vault that keeps them safe at this time of night.

As usual, several security officers and the site security manager were in this room and watching those monitors. They were all keeping a watchful eye for anything that might be out of order.

Joining them in the room tonight were two men that were not part of the regular crew. There were there under the direction of Scotland Yard, claiming to be armed with information that something unusual might happen on this very night that might put the Jewels at risk. What that risk was they would not disclose, which did not please the security manager. He did not like it when Scotland Yard got involved in Tower security affairs.

One of these men was Jason Elliot, a senior officer in Scotland Yard's anti-domestic terrorism division. A medium-built man, in his mid-thirties with brown hair and blue eyes behind his wire-frame glasses. He was never seen without a suit or being clean-shaven, and always looked professional. He had worked his way up through the ranks within the Yard. A dedicated person to whatever task that lay before him. He was a person with huge aspirations and an ego to match.

The other man was Oliver Calvin. A younger man in his mid-twenties. He was blond with a mustache to match. Full of ambition too and wanting to make a name for himself, he was Jason's faithful partner.

Circles in Stone

What was unknown to the others there was that these two men were both members of a secret order known as the Order of Divine Right or ODR, with male members, numbering around 400, located throughout the country. Many of those members were in well-placed positions, mostly in security services, police forces, and a few in city and town councils. The organization is a right-wing protestant order dating from the time of King James the First. The primary goal of this order was to end the monarchy and put the control of the government in hands of Puritan religious leaders. Among other things, they also wanted to destroy the pope and all things catholic and end all pagan beliefs and practices of every kind, first in England, then the UK, and eventually the whole world.

All members could be identified by the plain gold band ring on their right forefinger and a tattoo of a lion holding a cross on their left forearm. This was the main way they recognized each other.

As the midnight hour approached, Jason told everyone in the room to remain vigilant. One of the security officers looked at Jason and asked.

"What are we looking for sir?"

"I can't really say, but I am sure you will know it when you see it," he said. "Just keep a sharp eye out."

Then, shortly before midnight, a figure appeared along the waterfront just in front of the middle drawbridge. It appeared on the monitor to be a tall figure of about six feet or more, dressed all in dark clothes with a hood over their head that hid their face, and a cloak streaming from their shoulders. He or she was wearing knee-high black boots and long black gloves with silver buckle straps. Sporting a wide

3

belt embedded with shiny studs, the figure seemed to wear a pair of straps across their chest which formed an X shape, but they didn't appear to have anything on them.

Any other time of the year this person would have looked completely out of place, but tonight, not so much, as a lot of people dress in all manner of different fashions for New Year's Eve.

With CCTV cameras covering all areas of the tower, inside and out, Oliver was the first to spot him.

"Look there," he said to Jason. "What or who is that?"

"Could be just someone from a party trying to get a look at the fireworks," explained one of the officers.

"No, I don't think so," Jason answered as he looked closely at the screen.

"Look, whoever it is, they are not looking towards the river. They are looking straight at the tower gate. What time is it?" he asked as he turned to look at the clock.

"Five minutes to 12," Oliver answered.

"Keep your eyes on them," Jason ordered. "I believe this is what we have been looking for. I want all the cameras lined up between whoever that is and the Jewel house. This is our person; I am sure of it."

"Why the Jewel house," asked the security manager.

"Because the information I have says that is going to be the target," answered Jason.

"What do you think they're going to do?" asked Oliver, "One person can't just walk up, open the gates, and stroll in."

Jason looked at Oliver as if he wanted to slap him.

"Just keep a watch and make sure it's all recorded. Does everyone understand!?" He shouted so that everyone in the room could hear.

Almost with one voice came the reply. "Yes sir!"

All eyes were fixed on this dark character just outside the walls. Whoever it was just stood still facing the gate.

The minutes ticked away until there were only seconds left before midnight. The tension was so thick you could cut it with a knife. Both, because of the figure still outside the gate and because the New Year was about to begin.

Circles in Stone

The countdown began five, 4, 3, 2, 1, Big Ben let out its first deep bong instantly the first fireworks began to explode from the rafts on the river, along with the yelling coming from the crowds all along the banks and even inside the Tower complex itself.

At the very moment that the bell of Big Ben struck its first note and the first fireworks exploded, the figure outside moved toward the gate. Close enough to the CVTV now, that you could see it was a man with a beard.

When he got to the gate, he reached behind his cloak and pulled out what looked like two daggers. Stopping at the gate he then began swirling the daggers in the air as if he were cutting it. Suddenly, from the dagger tips, a trail of red light could be seen that landed on the gates that then spontaneously opened in front of him.

Everyone in the security room let drew in a gasp as alarms began going off.

The man ran forward through to the second gate and did the same. Once that gate was opened, he ran across the central yard alongside the central tower and up the stairs to the level in front of the Jewel House. Stopping in front of the Jewel house he again swirled his daggers and sent another flash of red light, that looked something like lightning, flying out from their tips. With that, the doors of the Jewel house flew open in front of him. Inside the same was repeated at every door, with them flying open at the command of his daggers. Before anyone knew what they were seeing, he was standing in front of the Jewel House safe that holds the Crown Jewels.

This time, swirling the daggers more intensity than before, a very blinding flash of red lightning was hurled at the safe door striking it with a deafening explosive clash as the entire safe door was encircled. The dial turned, the lights flickered and the safe door flew open. By now, more alarms were going off all over the place.

Everyone in the security room was talking to each other in a frantic conversation about who they should call or what they should do.

Meanwhile, Jason kept his eyes fixed on the monitors. Without looking away shouted,

"Keep your eyes on the crown jewels, especially the scepter!"

"He's after the diamond," shouted one of the officers.

Circles in Stone

They all froze watching the monitor. The figure, which was in plain view now, approached the crown jewels. Everyone expected him to break the bulletproof glass and grab the jewels. But instead, he simply looked at them and then scanned the room. He was acting as if he was looking for something. He did not act at all as a thief would. As he approached, a point closer to where the scepter was, something strange appeared on the monitors. Everyone could see that one of the jewels on the scepter was beginning to glow brightly.

"Is he using a laser?" the manager asked.

"No, Jason answered, "The scepter is responding to his presence."

"Responding to his presence?" Oliver asked surprised.

"Yes," replied Jason. It will be interesting to see which Jewel it is that is responding."

One would expect it to have perhaps been the diamond. But it appeared to be the crystal amethyst located just above the great diamond. As they watched, it grew brighter and brighter until you could no longer hardly see the scepter or anything else in the safe.

***

At that very moment, over 7000 miles away on an island in the middle of the Pacific Ocean, a 30-year-old 6 ft tall, 170 lb. man with blue eyes, and long brown hair, was relaxing on a chair in front of his house. He was making plans for the New Year's celebration he would be attending some 10 hours later.

Suddenly he felt a strange power engulf his whole body. It raised him to his feet. His hands extended themselves in front of him. A ball of blue fire formed in each of his hands. His hands moved close together forming a single ball of blue-white fire. Suddenly his hands turned over and the ball of fire shot straight into the earth disappearing and slamming him backward onto the ground. Stunned, he stood back up shaking himself back into some clarity. Things like this had happened to me before, he thought, but never on this scale or with such force. He knew something had just taken place someplace out of his reach or control. He was just going to have to find out what. He knew that the universe had shifted. How much he did not know.

***

Circles in Stone

Back at the Tower in London, the would-be thief rounded the corner closest to the scepter; the amethyst jewel in the scepter suddenly shot a ball of blue light in a straight line toward him. He was lifted into the air where he floated for a second and then, in a flash, he was mysteriously gone. The safe door could be heard slamming shut as well as other doors and gates all the way back to the place where he had entered the Tower. Then for a moment, everything went dark, including the lights in the whole Tower complex. The monitors all went dark as well.

After what seemed like a lifetime, but in reality, was only seconds everything came back on.

Fear and awe struck all those that watched what just happened, except for Jason. He had resumed looking at monitors. He had shifted his attention back to the one with the view just outside the gate where the man first appeared.

"Look there," he said, pointing to a place on the monitor. "There he is."

Sure enough, there was the intruder sprawled against the wall by the river. They watched as he stood up and ran in the direction of Tower Bridge.

"He's still alive," Oliver shouted. "And he is getting away."

"Yes," said Jason "And you won't ever catch him so there is no use trying."

The site security manager looked sternly at Jason.

"What the hell just happened and what the hell was that?" he asked.

"I can't tell you," Jason said. "What you just saw, as far as you and your men are concerned did not happen. You and all your men are not to speak about this to anyone outside this room. It is a matter of national security."

"What if he comes back?" he asked Jason in return.

"He won't," snapped Jason.

"What makes you so sure?"

"Because," replied Jason, "What he was after was not there. He was not interested in the Jewels."

"What was he after then?"

"I can't tell you that either," Jason said, "I can't tell you, not because I don't know but because it is classified. So, I need to make myself clear.

No one talks about what you saw or what you think you saw. I also want all the tapes of what happened, no copies. Got it? Get us those tapes and Oliver and I will be out of your hair for good."

The security manager objected but got the tapes and handed them over to Jason, who promptly put them in his briefcase and locked it. As Jason and Oliver left the room, Jason turned back and with a smile spoke.

"A Happy New Year to everyone."

By now, police had surrounded the whole tower complex. Jason, with all the tapes in his possession, along with Oliver, the tower constable, the chief security officer, and the site security manager were walking to meet the police at the main entrance. Jason stopped. Looked at all of them and repeated.

"Remember, what happened here stays here. I don't care what you tell them but don't say anything about what you saw here."

With disappointed faces, they all nodded.

The chief of police met them as they all came out.

"What is going on?" she asked the tower constable.

He looked at Jason then back at her and replied,

"There has been a major computer malfunction of our security systems. Do not worry; the Jewels and everything else are safe and the Tower is secure. We will sort it out. But thanks for showing up so quickly."

"Well, that is a relief; I suppose," she replied. "What a way to start the New Year."

Jason looked at the constable with a grin and gave thumbs up with his hand low to his side. With that Jason and Oliver walked away.

Music and singing came from all around as Jason and Oliver walked to the car park located across from the Tower. The flashing lights of the police cars, which were now slowly going out, seemed to add a festive look to the whole scene.

As they walked, Oliver put his hand on Jason's shoulder to stop his stride. With a concerned look on his face, he asks Jason,

"Well, you going to tell me what the hell went on back there?"

"You'll know soon enough," answered Jason. "Meanwhile this remains between you me and other senior members of the order. This is

Order business now. This must not be reported to anyone outside the Order. If anyone at Scotland Yard should ask you what happened tonight you must tell them nothing. You are to make your reports show the same. That the lead we received was a dead end."

"I thought this was a national security issue?" asked Oliver concerned.

"ODR business is always a matter of national security," Jason answered. "The sooner you understand that the sooner you'll move up."

"Yes sir!

"I will be calling an Order meeting in a week for all the senior members to deal with this." Jason continued. "I would like you to make the arrangements for that meeting in the usual place. Make sure you include a computer and screen for these tapes to be shown on. Can you handle that?"

"Sure, I can," Oliver assured him.

"Good then," said Jason. "I will let you know when it is to be held and see you there. But before you go why don't you take a day off and celebrate the New Year? I can assure you it's going to be an interesting one."

"Ok sir," Oliver said. "And a Happy New Year to you sir."

"To you too," Jason shouted back as they walked to their separate cars.

Chapter 2
The Meeting

Edinburgh has been a place filled with history for many people over a long period. At the center of this great city is the Castle, with its grand approach up the giant rock that protrudes above the city like a God-made obelisk reaching to the heavens. Battles were once fought here. For some, it is where they are still being fought. The seat of power for many in the past, and is the seat of power for many still. Such is the case for the Order of Divine Right. It is at this castle where they always held their most important meeting.

***

A group of men began to gather on the Plaza in front of the castle gatehouse, known as the Esplanade.

Among this group, were, of course, Jason Elliott and Oliver Calvin; the two men that were at the Tower of London on New Year's Eve. Also, there was Charles Stewart, the leader of the Order. An average-built man with neatly groomed brown hair, and hazel eyes. Not an imposing figure at 5'6", but his position in the ranks of Scotland Yard gave him the leadership needed. He had been elected twice to that position by the other members.

The others include John Coke, the group's information specialist, Edward Hampden, David Green, Allen Carter, Peter Walker, Scott Ward, James Wilson, Lee Bennett, and a newcomer to the leadership group, Lewis Hall, who was the new head of security. These men made up the 12 leaders of the Order of Divine Right. All major decisions were passed to these men before any action could be taken. But all decisions would finally fall to Charles Stewart. Whatever he decided, even if it went against the rest, would be final, without question.

As they were all shaking hands and chatting, and it was clear that everyone was present Charles spoke up.

"Gentlemen, it's good to see you all here, I do believe lunch awaits us inside. Shall we proceed?"

All of them proceeded to the gatehouse and across a small bridge guarded by two stone medieval knights.

Once through the gate, they went around the corner where the gatehouse manager met them.

"This way gentleman," he said with his hand extended out to guide them.

The manager led them through a door and up some stairs to a room on one end of the gatehouse. It was not a grand hall but it was grand enough, with its high arched ceiling and walls paneled in fine wood. At one end was a large cut stone fireplace with a coat of arms above it. The tables were arranged in a square shape with three seats on each side all facing inward. In the center on a small table was a large but old version of the King James Bible. In one corner of the room next to the fireplace in front of a window, Oliver had placed a large screen and a stand on which sat a computer.

Upon entering the room, Lewis Hall opened his case and pulled out some electronic gear. Going around the room he began scanning for eves dropping devices that might be hidden. He had been recommended for this leadership group because of his devotion to the cause and his expert knowledge of espionage and security. Giving the all-clear, they all took a seat labeled with their names.

Charles was seated in front of the fireplace; Jason was on his right and Oliver was on his left. Looking around and seeing how everything had been arranged so well, Jason leaned back and touched Oliver's shoulder.

"Well done, Oliver," he said. "Well done," he repeated and gave him a wink.

After a three-course meal, which included Mackerel as the main course, they all sat about chatting as the service staff cleared the lunch plates leaving behind only glasses and bottles of champagne. Once the staff had left Lewis got up looked out the doors and closed and secured them. Looking at Charles, he gave him a nod.

"Ok gentlemen," Charles called out. "It's time to get down to business. Before we begin let us have a moment of silence and raise a toast to our long-ago patron that was born right here in this castle."

Raising his glass Charles said in a loud voice,

"To King James!"

"To King James!" they all said in one accord.

A moment of silence followed.

With them all seated, they looked at Charles.

He stood up and speaking with a firm clear voice said, "Once again God has shown us that his hand is with us. As the great book before us says, God works in mysterious ways. What you are about to hear is one of those ways. This meeting is called because of new and profound information that has come to our attention by His grace. Information that could, and I am sure, will profoundly change our course as an Order. To present this information I now turn this meeting over to Jason Elliott, whom you all know."

Extending his hand toward Jason, he sat down. Jason stood up. Oliver also got up and went to the stand to operate the computer. A light came on the screen.

"Gentlemen I want you to watch this video," Jason began. "This is footage captured on New Year's Eve at midnight at the Tower of London where myself and Oliver Calvin were present at the time. Please watch it closely, we will play it twice, and then I will explain what we believe we are seeing."

Looking at Oliver, Jason gave a nod. The lights darkened and Oliver played the footage. As it finished there was silence, and then a bit of a murmur. Oliver played it again. When it ended and the lights came up Oliver sat down. Everyone had stunned looks on their faces. After a moment of silence, John Coke spoke up.

"Mind telling us what the hell that was?"

"That gentleman was pure unadulterated sorcery magic," Jason explained. "The kind of which has not been seen in the open in a very long time. We suspected it was still out there but now we know for sure."

Oliver, whose attention was peaked to the bursting point, asked, "Do you have any idea who he is?"

"Yes, we do," Charles said looking at everyone around the room who were now looking at each other.

"Well?" said Oliver. "Not to be rude, would you enlighten us and tell us what all this has to do with us?"

Jason looked at Oliver then at the rest of the room and began.

"He calls himself Master Rhyfel. He is a member of a secret society named The House of Morgan. They are said to be direct descendants of Morgan La Fay. Half-sister of Arthur, rival, and nemesis of the wizard Merlin, and most importantly they claim that the throne of Arthur is there's by right and therefore the throne of Great Britain. We in Scotland Yard have watched this group for a long time. They are serious about who they are and what they believe. After what we saw on New Year's Eve, we know for sure they are who they claim to be."

"He was after the crown jewels then?" asked Lewis.

"No," said Jason, "Something else, something he didn't find." Jason looked through the papers in front of him on the table and pulled up an image.

"THIS!" he said as he pointed. "This is a computer-generated image of what we believe he was seeking.

It was an image of what looked like an amber orb containing a tooth of some kind.

"And, what is that supposed to be?" Oliver asked.

"This is called The Jewel of Power or the Jewel of Authority, depending on who you ask," said Jason. "An amber orb about four centimeters in diameter containing a real dragon's tooth enclosed in it. This orb is said to have once been in the pommel of the sword Excalibur. That, of course, was the sword that gave King Arthur the power and authority to rule. It is also believed to be the orb that gave the sword its power. It is said, by some sources, that the orb was removed from the pommel just before the sword was returned to the Lady of the Lake. The orb was then given to Merlin by Arthur just before he died to be held by Merlin and all his descendants until there is a need for it again. What has been kept secret is that Merlin had children. By whom it is not known. How many children he had is also not known. As you all know the legend says that one day Arthur will return when the time is needed. It is believed that this Jewel, and the power within it, through the dragon's tooth that represents the Pendragon line coming to rule through Arthur. This same jewel and the power from it, are believed to be what keeps the monarchy in place to this day. Without a monarchy, any future Arthur would have no place from which to rule from. Whoever holds this Jewel would hold the power of authority and the power to rule over at least Great Britain and who knows perhaps the world. This is what he was looking for."

Oliver ever pushing to know more asked, "What made him think it was there?"

"Information was leaked out that the Jewel had been found and was going to be displayed with the Crown Jewels after the New Year began," Jason answered.

"Who leaked this information?" Oliver asked.

Jason looked at Charles.

"We did," Charles said.

James Wilson spoke up.

"If you knew this guy and his society was out there, why did you set him up to this? If this kind of magic is known to exist and gets out, this could be dangerous to our cause. You already know that pagan beliefs are on the rise at an unprecedented rate. This would only add a lot of fuel to the fire that is already burning out of control."

"We needed him to confirm or put to rest something far more important," Charles, answered. "What you believe about the story is of no importance. You are all overlooking the most important part of the video to us. It is not who he is or what he was doing or can do. It was what was done to him! The royal scepter amethyst Jewel shot a beam of light and power that threw him completely out of the Tower once he got close to it. A secret legend says that the amethyst crystal in the scepter is the one that Merlin once had in his staff. We now know this must be true. This also makes the rest of the story true. The only thing that could have triggered that reaction you saw was a member of the family of Morgan La Fey. The only way this could happen is that there is, out there somewhere, a direct descendant of Merlin, and they hold and still possess the Jewel of Power. Remember, Arthur came into being because of Merlin's power, this means that if Arthur is to return it must be by the power of Merlin. No Merlin, no Arthur."

Jason broke in, "If we don't find and destroy this descendant and his line and recover the Jewel of Power, what we are trying to achieve will all end, and the old ways will return, the monarchy will continue and we and our order will be redundant. However, if we, the Order, can find and hold the Jewel we will be able to reach every goal we are sworn to. The power will be ours. I know this all may be hard to believe but the evidence you just saw proves the legends and the Jewel are real. There is no way a member of the House of Morgan would have risked exposing himself unless he also knew the Jewel was real."

"So, what's the plan?" asked Lewis.

"We must find out who this descendant of Merlin is and where he is," Jason replied. "We must use all our resources and our connections to do this without revealing what we're doing. There is just one problem.

As all of you know, there is another secret society out there. They call themselves the Society of the Green Man. We have always thought they were just a bunch of Knight Templar wannabes but, with this new revelation, we now know they are far more than that. They are sworn to protect the crown and country and put their lives on the line, not only to protect those but also the Merlin lineage. Up until now, we thought they were just a militant group that needed an excuse to exist. This group is old, how old we don't know, perhaps to Arthur himself. They are rich and well-armed. We're not even sure who the members are or how many of them there are or where they meet. They are masters at creating dead-ends and false trails. We also believe they have members inside MI 5. But most importantly, they must not under any circumstances know what we have found out!!"

Charles spoke up, "We must move fast on this, and if anyone should ask. This was not a formal meeting; this was just a late holiday get-together. What we have discovered must not leak out. You all must be careful what you say and to whom you say it. Each of you will be informed of what your part will be. Use only our private communication methods. Are there any questions?"

There was no reply from anyone.

"Okay then, let's get to work. This descendant must have left tracks. We need to find them and follow them. We find the descendant; we find the Jewel. With the Jewel, we can form the world as we have dreamed. God's mission given to us will be fulfilled. Let's fill our glasses for the final toast."

They all filled their glasses with champagne and stood in silence with them in hand. Charles raised his high.

"To King James!!" he said with a loud voice.

"To King James!" they all repeated.

After the toast, they all filed out of the room to discuss what they had learned. Oliver finished taking down the screen and putting away the computer. Charles, standing next to Jason signaled Oliver to join them.

"Listen," he said, "When we get back to London we will meet and form a concrete plan to deal with this. For now, though I would like Oliver to arrange for surveillance of all the members of the House of Morgan. Also, see if we can find any new information about the Green Man Society. We need to know what they are up to as soon as possible. We must not underestimate either of these groups. Get whatever resources and manpower you need to get it done. This is our chance gentlemen, let's get it right."

"Yes sir," answered Oliver.

They then all shook hands together as if they were the three musketeers.

"Mind if I take some champagne with me?" asked Oliver.

"Not at all," Charles said. "Plenty left unopened. Have a safe trip back. I will see you in London."

Oliver grabbed a full bottle, raised it to Jason and Charles, and left the room.

Charles turned to Jason, "We must find out more about this Green Man Group. They are sure to know where this Merlin descendant is. I need you to work on that."

"Yes," said Jason. "And I think I know just the way to find out. There is another group."

"Oh please, not another group?" Charles broke in.

"Yes, I am afraid there is," said Jason. "They are a small woman's group called The Sisters of Saint Gwen. They are closely connected to the Green Man Society. They once ran a girls' school, but most importantly I know they are the record keepers for the Green Man group. Old manuscripts and such. I believe that is where we will find the information we're looking for."

Across the room, Lewis was picking up the last bits of electronics and gear. Charles motioned to him to join them.

Once joining them Charles asked, "You heard what we were talking about."

"Yes," he replied. "A group called the sisters of Saint Gwen?"

"That's right," Charles said. "I want you to find out everything you can about them. See if you can find out where the records are kept. That's what we very much need to know and what it would take to get access to those records."

"I'll get right on that sir," Lewis answered. "I will let you know what I find out as soon as possible."

"If you get a chance to get your hands on any relevant records before you inform us, do so without question. I authorize you to use whatever means necessary. Just get them," Charles told him.

"I will sir," Lewis replied. "And thank you, sir."

"What would that be for?"

"For the chance to be truly useful," he answered.

"You are already," said Charles. "In more ways than you realize. We are lucky to have someone with your talents on board. Particularly at this time, we are going to need all the help and skills we can find. Well, Jason and I need to catch a train back to London. We look forward to hearing from you and what you can find."

"Of course, sir," replied Lewis. "Have a safe trip."

They all left the room leaving Lewis to finish up. Lewis would spend the night in Edinburgh and catch the first train out in the morning to his home in Salisbury.

Chapter 3

Nemesis

Tintagel Cornwall whose name means, Village on the Mountain, located on the Cornish coast of southern England, has been a place of special interest for nearly 2000 years or more. The Romans left their mark there as a point along one of their many roads. Perhaps they were after the tin in the area needed to make bronze.

A point of land surrounded on three sides by the sea and 300 feet above the waves, the site soon became a place for a fortress. With a small sandy beach where goods could be unloaded at low tide, it was a place to be protected and controlled. Goods flowed up the cliffs and out into the plains of Central Britain and beyond.

One of the earliest masters of a castle built on this point was Gorlois, Duke of Cornwall. The year was around 473 and his beautiful wife thought to have been a member of a powerful family of the fae, had given birth to a girl giving her the name Morgan Le Fey, "Morgan the Fairy." A few years later, as the legend says, Uther Pendragon made war with the duke, and during a battle in which the duke was killed, Merlin the wizard disguised Uther to look like the duke so he could lay with the duke's wife without her knowing. From this union, Arthur was conceived. Thus began the Legend. But was it a legend? To those that lived it, it was real and still is to their descendants.

For some of those descendants, the belief that Arthur was not the rightful King of Camelot and Britain has lingered for 1500 years. The wound has never closed, but the pursuit to correct the perceived injustice remains. The path of this pursuit lies across English history like a scar cut with a sharp sword. Using the inherited magic passed to each generation from Morgan Le Fey. It has been used to try, in vain, to unseat the Kings and Queens of England. Always trying to lay open a way to place themselves on the throne and claim what they believe to be rightfully theirs.

From the Norman invasion in 1066, the White ship incident that sparked the battles between Matilda and Stephen, King John and the rebellion of the nobles, the War of the Roses, and then on to Henry the Eighth and Ann Boleyn. All of these are part of that scar.

When King James the First, was crowned it was a dark time for them, as James hunted anyone that wielded any form of magic as witches, put them on trial, and killed them. Because of this Oliver Cromwell was raised up, with hopes it would be easy to snatch power from him or his son. This too failed and the Monarchy was saved. It was always known why. The Morgans were aware of the existence of the Jewel of Power, and the power it held, and were also aware that it was protected by Merlin's line of descendants. But they never gave up hope in trying to override the curse.

That struggle and the dark magic they wielded were now in the hands of the latest descendant of Morgans. At the head of these descendants is Master Rhyfel, "Master of War." He and a small group of magic-wielding descendants that call themselves, "The House of Morgan," continue this long fight.

Master Rhyfel, the man that broke into the Tower of London on New Year's Eve, cuts an imposing figure. At six feet three inches tall with long coal-black wavy hair. He has one yellow eye and one green eye and is muscularly built at about 190 pounds.

He is usually dressed entirely in black except for the silver-studded belt with a gold buckle. A heavy silver chain hangs around his neck, on which, is a large black obsidian orb surrounded all around by bright red rubies. On the ring finger of each hand are silver rings each with a mounted green emerald. Just to see him would bring a shiver of fear along your spine.

When performing magic, as he did at the tower, he usually wears a black cloak. Behind the cloak mounted on X-shaped straps, among other things, are two daggers each with black obsidian orbs in their pommels. Each dagger has an eight-inch bronze blade with rune symbols etched their entire length.

Where most wizards use either a wand or staff, he uses these daggers to perform magic.

***

The place where he holds court is none other than Tintagel. The place where it all began so long ago and continues still.

Circles in Stone

The rest of the members look and dress as anyone else, except for the black obsidian orb pendants that each also wears around their necks. Though decorated in various ways to each one's taste, these orbs are not for ornamental purposes. They are magic scrying orbs. Used for all manner of divination and even communication between each other.

Only using first names, they only refer to each other and themselves as Lord and Ladies. Four couples altogether form the core of the family. Even though they are husbands and wives they individually can wield magic of every kind. Each member, including husbands and wives, is a descendant of the House of Morgan. Like any royal dynasty, they only marry known descendants. Each couple comes from a different corner of England.

Lord Ambrose and Lady Selma are from London. Lord Seamus and Lady Eris are from Cambridge. Lord Percy and Lady Ophelia call New Castle home. Lastly, Lord Remel and Lady Mira are from Sheffield. Of course, Master Rhyfel, not married, resides in Tintagel in a large house they call the palace, which is jointly owned by all members of the family.

Master Rhyfel had called a meeting of the house of Morgan to discuss the events of New Year's Eve. The meeting would take place in Tintagel at the Camelot Castle Hotel. A grand five-story building perched atop the great buffs of Tintagel just opposite the ruins of the once-mighty castle. The long-ago birthplace of Morgan le Fay and King Arthur. Here he and his court would plan and lay out a response to that event that began the new year.

Master Rhyfel was there to meet each one under the portico of the Hotel in front of the main tower in the center of the building. He escorted each couple into the Grand Hall, with its marble columns, great fireplace, and comfortable seating. In the center room is a large round table, a copy of the legendary round table of Arthur and his knights. Around the table are chairs with high straight backs carved in the finest wood and details, fit for any royal court.

The four couples took their seats around this table with Rhyfel sitting in the place where Arthur would have sat. They were served the finest meal that came from the Cornish Sea and surrounding countryside. Champagne is their beverage of choice served in crystal glasses worthy of any royal house.

After the meal, the staff cleared the table of everything except the champagne and glasses. Rhyfel signaled the manager, who then cleared the room of any other guests and secured it, so the meeting would be private.

With this done, Rhyfel looked around at his court. Without any words, they all stood, raised their glasses, and with one voice said,

"To the House of Morgan, To the House of Morgan, To the House of Morgan."

They then drank their glasses empty and sat down.

Rhyfel began to speak, "As you all know New Year's Eve did not go as we hoped. We, all of us, were deceived. Why we were unable to see this ahead is a puzzle but that is water out with the tide now. We were used. Because I was there, I know the one group that was responsible for this, The Order of Divine Right. The ODR is the only group to have anything to gain from what happened. They, like us, were unsure if the Jewel of Power was still in the hands of a Merlin descendant and if there were any descendants even left, or indeed if the Jewel had been lost. We had not seen or heard of any magic activity of the kind his line would wield in hundreds of years. We were beginning to believe that the reason we could not break into the royal house and take power was the results of the Church of England or other circumstances beyond or even out of our control. We now know, thanks to the ODR that the latter was the case. We also know that the Jewel does still exist and it is still in the hands of our nemesis, Merlin's line."

Lord Ambrose spoke up, "So where is he and it, and why haven't we been able to discern either?"

"Perhaps," said Lord Percy. "We have not looked in the right place. We always assumed it or he would have been close to home."

"I believe you may well be right," replied Rhyfel. "And with the world now vastly populated, it will be difficult, even for us, to discern far afield. But unless we find both him or her and the Jewel all further efforts to gain what has always been rightfully ours will continue to be futile."

"Do you think the ODR knows where it is?" asked Lady Mira.

"No, I don't," answered Rhyfel. "I don't think they know any more than us at this point which gives us the advantage."

"How you figure that?" asked Lord Seamus.

"Because," answered Rhyfel. "We have means to find out things that they don't. We know things they don't. We have been around a lot longer than they have. One thing is for sure. Someone knows where it is. It falls to us to find out. If we can find this Jewel, we will be closer to ending this long quest than we ever have been since Arthur was killed."

"Where do you suggest we start?" asked Lady Selma.

"The SGM might be the best place to find out," replied Rhyfel "I am betting, the ODR have ignored them but in light of what we have been enlightened to if anyone knows it will be them."

"The Society of the Green Man?" broke in Lord Remel. "They are like a paramilitary bunch of crazies from what I have heard."

"That may be so," Rhyfel said. "But if they are protecting both the Merlin line and the Jewel then they are not the crazies after all. Don't forget they have been around for as long as we have. There must be something to them to last that long."

Lady Eris jumped in, "I would suggest we keep an eye on the actions of ODR. We know more about their members than the SGM. We could tag one of them and scry that member and see what they are up to. They might possibly lead us to a way to get inside what the SGM knows."

"Great idea Lady Eris," Rhyfel answered. "I, therefore, put you in charge of that. I know how good you are at scrying."

"That's the only way you're going deal with the ODR, by scrying? That's it?" asked Lord Percy with a concerned voice.

"No," said Rhyfel. "I have foreseen that they will be coming to us for help."

"Coming to us, are you kidding?" asked Lord Seamus with an almost joking tone. "Why the hell would they come to us? We are everything they detest. They would destroy us at the first chance if we let them."

"Because they will need us," replied Rhyfel. "Without us, they stand no chance of getting close to the Merlin line let alone getting their hands on the Jewel. You don't think once they find this Merlin descendant, whoever they are, is just going to hand the Jewel over to them? They will be dealing with magic the kind of which they never imagined. That's where we come in. We are the only ones that can deal with that."

"Once they lead us to this descendant if they lead us to him or her, then what?" asked Lady Ophelia.

"We will deal with the ODR," Rhyfel said. "They are no match for our magic. But I do have one concern though."

"What's that?" asked Lord Ambrose.

"If this Merlin's line member was hidden away a long time ago to some remote corner of the globe, there is a possibility that he has a Draco with him, and that could be trouble."

"Are you saying he might have a dragon with him!!" shouted Lady Selma.

"Keep your voice down," reprimanded her husband, Ambrose.

"Well," Lady Selma continued, "who here knows how to fight a dragon? I've never even seen a book on how one would go about fighting one. No spells, nothing."

"That's because there aren't any," Lady Eris said looking directly at Lady Selma. "Magic does not affect a dragon. A dragon is the product of root elemental forces. Magic only flows from them, not to them or against them. No wizard can stand before them and win with magic. However, if a wizard or any person is bonded with one, the dragon will defend them to the death."

Lady Selma looking directly back asked, "Then how do you stop one?"

"With conventional weapons," replied Rhyfel. "Bullets, guns, arrows, things made from the elements."

"So, are we supposed to carry a cannon with us when we find this Merlin line wizard?" retorted Lord Percy.

"I didn't say they would have one or that there is one," replied Rhyfel. "Besides, a creature like that is very hard to hide, especially these days. Not going to worry about that right now. Deal with it when the time comes, if it comes. The real concern should be the SGM." Rhyfel continued. "We don't know enough about them. If they are as well-armed as I hear then a dragon will be the least of our worries. We need a plan. Got any ideas, Lord Ambrose?"

"We need to find a member," replied Lord Ambrose. "A high-ranking one would be best. Once we find them, we need to search out their weaknesses and even use spells on them if necessary to achieve what we need. Perhaps attach a scrying orb to them through some sort of jewelry. This would give us an eye on the inside."

"Sounds good to me," said Rhyfel. "I'll let you work out the details. Keep me informed on your progress. May I also suggest that Jason Elliott of the ODR be followed and tagged if possible? He is one of the ones that were there at the Tower. I, at least, picked that up before I got out. If anyone knows something it will be him. I sensed he is a bit of a hot head so be careful."

He looked around the table for a moment.

"Lord Remel and Lady Mira, you have connections that might help. Perhaps you could handle this?"

"Yes of course," they answered.

"Now if anyone else comes up with any other ideas?" Rhyfel continued, "Please let me know and I will pass it on. I believe our time has come for us to take back that which is rightfully ours. Let's make some history! Maybe the moment that our house has been waiting for all this time has finally come to pass. May our ancestors look down upon us and guide our paths. Let us make them proud!!"

After a moment of silence and again without anyone saying a word, they all filled their glasses and stood up and raised their glasses high.

"To the House of Morgan, to the House of Morgan, to the House of Morgan!" they all said with one voice.

They then all drank their glasses empty as before.

They all sat again except for Rhyfel, who spoke.

"A room has been secured for each of you for the night. All of you are my guest here in this wonderful modern castle so close to our roots. Please make yourselves at home. The manager will see to all your needs. Don't hesitate to ask for anything that would make your stay more comfortable. Let us not forget that we are all family here."

After those words, they all got up and began to part the table. Each one, in turn, thanked Rhyfel for his generosity. When Lord Ambrose and Lady Selma's turn came, Rhyfel leaned to Lord Ambrose's ear.

"I need to see you and Lady Selma in private if you don't mind,"

"Yes of course," he answered.

All the others had left the room except for Rhyfel. Lord Ambrose with Lady Selma, now standing by the window taking in the magnificent view it offered. Rhyfel approached placing his hand on Lord Ambrose's shoulder.

"Thank you for waiting," Rhyfel said. "What I would like to ask of you two is no light matter. I have thought carefully about this. You, Lord Ambrose, are the next in line if anything happened to me. When the time comes and where ever this takes us, I would like you Lady Selma to be with me there."

"Of course," they both answered at the same time.

"Thank you both, I knew I could count on you," he said, "I trust you both, and most of all I trust your magic."

"Thank you. That means a lot coming from you, Master Rhyfel. We are honored that you have asked us," Lord Ambrose replied with a humble tone.

"Just one thing though," Rhyfel said. "Don't tell the others that I asked you. Just tell them that you volunteered and I accepted your offer. I am sure you can understand why."

"Yes, of course, we understand completely," replied Lord Ambrose looking at Lady Selma who was nodding in affirmative.

"Great," said Rhyfel. "I am glad we got that settled. Now go and enjoy the evening."

***

The next morning after a splendid breakfast they all again thanked Rhyfel for his kindness and said they were excited to finally be doing something to further their cause. They each pledged their service to him.

The group then dispersed back to where they had come from.

Chapter 4

Rowland

After the meeting at Edinburgh Castle, Lewis Hall knew the train ride home to Salisbury was going to be a long one. Seven hours, but at least it was along the western side of the country. The first four hours took him through some of the most beautiful countryside in England. The majestic peaks of Cumbria would be on one side and the Pennines on the other side. Later as the train ran closer to the coast the Yorkshire Dales would be seen to the east. He would be changing trains in Birmingham and later in Bristol before ending in Salisbury.

The long journey gave him lots of time to think about what he had learned in Edinburgh and what lay ahead. The assignment that Charles had given him weighed heavily on him. He began to wonder why he accepted it. Was it the chance to prove himself to the Order or was it for the bigger picture he knew was ahead? Whatever the reason, he would begin to deal with it after he got home and had a good night's rest.

The Victorian Salisbury train station was a welcome sight. It was dark by now. Once at the station, he called a taxi to take him home which was in the outlying area of Salisbury. He lived in a fairly recent housing development. The house the taxi dropped him off at was a two-bedroom single-story brick-faced bungalow with an attached garage. The house set back from the street about 40 feet, giving it a nice front lawn that was kept meticulously tidy. There was also a large garden in the rear bordered by trees and a fence. This separated it from the house behind that faced the opposite direction. The houses on his street and the ones behind were not linked by a common road. The only way they were linked was by going to the main road and then onto a separate road that ran separately along the front of the two housing estates. This made the house more private except for the ones next to him; only hedges bordered them. The inside of the house was decorated simply. There were only the bare essentials for furniture.

He wanted to rest but he needed to change and have a good hot shower. He turned on the outside light, opened the garage door, and pulled his Audi A5 that was in the driveway into the garage. Closed the door and went inside. This was to let anyone that might be watching that he was home. He then turned on a small lamp in the front parlor room that could be seen behind the curtains from outside. This too was a sign that he was in residence.

He then retreated to the rear master bedroom carrying a small suitcase and without any lights on, he found a remote control that was on a bedside stand. Pointing the remote at the room's back wall, he pressed a series of numbers. A four-foot section of the wall slid to the side. Once opened, it revealed a square opening about the size of a standard shower. Taking the remote with him, he stepped inside. Pressing more numbers, the panel closed with him behind it. The cubical began to lower. Going down about 12 feet it stopped. The opposite side from where he entered was now open and looking into a seven-foot-high tunnel running over a hundred feet straight ahead toward the rear of the property.

Pressing another number on the remote he turned on the lights that lined the top of the tunnel. Lewis walked the length of the tunnel for about one hundred feet. The tunnel then opened into a small room. There was a table, a couple of chairs, and a washbasin built into a small counter. Above the basin, a mirror was affixed to a wall cabinet.

He put the suitcase on the table opened it and removed a smaller case with combination locks on it. Dialing the combination, he opened it and took it over to the counter next to the basin. There was not too much in it. Some tubes of stuff, cosmetics, scissors, and other grooming tools.

Lewis removed his shirt revealing the tattoo that all members of the ODR had, on their left arm. He removed the gold band from his right forefinger placing it in the case. He took a bottle of liquid from the case and then swabbed some over the tattoo. After waiting a few minutes, he took a small knife and scraped his arm next to the tattoo lifting the entire tattoo from his arm. Washing the place where the tattoo had been with water. He took some more of the same liquid but swabbed it on his upper right arm this time. Repeating what he had just done before, he lifted a film from that arm that matched his skin perfectly revealing a tattoo of the Green Man!

Circles in Stone

He then reached up and carefully removed a wig from his head that now revealed his military-style crew cut. Carefully, he next removed a part of his mustache. Finally, he popped out the brown iris contacts to reveal his blue eyes. Thoroughly washing his face and brushing back his hair he looked into the mirror and said with a smile.

"There you are, Mr. Theodore Rowland. Welcome home."

He then put his wig and all the cosmetics in the case and locked it. Leaving it there he walked the remainder of the tunnel to where it ended at a door. Reaching behind a light fixture he found a key and unlocked it revealing a set of stairs. Closing and locking the door behind him he went up the stairs to another door. Unlocking this he stepped into a small closet. Sliding a set of doors open, he was now in a bedroom on the ground floor of a two-story house. This is the house directly behind the one that the taxi had let him at on the opposite street. This was his real home. The lounge was decorated with fine leather sofas and chairs. These were arranged in front of a brick and tile wood-burning fireplace. Just off the lounge was an office. Next to the office is the dining room which had an oak table surrounded by matching oak chairs. The kitchen was roomy with all the most modern conveniences. On the second floor, there were three bedrooms and two full bathrooms.

He and the society that he was a true member of, had these houses built, and their adjoining tunnel.

This was Colonel Theodore (Ted) Rowland of the Society of the Green Man and a deeply placed spy in the ODR. He is a 52-year-old 5-foot 8-inch-tall ex-military man with brown hair and blue eyes.

Taking a gold ring with an amethyst mounted in it that all members of the Society wore, from a pouch in his pocket, he placed it on his right ring finger. Ted then went into his office and took a bottle of scotch from a cabinet poured himself a generous measure, and sank into his favorite lounge chair.

Toasting to himself he said, "And so let it begin."

Putting the drink down on the table next to him, he soon fell asleep.

***

Ted's phone went off at 7 am. He picked it up from the kitchen counter where he was eating breakfast. Looked to see who is calling, and he answered it.

"Good morning, Major General. How are you, sir?"

It was Major General John Wigmore, the head of the Society of the Green Man. He was a man in his late forties, 5'9" military build, and a cleanly shaved head. Dark framed glasses and a light brown mustache.

"Good morning to you Colonel," he answered back on the phone. "I trust the meeting went well. I hope you have some information for us."

"Yes," Ted answered. "This information will need our attention as soon as possible. I shall leave shortly and should be there within the next hour and a half Sir."

"Very well," Wigmore answered. "We shall see you shortly then. I am calling a staff meeting; we will be ready for you when you arrive."

"Very good sir," answered Ted and ended the call putting the phone in his front shirt pocket.

Ted finished his breakfast, took a quick shower, and headed to the garage where he kept his black, fully loaded Land Rover. Opening the garage door with a remote he backed out and left for headquarters.

Headquarters was located about an hour's drive north in the town of Marlborough. In the center of the town, is the landmark known as Marlborough Mound. This mound is also known as Merlin's Mound. Legend has it that it is the burial site of Merlin himself.

***

The mound is said to date to the Neolithic period. No one knows for sure who built it or why. Measuring over 62 feet high from ground level and 270 plus feet in diameter, this once dominated the landscape around it. It is certainly large enough to house a structure inside it without being noticed. The mound is now surrounded by the buildings of Marlborough College.

The headquarters is not located at the mound or near it but, known only to members of the Society of Green Man (SGM), they are located inside the mound itself.

The Green Man Society has been around in one form or another for over 1400 years protecting the line of Merlin and the English crown. Perhaps Merlin had been buried there or perhaps the name was a cover for those that protected his lineage. What better place to locate your headquarters than in a place that was formed for that very purpose? With that much time, a lot can be done without anyone paying attention or asking why.

Upon arriving in Marlborough, Ted parked his vehicle in the car park just opposite the college buildings that surrounded the mound. He walked across the road and past the college buildings to another small unassuming brick building. Ted used his ring as a passcode to unlock the door to the building. Every member's ring doubles as a passkey with a security chip mounted behind the mounted stone of each of them.

The door shut behind him as he headed down a set of stairs. At the base of the stairs sat an officer who operated a fingerprint-scanning machine. Ted placed his hand on the scanner and the door in front of him opened. Once inside, a corridor ran straight ahead leading to the main meeting hall. Off to the sides of this corridor were two other corridors running in a circle following the contour of the mound, an outer one and an inner one. Along these corridors were various offices, sleeping quarters, storage rooms, communication rooms, and weapons rooms.

There was also a floor above this one that is reached by a single-story lift or stairs from the central meeting room. On that floor was a single open ring containing lounges, restrooms, and a cafeteria. On the opposite side of the mound from where Ted entered and only accessed from within one of the college buildings, was a service entrance. This was for goods and supplies to enter through. Goods were put in a storage room in the college and brought in only by members. Security was very tight at all points.

Ted walked down the corridor towards the center room where Major General Wigmore met him.

"Greetings Colonel Roland, good to see you again," he said as he reached out his hand.

"Yes, good to see you too sir," replied Ted.

"Come to my office," Wigmore said. "I am having some lunch brought down to you and a few others. We can have the meeting there."

They walked across the large meeting room to the other side. Just off the corridor leading away was Wigmore's office. In his office were his desk and a plain table able to seat eight.

Already seated around the table were four men and a woman. Major James Rupert, Captain Joe Burton, Captain William (Bill) Bastwick, Lieutenant Martin Laud, and Lieutenant Jayne Roberts.

Ted greeted each with a handshake. He knew each of them well and had worked with them on different occasions.

Ted and Wigmore took their seats as Wigmore said, "Well Ted, tell us what you have learned."

"They know a lot," he replied, "But not everything."

"You have spent a long time to get this far into their organization," Wigmore said. "The timing could not have been better."

Ted went on to tell them what he had learned at the meeting. How they had lured Rhyfel into the tower and what they had learned by doing this. He told them he had smuggled out taped copies of the meeting including the video of the break-in at the Tower. He also told them about the ODR assignment concerning The Sisters of Saint Gwen.

"What they don't know," he said. "Is where he is or who he is. That is what puts the sisters and the archives they protect at great risk."

"This should be our first objective, to protect them and those records," Wigmore replied. "I would guess the Morgans don't know either then?"

"I would guess that they were as surprised by this as much as the ODR," said Ted. "But I guarantee their focus has now changed as well."

"Then this puts the sisters and records at double risk," replied Wigmore.

"You are right about that Ted," Major Rupert broke in. "I am not sure which is the more dangerous the Morgans or the ODR."

"That would depend on who would get the information first if either does get their hands on it," answered Ted. "If the Morgans were to get it first you can bet the ODR will be out of the picture. If the ODR were to get it, then the Morgans would try to get it from them or, worse yet, collaboration might be formed, and in that case, we would have to deal with both groups at the same time."

"Your right," answered Wigmore. "So, it is imperative that neither of them gets hold of any of the documents. So, we need a plan to find out which documents would be most dangerous and move them from the sister's archives to a more secure location, like here. Lieutenant Laud? I need you and Lieutenant Roberts to go to the sisters in the archive and tell them what we need and give them any help you can. They would know best which ones and where they are. Captains Burton and Bastwick, I need you two set up a security detail over there and put in place a transport detail to move the documents here once they are gathered."

"Yes sir," they all answered as they wrote notes on the pads they were holding.

"No unsecured phone calls use only private secure means of communication," said Ted in a firm voice. "You never know who is listening in or how."

Just then, there was a knock on the door.

"Lunch sir," called a voice from outside the door.

"Come in," Wigmore called back.

The door opened and two men each rolling a cart of food and drinks entered.

"Thank you, gentlemen," Wigmore told them. "Just leave them we can handle it from here."

"Yes sir," they replied as they left the room closing the door behind them.

Ted got up and opened a case he had brought with him, took out a scanning device, and scanned each cart thoroughly.

"Can't be too careful," he said. "They are all clear."

"I agree Colonel," Wigmore said. "Let's have some lunch everyone. Please help yourselves."

They all got up and helped themselves to a lunch of sandwiches, salad, fruit, and fruit drinks.

Following lunch, Wigmore spoke, "Well, you have your missions. I am sure you will carry them out with utmost urgency. Keep me informed and let me know if you need anything to carry them out. You are all dismissed except Colonel Rowland."

They all stood and gave a salute.

"Yes sir," they all said at different points as each left the room.

After they left Ted turned To Wigmore.

"You wanted to speak to me sir?" he asked.

"Yes," he said. "I have special orders for you. Ones that I think you will agree with. However, if you don't and have better ideas you must let me know and speak freely. Is that understood?"

"Yes sir, of course."

They both sat down at the table.

"First," Wigmore began. "You need to get back in touch with ODR and lead them to believe that you have gotten access to the archives of the sisters and are compiling the necessary information. You need to go to the archive site at Sarum College. You know the ODR will be checking, so you need to go disguised as Wilson Hall. I will arrange for them to let you in as him. That should convince them. Our client, you know who has been informed. He said he already knew something was up, which is not a surprise. He said he first found out on New Year's Eve by means that he did not disclose."

They both gave a small laugh.

"Not surprised at that either," Ted commented.

"So, the next part of your mission," Wigmore went on, "Is that I want you to go to the islands. Meet with our members there and formulate a plan to protect him, if necessary, from whoever might find out where and who he is. I am hoping that it will not come to that. But if it does, I want to be ready and I want our best man on the job."

"Yes, of course, and thank you, sir".

"However," said Wigmore. "To maintain cover, I would like you to travel as a tourist and was thinking that you could take your daughter Sarah with you."

"Sarah?" replied Ted with alarm in his voice. "I don't know. If all this blows up, she could be put in danger. I don't know if I like that idea or if she will either. Besides I can't just make her come. All I can do is ask her?"

"Thank you, Colonel."

"With your permission sir, I would like to visit Sarah before I go back to Salisbury and on to Sarum College. I would like to spend the night at her place. I not only have not seen her in a while but I could ask her about the trip while I am there. I am just not sure how I am going to do that without revealing the real reason for the trip." am sure you will find a way as you always do," Wigmore replied. "So of course, you may go to see her. But I do need you on this mission as soon as possible. We have no idea how much time before our adversaries make their move."

"Yes, I understand," replied Ted." I will head back to Salisbury the next day and see about getting those documents."

"Very well," Wigmore said while slapping Ted on the shoulder.

The two men got up, shook hands, saluted each other, and parted.

Chapter 5

Sarah

Ted spent the night in the Green Man complex within the great mound. The sleeping quarters were very comfortable. It was also a peaceful place for Ted, as he felt protected there from those, he knew would like to do him harm, especially from the ODR if they ever found out who he actually is.

He rose early to meet with other members about the other ongoing operations as well as help to put together the details of the upcoming missions. After some lunch and saying another goodbye to Major General Wigmore, he left for his daughter's home.

***

It is around an hour and a half drive from Marlborough to Sarah's house in Glastonbury, going across some of the most historic lands in England. He was crossing Salisbury Plain, with sites like Stonehenge, Avebury Circle, and Salisbury Hill. He would be driving through southern Wiltshire, then into Somerset with its hills also filled with legends and history. Glastonbury itself is famous for the Abby where King Arthur and his wife are supposed to have been buried.

Ted had bought the house for his daughter there as a gift when she finished her studies at Oxford. She had received a DPhil in anthropology and archaeology. She inherited a large amount of money from her late mother's estate. She didn't have to work but found her research very fulfilling. She now focused on the studies of ancient people; their myths and stories, and how they fit into history. This area of England was the perfect place for this with all its myths going back thousands of years. The myths of Arthur and Merlin were only one of many.

Ted could not tell his only child what he knew to be more than a legend. He knew well enough that not only would this scare people but, in Sarah's case, put her in danger. This is why he is hesitant to take her on the upcoming mission. With all this new information and new players, there were just too many unknowns.

Circles in Stone

As far as Sarah knew, from what she had been told, was that her mother died just after giving birth to her and Ted had adopted her as an infant. Raised and schooled by the sisters of St Gwen while her father served in the military. He made it a point to always spend as much time as possible with her. He always provided for Sarah on all levels. He always made sure she knew he loved her with every bone in his body. He had also given her the Sir name of her mother. This makes her Sir name Harper. Her full name is Sarah Harper, not Sarah Rowland. Ted not only did this to honor her mother but he knew it would be a line of protection between him and her in his line of work.

Sarah's house was located on the outskirts of Glastonbury. A two-story brick farmhouse, that had been renovated just before Ted bought it. Out the front window was a perfect view of the Glastonbury Tor. There were gardens and trees on the other sides of it giving it a feel of a country estate. Ted always paid a gardening company to maintain the grounds and do any necessary maintenance, so that his daughter could focus on her work.

Inside the house through the front doors is a short hall. Straight ahead is a staircase leading to the second floor. On the right is a large living room with a large tile-faced wood-burning fireplace. On the opposite side of the hall is a doorway leading to a large dining room decorated with oak paneling. In the center is located a large oak table surrounded by matching chairs. Further to the rear of the hall and on the same side as the dining room was a modern kitchen. Opposite that is a full bathroom. At the end of the hall is a door leading to the rear garden with a large paved patio. On the second floor of the house, there are 4 bedrooms along with 2 full bathrooms.

Ted had called Sarah on a phone that he only used for talking to her to let her know he was coming. She sounded excited that he was coming and was arranging a special dinner catered at the house for them.

When he finally arrived, Sarah was standing by the door to greet him.

Sarah is a 28-year-old 5'8" very attractive woman. With long wavy brown hair and bluish-green eyes, she stood out, as Ted would say, as a star in an empty sky.

When Ted got out of the Land Rover, Sarah ran and threw her arms around his neck.

"Oh Dad, I am so happy to see you!" she said as she kissed him on the cheek.

"Me too my sweet Sarah, it is always too long between our visits," Ted replied as he also kissed her on the cheek and held her tight in his arms.

Pulling back a bit but with arms still around each other Sarah enticed him.

"You're staying the night? That is wonderful. Come on let's go sit in the garden while the sun is shining. I have your favorite ale on ice waiting for you."

"Oh, now that sounds wonderful," Ted said with a big smile.

They walked to the garden through a side gate, Sarah's arm still around his neck.

In the rear garden on the stone patio was a table with a large umbrella mounted through its center. Around the table were four comfortable garden chairs. There was a small side table next to the large table on which was a bucket filled with bottles of Ted's favorite ale surrounded by ice. Ted sat next to the table with the bucket on it and Sarah sat next to him where she already had a bottle of white wine and a glass sitting on the table. Sarah filled her glass with wine as Ted popped the top off a bottle of ale.

Each holding their drink and looking at each other Sarah asked, "What shall we toast to?"

"I let you decide. You provide the drinks; you get to choose."

Sarah, still holding her glass up, thought for a moment.

"I know," she said with a large grin.

"To things yet to be discovered."

"To things yet to be discovered," Ted repeated as he clicked his bottle of ale to her glass of wine and they each took a drink.

Ted relaxed back in his chair with his eyes closed simply enjoying the peace and quiet. After a long silence, he finally spoke up.

"It's so peaceful here. So quiet only the wind and the birds."

"Why don't you come and stay here for a while?" Sarah inquired. "I could take some time off and we could spend time together.

Ted saw his chance in what she said.

"As much as I do love it here perhaps what I am really in need of is a long vacation someplace far away."

"How far?" asked Sarah with her probing.

"I don't know, how about Hawaii? That's far away," replied her father with his eyes still closed.

"That's far away all right. Why don't you go?"

"I just might. However, I do not want to go alone. How about you come with me?" Ted said opening his eyes and looking to see her reaction.

"Are you serious?" she asked, looking back at him with a half-shocked half-questioning stare.

"Yes, I suppose I am," Ted said looking back at Sarah with both eyes fully open and head up.

"I don't know. We just started a new dig of possible Roman connections here in Somerset. This could be an important find," Sarah said looking away as if to the site.

"Oh, come on," her father said. "A vacation is your idea. We would be able to spend time together and see new places. I know how much you like to travel. Besides, the Romans have been there for nearly two thousand years. I am sure they will not be going anywhere now. It will be great fun and who knows maybe some great adventure will await us there."

"I have to admit," she answered. "I have always wanted a chance to go to America and study Native American and Hawaiian culture. I always found it fascinating how the Hawaiians traveled so far across the vast Pacific and settled in those remote islands long before any modern navigation devices."

"You will go with me then?" said Ted as he sat fully erect in his chair.

"When are you planning on this trip?"

"How about next week? How would that be?" replied Ted. "I have some stuff to clear up before I can leave but I know I can arrange it.

"It is a bit short notice but I might manage it if you're serious.

"I am very serious," Ted replied with an excited tone.

"Not much time to find someone to manage the new dig but I think I know someone I could put in charge. I suppose I could turn it into a work trip as well," Sarah said with more excitement in her voice. "Hawaiian culture is ancient and filled with myths. I could write a paper on it."

"Yes, and who knows, you might even meet someone to your liking," Ted replied with a bit of slyness.

"Really Dad," Sarah shot back with a sharp tongue. "Don't think that will ever happen with my condition. Why did you have to bring that up? You know how much it hurts me to be like this. Perhaps it is why I prefer digging up the dead. At least I can't hear their thoughts."

What Sarah calls her condition was her ability, or curse as she saw it, to hear others' thoughts. Having this all her life made being around crowds difficult. If she were within twenty feet or less the thoughts would be loud. This also made dating difficult if not impossible. The few men she had known soon walked away as she would always know what their real motives were and would confront them with them.

"I'm sorry," Ted said with a soft tone. "It's something you must have inherited from your mother. I knew her well enough to know she had the same problem but she managed it somehow. When we first met, she told me about it. At the time, I thought she just had great intuition, in time, of course, I came to understand it was more than that. I have told you this before so it is nothing new. You do remind me of her so much. I am sure you will find a way around it somehow just as she did."

Sarah replied, "I am getting better at turning it off and on. It is keeping it turned off that is the hard part. If I could just find someone like you, Dad, it would be great, never being able to hear his thoughts, like a normal person. I never have been able to figure out why I can't hear your thoughts."

"I am guessing that knowing you since a baby may have something to do with it," he answered.

"I know you told me that hundreds of times, but I am not sure if that's it. That is enough about that. How about we have a nice steak for dinner?" Sarah said with a spark in her voice. "I had Ann pick some up and she is grilling them with mushrooms, I know it is your favorite."

"Ann?" Ted questioned.

"Yes, Ann my new housekeeper I told you about."

"Oh yes, I forgot," Ted replied with an embarrassment in his voice.

"There are times I wish I could hear your thoughts. Just so I could know if you heard what I told you with my real voice."

They both laughed.

Ann served dinner on the patio table, as the sun was getting lower in the sky, which was now turning a wonderful pink-red color. Dinner was, as Sarah had promised, his favorite. Sirloin steak, done medium, with grilled mushrooms on the side. There were also baked sweet potatoes and cherry ice cream for dessert. All washed down with dark ale for Ted and white wine for Sarah.

Ann did not eat with them. She said she had to get dinner for her husband at her home located in town. She told Sarah to leave the dishes in the kitchen she would be back in the morning to take care of them. Having dinner with her father was wonderful for Sarah. She most often would have dinner alone while going over paperwork.

During dinner, Sarah talked about her work, the latest dig, what they had found, and what possibly still be buried. Ted enjoyed his steak while listening to her every word. He found it fascinating as well as felt happy to see that she so enjoyed her work.

After dinner, Sarah cleared the table and lit some candles that were on the table, as it was now getting dark. Sitting next to Ted, she hooked her arm in his in a kind of chair hug.

Ted looking at her said, "What shall we talk about?"

After a moment of quiet Sarah answered, "Tell me more about my mother."

"What can I tell you that I already haven't?" he asked.

"Did you love her?"

Ted was silent.

"I'll take that as a yes," Sarah said responding to his silence.

"Her family didn't like me much. I can say that one thing is for sure. They told me I was not her kind. I would never fit in. They said they would never allow us to marry or live in peace if we did," Ted replied with a tone of bitterness.

"Did she love you?" Sarah asked looking into his eyes.

"I believe she did," he answered. "Giving me you to take care of and love I have always taken as a sign that she did. I have always tried my best to honor that by taking care of you."

Sarah looked up at him with a smile. That told him all he needed to know.

"Why do think her family didn't like you?" Sarah kept pushing.

"Why is this important to you?"

"There comes a time when one wants to know where they come from and what their roots are and besides," Sarah continued "We're going to be going on a long trip with a lot of flying involved. What if we crashed? Would you want me to die not knowing things?"

Ted looked at her. She was grinning at him in a way that let him know that she was not worried about crashing but just wanted the answers anyway.

"There was something about a long family line that was unbroken in some way," Ted answered. "That marrying outside that line, in their eyes, would somehow diminish the line. So, in a nutshell, I was somehow not of the right line or was not pure enough for her. Somehow, I would taint their precious bloodline. From what I saw, they always saw themselves above everyone else. I am sure they still do. Your mother was not like that though. If there was a night, it was them, if there was a day it was your mother. She always wanted to help those less fortunate than her."

"Why won't you tell me who they are?" Sarah asked as if she was miffed.

"They are bad news, always have been, and always will be," he answered. "As I have told you before, your mother made me promise to never tell you. If she found it necessary to ask me to do that, then I would trust her if I were you. I know you believe you have a right to know and you could be right, but I must keep my promise to her."

"I know you said that one day you would tell me about my birth father. When will that be?" she asked.

"When the time is right," he answered. "You will have to trust me on when that will be for now. Besides, it is getting cold out here. Think it is time we went in. Don't want you catching a cold before going on our trip."

They both got up and went inside. Sarah fixed them both a cup of tea. Ted made a fire in the large fireplace in the lounge. They spent the rest of the evening watching old movies on TV and just enjoying each other's company.

In the morning, after a good night's sleep, Ted found Sarah in the kitchen making coffee and fixing his favorite breakfast of bacon and eggs on toast. Ann had already arrived and was cleaning up from the night before.

Sarah spent most of the morning talking about what clothes she should bring on the trip. Ted suggested she should go online and search it out. Suggesting that perhaps she should take very little and buy what she wanted to wear there. That way she would blend in more and not look so much like a tourist.

"I think I will do just that," Sarah answered. "If you promise to come shopping with me when we get there?"

After breakfast, she walked him to his Land Rover as he left the house.

"Listen," he explained, "I will call you and let you know the details. I will take care of all the arrangements so that you only need to worry about packing. I will be out of phone contact for a couple of days. I will call you first with all the dates and times."

She hugged him around his neck.

"Love you," she said as she kissed him on his cheek.

"Love you too."

When they separated, she looked at her father and said, "You know what Dad?"

"What?" he asked not sure what to expect.

"I am beginning to get excited about this trip."

"Wonderful," he replied. "I can't wait for it myself. I will call you in a couple of days."

He climbed into his Rover and drove away, waving at each other.

Chapter 6

The Car

As Ted drove the one and half hours back to his house in Salisbury, he thought a lot about the upcoming trip to Hawaii. He wished he could have told the truth to Sarah; not only about the reason he was going but also about her mother and her mother's family. He also thought about the real danger it could bring to her. Taking her on this trip had enough possible danger as it was. As he thought more about it, he realized he was worried about things that have not happened and may never happen. He made up his mind, that even though he was going there on a mission he was going to try to make this as much fun for Sarah as possible.

Before he knew it, he was on his home street. He decided to drive by the front house first to see if anything was out of order. The house looked fine but he did notice a car that was not familiar to him parked just past his driveway. The thing about living on a street in an area like this was that you get to know the cars that belong and those that don't. This one did not belong.

He decided to drive around again to get a better look at it. As he circled around, he thought he saw a person duck down just as he approached. He dared not slow too much as it might make himself look suspicious. He did make note of the car. It was a silver two-door, Vauxhall Astra. He took note of the plate number as he drove on, to his main house.

Once there he parked his Rover in the garage and looking both ways down the street, he shut the door. Inside he went to a small desk where he kept a laptop computer. It was connected to the CCTV cameras that he had on both houses. He adjusted the one on the front house to aim at the car. Sure enough, there was someone in the car. He now reviewed recordings from days past. Everything appeared ok until the day before. It appeared the car was there all day until around dark and then left. It then returned around 9 am and had been there all day except for a couple of times when it left for a few minutes and returned. It was clear that someone was watching the house.

Circles in Stone

He decided it would be good to make at least a show. He went down into the tunnel connecting the two houses and stopped at his changing point and put on only the wig, glasses, and mustache. Going the rest of the way and up into the front house, he grabbed a sports jacket and a bag of trash from the kitchen. Went out into the garage and opened the door. Without looking directly at the car, he put the trash in a wheelie bin and rolled it just outside the garage door. He then looked directly at the car. Again, there appeared to be no one in it. He smiled to himself. Went back into the house turned off some lights and turned some others on. He went back to his real house stopping just long enough to remove the wig and mustache.

Once back in his house, he poured himself a drink and fired up his main computer. He ran the number plate of the car. It turned up as registered to an offshore oil company. He thought to himself, why would an offshore oil company be watching his house? The only conclusion he could come to was that it was a front for someone else that didn't want him to know who they were.

He decided to deal with it tomorrow. He put a frozen lunch in the microwave and spent the afternoon making the arrangements for the trip to Hawaii, flights, hotels, and rental cars. He also called Wigmore to see if he had arranged for the sisters to receive him as Wilson Hall. Wigmore informed him that he had and that they would be expecting him in the morning.

He did not tell Wigmore about the car. He had decided to deal with that himself, in case it was nothing to do with the mission. Just as it got dark, he checked to see if the car was still there by way of his computer. Sure enough, just like the night before, it was gone.

***

In the morning after some coffee and a quick breakfast, Ted used his computer to check to see if the car was there. It was just after 9 am and, just like the days before, the car had returned. He now knew he was going to have to deal with this. So, he began to collect things he might need in confronting this car and whoever was in it.

First, he went to his safe hidden behind a chair in his lounge and below a small bookcase. He retrieved his G-17 9mm handgun and shoulder holster. He had two clips for it. One had real bullets and one

44

with rubber. After thinking for a minute, he decided to take the one with the rubber bullets. The only one that would know he didn't have real ones would be him. He then went to the tunnel.

This time he had to put on the full disguise. He would once again be Lewis Hall.

Before leaving the tunnel, he went to a metal locker he kept in the tunnel. Unlocked it and removed a metal ammo box with a handle on it. The box contained specially designed car stoppers. There were rectangular-shaped metal blocks. Each had explosives inside that were set off remotely. They had thick high carbon steel tops and bottoms weighted with lead. The centers were filled with rows of projectiles. They resembled some kind of a metal sandwich. The purpose of these is to be dropped on a road in front of a speeding car. They would land flat with the minimum roll and when set off would shoot out projectiles in every horizontal direction and flatten all the tires on the vehicle without harming the occupants.

He was hoping it would not come to either the gun or these car stoppers. But Ted was never one to rule out anything. Better to be prepared than not and regret it. He put on the shoulder pistol holster with the gun in it and a sports jacket to conceal that he had it. Taking the rest of the gear he went to the garage where his Audi A5 was waiting. He put the ammo box with the car stoppers in on the front passenger seat and unlatched the lid. Taking a belt, he strapped it in as if it were a passenger.

He opened the garage without looking at the car acting as if it was not there. Pulling out and closing the garage door remotely he turned on the road in front of the house. Again, he acted as if he did not notice the other car.

After making the first turn out of the housing development where the front house was located, he noticed in his mirror that the car was behind him but keeping its distance.

Ted decided to detour to a local grocery store and get a sandwich. Not that he wanted one, but this would give him a chance to see if it was truly following him and get a better look at the car. He pulled into the shop's parking area, got out, and went inside. As he was paying for the sandwich, he looked out the door of the store and noticed that the other car had pulled in and the driver was pretending to read a newspaper.

Whoever this was, Ted thought, he was no pro. At this point, he decided he was either going to lose this guy or find out who he was. Confronting him in a public place would not be a good idea.

The Sisters of Saint Gwen archives were at Sarum College, just a few miles from Ted's home in Salisbury. He knew he couldn't go straight there but he did know where he could find a remote road just outside town. He would either lose this guy on the way or confront him there if he followed.

Pulling out of the market he headed north on the A354 toward the river Avon. The Astra pulled out as well and was following a few cars behind. Ted crossed the bridge over the Avon where a roundabout was just ahead. When he approached the roundabout, he signaled left. Watching the Astra, he saw that it too had signaled left. When Ted entered the roundabout, instead of turning left he continued around and onto Churchill Way. He saw the Astra follow suit causing a few drivers to blow their horns.

Ted now increased his speed to nearly 80 mph as he headed for the next roundabout that intersected with the A36. He again signaled as if to turn right. He got into the far-right lane as if he were going to follow it around to A36 South. But without even slowing he shot across it to the A36 north. Just missing a lorry as it was making the round. The lorry driver let Ted know he was not thrilled with his move by blowing his horn. The Astra had to slow for the traffic but also shot across in pursuit. Ted now floored it. He was doing nearly 90 mph. The Astra too had now pushed into high speed. Ted now knew the chase was on.

As they headed up the A36 at over 90 mph, they were both weaving back and forth in traffic. Other cars were swerving and blowing their horns at the near misses. Ted realized there was too much traffic for this to go on as it was. Some innocent person could get hurt. Steering with just one hand, Ted reached into the middle console and pulled out a blue, police-style light. Still driving with one hand at 90, plugged it in the USB plug and placed the light on top of the car where it was attached with a strong magnet. He then reached under a dash and flipped a switch. A police siren came on.

Circles in Stone

At least, even if it were not real it would clear the traffic ahead. Cars immediately began to pull to one side so Ted increased his speed even more. The pursuing Astra, on hearing the siren began to slow. But shortly realized he was being duped and floored his car. Both still doing over 90 mph while fast approaching another roundabout. Ted shot straight across again onto the A30. He didn't bother to signal this time. The Astra repeated the move following about a quarter-mile back.

The pursuit continued at this rate to the next roundabout where they each shot across in turn. Even with the siren and flashing light, there were plenty of near misses with other drivers.

A short sprint to the next roundabout but, this time, Ted made a hard left onto the A338, his tires squealed as the Audi slid around the turn. Just as he made the turn, he saw a bus was stopped ahead. Even with a curve just ahead Ted took the chance and went around the bus doing nearly 80. Looking behind he noticed that this had put some distance between him and his pursuer.

Ted did not let up. He took advantage of the gap. At the end of a straight part of the road, Ted noticed he could still see the Astra hot on his tail. As far as Ted was concerned, he was leading him right where he wanted him.

To the next roundabout with a hard fast left, over a railway bridge where his car became almost airborne, and to another roundabout, and a hard right this time. Tires were squealing at every turn.

Still, on the A338, he slowed a bit as he sped through the village of Winterbourne, but never below, or even at the normal speed limit. The flashing light and siren truly helped through areas like this.

By now people, seeing the other car behind would have assumed it was another police car. Also, by now Ted had about a half-mile advantage on the Astra.

Just before the sharp bend that led through the village of West Gomeldon, Ted slowed a bit to make sure his pursuer could see him. He was close to Ted's trap now and he didn't want to lose his quarry.

At the West Gomeldon roundabout, Ted shot straight across onto Down Barn Road. This is where Ted would spring his trap.

About a mile from the roundabout on a straight section of the road, where you could see half a mile in each direction, Ted put his trap into action. He abruptly slowed to about 50. Reaching into his ammo box which was still secured to the seat, he grabbed 4 of his car stoppers. Passing them to his right hand he reached out his window and as carefully as one can at that speed, dropped them and watched them in his mirror as they hit the road. They dropped almost perfectly in the middle of the road.

Still doing about 50 mph he went about 200 yards. Pulling the handbrake up hard and steering hard to the right he put the car into a full 180 degrees. Slamming on the foot brake and the clutch, he came to a hard stop facing his pursuer he could now see him coming at a good speed towards him.

Pulling the remote control for the stoppers out of the ammo box, Ted waited.

It was not long before the Astra was right where he wanted him. Just as the car passed over the stopper blocks, Ted pushed the remote. A blast followed. Ted could see the tires blow. They had worked perfectly. The Astra tried to maintain control but was soon off the left side of the road against a fence.

Ted wasted no time. He punched his car in gear and pulled up next to the now ditched Astra. Stopping his car, locking the parking brake, and opening his door as if all in one motion, Ted jumped out of his car pulling his G-17 from under his sports jacket. He approached the Astra with his gun pointed at the driver who was still in the car.

"OUT OF THE CAR AND KEEP YOUR HANDS WHERE I CAN SEE THEM!" Ted shouted just as the driver was opening the door.

The driver of the car was a young well dressed, blond-haired man in his mid-twenties. He looked shocked that he was now the prey.

"Put your hands on your head and keep them there."

The man complied.

"Roll the window down on this door," Ted demanded.

"What?" said the driver surprised at such a request.

"Do it!" Ted demanded as he kept the gun pointed at him. The driver again complied. Ted reached into his back pocket and pulled out a set of handcuffs.

"Give me your left hand," Ted demanded again.

The man got out of the car and did what Ted asked. Ted put one end of the cuffs on the man's left wrist and then put the other end on the doorframe where the window had been. Ted now lowered his gun, keeping it in his right hand with his finger in the trigger hole. Still holding the gun, he frisked the man for a weapon. He found only a phone in his pocket. Taking it out, he threw it on the seat of the car. He then positioned himself in front of the man and, looking into the man's face he demanded.

"I want the answers to the following questions and I want them in the order in which I will ask them. First," he continued, "Why were you watching my house? Next, why were you chasing me? Last and most importantly, who sent you and why?"

The man did not answer. He just looked away.

Ted stepping even closer to him put the gun to the man's groin.

"Now," said Ted looking sharply into his eyes. "You are going to answer me. I won't kill you, but I will make it impossible for you to make babies or even have fun trying. Do I make myself clear?"

"OK, OK," the man said with fear in his voice. "I was ordered to."

Just as the man was to speak again, Ted noticed he was wearing a gold band on his right forefinger.

"Wait," Ted broke in. "Are you a member of the Order?"

"Yes," he answered.

Ted grabbed his left hand and rolled up his sleeve and there was the tattoo of the lion holding a cross. Stepping back Ted looked at him sternly.

"Now, I want to know who ordered this. I am assuming it was a member. I want to know who?" Ted demanded.

"It was Mr. Elliot."

"Jason Elliot ordered you to watch my house and follow me? But why would he do that?"

"He had not heard from you in a couple of days since you got home and said you had not moved on the plan fast enough and wanted to know what you were doing," was the man's reply.

"Well, that son of a bitch. Where is he now?" Ted shouted back.

The man did not answer.

"Where is he now?" Ted asked again, this time doing a reload of his gun while looking at the man.

"At Sarum College," he said. "Mr. Elliott said he was going to do what you should have already done."

"Shit!" shouted Ted as he went over to Astra.

Ted grabbed the man's cell phone from the seat and put it in the man's front pocket. Reaching into his own pocket Ted pulled out the keys to the handcuffs. Putting them on the rear window well out of reach, he told the man.

"I guess you should call for help. I suppose you should also call Elliot. When you do, tell him I will deal with him personally. Also, if I were you, I wouldn't tell him much about what happened here today if you value your position in the Order."

Leaving the man handcuffed to the car Ted got into his car, pealing his tires, he spun his car around and headed for Sarum College.

Chapter 7

The Archives

On the way to Sarum College, Ted was thinking about how he was going to confront Jason. He had been given the assignment of retrieving the information from the sisters there by Charles directly. The fact that Jason had his house watched and someone ordered to follow him was more than troubling. Yes, he was a spy but, he had to think as if he wasn't. What he didn't know was how much Jason knew. Had he suspected he was a spy or had done as the man said he did? He knew Jason was an impatient man.

He decided the best course of action was to assume that Jason did not suspect him but had just wanted him to move faster. He would see how that went and deal with it.

From where Ted left the man cuffed to the car to Sarum College was about seven miles. Ted had turned off the siren and taken in the police light. He did not want to attract any more attention.

***

The Sisters of Saint Gwen went back just after the Norman Conquest. Naming themselves after Guinevere, King Arthur's wife who herself had become a nun after the incident with Sir Lancelot.

The Normans had brought a strong Christian faith with them believing themselves sent by God to rule England and were determined to wipe out any reminders of the old religions. So, a group of women of the old faiths decided that they needed to preserve the belief and history of those faiths as best they could. Posing as nuns they set up a convent and later a school, to carry out their mission.

The original school had been set up in the city of Sarum located atop an old Iron Age hill fort. Today it is known as Old Sarum. The Normans had built a motte and bailey castle on the old hill fort and within the fort had also built a cathedral that was finished by 1092.

This is where the sisters had first set up their convent.

Some ancient documents that the sisters had in their archives, told that Arthur and Guinevere had visited the hill fort. This was to have happened while touring the lands of what was then part of Camelot. To the sisters, it made good sense to build in such a place.

The Sister's convent remained there until the new Salisbury Cathedral was completed in 1227. King Henry III issued a city charter for the New Sarum after the city that had sprung up around the new cathedral. The dismantling of the old cathedral on the hill fort supplied materials for the new one.

New Sarum remained its name on paper until only 2009. That's when a new city charter officially changed the name to Salisbury.

The college, which has always been a school of theology, for which it is known today, kept the old name. The college is in the heart of Salisbury directly across the street from the famous cathedral.

It was next to this college that the sisters had set up a school for girls a long time ago. Ted's daughter, Sarah, had attended that same school.

The school closed shortly after Sarah had left. The Sisters continued to maintain the archives of ancient documents and artifacts. This has been done under the support and direction of the Society of the Green Man. It is in this archive that the SGM keeps its most valuable documents. Among these documents are the records of what was known of the Merlin lineage.

The archives were now the focus of those that wanted this information. They hoped it would lead them to the location and name of the descendant of the Merlin line and the Jewel of Power.

***

Making sure no one followed him; Ted drove to a car park on the other side of the cathedral from where the College was. Reaching under the dashboard he flipped down a secret compartment where he kept a private phone for contacting the SGM. He called Major General Wigmore directly and asked how the arrangements were going to get the documents from the sisters' archive.

Wigmore told Ted of the arrangements with the sisters and that the SGM units should be there within the hour. Ted then told him what he had learned from the man in the car and that the ODR was most likely already on site.

"Oh shit!" Wigmore shouted back on the phone.

"That's what I said," Ted replied. "You better stop them before they get there. We don't want a firefight in the middle of the city."

"Yes, of course," responded Wigmore. "And what's your plan?"

"I am going there as planned and see what, if anything they have. I believe we must proceed as if we knew nothing about the knowledge they acquired during the break-in at the Tower. If they even sense that we were onto them things could get ugly real fast."

"I agree," Wigmore said. "But I will hold the units back just far enough to be out of sight. You call or signal or whatever you need to do if things go south and I will send them in to clean it up. Is that clear?"

"Yes sir," Ted answered. "Give me at least a couple of hours. If you don't hear from me, do what you must."

"Okay, but be careful."

Ted ended the call and put the phone away. Taking a deep breath as he sat back into his seat as if to prepare himself for what was ahead and said to himself.

"Well Mr. Hall, let's see what kind of shit we can get into."

Ted gathered himself together and drove around to the other side of the cathedral onto North Walk where the Sister's home and the archives were located. He pulled into a parking space on the cathedral side of the road. There were several cars already parked there. Most he did not recognize but at least one he did. He knew it was Jason Elliot's. Getting out of his car he approached the front gate of the sisters' house.

The house was a large medieval flint and block stone building. It had large rectangular stone-framed windows. There was a stained-glass window high in the gable in the shape of the Sisters' crest which was a circle Celtic cross in a blue field with a red dot on each point of the cross. Every sister also wore the symbol as a pendant.

Circles in Stone

On getting to the gate leading to the Sisters' house, two men that were standing guard stepped to the center of the gate blocking his way. They did not speak to him. He looked at their hands. They both had gold bands on their right forefinger. Seeing this, Ted rolled up his coat and shirt on his left arm and showed them the tattoo on his forearm. They looked at each other and stepped aside. There was another man at the entrance door of the building. Again, Ted showed his tattoo and the man opened the door and let him in. There was no one in the entrance hall, however, he could hear voices coming from what he knew to be one of many libraries. Ted headed toward the voices.

This library was a large room filled with old but very comfortable-looking furniture. The walls were lined with bookcases filled with books from floor to ceiling. At one end of the room was a set of large double doors. Ted had been in this room many times and knew those doors led to a staircase down to the special archives. Normally these doors were closed. They were now both wide open.

Two of the Sisters were standing near the doors. Upon seeing Ted, disguised as Lewis Hall, they came over to him. He of course knew them both. It was Sister Rose and Sister Helen.

Sister Helen leaned over to him and kissed him on the cheek. As she did, Ted whispered in her ear.

"I know what's going on and you will be alright. Just remember I am with them for now and act as if you met me once before inquiring about documents a couple of days ago. I also need you to whisper what I just told you to the others."

He pulled back and gave her a wink.

She then spoke with a loud voice,

"Good to see you again Mr. Hall. Please make yourself at home. Perhaps you would like some tea."

"That would be very nice, thank you," he replied.

Sister Helen took Sister Rose by the hand and led her out of the room whispering in her ear as she went.

Ted then heard someone coming up the stairs that went down to the archives. Before they came through the door, he could see it was Jason.

"Is that you Lewis?" Jason said as he came through the doors. "It looks like we're doing your job for you."

Ted walked briskly over to him, grabbed him by the collars of his sports coat, and almost lifted him off the floor.

"You may be some high-up asshole in this Order but no one treats me like you have," Ted said, with a tone of anger and showing his teeth. "If you were anyone else you would have been sucking swamp water by now. I was given a mission and I was working it my way. You put a watch on my house and had me tailed. By now you know that didn't turn out so well. What I want to know is if this was your idea and does Charles Stewart know what's going on?"

With Ted still holding him firm and Jason trying to free himself, Jason replied.

"Charles only wants results; he doesn't care who gets them or how."

"We'll see about that!" Ted said still speaking through his teeth as he slowly lowered Jason. "And what method did you use to get in here? Guns blazing, I suppose. Frightening these poor women, who have no idea what's going on."

"No of course not," Jason answered. "You underestimate my powers of office. I simply told them that we had reason to believe that there are documents stored here that are relevant to an ongoing terrorist plot that we are investigating."

Ted looked at him with contempt but did not want to push his luck. He knew by now that they had no information as to who he really was or that the SGM knew anything about what they were up to.

"Come down to the archive room and help us finish up," Jason said heading back toward the stairs.

Located at the bottom of the stairs there was a large metal door, which was now open, that led into the special archive room. It was a very large room that was humidity and temperature controlled. The fact that the door was blocked open irritated Ted because of the damage this could cause to some documents. But he could, of course, say nothing.

The walls were lined with row after row of shelves with books and scrolls. In the center of the room was a very large table that now had old books and documents sprawled on it.

Around the table were two more men and a woman. The woman was Sister Clara. Ted knew her very well he also knew that she was the one Sister that knew more about what was in this archive and where to find it than anyone else. The men were two more members of the order. One was Oliver Calvin; Jason's right-hand man and the other was John Coke.

When Sister Clara looked up and saw Ted disguised as Lewis. Ted winked at her and she went immediately over to him.

"Hello Mr. Hall, Mr. Elliot said you might be coming," she said as she kissed him on the cheek.

Ted whispered back in her ear that everything was ok and followed her back to the table where Oliver and John were looking over and taking photos of documents.

"What do you think John?" Jason asked.

John Coke seemed to be the point man on the documents.

"I am beginning to see a pattern about where this descendent might be," John answered. "A lot of it doesn't make sense. There is a gap in where they might have gone after a certain point. There was an attempt to cover the trail going back hundreds of years. It looks as if there was more than one descendant at one point. It all seems very confusing. The information about where he or she might be now, I believe, is in what we have. I just need to sort it out. What is a blank, is who this descendant is today."

"From what you can make out, are they here in Britain someplace?" asked Jason.

"No," John replied. "From what I can tell, so far, the person we are looking for may well be on the other side of the world. Perhaps in South America, Russia somewhere, or maybe even beyond. The descendant we are looking for left Europe sometime in the early 17th century."

Oliver broke in, "This person could be anywhere in the world by now."

"Yes, but I have some more modern references referring to them. Those references put them still where they last landed, if they are the true heir, I can't be sure," answered John.

Ted was now looking at all documents, maps, and books that the rest of them were looking at. He had seen these many times before but, of course, pretended that he never had.

Looking at Ted (as Lewis), Jason asked him, "What do you think Lewis? Is any of this making sense to you?"

Ted still looking at the table said, "I am afraid not. This is just interesting to look at but it's out of my expertise, I am afraid."

Ted stepped back and looked around the room as if searching for something. He glanced at Sister Clara. Jason noticed the glance.

"You think there might be more stuff in here that is relevant?" asked Jason looking at Ted and then at Sister Clara.

"How would I know?" answered Ted "There is a lot of stuff in here."

"What about that sister Clara?" asked Jason looking sternly at her.

"I have given you all I know about the subject you asked about," she answered with a bit of fear in her voice.

John broke in, "There might be more here, but we could be here for months, even years trying to find it."

We don't have that kind of time," Jason snapped back. "Can we get what we need from what we have?" he asked, looking at John.

"With some old language deciphering and overlaying these old maps with new ones, I believe I can give us a good lead."

"Okay then, let's take what we got back to London and work with it there," Jason said while filling a large case with as much of the stuff he could from on the table.

"I only hope it's enough. We won't be able to come back for more."

"Why is that?" asked Oliver.

"Because," Jason replied. "Our good Sisters here are sure to inform their benefactors of what just happened here. I can assure you the SGM will be hot on our ass now. We have just exposed our plan and what we are looking for to them. As they say, the cat is now out of the bag."

They completed packing up what they had and left the building. Ted was the last to leave. He took time to reassure the Sisters that everything would be ok and nothing was their fault.

On the way to their cars, Jason caught up to Ted. Stopping him on his way he spoke to him.

"Listen here Lewis, I just wanted to say I am sorry about what happened. I meant no disrespect. I am sure you had a plan and it was a fine one but I felt we needed to get a jump on this before we got found out. I hope this doesn't hurt our working relationship."

Looking directly at him Ted replied in a stiff voice,

"First, I don't work for you. I work for the Order. Second, I don't take orders from you either. I take orders from Charles. I was doing the job I was asked to do in a way I felt best. So as far as a working relationship goes? At this moment there isn't one."

Jason stood there stunned. He had never been spoken to like that before. Ted turned and walked toward his car, stopped abruptly then turned back toward Jason.

"There is something you can do for me, Jason," Ted said. "When you get back to London you can deliver a message for me to Charles. Tell him that thanks to you, I am going on holiday and will be out of touch for an indefinite amount of time. Tell him I will let him know when I get back."

"You can't go on holiday now in the middle of all this," Jason yelled back.

"Oh, yes I can and I will," Ted yelled back as he got in his car and closed the door.

Once in his car, Ted breathed a deep sigh of relief. That went better than expected he thought it would. Ted started his car and drove back to his front house. Pulling the car into the garage and looking at his watch, he could see that the two hours he promised Wigmore were almost up. Taking out his hidden phone, he called him.

"You can call off the troops sir," Ted said when Wigmore answered the phone. "But you need to send someone to the Sisters to make sure they are alright and protected."

"Yes of course, glad you're ok," Wigmore answered. "How much do they have?"

"Enough to find out where he is I am afraid. It will take them a while to figure it out, but I am sure they will. What they don't have, thanks to Sister Clara, is who he is."

"Okay," Wigmore answered. "I will inform the island units. What about you, how did you leave your position with them?"

"I told them I was going on holiday and there was nothing they could do that would deter me. I made it look to Jason like it was because of what he had done. This has worked out to our advantage. Oh yes, and I did manage to convince Sarah to come along."

"Well done," Wigmore said. "Well, in that case, you better pack. I wish you a good trip and don't forget to keep me informed."

They both ended the call at the same time.

Chapter 8

Alex

Almost 7000 miles from the islands of Great Britain, and in the middle of the blue Pacific Ocean are another set of islands. They hold the claim of being the most remote islands in the world. Further than any other group of islands on the globe to a major landmass. These are the islands of Hawaii. With 137 islands, only eight are considered habitable to humans. They are so remote that no humans had set foot on them, until around 900AD. These were seafaring Polynesians exploring the vast Pacific in double-hulled canoes without the aid of a compass or maps. Reading only the waves and the stars, they found their way there and made them their home. These explorers became the Hawaiians.

These islands are the tops of great volcanoes that began as cracks in the seafloor, spilling out vast amounts of lava and creating giant mountains whose crowns rise above the ocean.

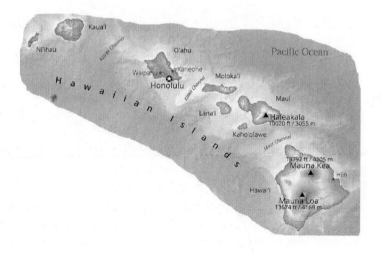

Starting from the far west, where the main islands are the oldest in the geologic age, is Ni'ihau, known as the forbidden isle. No one goes there except by invitation.

Next to it is Kauai, the garden isle, known for its lush greenery and flowing rivers.

Moving east, you come to O'ahu. The most populated of all the islands, but not the biggest. This island hosts Honolulu and Waikiki with its famous landmark known as Diamond Head.

Further east and within sight of the eastern shores of O'ahu is the island of Moloka'i. Known as The Friendly Isle, it is a long narrow island with the highest sea cliffs in the world.

Next along is Maui, the valley isle. A valley separates its two mountains. There are the West Maui Mountains on one side and looming over the eastern side of the valley is Haleakala. Last erupting during the 18th century, is still considered an active volcano.

Just a short way to the south of Maui is the island of Lana'i, it was once covered in vast pineapple fields.

Further south but still within sight of Maui is Kaho'olawa. People no longer live on this island because the Navy used it for bombing practice during WW2.

Going still east and south is the last of the main islands. This is the largest of the islands by far. Its size is so vast that all the landmass of all the other main islands could fit on it and still have room to spare. This is the Island of Hawaii, holding the namesake for all the islands. To the people of Hawaii, it is simply known as The Big Island.

The island has five massive volcanoes. The oldest and now extinct is Kohala.

Next to that one, is the towering Mauna Kea. At nearly 14000 feet above sea level, it often has snow on its summit. The meaning of its name in English describes it well, White Mountain.

South of these and hugging the western coast of the island, is Hualalai, meaning head in the clouds, its 9000 ft plus peak is seldom seen for the clouds that cover its summit. Located east of Hualalai stands a volcano called Mauna Loa. Meaning long mountain, it is not only long but also truly massive, considered the tallest and most massive mountain on the planet. Its summit is over 13000 ft above sea level. With its base reaching down to the seafloor where it was born, it is taller than even Everest. On its side and hugging Mauna Loa like a child, is Kilauea, the most active volcano in the world.

It is here, near its 4070-foot summit, lives the focus of so many people so far away, Alexander Michaels, the long-lost last direct descendent of the great wizard, Merlin.

Known by his Hawaiian name, Alika, and called Alex by his friends. With his long brown hair, blue eyes, and 6'2" frame he looks a young 30 years old. Having graduated with a BSc from Open University in Earth Science and living on an active volcano and working as a geologist, it is all a shoe fit to wear.

His family goes back 20 generations on this island. He is well aware of who they were and who and what he is. The only other ones that know who he is, are of course, are the members of the SGM, sworn to protect him. Not just him but those that came before him. But even the SGM had no idea precisely where this part of the line was until after the arrival of Cook on the Big Island in 1779. Back then the SGM was known by a different name, they were called the Knights of Merlin. By the time of Cook's visit, Alex's descendants had already been on the island for 160 years.

His first ancestor to arrive on the island came ashore on the western side of the island at a place called Keei, in the district of South Kona. They were survivors of a Spanish shipwreck.

Those ancestors were Michael Dee and his wife. Michael was, the thought to be dead; son of John Dee, who was Queen Elizabeth's 1st astrologer. Known as the queen's conjurer, John Dee was, in fact, a wizard in the Queen's court. Some believe he called up the storm that helped to destroy the Spanish armada.

With the death of Elizabeth in 1603 came James I and his war on witches. John Dee saw the rising threat and decided to do something to protect the line. His firstborn son Arthur Dee was already trained in the arts of magic. This would make him a target for James and, since he was already well known, another way had to be found to preserve the line. Because Arthur's father had foreseen the coming threat while he was in Elizabeth's court, he put the plan into action by hiding his second son under the veil of having died at birth.

When John died in 1609, the plan was passed to his son Arthur. As soon as James came to the throne in England, the hunts began. Arthur almost became a victim of them. King James had Sir Walter Raleigh, a friend of the former queen, put in the tower of London on trumped-up charges of conspiracy. This is when Arthur Dee saw his chance.

Among his father's books and manuscripts were Dutch maps the Spanish had made that showed the islands on it and where they were supposed to be located. Since the English did not have these maps, nor did they trust Spanish maps, this would be the perfect place.

Using what influence Arthur still had in the royal court, or perhaps James' fear of him, he convinced the king to release Raleigh and send him on a mission to find Eldorado, the famed city of gold, in South America before the Spanish did. Using much of his family's wealth and the fact that he had saved Raleigh from certain death; Arthur put his brother Michael with his wife and a few others on Raleigh's ship. Arthur then laid a trail, though hidden in story and myth, to where he had sent the true line of Merlin. With this now accomplished, Arthur got King James to assign him as a physician to Tsar Michael of Russia. This may have well saved Arthur's life.

Circles in Stone

In 1617 along with maps and crates of books, Raleigh set sail for his search for the city of gold. Raleigh also had clear instructions from Arthur to make sure that Michael got to the islands he had seen on the maps. While in South America, and with much silver, Raleigh convinced a Spanish Captain to take Michael and his fellow passengers to their final destination. What happened to Raleigh after that is now history.

In 1620, the Spanish captain did get them to the islands but refused to land. Whether it was out of fear or some sinister plan is not known. This is when Michael, a now very accomplished wizard of the elements like his father, called up a storm. This storm drove the ship upon the rocks along the south coast of Kona.

Most of the crew was lost. Among the items that were recovered from the wreck were the books sent with them by his brother. These would provide the education to the generations of Merlin's line that would survive in this remote, but safe paradise.

This is how Alexander's ancestors came to Hawaii.

It was not long after Michael Dee arrived; that the Hawaiians realized he had great powers of magic. They soon gave him the name Ke Ahi, meaning "makes fire", because he could make fire with his bare hands. Although he told them that his name was Michael Dee, his new name became Ke Ahi Michael. Therefore, over the generations, Michaels became the last name.

Because he could make fire with his hands, the Hawaiians were sure there was a connection between him and Pele, the Goddess of fire that lived in the volcano Kilauea. Soon, he also was adopted as a kahuna, a Hawaiian holy man. The chiefs moved him to the summit area of the volcano to be close to the Goddess Pele and allotted him land for a home there not far from a large lava tube, where they said, a great Mo'o, a giant lizard, had recently moved into. It is on this land where Alex has his home. There Michael and his descendants would remain, hidden but protected until the arrival of Captain Cook.

Through training and teaching down through each generation, including his father, Alex had become a fully powerful elemental wizard and a master artisan of all kinds of magic and divination.

Having been to England himself several times, he had collected even more books on the subject. While there he visited the Sisters' archives and the SGM complex. This had given him a much broader knowledge of who he was, and what kind of future he might face.

***

Shortly after Alex had the experience on New Year's Eve, he contacted a member of the SGM that lives in Hilo on the island. This was Colonel Jack Fairway. Alex had also done his own magical scrying to see if he could decipher what had taken place. It didn't take long for him to see what and who was responsible. A couple of weeks later Colonel Fairway told Alex what SGM had learned at the meeting Ted had attended undercover with the ODR.

For Alex, all of this was going to mean life-altering events were coming his way. He knew someday this might happen but he was hoping, as each generation did, that it would be in the next generation. With all the implications this could mean, Alex knew that he must focus on what might be directly ahead.

Alex also had just received the most updated information from the SGM. That the group known as the ODR had taken information that could lead to Alex's location. Though the ODR had possible information as to where he was. They did not have anything yet about who he was. With this knowledge, it was recommended by the SGM that he do nothing that would draw any attention to himself. Alex now also requested a face-to-face meeting with Colonel Fairway to discuss plans and strategy. Phones could not be trusted. The meeting place must be well known to each of them but not well visited by others. It was agreed to be Laupahoehoe point. A state park located in a valley on the northeast coast of the island. Once a thriving community, it was struck by a tsunami in 1946 destroying the village and killing 159 people. A tragedy from which it never recovered. Known and used by mostly locals it would be the perfect spot. Fairway also suggested they buy a lunch and beer. A picnic in a park would be the best cover.

The next day Alex loaded a cooler full of food and beer into his Ocean Blue Jeep Wrangler 4x4 and set out for the park. It is an hour and a half drive from his home. However, any drive in Hawaii to anywhere is usually a pleasure, even if you have lived there all your life.

Fairway, who was already there when Alex arrived, rushed over to him as he got out of his Jeep.

Circles in Stone

Jack Fairway, a retired US Naval Commander, stood 5 ft 6 in with dark brown hair. It was rare to see him without his dark sunglasses. Born and raised in Hawaii, he joined the SGM after his retirement because he believed in the British monarchy and he wanted to help local law enforcement control the drug flow into the islands.

"So good to see you again Alika," Fairway said greeting him with a Hawaiian handshake and hug. Fairway always called him by his Hawaiian name.

"You too Jack, my friend," Alex replied. "Come; help with the cooler, I brought plenty good grinds and beer for us my friend."

They carried the cooler to the picnic table Jack had already chosen for them. Alex opened the cooler and pulled out 2 beers and a plate of smoked meat to have as a pre-lunch snack. Jack had already taken out his Swiss pocket knife and opened the bottles of beer.

Raising their beers and clinking them together Alex said, "To the unknown future."

"You got it, my man."

They both sat down and started snacking on the smoked meat Alex had brought.

"Oh wow, ono kind meat, you make em yourself?" Jack asked Alex.

"No, I got one friend that snare his own pig and smoke da meat himself. He make his own sauce but no more share the recipe with me," Alex replied laughing.

Both were now speaking in a form of local Pidgin English. They did not always speak this way. They both being born in Hawaii, and it was how the locals would talk. However, schools did not allow it spoken in them.

After snacking on the meat and some boiled peanuts that Jack took out of his cooler, Alex turned to Jack. With a serious look on his face, he asked,

"So, my friend what plan you got to deal with all this? You know this be some serious kine stuff, could get nasty."

"What kine nasty you talking bout?

"Da kine you never seen before my friend," Alex replied. "If da House of Morgan come here, I am fraid dat they not gunna care bout using magic. They gunna use it like army use bullets to get what they after. Am sure not gunna be just one of em that come either."

"How do we stop dat kine shit?" asked Jack with alarm in his voice.

"You no can without my help," Alex answered. "I be the only one dat can spot em. Once I do spot em, it be up to you to keep em separated from each other. Must not allow em to work together if a battle happens. So, I need for you gather you best men for this. Need for em to work as team."

"What bout da ODR?"

"I let you deal with em direct. You know more bouts how they operate. Besides, they no more the magic so can deal with em usein conventional ways."

"You has point there. I hear dat one of our best be on his way here. He can work both sides da fence. It be good thing he be from our side of dat fence. I think you heard of him already."

"You means Ted Rowland?"

"Yep, dat be him. He knows how deal with da ODR better dan anyone I knows."

"Den maybe best you when put him in charge of dat part of any operations," suggested Alex.

"Yep, I think dat be a good idea."

"I needs you and da best locals to be workin with him. You needs peoples dat know da area and who can tell da ones no more fit in, dat sort thing."

"I get your meaning," Jack replied. "I got just da guys. I let you know who dey be so no more mix-up when time comes. I know it not sound like much plan but we no more to work wid yet. Maybe when Rowland guy get here, he have some betta ideas. But I do my best to work wid what we knows already."

"Sounds good to me. Now, let's get out those grinds I brought. Time for cow cow."

Alex emptied the cooler of food on the table while Jack opened a couple more beers. After filling themselves on poke, lomi lomi salmon, and other Hawaiian favorites, they packed up and parted separately so as not to bring any suspicion on their purpose for being there.

Circles in Stone

On the long drive back to his home on the volcano, Alex thought about the plans they had so far laid out. He then had an idea that might help and add to the confusion of the enemies that might come. He would go to Kona, to his house over there. It looked much more normal both inside and out than the one outside the village of Volcano where he lived. In fact, he thought, he could do one better than even that. He would book a room in one of the grand hotels on that side of the island. He would be even harder to find in a crowd of tourists. He could place a magic shield around his Volcano home making it invisible to anyone that went looking for it. Yes, it would seem strange for the people that lived up there. But lots of strange things happen up there. People just take it in stride. If the ODR or Morgans did find his house in Kona they would not find him. They don't know what he looks like so living in a hotel would give him a double advantage.

I shall get hold of Jack in the morning and tell him his plan, he thought to himself. He was sure he would go along with it. Satisfied with this idea Alex relaxed as he drove home where he would prepare to put the plan into action.

Chapter 9

The Trip

After leaving the Sisters of St Gwen's place at Sarum College, Ted went straight back to his front house. It was time to prepare for his trip.

Parking his Audi in the garage, he double-secured the door. Going through the house he set several alarms and made sure all the CVTV cameras functioned properly. He went to the lift that took him to the tunnel that connected the two houses. When he stepped into the lift, he activated a second panel that came between the bedroom wall panel and the lift. This panel looked like a brick wall. If by some chance someone were to find the bedroom panel and open it, they would see what appeared to be a brick wall.

Once in the tunnel, he once again removed his disguise and became the real Ted Rowland. Putting fresh disguise cosmetics in his case, he went to his main house to continue making arrangements for the trip ahead and to pack. He would spend the following day doing just that. He called Sarah and told her to begin her packing. He would be there the day after next.

***

Ted always traveled light. Something he learned in the military. You should carry only what you need to get by if stranded on a journey. For him, that would mean only a couple of shirts, extra underwear, two pair of trousers, and some toiletries. Everything should fit into one case.

If it were anywhere else, he was traveling to, he would take his gun. Since Hawaii is part of the USA, he knew it would be easier to travel without it. He also knew the units in the islands had all the weapons he might need. There was never a shortage of guns anywhere in the US.

Just before leaving, he called Sarah. She told him she could be ready by the time he arrived. He told her not to hurry because the flight out was not until the morning. discuss any other details about the trip on the phone; he did not trust that the phones were secure. He put his one case in his Land Rover, secured the house, and left for Sarah's.

Circles in Stone

The hour-and-a-half drive seemed long this time. Perhaps because he was somewhat excited about going on this trip with Sarah or perhaps, he now knew things well might get messy in Hawaii. The idea of the ODR getting there, or even worse, the House of Morgan, gave him great concern. Because everything depended on what these groups might do was like going into battle with no idea where the enemy would come from.

When he arrived at Sarah's house, she did not come out to greet him. He knocked on the front door and heard her call down to him to come in. She told him to make himself comfortable and that there was still ale left in the fridge. He grabbed a beer and went across the hall into the lounge. After about 30 minutes, Sarah came down from upstairs and greeted him with a kiss and hug.

"I think I'm ready," she said. "I managed to keep my packing down to one large case."

"Well done, travel light, travel fast, is my motto," Ted replied smiling.

"You will have to help me shop when we get there, as you promised. I will help you find something to wear too," she answered. "I am sure you don't have any aloha shirts in your case."

They both laughed at the idea of them shopping together. Just then, there was a knock on the door.

"Dinner is here, I think. I ordered Chinese takeaway for us. Hope you don't mind?

"Not at all. You know I love Chinese. It will set the mood for the trip. I hear that you can get the real stuff in Hawaii."

Ted answered the door and retrieved the food. He took it to the dining room where Sarah was already setting out plates and chopsticks.

During dinner, Sarah talked about sites she wanted to visit but was unsure about the length of their stay. Ted told her that he had bought open-ended tickets so could stay up to 120 days which is when visas would run out. He also knew he could extend the visas if he needed to.

"Don't think I can stay that long. I don't think the Romans will wait that long for me," Sarah said laughing aloud.

"Those damn Romans," Ted said laughing too. "They are always in a hurry, even after they are dead."

It felt great to Ted to be with Sarah like this. He was wishing this could have been a real holiday. Perhaps he would take one after this was all over. He was also secretly hoping that nothing would happen and that this would turn into a real holiday after all.

After dinner, Ted got Sarah's case from upstairs and took his from the Rover, putting them both by the front door. He then parked his Rover inside the empty bay of Sarah's attached garage. Later as they both were relaxing in the lounge; Ted gave Sarah the trip details.

A taxi would be taking them to Gatwick Airport early in the morning to get an 11 ½ hour first-class flight to Vancouver, Canada, with one short stop in Calgary. They would be spending the night in the Fairmont airport hotel in Vancouver. The next morning, they would catch another first-class six ½-hour nonstop flight to Honolulu. Ted had booked two ocean-view rooms at the Royal Hawaiian Resort on Waikiki Beach. Known as the Pink Palace of the Pacific, it is one of the most famous hotels in Hawaii. Ted spared nothing. Wigmore assured Ted that the SGM would cover all expenses. For them, money was never an issue. Along with the flights and the rooms, he had also reserved two rental cars to be waiting for them at the hotel, one for himself and one for Sarah.

They both retired to bed early knowing the taxi would be there well before sunrise. Sarah would not get much sleep. However, Ted, being ex-military, received training to get sleep no matter the pressure.
***

Ted rose before the taxi arrived and prepared 2 cups of coffee to drink on the way to the airport. The taxi arrived just as Sarah was coming down the stairs. Ted handed her the cups of coffee as she headed out to the taxi. He then loaded the cases into the taxi, set the alarms, and locked the house doors. When he got in the taxi, Sarah handed her father his coffee as they set off.

Very little conversation took place during the 2 ½ hours trip to the airport. After finishing her coffee, Sarah nodded off to sleep.

With Ted's skill in traveling, it all went very smoothly through check-in and boarding. Sarah now fully awake was pleased with the first-

71

class seating on the plane. She even felt sorry for those not traveling that way.

Soon they were taking off into the morning sky with the sun chasing them from behind. Sarah had a window seat so she could watch as they climbed above the clouds that looked like pillows of cotton wool below them. Ted and Sarah were offered drinks and snacks even before the plane reached cruising altitude. Foldaway screens had all the entertainment that one could want. Movies, TV shows, news, and even a map showing how far along you were in the flight.

Breakfast was served once the plane reached cruising altitude. After that, more snacks and then lunch. With all of this, the hours seemed to have slipped away. Soon it was time to land at their first stop in Calgary. This was a short stopover. Off the plane for an hour and back on. It was now only a short hop to Vancouver.

Once in Vancouver, a check through customs and then on to the hotel.

While walking through the airport terminal, Sarah became mesmerized by all the wonderful Native art displays. She told her father that once they were checked in, she must come back and have a good look around. He agreed.

After check-in and having a quick shower, they went back to the airport for a proper look around.

Sarah pulled out her camera and could not stop taking pictures of all the wonderful displays.

To her, this was at the heart of her studies, myth art, and history all combined in single images. Along with the displays of native art, there is also a two-story fish aquarium near the center of the airport. Ted sat near it and enjoyed watching the fish while Sarah was wandering about excited by all the exhibits. Ted told Sarah that if she wanted to wander off on her own to do so. He would stay where he was so she could find him later and they would go have dinner.

"Are you sure?" she asked him.

"Yes of course, please go and enjoy yourself," Ted reassured her.

Soon Sarah was out of sight.

As Ted sat watching the fish and the people, someone in the crowd caught his eye. He looked again more intensely. He knew them. It was Captain Bill Bastwick. One of the members of SGM from the meeting he had at the complex. It was not long before Bill also spotted Ted sitting there. Looking around with caution, he approached Ted and sat opposite him on a bench. Without speaking and all the while looking around, Ted finally broke the silence between them.

"So, Bill, how is your holiday going?" asked Ted.

Realizing Ted was speaking a sort of coded conversation he answered.

"Very well thanks, it was nice for the boss to send me on this holiday. I needed one. But he also told me to be on standby in case I was needed for anything. He meant to tell the other people on the staff but said they would be informed after I arrived at my final destination."

"Yes of course," Ted answered. "I think I can understand why the boss would do that. Are you staying here long?"

"Two days, then flying directly to the final destination. I think I am supposed to meet some staff there."

"Two days here in Vancouver? That sounds like a holiday unto itself. I hear it is a beautiful city."

"Yes, I intend to take full advantage of my time here before continuing to my destination." I would like to stay longer but the boss said I will be needed where I am going as soon as possible."

"I suppose the boss would know best," Ted said as he smiled at him. "I will call the boss once I arrive. Perhaps new information about the deals will be revealed."

"Any new information would be helpful with this deal," replied Bill grinning.

Circles in Stone

"Enjoy your stay here in Vancouver," Ted said. "Hope you have a good flight out."

"Thank you," Bill replied as he got up. "Same to you, see you at the meeting."

Bill walked off and disappeared into the crowds.

Sarah returned after a while thrilled with what she had seen. It was all more than she would have expected from being in an airport. She sat with her father for a while telling him what she had taken pictures of, and at the same time enjoyed watching the fish in the aquarium.

Ted was hungry now so they were off to the restaurant located in the Fairmont Hotel. Sarah dined on grilled chicken, while her father had an Angus beef burger with mushrooms. Cheesecake for both was for dessert. It was all chased down with California white wine for Sarah and draft beer for Ted. While eating their meal they watched the sunset behind the mountains on Vancouver Island. It was a wonderful close to the first leg of their trip.

The next morning started with a fine breakfast at the same place they dined the night before. They then went back to the airport and checked in for the second leg of their journey.

Soon they were airborne heading over the mountains of western Canada and out over the vast blue Pacific Ocean. This flight was shorter than the last one, but still 6 ½ hours. Movies, food, and drinks again seemed to make the time pass faster.

Five and a half hours into the flight, Sarah could feel the plane begin to descend. She was now watching intently out the window for those specks of land in the middle of the vast ocean below. After an announcement to prepare for landing Sarah began to see silhouettes of land appear. Soon they became bigger. They were much bigger than she had imagined. She could see huge mountains in the middle of them and strips of white lines she knew were beaches around some of them. As the plane flew lower, craters in the center of large hills could be made out. She realized these were old volcanic cones. The water around the islands was bluer than she had ever seen water. It looked as if were painted. It was so clear that she could see the rings of coral from the plane.

Circles in Stone

As the plane circled for the final approach to Honolulu, Sarah got her first real view of the island's most recognized landmark, Diamond Head. She now knew for sure she was about to land in Hawaii. Her heart was filled with excitement. She reminded herself that so many people dream of making this very trip. How very fortunate she was.

It seemed like it took forever for the plane to reach the terminal once it had landed. She and her father were some of the first ones off the plane. As she stepped into the jetway she was hit first by the heat. It was, after all, winter when they left England. It was not a stifling heat. The air felt heavier but it seemed to be filled with all manner of scents. It almost seemed as if she could breathe easier.

The walkways from all the boarding areas were open to the outside. No windows anywhere. She thought to herself that she will always remember the sensations she was experiencing at that moment. Looking at her father she noticed he was smiling widely. Sarah reached over and took his hand the way she once did when she was a small girl. She almost wanted to pinch herself to make sure it was not a dream.

Going through customs was smooth and uneventful. People were very friendly and everyone seemed to be dressed in colorful Hawaiian prints. She could smell the strong perfume of flowers in the air.

Once through customs, it was now time to collect their bags. As they approached the baggage area Ted notice a man holding up a sign with their names on it. It read Ted and Sarah Harper. Ted waved at the man who approached and placed a lei around each of their necks and, at the same time, hugged each of them touching his cheek to theirs. Ted's lei was made of some sort of black nuts. Sarah's was made of Plumeria blossoms, whose powerful fragrance now filled the space where they were.

"Aloha, welcome to Hawaii," the man said. "My name is Ka Koa. I will be taking you to your hotel."

"Thank you very much," replied Sarah and Ted at the same time.

"I hope your flight was a pleasant one?" Ka Koa said. "We will be on our way as soon as we collect your bags."

"Fantastic," answered Ted.

Ted had noticed that Sarah had not stopped smiling for even a moment since she got off the plane. Despite his reservations, he began to feel that the trip had been a great idea. Just seeing his daughter smiling so much was worth everything to him.

After collecting their bags, Ka Koa took the cases and told them to follow him to where he parked the car.

Once in the car and on their way, Ka Koa told them it would be about a 25-minute journey to the hotel. Sarah noticed how strange it was for the car to be on the other side of the road. Looking out the window she noticed the mountains, they looked so strange but so beautiful. The coconut trees and many others she did not know made it feel as if she was in another world. Compared to England, for Sarah, it was.

As they approached the Waikiki area Sarah also noticed how many very tall buildings there were.

"Are those all hotels?" she asked Ka Koa.

"Yes, most of them are," he replied. "Yours is one of the finest in Hawaii."

Sarah had no idea it was so crowded. Her smile diminished a bit at the thought. Ted also noticed her change of expression. Ted knew because of her condition that crowds could be a problem.

Soon they arrived at the Royal Hawaiian Hotel resort. Going inside it truly did look like a royal palace from glory times gone by. It did not have the feel of a hotel at all. The sites and the smells filled Sarah's and Ted's senses. Her smile returned. Sarah soon spotted a view of the beach through the open doors. She could hear Hawaiian music. She wanted to go straight out there but thought she had better change first.

Circles in Stone

The separate rooms Ted had booked were next to each other but both had stunning views of Waikiki Beach. From their balconies, they could see all the way to Diamond Head. The ocean breeze flowed through the open door and into the rooms like a wide but gentle river. The sound of Hawaiian music and the waves rushing ashore flowed up to her room and blended like a well-mixed drink.

Before Sarah changed to start exploring, she sat in a chair in front of the open door overlooking the beach. With her eyes closed, she took in all the wonderful sensations and smells of paradise. For these moments, England, the digs, and the whole rest of the world just vanished. Hawaii, she thought, "I am here and ready for whatever you have to share."

Chapter 10

Chaos

As the SGM was making plans for what they saw as a possible coming storm, others were still trying to decide what to do. The ODR planned another meeting. This time in London, and just a 10-minute walk from Scotland Yard where many of its members worked. The ODR made it a policy to never discuss order business at the Yard.

The Sofitel St. James hotel is where the meeting is to take place, in their Belgravia Suite. It was a modern private meeting room on the lower ground floor. Seating just 12 with a center table and chairs all around, it was the perfect size for those members that had been called. The suite was booked for two days of meetings. The first day's meeting would have only six members attend.

Chair of the meeting was Charles Stewart, of course, the head of the ODR. The others were Jason Elliott, Oliver Calvin, John Coke, James Wilson, and Lewis Hall.

The first two to arrive were Charles and Oliver. Jason soon arrived followed by the rest except for Wilson Hall aka Ted Rowland. As each got a drink and was taking their seats, Jason noticed that Charles was looking at his tablet very intensely. After they were all seated no one was speaking as Charles continued to look at his tablet. From the expression on his face, he was not happy with what he was seeing. Finally, he closed the tablet and looked at everyone.

"Is everyone here," he asked. "Where is Lewis?"

Looking directly at Jason with a burning glare, he asked again, "Where is Lewis?"

Jason looked back at him and then around the room like a deer caught in headlights.

"He won't be here sir," Jason answered. "He wanted me to deliver you a message."

"Oh, is that right?" asked Charles while still staring at Jason. "And what would that message be?"

"He said he was going on holiday," replied Jason

"Going on holiday?" Charles shot back. "Now why would he do that at a time like this? Right now, when we need all the good men we can get."

Jason and the others could see that Charles's face was turning a bit red.

"It wouldn't have anything to do with what I was just watching, would it?" replied Charles with an almost angry tone. "A car chase involving one of our men after he was caught watching his house. Now I wonder who would have ordered such a thing. I know I didn't!"

Jason was about to speak but before he even got a word out Charles slammed his fist on the table. Looking straight at Jason, his eyes were blazing with anger.

"Don't you dare speak Jason!" Charles snarled. "I gave the mission to retrieve the documents from the Sisters' archives to him myself. What or who gave you the authority to override those orders? You are not the head of this Order; I am, voted in by the majority of our more than 400 members. You had no authority, no reason, nothing, to do what you did. Now one of our members, whom we need the most, is out of touch and another of our members is dead!"

"Dead!?" Jason blurted in. "I didn't kill anyone or order anyone to do so."

"That much may be true," Charles answered. "But because of your actions, someone is!"

"Who, how?" asked Oliver.

"The man you sent to spy on Lewis," Charles replied staring at Jason.

"Who did it?" asked John Coke. "Was it the SGM?"

"Don't be ridiculous," replied Charles. "They are not that stupid. I just found out today that it was one of the Morgans. They are the ones that sent me the video taken from the man's car cam of the chase. They arrived at the site of the car off the road just after Lewis had left. It seems they have been following some of our members and Lewis was one of them. Finding the man handcuffed to the car they released him and began to question him. Our man, or should I say, your man, went to the boot of his car pretending to retrieve information to give them. He instead pulled a gun. Some kind of skirmish followed and he came up on the short end of their magic."

"Then it was Lewis's fault, not mine," shot back Jason.

"Don't you even try to crawl away from this Jason," Charles snarled back at him. "If you would not have overridden my orders and put that man on Lewis's tail, this man would still be alive. Even if the Morgans would have caught Lewis, I am sure he would have been able to deal with them."

Everyone in the room was stunned. Finally, James Wilson said that it would be a good idea to have a moment of silence for their fallen comrade. Charles agreed. After the silence, Charles gathered his composure and got down to the reason for the meeting.

"Despite the way it was done, information was retrieved from the archives," Charles told the group. "With the help of others, John has been able to decipher valuable information from what was gathered. I am going to ask him to share what he has learned with you as he has already done with me."

John Coke switched chairs with Charles at the front and flipped open his computer that was already in place. The built-in screen behind him lit up with his desktop in plain view. After opening a few files, a bunch of dates, maps, and other information appeared on the screen. John meticulously went over how he had gleaned information from the documents and maps that led him to his conclusion.

"Based on everything I have just shown all of you," John said. "I do not doubt that the person we're looking for, the last living direct descendant of Merlin's line, is in Hawaii. Now I am not sure which island. We also found no information about who this person is. But, I repeat, I am positive beyond any doubt that we will find him or possibly her residing in Hawaii."

"How do you suggest we find this person there if we don't know who or which island they are on," asked Oliver. "The haystack may be much smaller but it's still a big pile of hay."

"Whoever it is, they and their family have been there a very long time," Charles said. "With that much time, they are sure to have left tracks. What we need is a good tracker."

"Who do you have in mind?" asked Jason.

Charles looked around at everyone and his face became almost pale.

"Considering what we have just learned today," replied Charles. "I feel like I may have created chaos for us. Two days ago, I contacted the Morgans."

The room came alive with moaning and stirring.

"What?" John asked. "Why them? They killed one of our own. You are right. This is madness and chaos. I am sure we could do this without their help."

"I know, I know," said Charles. "At the time I had no idea what they had done. But I did and still do think we can use them. They are the only ones that can read tracks left by someone that uses old magic. We also outnumber them. We must look at the big picture now."

"They track the magic trail and we track them," said Jason. "Once we find this descendant, we overwhelm them?"

"We will have to play it closer than that," replied Charles. "There is the SGM to deal with too. Before we go too far let's see how the Morgans are to deal with. I have invited them for a meeting in this same room tomorrow. I want all of you here. Once we have them here and see how that goes, we will be in a much better place to make real plans."

"I don't like it," James Wilson said with great nervousness.

Jason jumped in, "This is a public place. They would never think of doing anything here. There are cameras everywhere and many of us are from Scotland Yard. I am sure they are smarter than that."

"Jason is right," replied Charles. "That is why I called the meeting here, on our turf. The meeting is at 10 am, I want you all here in this room by 9. I will greet them in the lobby and bring them down here."

"Shall we come armed?" Oliver asked.

"No," replied Charles. "They would sense that in a heartbeat. But I do want our own extra cameras set up in this room. I want them in plain sight. God, I wish Lewis was here. Since that's not going to happen, I put you, Oliver, in charge of that."

"Yes sir," replied Oliver. "I will get right on it."

"I want you, Jason," Charles said looking directly at him. "To see if you can find Lewis. Credit card traces, CCTV, do whatever. You lost him, now you find him!"

"I will do my best," answered Jason, secretly not wanting to follow that order.

"So," said Charles. "Let's all get to work. See you all in the morning and don't be late."

They all got up and left the room in silence.

***

The next morning everyone was back in the room at 9 am as Charles had asked. Oliver was putting last-minute checks on all the cameras and recording equipment. Charles set up the seating so he would now be close to the door. The Morgans would be seated on the backside of the table. He was trying to make sure that if anything did happen that he and his men had a chance to escape. He also wanted the Morgans to feel boxed in.

Charles took Jason aside to ask him if he had found any trace of Lewis.

"I spent all of the rest of yesterday and half the night running every check I could think of," replied Jason to Charles's inquiry. "He either covers his tracks well or he doesn't leave any. I found nothing."

"Too bad," Charles said. "That's really too bad.

The truth was that Jason had made little effort to look for Lewis. In his mind, if Lewis never came back would be fine with him.

At 9:50 am Charles left the meeting room and went to the lobby. As he arrived in the lobby just as he saw Master Rhyfel and four others enter through the street-level door.

Lord Rhyfel looked much different than he did in the video from the Tower that Charles had seen. He was dressed in an all-black suit, with a black shirt. His hair was pulled back. His beard was well-groomed. He looked the gentleman, though an exocentric one, a gentleman just the same. He approached Charles as if he knew him. He shook his hand without saying anything and turned toward those following him.

"Mr. Stewart I would like you to meet four of my family members," he said, as he stretched out his hand toward them. "This is

Lord Ambrose and his wife Lady Selma and this is Lord Seamus and his wife Lady Eris."

The women were all dressed in very fine suits as well as the men.

"It is my pleasure Gentlemen and Ladies," responded Charles. "Please come this way. The meeting room is on the lower ground floor."

Once in the meeting room, Charles introduced everyone. They all took their seats except James. He was fixing drinks at the bar that the hotel had provided in the room.

"Can I please get anyone a drink? asked James with an open-to-everyone question. Rhyfel spoke up first.

"Yes please," he said. "A Scotch on the rocks would be great."

After making his drink along with others who followed, each with their own request, James took his seat.

There was an awkward moment of silence before Charles broke it.

"Can I begin with_?"

Rhyfel interrupted him.

"I noticed all these cameras and recording devices in this room that I am sure are not part of the decor. If you think this is a deterrent to us you are very much mistaken. You very much underestimate our powers. Electronics are some of the easiest things for us to disrupt. So, I am assuming these must be here so no one forgets what is said here."

"Yes, of course," responded Jason nervously. "We record all our meetings in this way. That way there are no mistakes about what was said later."

"I thought so," Rhyfel replied with a grin that let him know he knew it was a lie. "I believe we have met once before. Not in person, but at a New Year's Eve celebration in the Tower of London?"

Jason's face turned red. How did he know? It made a shiver run up his spine.

"Enough of that," blurted Rhyfel. "Let's get down to why we are here. We believe you want our help in some way?"

"Perhaps we can work together for the same goal," replied Charles. "We both seek the same thing. If we help each other, we might work out a way to share in the benefits."

All the Morgans suddenly broke out in laughter at the same time. Jason realized it was arrogant laughter.

"I am going to tell you what you know and what you think we don't know," Rhyfel said as he leaned onto the table. "We already know where he is. We know "they", are a "he", and we know what he is capable of. We know where you got the information. We also know you have no idea what you're doing. What you also don't know is that we tagged one of your own to get the information you thought no one but your Order had."

"What do you mean tagged?" snarled back James. "Who has been tagged, as you say?"

"Who, only I know," Lady Eris said. "They don't even know who they are. I plan to keep it that way."

"Do you know what these are?" asked Lord Ambrose as he held up the black orb that hung around his neck. "These are scrying orbs. Once we tag someone, we can see everything they are doing and hear everything they are saying at any time, no matter where they are. They are the CCTV of old ways."

"What we are saying is," Rhyfel said breaking in. "There is nothing you can offer us. But I will give you a word of caution. Don't get in our way. You are in way over your heads. We have more respect for the SGM than your group. As hard as we tried, we couldn't even tag any of their members. I'd watch out for them too if I were you. If you know what's good for your order, you should consider quitting while you're ahead."

"There are a lot more of us than you," blurted Oliver. "You bleed just like us. I wouldn't underestimate us if I were you."

"Careful there," Rhyfel answered back with a snarl. "You pull a weapon on any of us and you will end up like your member in the car that tried it."

Suddenly Rhyfel reached inside his suit coat and pulled out one of his daggers. Slamming it on the table he looked around the room with mean determination.

"Let me make something clear," Rhyfel said with a stern yet frightening voice. "You think you're safe here? You are not. If I was so determined, I could knock the lot of you out with one pass of this and set this place ablaze. Then walk out of here with no one knowing what happened except that a fire broke out and you poor souls got trapped behind a locked door. So, I think you better rethink any ideas you might have of us sharing anything with your Order. I think this meeting is over. Don't call us again."

Rhyfel put the dagger away as he and the others of his group got up to leave. The members of the ODR sat frozen in their chairs not knowing what to expect. Rhyfel pulled his suit coat closed and picked up the glass that still had Scotch in it. Swallowing the rest of it down with one gulp he slammed the glass down on the table.

"Thank you for the drinks," he said.

The Morgans then all left the room.

The ODR members sat silent for a while. Jason got up and checked the hall to make sure they were gone. He closed the door and sat down still stunned. Finally, Charles spoke.

"Well, that went well. At least we're still here and alive."

"You thought we could work with them?" John asked. "You almost got us all killed!"

After calming himself down, Jason spoke up, "I think we can still do this. This was meant to scare us off and not even try. Think about it. If we were no threat, why would they have even bothered to meet with us? They are weaker than they are letting on. If we don't try, we might as well disband as an Order."

"Jason is right," said Charles. "God is with us. We have resources. We have the means. All we need is the will. I say we go for it. What happened here in this room should never leave. I want all the recordings destroyed. We also need to see if we can find out who they tagged and how."

"What we need to do is get our best men and make plans to go to Hawaii," Jason said. "Perhaps even make it look like we have given up. Once there, we watch them. I still say they will lead us to him."

"Get me a list of men you need and make arrangements," Charles said looking at Jason.

Whatever plans we make must include dealing with the SGM. We also need to find someone to replace Lewis for now. I put you in charge of that Jason. But this time you don't act without my approval."

"Yes sir," answered Jason as he and the others got up and left the room.

Chapter 11

O'ahu

After a day of relaxing from the time change between Hawaii and England, Sarah did as she promised. She took her father shopping. Just across the road from the Royal Hawaiian Hotel is the International Market Place. If you wish to shop for all things in Hawaiian dress and many other tourist-centered items, this is the place.

It was not long before Sarah had found several beautiful Hawaiian print dresses, bathing suits, and shoes. Next, she found several shirts for her father that she said fit his personality. He was happy to go along with her. He was so glad, not only to spend time with her but to see her happy. They then went back to the hotel to change into their new clothes.

Ted checked his SGM private phone after he changed. There was a message on it from Major General Wigmore. It said that there was to be a meeting of the Hawaii unit heads in Waikiki tomorrow at 10 am at the Na Koa Room in the Outrigger Hotel.

Ted had earlier sent a message to Wigmore letting him know where he was staying. The Outrigger was right next door to the Royal Hawaiian. He had to now figure out how to go to this meeting without alarming Sarah. After all, she thought this was his vacation and she was along for the ride. He then went to the front desk for some tourist information. He was formulating a plan.

She had told him, before they left England, of places she wanted to visit. On her list were the North Shore surfing beaches. The winter was the perfect time to watch world-class surfing. It is when the waves were the largest and surfers come from all over the world to ride them. Knowing this, he made arrangements for her to go on a tour there the next day. The tour would take most of the day. He bought the tour and decided to present it to her as a gift.

He was waiting for her in the outdoor Mai Tai Bar located right on the beach in front of the hotel. Sarah soon arrived in one of her new outfits. He promptly ordered himself one of the local ales and Sarah a Pina Colada. Finding a table under a large umbrella next to a palm tree, they set down to relax.

Sarah looked well into the scene with her Hawaiian dress, sun hat, and sunglasses.

"The smell of the sea here is so different," Sarah said as she sipped her drink. "Like it's fresher or something."

"It does smell different," replied Ted, sniffing the air. "It smells like suntan lotion to me."

"That's the people silly," Sarah said laughing.

"Speaking of people," Ted said inquiring. "How are you doing?"

"I am holding my own. Most people seem to be in their own vacation world. The thoughts are noisy but not intrusive."

"I got a surprise for you," Ted said looking at her with a smile.

He handed her the tickets for the tour to the North Shore to watch the surfing. She looked at the tickets and smiled widely.

"You remembered," she said as she leaned over and kissed him on the cheek. "But this is for only one person. Aren't you coming?"

"No, I don't care much for watching surfing. Think I'd just like to stay here, drink beer, walk the streets, and maybe girl watch."

Sarah laughed at the last part. It was hard to think of her father girl-watching. She only ever saw him as her father.

"Was only teasing about the last part," he said laughing.

"Why? You are a man. I suppose it is something men do."

"Afraid a bit old for that now my dear," Ted replied as he took a swallow of his beer.

"Never too old," Sarah said winking at him.

They both laughed.

They spent the rest of the day eating Hawaiian snacks, drinking tropical drinks, and listening to the band playing Hawaiian music. At one point close to dinner time Sarah stood up, and to her father's surprise, took off her dress revealing one of her new bathing suits underneath. She threw the dress in her father's lap and took off for the sea running full-on into the water. Ted laughed as he watched her frolicking in the waves. He so much wished he could just walk away from the real reason he was in Hawaii and just enjoy his daughter's happiness. He knew too many others depended on him and the stakes were too high to entertain the idea any further.

After Sarah's swim, they went to their rooms to change for dinner. Ted had made reservations at Sky Waikiki restaurant with its great sunset views overlooking Waikiki from a rooftop.

At dinner, Sarah watched the breathtaking sunset as she dined on baked Ono fish and Ted had steak as usual. They stayed drinking and listening to music while watching the tropical nightlife whizzing by far below them.

They both retired around 10 pm. Sarah went to bed excited about her upcoming trip to watch the surfers and Ted thought about the meeting that would take place in the morning.

***

Both rose early in the morning and had breakfast in the Surf Lanai restaurant located in the hotel. Sarah did a quick change to get ready for the tour, which was leaving at 9 am. Ted saw her off and teased her.

"Now don't fall in love with any surfer dudes. Their lives are full of too many ups and downs."

"Very funny Dad," Sarah said as she got into the tour van.

After waving goodbye to Sarah, Ted went to the beach for a while to watch the waves and see all the surfboards and kayaks being prepared for the day ahead. He then wandered to the Outrigger Hotel at about 9:30. He walked around the lobby for a while looking over the outrigger canoes on display.

He was suddenly startled a bit by a familiar voice behind him.

"Aloha Colonel Rowland," came the voice.

It was Captain Bill Bastwick whom he had last seen in the Vancouver airport.

"Aloha to you Bill," Ted responded with a smile. "Good to see you again."

Just as they were shaking hands someone else spoke. This voice Ted did not know.

"You must be Colonel Rowland; I am Colonel Jack Fairway. I have heard a lot about you. General Wigmore sent me a photo so I would be able to recognize you."

"This is Captain Bill Bastwick," Ted responded as he shook his hand. "He is part of our England division."

"Aloha to you both and welcome to Hawaii," Jack answered. "If you both would please follow me to the meeting room, the others are already in there."

The Na Koa room was small but private. Seating only 12 it was usually used for board meetings. The room came with a portable bar and snacks. It was the perfect setting for the meeting.

The other four men that were already in the room stood up as soon as the three of them entered.

Jack introduced each of them. There was Major Pika Johnson, Major Kaimana Parker, Captain Aolina Kim, and Lieutenant Makani Wilson.

All these men were from Hawaii and had served in the United States military at some point. They were recruited by the SGM for their belief in the sovereign right to be ruled by Kings and Queens as their beloved Hawaii once had been. They believed that the cause of the SGM would someday lead to the return of Hawaii as a sovereign nation and once again be ruled by Kings and Queens. The historical connection to Great Britain is well known. It is why the Union Jack is part of the Hawaiian Flag to this day.

After all the introductions, and everyone had a drink in front of them, Jack opened the meeting.

"It appears that the ODR has now figured out that our man is here," Jack began. "Our latest intelligence says that they know he is here on the islands but they do not know where. It has also revealed that they tried to recruit help from the Morgans, but that meeting did not bear any fruit they hoped. The other thing that we have learned is that Morgans also know he is here and they are also planning to come here."

"So, our worst fears have come true then?" asked Ted. "What about the ODR? What do we know of their plans?"

"After the meeting with the Morgans they went mostly silent," replied Jack. "The General told me that every channel of information that normally comes out of them suddenly dried up. Evidently, the meeting with the Morgans shook them. The one good thing we did learn is that there will be no collaboration between the ODR and the Morgans.

"I am not surprised," responded Ted. "It's a wonder that ODR members got out of that with their lives. But the silence does tell me something. It means they are most likely restructuring and they will be more determined than before. You can count on them coming here. They don't want us or the Morgans to know what they are up to."

"Has Alexander been informed?" asked Bill.

"Yes," replied Jack. "Anything we learn is given directly to him."

"Where is he now?" asked Ted. "Is he working on a plan?"

"Yes, he was," replied Jack "He came up with a very clever one. He has two homes, one on either side of the Big Island. He is using some sort of spell to hide the one in Volcano and is leaving the one in Kona exposed. Meanwhile, he is booked into one of the resorts as a tourist."

"Well done," said Captain Kim. "That's some good thinking on his part."

"He has not told us which one at this point," Jack said. "He contacts me daily through different methods. This way, he says, we can concentrate on dealing with the others and not on protecting him directly."

"I agree with him fully," replied Ted. "What we need to do first is to put a watch on the airports. It is the only way any of them are going to get into the islands. I doubt any of them would use cruise ships. We need watches on all four airports where international flights come into."

"You are right Ted," responded Jack. "Major Parker, you will oversee setting up those on the Big Island's airports since you are from there. Major Johnson, you will be in charge of Maui. Lieutenant Wilson, you will be with Captain Kim and Captain Bastwick to cover the airport here. Get whatever men you might need from the units from the island you're on. Photos of known members of the groups will be given to each unit. You are to report anything, and I mean anything to either Colonel Rowland or myself."

"When you do call in," Ted followed. "Use only SGM phones and send coded messages when possible. No military-looking clothes. None of the members of these groups know any of you from here so this is a decisive advantage. I will stay here on this island for now and Colonel Fairway I feel it would be best for you to return to the Big Island and be closer to where Alexander is."

"I agree with you," answered Jack. "I will coordinate with our units there to be prepared for whatever comes. This is our turf and this is our main advantage. We must exploit it to the fullest."

"Absolutely," Ted said. "From what I can already see, the best camouflage here is to blend in. Standing out not only gives you away but also makes you a target. I am sure you already have photos of the Morgans. One thing about them is that they are easy to spot, they like standing out."

"Yes, we have had photos of them for a long time," replied Jack. The General sent some updated ones of them not long ago."

"I think that is it then," Jack said. "Thank you all for coming. Let's get to work and get this net spread as fast as we can. It's time to go fishing gentlemen. The meeting is now closed."

They all stood and shook hands again, got some more drinks, and finished off the snacks. They each left one by one until Jack and Ted were the only ones there.

"What do you think?" asked Jack.

"A fine bunch of men. The plan sounds clean. I guess now we just wait."

"You enjoying your stay so far?"

"As you know I have my daughter with me. It was the General's idea. She is enjoying herself so far. I worry about her safety if this situation blows up. I didn't like having to deceive her to get her to come."

"I understand completely, I have a wife and daughter myself. I can never tell them everything. But it's the nature of our business. Someday if they find out what we do and have done I think they will understand."

"I suppose you are right. How about another drink out where we can watch the waves?"

"Would love to but I got a plane to catch back to the Big Island. Perhaps we can when this is all over. We can swap war stories."

"Sounds like a date," answered Ted.

They shook hands and saluted each other as they parted.

After the meeting, Ted decided to walk around Waikiki. After finding some fast-food lunch he happened upon the Fort DeRussy Army Museum, right there in Waikiki. There were lots of displays and history of Hawaii during World War II. Ted found it most interesting.

Before long the day was gone. Sarah would be back soon. So, he headed back to the hotel, ordered a drink sat down, and watched the waves. He had seen a nice place to eat in the Outrigger Hotel called Dukes, named in honor of Duke Kahanamoku, one of Hawaii's most famous surfers. Ted thought it would be a great treat for Sarah after a day of watching surfers. With that in mind, he made reservations there for them for dinner.

Sarah returned just before sunset all excited about her day. She found her father still sipping on a drink by the beach. He told her about the dinner plans and she could tell him all about it then. She agreed but said she must change first.

At dinner, she told him all about the huge waves and the men and women brave enough to ride them. She was pleased that her father had picked Dukes for dinner. Sarah asked her father about his day. He told her about finding the military museum. She was happy that he found something of interest to him also.

For Sarah, it had been a perfect day in paradise. For her father, it had been an interesting day but also filled him with concern. But he also knew that worrying about things that have not or may not happen was a waste of time. Sarah was happy; he was hoping it would stay that way.

They spent the rest of the evening listening to live Hawaiian music The music, the waves rushing on the shore and the flicker of the Tiki torches in the breeze, made all those worries vanish, for a while at least.

***

The next morning at breakfast Ted asked Sarah if there was anything special, she would like to do that day. Ted wanted to get in as much time with her as possible before things might get serious with the mission.

"No, not really," she answered. "Why don't we do something together you would like?"

Ted thought for a while as he ate his pile of eggs and bacon.

"Well, there is something I'd like to see if it would not bore you to death," he answered after a long pause, "I would like to visit the Pearl Harbor memorial. What happened there is what finally brought the Americans into WW2. I would like to see it firsthand."

"That sounds interesting," Sarah responded with a bit of excitement.

"Great, I will get one of those cars I rented and will see if I can drive us there without causing a panic on the road."

Sarah laughed. Having already ridden in vans to the north shore she could see that driving in America could be an adventure all its own.

Following breakfast, they both changed for the day out. Ted got the car out and picked up Sarah at the lobby entrance. Ted drove the car as if he had always driven in the US. He had driven on the other side of the road in other countries when he was in the military so this was not all that new to him.

Both Sarah and her father found the tour of Pearl Harbor very interesting as well as moving. Reading all the signs and looking at the many displays seemed to make the events there seem more real than just reading about them in history books.

Sarah very much liked the boat ride to the Arizona Memorial. Once there she became very somber as she saw all the names of the sailors that lost their lives. She could hear the solemn thoughts of the other visitors as well. She forced herself to turn off those thoughts.

She and her father stood next to each other as they looked down at the sunken ship below them. They were both thinking about those that never made it out of the ship when it went down. When Ted saw oil surface from the wreck below, it reminded him that it was not all that long ago this all happened.

Once the tour had ended and they drove back to the hotel, the day was over. They dined at Duke's again and watched the sunset. Another day ended in paradise. The day's tour at Pearl Harbor reminded them that Hawaii was not always a paradise. Ted understood it still was not for some.

As the sun set and Sarah sat with him, he enjoyed the moment, wishing it would never end.

Chapter 12

Operation Cook

General Wigmore was right. The ODR had almost gone silent. After the failed meeting with the Morgans, everything changed for the ODR. The first thing that happened was an election was held for the leadership. Charles ran to hold his top position, but it was Jason who challenged him. This is a position that Jason had felt he deserved for a long time. He had a loyal following but it proved not to be enough. The meeting with the Morgans worried some about Charles's leadership. They wondered if the idea of dealing with those that used magic was good for the Order or perhaps violated the Order's principles. It looked like that Jason might have a fair chance to win. But when it became known that Jason was partly responsible for the loss of one of their members, by ordering the surveillance of Lewis Hall without permission from Charles, it cost him the election. Jason blamed Lewis for the death of the member and now he blamed him for his loss of the election and made little effort to find him despite Charles's continued insistence. What worried Charles was that the records of the election showed that Lewis, for the first time in many years, did not vote. He even wondered if something may have happened to him. He had his suspicions that Jason had been involved but, with no evidence, he did not pursue it any further. Charles finally, out of desperation, asked someone to check Lewis's home. When they knocked on the door there was no answer, so they tried a window. That's when alarms went off and police soon showed up. It took some calls to and from Scotland Yard to clear that mess up. After that, there were no more attempts made to locate Lewis. It was now clear he did not want to be found and for this Charles blamed Jason. Charles also knew he did not want to dissuade Jason. He was, after all, the most focused and dedicated member even if at times he was a loose cannon.

After the election, they re-evaluated their strategy and made a lot of changes to the way they operated. Though some disagreed, many still believed that it was a call by God to retrieve the Jewel of Power. The fact that they had survived the encounter with the Morgans' was evidence to many of them that they were protected and that providence was on their side. But it was now clear that they were not up to the challenge of retrieving it by doing things the way they always had.

The first thing they did was to purchase new phones for all the 400-plus members of the Order. They then developed coded and secure systems to communicate. Messages were now being sent to each other either by Post or by messenger using a type of Morse code. The Morse code texting system consisted of using two different letters each day. For example, one day, the letters might be T and X. So, Ts would represent dots in messages, and Xs would be dashes. An SOS would look like, TTT XXX TTT. The new letter format was to be mailed to each member in the post once a week before it was implemented.

There were to be no more high-profile meetings to be held in highly visible or public places. Meetings that had to take place, were to be scheduled in members' homes or other secure facilities.

The hunt for the tag the Morgans had told them about took a while but also became fruitful. Using the clues that the Morgans gave them about the orbs they wore at the meeting they were able to trace the tag to James Wilson. He had received, in the post, a crystal lapel pin he thought was a gift from a charity he'd done work for in the past. In the thank you letter; he was asked to wear it to show he had been honored by them. After an investigation, it turned out the charity didn't give out such awards. It was then determined that this was the tag sent to him by the Morgans. Charles then ordered a review of all such gifts given to senior members. Jason suggested the tagging device be placed in a fish tank in his office. That way it would appear to still be active to the Morgans. But anything the Morgans might receive would be blurred and garbled. He surmised that if they destroyed it, the Morgans would be aware that it no longer functioned and were sure to attempt to tag someone else. James was not reprimanded for the tag because everyone realized that anyone could have fallen for the same scheme. They also made it a policy that no one in leadership roles was to receive gifts from anyone without it first being cleared by all other senior members.

Charles finally ordered a replacement to be located for Lewis. After a search among their many members, Jason located someone that he thought would fit the bill. A man named Edward Goddard. He was an ex-military security officer and had also served as a travel liaison for high-ranking officers. He knew everything there was to know about arranging travel to anywhere in the world. Others that knew him gave him the nickname "The Finder", because if you needed something he had a knack for finding it, no matter where he was. This is just the kind of man the ODR needed at this time. Jason also made sure he was loyal to him personally and would take orders from him without question.

They now also broke from an unwritten rule that before had always been followed. The rule stated, that no Order business was to be talked about by members of Scotland Yard or other agencies while working there. Not only would this be put aside but they would now use the Scotland Yard resources to carry out their plans. Instructions and methods were put in place that when anyone used Scotland Yard or any other government agency resources, they must wipe clean the trail of using them, even if it meant destroying entire computer hard drives.

Charles, through his position at the Yard and with his influence with MI5, managed to get the Morgans listed on the terrorist watch list. This meant that the Morgans could be watched and followed by both Scotland Yard and MI5. Any information about them or their travels within the country would be reported back to Charles directly. With this new power, the ODR could now restrict any travel plans, attempted by any of the Morgans, to leave the country. The ODR knew they would still eventually need them at some point to track the magic of the Merlin descendant. The ODR had every intention of letting them travel to Hawaii at some point for that purpose, but now they could control when that would be. Charles had to make sure that the ODR had a base established there first.

Charles also tried to get the SGM listed as a terrorist group but this failed at every turn. Even he was not aware that there were members of the SGM working in Scotland Yard and MI5. These people reported directly back to General Wigmore. This action often gave the SGM a window into what the ODR was planning. After this action failed, Charles was smart enough to realize why. This was the reason the order to leave no trail when using Yard resources. He knew if SGM found out that Yard resources were being used they could cause real problems for the ODR members working in Scotland Yard. The ODR knew that the eyes and ears of both, the Morgans and the SGM would be now on them, so what they did had to be kept as quiet as possible. The suggestion of Rhyfel to give up was now being turned into a strategy. Go silent and make it look like they had indeed given up or at least that they had backed off the pursuit for now.

It all looked good on paper but the ODR had completely underestimated the SGM. It did not take long for the SGM to pick up the ODR trail and start to unlock their plans.

***

The ODR's plans to get to Hawaii were in full swing. The new man, Edward Goddard was assigned to organize and implement these new plans.

The first part of the plan was for Edward Goddard to go to Hawaii first. He would fly to Honolulu and then on to Kona on the Big Island. All further flights would be direct to the Big Island on direct flights to Kona, bypassing Honolulu, in hopes of not being detected by the SGM which he was sure already had people there. Goddard's job was to find a place where the ODR could set up a headquarters in the islands from which they could operate. Even though they did not know where the Merlin descendent was located, the idea was for the ODR to set up in a place that had good resources but would draw the least attention. Those headquarters were to be on the Big Island, thinking it would be out of the view of those that might be watching for them. He was also to arrange all further member flights in and find them lodging. His plan was to first bring in four of the top men of the ODR. He would do this over a period of one month. One would fly in every week or so. The timing between them would be staggered. The staggering would hopefully throw off anyone that might be watching the group members' movements. The one-month time-space would make it look as if they were not being serious about searching even if they were discovered.

Following Goddard, the first to fly in would be Jason Elliott. He would oversee the setup of the new headquarters and communications. One week later, Oliver Calvin would come. His mission would be to acquire weapons. After that John Coke would arrive to study terrain and history, looking for traces of where the descendant might be located. Lastly, Pete Walker would arrive. He would control and oversee all security and also when and how the Morgans would arrive when the time was right. Being able to control the Morgans' travel plans gave them lots of time. Being in a hurry had already cost them dearly. They would not make that mistake again.

All four would take the same 25-hour flight out of Edinburgh, with stops in Amsterdam and Los Angeles and then on to Kona. Once arrived, Goddard would have arranged for a rental car for each of them to be picked up at the airport and a place for each one to stay. They would not all stay at the same place but would be near enough to each other to make quick contact if necessary. They called this grand plan "Operation Cook" after Captain James Cook the person that truly put Hawaii on the map for the first time.

History records that Captain Cook died only a few miles south of Kona on the Big Island when attacked by the Hawaiians after he touched a chief in a skirmish.

The use of the powers of Scotland Yard by the ODR was not playing well for the Morgans. Rhyfel had tried several times to get flights out to Hawaii. Each time he had been stopped by immigration for all manner of reasons. It soon became apparent to him that somehow the ODR was behind it. Trying to find a way around this was becoming frustrating, to say the least. They tried to find out what the ODR had done. That proved to be almost impossible. Scrying had become useless. The ODR at times appeared to have fallen off the earth. Even the old magic was proving no match for the new magic of the Internet, computers, and endless paperwork. They were soon all scouring through old books of magic in all their libraries looking for spells that might transport them to the islands without the use of modern transport. So far, no such spells had been found. The closest thing they found was a spell for manifesting one's image to another place but for even that to work there had to be a person of like powers to receive it. Their false sense of security in magic, which they thought was invincible, was now beginning to show itself.

Lord Ambrose meanwhile, had taken up another source of study. This was of Hawaii's history, landscape, maps, and customs. He even began to investigate the Morgans' own history believing there might be something that might prove useful. He had become convinced that there was more information about this Merlin descendant than what they had gotten so far from other sources. To do this he turned to the new magic of the internet and modern books of history. He was confident that they would get to Hawaii at some point and this knowledge would become useful. Using this time of delay, as he saw it, could come to serve them later.

He had already told Rhyfel that he had seen a vision. In this vision, a rope of fear had been turned into a rope of control and was now being used by their enemies to tie them up. Unfortunately, this rope had been supplied by the Morgans themselves. He told Rhyfel, that it would be best not to fight the rope but to just hold onto it. That those same enemies would pull them into the place they want to be and once there the rope could be cut. Rhyfel trusted Lord Ambrose's visionary powers. He told him he would take it under serious consideration.

Despite the vision, Rhyfel was going to continue to poke at the wall of their travel prison looking for any weakness. Perhaps, he thought, somehow the ODR had left a weak spot. All he had to do was find it.

***

The SGM was now using every means possible to keep track of both the ODR and the Morgans. They were sure that both were going to make a move.

Shortly after the meeting, Ted had with Jack and the others in Waikiki, he was informed of the Morgans being put on the terrorists' watch list. Ted knew at once who was responsible for it. General Wigmore also told him that a rash of new phones had come online all linked to members of the ODR. Shortly after monitoring these phones, it was clear that a code was being used to send messages. It didn't take long for the SGM's code breakers to crack it. Most of what was being sent seemed to be of little importance. The fact that they were now using new phones and a code indicated to Wigmore and Ted that they were planning something. Wigmore told Ted that nothing had been deciphered yet about what those plans might be, but he would alert Ted as soon as they learned anything new. He also told Ted that he was sure that the ODR was going to try to use the Morgans in some way. It was clear for now that the ODR was pulling the strings on the Morgans. Ted assured the General that they would keep their vigilance in Hawaii no matter how long it took.

Circles in Stone

Ted hated to wait for things like this. However, he also knew that if he had to wait, where he was now was a great place to do it. He knew at some point that the mission would become truly active. In any other circumstances, he would focus on the mission. His daughter being this close to where all the action was, gave him great concern. This was the first time he ever felt torn about what he was doing. He could miss something that could make the difference between her being safe and being in danger. Even after seeing how much joy this trip brought Sarah so far, he was still not sure if it had been the right thing to do. It was now too late to wonder. He would have to deal with everything as it came. He knew if he thought too much about whether the decision was right or wrong, it would take away his focus on the here and now. That, he knew, could be more dangerous than any past choice that he already made. What Ted wanted to do, was to get Sarah to go out on her own more and meet new people. Perhaps she would find someone that encourages her to be more socially independent.

Chapter 13

The Dukes Idea

Ted and Sarah had been in Hawaii for nearly two weeks by now. They had toured many of the well-known sites on the island of O'ahu. Places like Diamond Head State Park, Dole Plantation, and Punch Bowl Crater. They spent one whole day at the Polynesian Cultural Center and another day swimming at Hanauma Bay. A visit to the Iolani Palace, the only royal palace on American soil, reminded Ted of the reason why he was really in Hawaii.

Even though Ted found it difficult waiting for things to happen when it came to the mission, he was more than grateful for all the time he had to spend with Sarah.

Sarah was enjoying all the time they were spending together, though it did seem strange to her at times. Her father had always been away a lot on missions or in the military. This was the longest they had spent together at one time that she could ever remember. She was seeing a side of her father that was new to her. She saw a more playful side as well as a curious side. He was always encouraging her to try new foods and learn new things to do.

Ted was now seeing his daughter as a woman. He had always seen her as somehow a child before. She was reminding him of her mother more each day. He was now thinking of her having a family of her own someday. He was wise enough to realize that would not happen if he was always around. He also knew that one day soon he would have to concentrate on the mission and would not be by her side. Every chance he got he would encourage her to spend some time on the beach alone, to just be herself by herself. She often would take his advice but would return looking a bit sad. Ted was sure her condition was causing the sadness. The beach was often crowded and that did not help. Just lying on the beach was not such a good idea for someone like her. She needed to be doing something to keep her mind focused.

One evening while they were having dinner at Dukes, he had an inspiration. It was eating at Dukes that had inspired the idea he was about to share.

"You know how you like to watch surfing?" Ted asked her.

"Yes," Sarah answered with a curious tone.

"Well, why don't you learn to do it yourself?"

"Surf?" she answered surprised.

"Yes, there are plenty of signs around advertising to teach it. You could get a feel for what it is really like. I think you would be great at it."

"I suppose the Duke whispered that idea in your head," Sarah said laughing.

"Well in a way you could say that. I was thinking about the Duke being a great surfer and how much you like to watch it and the idea just sort of came into my head. This is the perfect place to learn. Learning to surf on Waikiki Beach in the shadow of your hero. What could be more classic?"

"You are my hero, Dad, and always will be. But to be honest, I had thought about it, learning to surf I mean," she responded with a sly smile.

"Well, there you go. You can sign up in the morning. By nightfall you will be ready for the North Shore," Ted said with a laugh.

"Ok, I will try it. But no laughing when I fall."

"I promise," replied Ted. "I never laugh when people fall when trying to learn something new. The Gods know too well how many times I have fallen in my life and am sure there will be more in my future."

***

The next day began at another all-you-could-eat breakfast counter. Ted had now decided he liked American bacon, sausage, and Western-style omelets. Sarah loved all the tropical fruits like papaya, star fruit, fresh pineapple, and Kiwi. Ted teased her about eating all that fruit, that she would become a fruit cake. She teased him back by saying he was going to turn into John Wayne.

After breakfast, they strolled down the beach and started interviewing different places about learning how to surf. They both always took things like this on a serious level.

After talking to several operators and listening to their thoughts, Sarah decided on one she could trust to do the best job safely. Ted paid for two days of lessons that were to begin that afternoon.

Heading back to the hotel to change Sarah thanked her father for the idea.

Sarah decided to have a light lunch before going to her first lessons. Ted told her he would let her go on her own so she would not be nervous about him watching, which she thought was a good idea.

Ted wished her luck and returned to his room to get in touch with Wigmore to find out if there had been any new developments.

When Ted got to his room and checked his special SGM phone, he saw that he already had a message from Wigmore to call him. He immediately called him back on his direct number.

"Good evening, General," Ted responded when Wigmore answered. I know it's late there but I returned your call as soon as I could."

"Yes of course," the General answered. "The time difference can be a challenge sometimes. But we have some new information. It seems that the ODR has replaced you, or I should say, Lewis Hall. His name is Edward Goddard. We ran a background on him and it seems he is a very capable man. His main specialty is logistics. Our intelligence says he is on his way there. He should be arriving within a day or so. A full description of him will be sent to you via messenger after this call. I need not tell you to delete the message once you make a hard copy of it. Remember, do not make direct contact. What we need is to see what they do and where they go."

"Of course, General. I will pass this on to all our eyes on the ground here. I will keep you informed of his movements here, once he arrives of course."

"I know you will Ted," answered Wigmore. "It looks like they are beginning to make a move on the situation. Thanks for the return call. Enjoy the rest of your day."

"Thank you General, we will handle it here. Have a good night, sir," Ted said as he ended the call.

As soon as Ted got off the phone, a message came through from Wigmore describing Goddard. It read as follows: white male, 5'4", dark brown curly hair, brown eyes, silver frame glasses, carrying a walking stick with a brass lion head on the top. Often carries a black briefcase with gold studs along its edges.

Ted immediately contacted all units on the island of O'ahu, where he was, and then Jack on the Big Island who would contact everyone on the other islands. Ted made it clear to everyone that no contact was to be made with Goddard. They were to only track his movements and report back to either him or Jack. When Ted contacted Jack to inform him of the Goddard situation, he also asked him to investigate arranging a base of operation on the Big Island. He was aware that at some point the Big Island would be the focus of all activity. Jack agreed but informed Ted that they already had two locations on the island. But he did suggest that they should have another one in Volcano Village, closer to where Alex's main home was located. Jack reminded Ted, who had not been to the island yet, that it was much bigger than the other islands and separated down the middle by two massive mountains. Ted took Jack's advice but added that all the bases should be fully supplied and stocked. When the time came, they could not be wasting time and resources moving what might be needed from one base to another. Jack agreed and said he would get on that as a priority. Ted also asked Jack if he had any idea yet where Alexander was staying. Jack told him that he did not and that was a good thing and should stay that way for as long as possible. Ted was in full agreement with that.

By the time Ted finished with all his communications, it was already drawing on the evening. Sarah would be back soon from her day of surfing lessons. Ted went down to the Mai Tai lounge and ordered a beer. He found a nice chair to relax in so when Sarah arrived it would look like he had spent his day just doing nothing but watching people and waves.

He had not waited long when he spotted Sarah coming toward him, wearing a beach wrap and her wet hair hanging straight. She stopped at the bar on the way to her father and ordered a Pina Colada. She sat down in the chair next to him. Ted noticed that she looked exhausted.

"Did you have a good day?" Ted asked with anticipation.

"Yes," replied Sarah with a tired voice. "I never realized how much work surfing was. It is far more than just jumping on a board and going for a ride."

Sarah's drink arrived and she took a long drink of it. The straw was the only thing stopping her from just gulping it down.

"Did you get to ride a wave?" Ted asked still inquiring.

"Yes, I did. Several of them and even managed to stand a bit on a couple of them though not for very long."

"Wow, that must have been trilling. I am impressed."

"I was too scared of falling to feel the thrill, but just the same I am rather pleased with myself," Sarah said as she took another long sip of her drink.

"How was your instructor?" asked Ted with a grin.

"He is very intense. He loves what he does and is very focused on teaching others what he knows. There was so much to take in, but he wasn't critical. He kept saying that you can't fail if you're having fun."

"I like that attitude. That is a good thing to remember. And what about your condition?"

"It didn't seem to be a problem after a while," Sarah answered with a surprised tone. "I was so concentrated on what I was learning and trying to take it all in it seemed to be blocked. I was so focused on paddling the board at the right time and watching the waves, it seemed like a door was closed to hearing anything else."

"I thought that might be the case," Ted said smiling. "Your mother found the same thing happened to her. I am so glad you discovered it on your own."

"I didn't realize it until just now, when you asked about it," Sarah answered with a puzzled look. "I will have to think on that to see if I can use it in a controlled manner."

"I am sure you will find a way," Ted said still smiling. "So then, I guess more lessons tomorrow? Now that you have the basics you can concentrate on having more fun."

"Yes," Sarah said as she sipped the last of her drink. "I think I will order something from room service tonight for dinner. Take a long hot shower and just rest, if you don't mind Dad?"

"Of course not. You do look tired. I think I will go try a steak at the Steak House I saw on the main street."

Sarah got up and went to her room. Ted stayed and finished his beer but was thinking how pleased he was that his idea of taking surfing lessons had paid off.

Ted enjoyed his steak and went back to his room. He went to bed pleased that the day turned out well. Sarah had learned something wonderful and the mission he was on seemed to be on the move. He also thought he would somehow slowly let Sarah know that he was working on a mission. He would start on that in the morning.

***

The next morning Ted and Sarah enjoyed a quiet breakfast. Sarah was excited about going to her lessons. Before she left, Ted decided to open the gate to her about the mission.

"I have to tell you something Sarah," Ted began. "I got a call yesterday from my boss. He has a mission for me to do while I am here. Nothing much, just wants me to do some monitoring of possible foreign agents using the islands for a base. That's all I can tell you right now."

Ted watched close at Sarah's face for her reaction. To his surprise, she just smiled.

"That's wonderful Dad," she said. "I was worried about you. You need something to do. You get too much enjoyment out of your work to simply stop. You can only holiday for so long. It's not your style. We have been enjoying our time together and it is wonderful. So, I am pleased. Remind me to thank your boss if I ever meet him."

Ted was very surprised by her reaction. He breathed a sigh of relief to have that pressure off his mind.

"I will have to remain here in Hawaii on this island for the time being," Ted told her. We can still do things if you like."

"Well," answered Sarah. "I have been thinking about doing the work I promised I was going to do before we came, the study of ancient Hawaiians and their culture. I have been doing some research on the computer about that and it seems that the best place to do that is on the Big Island. If you don't mind, I'd like to go there on my own and do that research. If you could arrange for me a place to stay, I would be so grateful."

He was once again, taken by surprise. She was so like her mother he thought. So independent and was not shy about doing what she wanted

"Of course," Ted responded with a smile. "Do you have any idea where you would like to be over there?"

"Yes, I would like to be on what is called the Kona side. There seem to be a lot of ancient sites there. But I don't want to be in the middle of a town. There is a resort hotel not far from an ancient heiau toward the north end of the island. I think it's called the Hapuna Beach Resort. Right now, I must go to my lessons, but can let you know this evening."

"I will look it up while you're out," Ted told her as she walked away.

"Thank you, Dad," Sarah shouted back. "Love you and thank you for understanding."

"Don't forget to have fun," Ted shouted to her as she ran down the beach.

Ted sat for a while very stunned by what had just happened. That was far more than he could have ever expected. He was also glad of her choice of location on the Big Island. From what he had learned about the island, he knew it was a long way from Volcano where he knew Alexander lived and could become ground zero at some point.

Ted spent the day doing very little. He checked in with Jack on the Big Island who told him he had located a place that might make a good base of operation just outside the village of Volcano. Ted was pleased with the progress and would keep in touch.

After the call, Ted checked on Hapuna Beach Resort for Sarah. It was just as she said, located near the ancient Puukohola Heiau. He then canceled Sarah's rental car in Honolulu and booked one for her to pick up at the Kona airport. He booked an Ocean View Suite for her, with an option to change if she wanted to. He would later confirm dates after he asked Sarah when she would like to go.

Ted then retired for the rest of the day at his favorite table at the Mai Tai Lounge.

Sarah soon came back looking wet and tired but also very happy. She ordered a Mai Tai at the bar and joined her father. As she sipped her drink, she told her father how the day started, a bit rough but soon she was riding waves on her own. She said she understood now the thrill of it all, feeling the uncontrollable power of the sea pushing you along. She understood why it could become addictive.

Circles in Stone

Ted told her of the arrangements that he had made and that they awaited her approval and dates. He told her that the hotel was located at one end of, Hapuna Beach, one of Hawaii's most beautiful beaches. He also mentioned that Hapuna Beach was also a great place to surf.

After a dinner of Chinese takeaway in her father's room, Sarah went over the details of the arrangements he had made for her. She decided that she would leave the day after next. She wanted to spend one more day with her father before she left. They decided that they would spend the next day at Honolulu Zoo. One of the places they had not yet visited.

Chapter 14

New Island

The next day after Ted had confirmed all the arrangements for Sarah's stay on the Big Island, they spent the day at the Honolulu Zoo. It was smaller than many zoos' in the UK that they had visited in the past; it was very good just the same. They learned how animals from outside Hawaii were dangerous. How many of them had already damaged much of the natural wildlife and plants of Hawaii. They were told that snakes were a particular worry. There are no wild snakes in Hawaii and it was the hope that it would stay that way. Sarah was hoping the same, she did not like snakes.

After a wonderful day out with her father and another dinner at the Sky Waikiki rooftop restaurant, it was time for Sarah to pack for her flight out to the Kona on the Big Island the next morning.

As she packed, she felt sad to be leaving her father behind but she was also excited about what she might learn while exploring another island on her own.

***

Sarah's flight out was a 9 am. The flight would take only about 45 minutes.

In the morning just before Ted left his room to collect Sarah's cases, he had a call from Wigmore. The SGM had intercepted a message that the ODR's man, Goddard, would be landing in Honolulu at 10 am that very morning. Ted thought to himself the timing could not have been better. Ted then called his men that were watching the airport and made sure they were on full alert. He informed them he would be joining them shortly but did not say anything about taking his daughter there.

Ted gathered Sarah's bags and took them to the car. He drove around and picked her up at the hotel entrance where she was waiting for him.

The conversation was light between them on the way to the airport.

"Are you excited?" asked Ted with a tone of apprehension.

"Yes. But I am also nervous."

"You will be fine," Ted said reassuring her. "Just think of it as another dig, just far away from home."

"I suppose that's a good way of looking at it. Just another work assignment only in a different country," Sarah said with a bit of excitement. "I know we won't be far apart really, but I just wanted to thank you for bringing me on this trip. I realize I needed this as much as you did. It has all been so wonderful."

"I am so glad you enjoyed it so far. It has been wonderful for me too. I do love you Sarah and it has always been my wish to see you happy."

"I love you too Dad," Sarah replied with a huge smile. "You really are the best dad ever."

They were both smiling as they arrived at the airport.

The part of the airport where flights leave for the other islands is separate from the main international airport. Locally it is known as the Inter-Island airport. Flights leaving from it only go to the other islands and back and nowhere else. Ted dropped Sarah off at the front to get checked in while he parked the car. He returned to say goodbye and make sure she was all booked through without any trouble.

"Make sure you call me once you arrived," Ted told her as she walked away toward her gate.

"I will, I promise," Sarah yelled back as she disappeared into the gate area.

Ted was sad to see her go but was proud that she had grown into such an independent and confident woman.

Ted now made his way to the main international airport terminal. He and other members of the SGM units all had special passes to allow them into the gate areas without boarding passes.

Just after he entered the main terminal, he spotted Captain Bastwick. When Bastwick spotted Ted, he began to walk toward him, but Ted signaled him not to. Ted ducked into one of the empty gates and called Bastwick. He told him not to acknowledge him and asked him to tell Captain Kim to do the same. He said he would cover one end of the airport and they could cover the rest. This way Goddard would less likely to slip past them.

Not knowing which flight would not make this easy. The only advantage was that not too many flights from the west came in that early in the day. So, the focus would be on flights arriving around 10 am from cities on the west coast of the US and Canada. After checking the arrival monitor, Ted thought the best chance was a flight coming in from LA arriving at just before 10. He decided to focus on that one.

As it got close to 10, Ted thought about Sarah and that she must be arriving in Kona about then.

***

Sarah was, in fact, just getting ready to land at the Kona airport. On her flight, she enjoyed the view out the window and seeing the islands below one by one as they flew by them. Looking out her window as they approached Kona, she was amazed at what she saw. Expecting the usual palm trees and greenery, she saw nothing but blue water up against the black rock. Though she had never seen any before she knew they must be lava fields. They were almost totally devoid of any trees or vegetation. For a moment, she wondered if this was the right island. The announcement by a flight attendant to get prepared for the landing in Kona assured her it was the right one. As the plane turned and made its approach to the runway, she could now see in the distance the towering volcanic mountains that made up the island. To Sarah, these mountains were incredibly huge. She could not have imagined such a sight. The wide lava fields, and the massive volcanoes, gave Sarah the true sense that this was indeed a new island.

Once they landed, she saw that there were no jetways, just a cluster of buildings on the end of the runway. She deplaned down a staircase onto the pavement with lines to direct everyone which way to go. While walking toward the terminal building, she was hit by the heat. Not the kind she felt in Honolulu, but an almost searing dry blast as if from a hot oven being opened. She could see that there were palm trees around the buildings and though out the airport complex. But she knew they must have been planted. They looked out of place on this vast lava plain. Sarah followed everyone to the baggage claim area where she collected her bags. Put them on a cart and headed for the car rental area to collect the car her father had reserved for her.

***

Circles in Stone

Back in Honolulu Ted was sitting outside of the gate where the flight from LA had just arrived. From where he was sitting, he could see every person as they entered the terminal from the plane. It wasn't long before he saw Goddard. The fact that he was one of the first ones off the plane told Ted he had flown first class. Goddard matched the description the General had sent him perfectly. He wondered if that had been on purpose or was the ODR just sloppy. Ted decided that they were just confident that no one had yet broken their code.

Ted immediately sent a text to the other units that were in the airport. He knew Goddard would have to collect his baggage but after that, no one knew where he would go. Therefore, the focus was now on the baggage claim area for that flight.

Ted and the others got to the baggage carousel for that flight before any of the passengers. They spread around at different points but in a way not to look obvious.

Soon Goddard, along with the other passengers from his flight, arrived and collected his bags, and headed to the terminal shuttle waiting area. Ted went over to one of the other members of the SGM that was holding a bag to make him appear to be just another passenger. Ted took the bag from him. Looking down at his phone, as so many other people were doing, he followed Goddard out to where he boarded the inter-terminal shuttle. When Goddard boarded it, so did he. They both rode the shuttle until it reached the Inter-Island terminal near where he had dropped Sarah off. Goddard got off there, along with the other passengers. Ted now knew he must be headed to another island. All he had to do was follow him to the gate from where his flight would depart.

To Ted's surprise, he did not go to the regular gates as he had expected him to. Instead, Goddard went to a private charter desk. It was now clear to Ted he was taking a private flight to another island, which one he didn't know. There were no monitors at such gates telling what flights went where. Ted waited outside the terminal for Goddard to check in and board the plane. Once he saw the plane begin to taxi away Ted decided to use the direct approach to find out where he was headed. He approached the counter and took a wild guess.

"Was that the flight to the Big Island I just missed?" Ted asked the woman behind the desk.

"Did you have a seat booked?" the woman inquired back.

"No. I was just hoping I could have gotten a last-minute seat and get there early."

"That flight is going to Kona on the Big Island." answered the lady. "I can book you on the next one if you like?"

"No thank you. I'll just catch one of the other flights but thank you for your help.

"Mahalo, have a good flight," she said as Ted walked away.

As soon as Ted was out of her view, he called Jack on the Big Island and informed him of what he had just learned. Jack assured him he would have his people on the ground to pick up his trail as soon as he landed. He asked Jack to call him as soon as he found out where he was staying. He was hoping it would not be anywhere near Sarah.

This action by Goddard had taken Ted by surprise. His first concern was if the ODR had learned where Alex lived or was this move a diversion to hide what they were up to on the islands. Not being sure he called General Wigmore and filled him in. Wondering if he should now go to the Big Island, the General told him to stay put for now in case more of the ODR came in there. They might be setting up several bases on different islands to get better coverage. Ted had to agree with Wigmore on that point. After the call, he decided to return to his hotel and wait for any further news.

***

Sarah now got the car that her father had reserved for her. The first thing she thought was how grateful she was that it was white. In the intense sun, even a white car felt hot. Learning to drive this car she hoped was not going to be too much of a challenge. She had never driven a car outside England. She got in the car and began to check where everything was located. With the steering on the opposite side of those in the UK, she needed to orient herself with everything. The first thing she noticed is that it was automatic. She had never driven an automatic before. After starting it up, she found the Stat map and typed in her hotel's name. Next, she found the AC and turned that on. The stat map clearly showed her which way to go from where she was. It looked simple enough. What she did not expect was the hotel would be 40 minutes away from the airport. Wow, she thought, "That is almost as long as my flight was from Honolulu."

She started slowly at first and soon found that not shifting was nice. Stopping and going with no clutch was easy. Soon she was out of the airport and on the main highway. It was what people in England would call a carriageway. She was amazed at how wide the road was, with verges wide enough to drive a car on them.

The landscape she was driving through took her completely by surprise. There was mile after mile of almost barren lava. Some she could tell were older by the brownish-red color and others were black as if they had been put down only months before. The bare lava in places gave way to vast areas of brown grass. It looked very much as she would have imagined a desert would look. There were no trees anywhere except for an occasional cluster of palm trees along the seashore, which was in view almost all the time. About halfway to her hotel, she saw a parking area labeled scenic point. Sarah could not resist stopping.

When she got out of the AC-filled car the blast of heat she encountered almost took her breath away.

Once out of the car, the view she saw was well worth stopping for. Even the heat did not deter her from taking a great many photos.

Looking toward, what she knew was the west, she could see a brown rocky landscape covered in half-green half-brown grass that ran from where she was all the way to the sea that looked to be about a mile away. At the edge of the deep blue-colored sea, she could see a cluster of palm trees.

Looking north the landscape went from light green to a dark green that ran off into the distance and up what appeared to be a low mountain that was also green up to its summit.

To the east was an even bigger mountain. This one, though far away, Sarah could see its top was covered in snow. She thought the contrast looked like something out of a surreal painting. Toward the south, there was another mountain. This mountain appeared closer. The top of it was covered in clouds.

Sarah took many pictures of all the different views. Other people had also stopped to take pictures as well, so she fit right in.

It was here that she decided to call her father. After telling him she had arrived alright and got the car without any problems she couldn't help telling him all about the views she was seeing from where she was. He was excited for her and told her he hoped to join her there as soon as possible.

After the call and despite the heat, she just sat on the stone-built wall around the car parking area taking it all in. She thought to herself if anyone were to have asked to describe Hawaii, this kind of scene would not have ever entered her mind. Even with its almost desolate look, it had a beauty that seem to beckon to her. She felt as if she wanted to walk across every inch and climb to the tops of all the mountains. Or at least walk across the half rock, half grass plain to those palm trees down at the edge of the sea. The heat bearing down reminded her that she would probably die of thirst before she ever reached them. It made her laugh aloud to herself.

Once back in the car, the AC felt nice.

After another 20 minutes of driving, she reached the turnoff for her hotel, the Hapuna Beach Resort. The drive to the hotel wound through a golf course that she quickly determined had been built out of the old lava fields. Green patches, clearly watered, contrasted sharply with the areas that were not.

All around the hotel were a large number of coconut trees as well as other trees she did not recognize. The whole area looked like a large, very well-groomed garden. Flowers of all sorts had been carefully planted. This looked like the Hawaii she was already used to seeing in Waikiki.

She pulled her car to the front lobby. A person came out and welcomed her with a Lei made of orchids. They took her cases from the trunk of the car and offered to park the car for her. They told her when she needed her car, they would retrieve it for her. This was all so posh to her but she accepted it all with gratitude. She never once forgot that her father was responsible for it all.

Soon the bellhop escorted her to her ocean-view suite located on the third floor. It was much bigger than most people's flats back in England. She, for a moment, felt ashamed for having so much space for just one person. The views were stunning.

Circles in Stone

There were balconies, called lanai in Hawaii, off every room. Each one was lined with violet bougainvillea flowers. She could hear the waves washing ashore along a white sand beach that stretched out from the hotel directly in front of her. She knew from the signs she had seen getting to the hotel that it was Hapuna Beach. The one she had read about when she had researched the hotel back in Waikiki.

Sarah right then, decided what she would do with the rest of the day. First, she would check out the restaurant for lunch, and then explore this beach. Perhaps rent a surfboard and put into practice what she had learned in Waikiki. It was time to begin exploring and enjoying this new island.

Chapter 15

Have We Met?

Immediately after Jack received the phone call from Ted about Goddard's flight to Kona he sprang into action. Jack by chance, was on the Kona side of the island at the SGM base there. He was only a few miles from the Kona airport when he received the call from Ted.

He called his men that were on watch at the airport and told them to check times for all private flights coming from Honolulu, and informed them he was on his way there and would arrive in a few minutes.

When Jack arrived at the airport, he contacted the head of security, which he knew well. The SGM had very good relations with all the airport security. In the past, the SGM had helped in covert operations dealing with illegal drugs and others with high-profile criminals trying to hide out in Hawaii.

Jack told the security head he needed to insert himself as a porter at the airport. This way he would help Goddard with his baggage and perhaps pry some information from him with casual conversation. The chief had no problem with that and called the person in charge of all the porters to get a Jack an aloha shirt that matched all the other porters working there. Jack's men had already located the flight and the location it would be coming in to deplane.

Jack made it to the area barely in time.

As the baggage handlers were unloading the plane, Jack was there to meet them with a baggage cart. Watching the passengers deplaning, Jack knew in an instant which one was Goddard. Only five other people had arrived on the flight.

Jack quickly rolled the cart to the baggage claim area and waited for Goddard to come to collect his. Other porters arrived to help each of the other passengers with their bags. A signal was already arranged between them and Jack made sure no one would help Goddard except him.

As soon as Goddard reached for his bags, Jack intervened.

"Are these your bags sir?" asked Jack as he reached to take them. "Let me take them for you sir."

"Thank you," Goddard responded to Jack's actions.

"Aloha, welcome to Kona," Jack said as he loaded the luggage on a personal trolley. "I hope your flight was a pleasant one."

"Yes, it was a nice flight," Goddard responded. "Thank you for asking."

"Are you picking up a car or is someone picking you up?" Jack asked as they stopped at the curb just outside the terminal.

"I called the car rental just as we landed," answered Goddard. "They should be here any moment. They told me it is a Ford escort."

Just as Goddard had finished speaking, Jack saw the car approach.

"I believe this is your car now," Jack said looking at Goddard.

"Yes, I believe it is."

"Great," responded Jack. "You get in and I will put your bags in the trunk."

The driver of the car popped open the trunk as Goddard climbed into the passenger seat. Just as he loaded the bags into the car's trunk, he reached into his pocket and pulled out a small GPS locator. He turned it on and slipped it just under the cover that was over the spare tire. Closed the trunk and went around the side of the cars where Goddard was holding some money for a tip, as is the custom to give all porters in the US.

"Mahalo, have a great stay here on the Big Island," Jack said as the car pulled away.

Jack knew that the driver would take Goddard back to the rental area to sign some papers. After that, Goddard would have the car to himself. The SGM will now be able to track the car's movements for at least a week. Jack called the SGM's office on the Kona side to inform them to begin tracking.

Jack went to the security office in the airport to return the shirt and thank the chief for his help before heading back to his office at the headquarters.

***

Sarah was doing just as she had decided once she had reached her room at the hotel. She found a restaurant called; Naupaka Beach Grill located right next to the beach. There she would have a light lunch. The Chinese Chicken salad and a passion iced tea. It was perfect for a hot day on the beach. She studied the hotel brochure while eating. To her surprise, there were three different restaurants to choose from located around the resort.

While she was dining on her lunch, she noticed a man looking at her. Not in a bad way, but in a way a man would look at an attractive woman. It was not strange to her for this to happen. What was strange is that she could always hear their thoughts. She even sometimes used this to her advantage to tell how she looked to others. She was well within range to be able to hear any thoughts. However, there was nothing. Perhaps it was the trip or something else. She put it out of her mind and continued to enjoy her salad.

She kept glancing in the man's direction to see if he was still watching. He sometimes looked away just as she looked at him. It made her giggle to herself. The man finished a drink he had and put the glass down. He looked intensely at her. All at once, she heard a voice in her head as if it was over a loudspeaker.

"Have we met?"

She was looking directly at the man so she knew he had not spoken. The voice did not come through her ears. This was a thought. But not a subdued thought, the kind that she was used to hearing. This thought went through her head like a thunderbolt. It was so loud and so clear that she put the drink she was holding down on the table and covered her ears.

Sarah began to wonder if something was suddenly wrong with her. Then suddenly, just as before, she heard the voice again.

"Sorry," the voice came. "Didn't mean to intrude. Don't worry, you'll be ok."

Sarah knew this time the thought was coming from the man. It scared her. It was in the form of a conversation. She took another drink. She felt flush. She was not sure if she should run or fight. The man had now gotten up and was coming toward her. He was smiling. The smile made her feel less afraid. Without any further thoughts, he came over to her table, pulled out a chair, and sat down. She felt like a bird in the glare of a cat. Yet his smile somehow was disarming.

"Aloha, my name is Alika," the man said in a natural voice as he held out his hand to her.

"Hi," Sarah said in a half-shy half-scared voice while shaking his hand.

"Sorry about before," Alika said. "I have never come across anyone that could hear my thoughts before. The "Have we met" was just me sending a test to see if it were real. Sort of like a person standing at a microphone saying testing one-two."

Sarah just sat there not sure what to say. He can hear my thoughts. That thought scared her.

"What's your name?" asked Alika.

Sarah sat silent. She did think her name in an answer form.

"It's alright if you don't want to tell me," Alika said with an almost shameful tone. "If you want to be left alone, I understand completely."

Alika started getting up to leave when Sarah finally spoke.

"Sarah, my name is Sarah"

"Aloha Sarah," Alika said with a smile now on his face. "Welcome to Hawaii. I told you my name is Alika. That is true, sort of. Alika is my Hawaiian name. My birth name is Alexander. Everyone calls me Alex."

"What just happened a few minutes ago?" Sarah asked with confusion clearly in her voice.

Alex looked at her puzzled for a moment.

"Oh my God," Alex responded, looking surprised. "That has never happened to you before, has it? That was the first time you knew someone could hear your thoughts."

Sarah, looking down at the table hesitated.

"Yes," she said in a quiet voice. "I suppose it is."

"Don't worry. It was not the first time I knew someone could hear mine," Alex replied. "I have to admit, it is strange when it first happens. But I am used to strange."

Alex saw the expression on Sarah's face look worried. It took a moment but he soon realized why.

"Oh, my goodness," Alex said. "You're wondering if I am hearing all your thoughts now. No, no, I turn that off as soon as I noticed it alarmed you. When I do that, you can't hear mine either. That's the way it works, I guess. This makes it somewhat good. If you can hear mine then you know I can hear yours and vice versa. I have learned to turn off projected thought entirely. Something my father taught me. The book I have says there are two kinds of thought. The ones that we project and the ones we keep to ourselves. Learning to separate them from each other took a long time. For me, if I engage in voice talking, I can't project or receive thoughts."

Sarah suddenly realized it was the same for her. A smile returned to Sarah's face at last. She felt as if she had been holding her breath the whole time and could finally breathe. Sarah was surprised to hear there was a book on the subject. She suddenly did not feel alone with her condition. She wanted to ask for the book but that seemed to be a bit forward to her. Perhaps if she got to know Alex a little better, she could glean even more information about the subject.

They both sat there taking in what had just happened. To Sarah, there seemed to be more questions banging around in her head than answers. To Alex, it was like finding a diamond in a pile of crushed glass. Alex finally broke the silence.

"I think I need a swim," he said as he stood from the table. "It has been more than a pleasure Sarah and I _."

"Mind if I join you?" Sarah said interrupting him mid-sentence. "I was planning on going for one after lunch anyway."

"Would be honored," Alex replied with a broad smile on his face. "You won't find a better swimming beach in all the islands in my opinion."

Alex hurried back to his chair to get his beach towel and headed for the rows of beach loungers that were on the beach facing the ocean. He threw his towel on one. Sarah swallowed the last of her drink and headed off in the same direction. Where Alex put his towel Sarah thought there were four lounges empty, but now it appeared to be only one. It was next to the one Alex had chosen. Must be the sun she thought. She put her towel on the beach lounge and followed Alex toward the waves.

The beach was beyond Sarah's imagination. There was no coral, no stones. Not even a pebble. Perfect, fine, white sand, this was even better than Waikiki. There were plenty of people but it was not crowded. The shore along the beach was lined with coconut trees and further inland there were some larger trees, but she didn't know what kind. The beach must be nearly a half-mile long, she thought trying to take it all in. To her, this was the picture-perfect beach. When she looked inland, she could see the top of the volcano, Mauna Kea, covered in snow. The contrast could not be more dramatic. A crystal blue ocean rolling upon a perfect white sand beach lined with palm trees and a snow-covered mountain for a backdrop. Sarah felt like she was inside a living postcard.

Sarah watched Alex for a while as he swam and would just float on the waves until they almost washed him ashore. He would then repeat the cycle. His past shoulder-length hair was nearly as long as her own hair. He kept it pulled back in a ponytail while he swam. He had a rugged look to him. His skin was dark but not as dark as native Hawaiians she had seen. In all, she thought him rather attractive.

Alex was the first to leave the water and retired to the beach lounge he had chosen. Putting on a light coating of sunscreen he laid back to relax under the afternoon sun.

Sarah stayed in the water a bit longer to enjoy the surreal views until she could feel the sun beginning to cook her skin. She two went to her beach lounge that was next to Alex. He opened his eyes just long enough to see her putting on sunscreen and lying back with her sunglasses and hat on. As she lay there listening with her mind open, the silence was almost eerie being this close to another person without any thoughts coming in. The only other person she had ever experienced this with was her father. After a while, she felt herself drifting off into a nap.

After laying there for about half an hour, Alex got up. This stirred Sarah out of her nap. Alex saw her stir so he made an invite.

"Would you care to join me for a drink at the bar?" he asked. "They do have some wonderful cocktails here."

"Yes," answered Sarah "Could use a nice cold drink after being cooked in the sun."

"Great, see you there," Alex said as he collected his things and walked toward the hotel.

Sarah got up collected her wrap and hat and walk in the same direction as Alex. About halfway back, she realized she had left her sunglasses on the lounge seat. She hurried back to where she had been laying and stopped suddenly in her tracks. She could see her glasses where she left them. Instead of the two lounges where she and Alex had been laying, there were now five. She looked around to see if anyone had moved them. However, there was no one else there. Besides, there would not have been enough time for anyone to move them there. She stood puzzled for a moment. Then collected her glasses and headed for the bar where Alex was. When she arrived at the bar Alex could see she looked puzzled.

"Is there something wrong?" asked Alex.

"Not sure," Sarah responded, as she glanced one more time back to the beach. "It's been a wonderful but strange day. I think I could really use that drink."

Sarah ordered her favorite, pina colada, and asked the bartender to make it a double. Alex ordered a Kona Longboard lager. After the drinks arrived, Alex decided to begin the conversation.

"Before I ask you anything about yourself," he began. "I think it would be proper for me to tell you a little about me first. I don't think it would be right for a lady to answer questions to a man she just met without knowing a little about that man first."

Sarah gave an approving nod as she took a long sip of her drink.

"My last name is Michaels. I was born and grew up on this island, as did many generations of my family. I have two homes here. One is located outside Kailua Kona and the other is in a village on the other side of the island. Both my parents died in a private plane crash a few years ago. They were exploring the Mauna Loa volcano from the air. No one is sure what when wrong but things like that happen.

I work as an Earth Scientist on the Kilauea volcano. I am not, or ever have been married. No brothers or sisters living. Had one sister but she died of a bad heart when she was young. I am staying here in this resort because I like to hide away sometimes and just be a tourist without leaving the island. How's that for a start?"

"That will do for a start I guess," Sarah said with a smile. "What do you want to know about me?"

"Do they have last names where you come from in England? You are from England. I can tell from the accent. I would say someplace in southern England, outside London. Perhaps, I would guess, not far from Somerset."

"That's impressive, from just hearing an accent."

"I have been to England several times to study. So, what brings you halfway around the globe to our islands?"

"I came with my father on a holiday. He is still on O'ahu doing some military job for his boss. He doesn't tell me much about what he does. I came over here to this island to write a paper on ancient Hawaiian history. I understand this island is a good place to do that. I do anthropology and archaeology and my last name is Harper."

"Wow that's impressive, Alex said with a surprised look. "It just so happens that I have some connections that could get you a personal tour of the Pu'ukonola Heiau, which is located just up the coast from here if you're interested?"

"Really?" asked Sarah with excitement. "Of course, I am interested. That place was on my list of places to look at. When could you arrange it?"

"Tomorrow, if you like? I just need to make some calls. I want you to know I would normally ask you out to dinner tonight but I have some things I have to do. That includes making those calls for you. What do you say that we meet for breakfast at about 8 am and go from there?"

"That would be wonderful," Sarah answered. "I do need to unpack and have a rest. It has been a very interesting day, to say the least."

"I will see you in the morning then," Alex replied as he got up to leave. "I look forward to showing you around. Oh, and you're not the only one that has found the day interesting."

Sarah watched as Alex disappeared into the lobby. She sat there finishing her drink thinking about what she said to herself when she first arrived in Hawaii. About being ready to share whatever Hawaii had to offer. This was more than she could have ever imagined. She was beginning to realize that Hawaii was, perhaps, a truly magical place. She finished her drink and returned to her room to contemplate all that had happened and get prepared for tomorrow and what possibilities it might bring.

Chapter 16

Find A Way

When Alex returned to his suite, he called Jack for the latest developments. This is something he did every day. However, he never revealed where he is staying.

Jack informed him of Goddard, who he was and that he had arrived on the island, and that they had tagged his car. They should soon know where he was going to be staying. Alex was a bit alarmed at this but trusted the SGM had everything under control. He did ask Jack to send him a full description of Goddard in case he should encounter him by chance. Jack said he would do so as soon as their call ended. Alex told Jack that he would be out of reach the next day and night for personal reasons but would contact him the following day. Jack was not bothered by this and assured Alex everything was being handled. As soon as the call ended, the full description of Goddard arrived on Alex's phone.

***

The next morning Jack received information confirming the location of where Goddard was staying. Goddard had moved into a condominium located in a place called Kona Sea Ridge. Jack knew the place well and ordered the place watched.

He then called Ted to inform him of the latest. Ted told him he would call Wigmore and fill him in.

It was a late hour in England when Ted called Wigmore. Wigmore always answered despite the hour.

"Good morning, Colonel," Wigmore said with a tired voice. "What's the latest?"

"Colonel Fairway just informed me they successfully tagged Goddard's car and have now confirmed where he is staying," Ted answered.

"That's good news then?" replied Wigmore.

"Yes General. I still believe I should go to the island to assist Jack. I don't believe this island is going to be the focus."

"I am not so sure," Wigmore insisted. "We have no information leading us to believe they know that Alex lives on the Big Island."

"Hear me out General," Ted implored. "Whether they know if Alex is there or not, I do not believe is the point here. I think that there are going to set up a base of operation over there. That island has two main international airports that fly people directly from the west coast of the US. They would expect us to watch the Honolulu airport. I believe they would think we would ignore the other airports on the outer islands. They needed to get Goddard there to find a location for the base. If I were setting up a base, it is what I would do. You wanted me here because you said I was the best man for the job sir. I am trying to do the best job. So, with due respect sir, I believe I could do that job best over there."

"Alright then, Wigmore replied with a tone of submission. "What about Honolulu?"

"I will put Captain Bastwick in charge here. He is more than capable. Besides, if things change, I can be back on this island in an hour."

"What about your daughter?" Wigmore inquired.

"She is already on that island. She went there on her own to do work."

"I now understand why you want to be there all the more," Wigmore replied. "You should have said so in the beginning. But I must insist that you must keep separate from her while you are there. If the ODR were to discover the two of you are connected, they may well try to use that to their advantage. That could put both of you in danger."

"I completely agree with you sir. I am sure she will understand. She always understands. I will fly over first thing in the morning."

"Very well Colonel," Wigmore said. "As always keep me informed. Have a good day."

"Yes sir. Have a good night," Ted answered as he ended the call.

As soon as he ended the call with Wigmore, he called Sarah who was just about to go to breakfast. He explained as much of the situation as he could. He would find a place of his own away from the hotel where she was staying. Ted was right. She understood as always.

Sarah did not tell her father of her plans for the day. Nor did she say anything about meeting Alex. She did not want her father asking too many questions and she was not sure how she would answer them if he did. She said goodbye to her father telling him she was going on her first research trip.

After the call with her father, Sarah met Alex in the restaurant called Ikena Landing. Alex was already there having coffee. Sarah sat down at the same table. All was quiet in her head so she felt pleased.

Sarah ordered banana waffles and coffee. Alex ordered a local breakfast called Loco Moco. White rice topped with a beef hamburger smothered in brown gravy and then a fried egg on top of that. Sarah looked at it almost with disgust. Alex saw the look and smiled.

"Don't knock it until you try it," he said with a laugh.

"No thank you," Sarah replied with a chuckle. "I think my father would enjoy it though, especially if you added some bacon."

"Oh, you're right. I have done that myself. It is much better with bacon. What do you think about getting a picnic lunch? They will make one here if you want."

"That sounds nice. That way we can make a day of it without interruption."

When the waiter came back to check on them Alex let him know they want to order a lunch to carry. He promptly returned with a menu for takeaway lunches. While waiting for the lunch order to arrive, they sat quietly drinking coffee. It seemed so strange to Sarah to sit with someone other than her father and not be bothered by hearing all the noise of thoughts coming into her head.

"You don't talk a lot," Sarah said after finishing her coffee.

"Be careful," Alex said with a laugh. I can talk your head off if you inspire me. But yes, as a rule, I listen more than talk. If a person is talking, they cannot listen. The universe is always speaking to us. If we are talking all the time, we miss what it is saying to us. That is my experience anyway."

"Interesting way of looking at things," Sarah replied. "I never really thought about the universe as talking.

Just then, the lunches arrived. Alex thanked the waiter and took them as he got up to leave.

"My jeep is out front waiting for us," Alex said as he headed for the lobby.

Sarah followed just behind him carrying her case that contained a camera, sunscreen, and writing material. Both climbed into his jeep and were on their way. It was another hot day and Sarah was grateful for the AC in his jeep. It was only 4 miles to the Pu'ukonola National Historic Site. The entire Heiau site is under the protection and guidance of the US National Park Service.

After parking the jeep, they both walked toward the visitor center where Ranger Ken met Alex just outside the center.

"Aloha Alika," the Ranger said as he and Alex shook hands. "Good to see you again my friend and this lovely lady must be Sarah you spoke to me about. Welcome to the site."

The Ranger shook Sarah's hand and handed her some pamphlets.

"This is some information I think you will find useful on your tour." Ranger Ken said. I hope you brought plenty of water. It's going to be another hot one."

"Thanks for reminding me," Alex replied. "Got to go back and get my backpack from the Jeep. Be right back."

Alex hurried back to the Jeep and retrieved his backpack filled with water and snacks. When he returned Ranger Ken led the way.

"Let's begin your VIP tour around this very historic site," Ranger Ken said. "Just follow me."

The first thing that struck Sarah was how dry and barren the landscape looked. Brown grass and reddish-brown rocks dominated the ground. The only trees were near the sea and around the visitor center. When she heard that it took thousands of people to build the heiau, she wondered how they would have fed such a number in such a landscape.

Ranger Ken told her that the landscape back then was much greener. The gradual shift in the trade winds has caused a decrease in rainfall.

She noticed wild goats climbing on the heiau and the surrounding area. Ranger Ken told her that Captain Vancouver first brought the goats to the islands.

Sarah was also surprised to learn that British men and guns helped King Kamehameha in his final conquest of all the islands. The site reminded her of Celtic hill forts but without defensive ditches. The idea of a human sacrifice taking place to dedicate the temple made her realize that humans everywhere are the same at their roots in so many ways. The whole experience gave Sarah a completely new view of Hawaii and its rich history. It also gave her an insight into a connection between Hawaii's history and that of England, and even her own.

Alex of course knew all of this and much more, but kept silent. He knew his ancestors witnessed all of this history firsthand. He also knew, but could not say, that one ancestor knew King Kamehameha personally. He was aware that, that same ancestor, was partly responsible for the disaster that befell the King's enemies on the slopes of Kilauea. This happened when an ongoing ash explosion from the volcano was combined with a storm conjured by this descendant causing the death of enemy forces that were opposed to Kamehameha. This information was not common knowledge and Alex was committed to keeping it that way.

The tour lasted all morning it ending back at the visitors' center. Sarah was very grateful that Alex had brought plenty of water. She had never experienced such heat in her life.

Alex thanked Ranger Ken for the tour and reminded Sarah it was now lunchtime. Alex went back to the Jeep and retrieved two folding chairs and a cooler containing the lunches. They decide the best place to have lunch was at nearby Spencer Beach Park. The park is just a short walk from the visitor center. It has large trees for shade from under which they could watch the waves while enjoying lunch.

After eating, they both sat in the cool shade watching a few surfers riding the waves. Suddenly Sarah jumped to her feet and pointed out across the waves.

"Was that a whale spout I just saw?" she asked with excitement. "Look there is another one."

"Yes, they are," Alex said still sitting. "This is whale season. The Humpbacks have come to Hawaii to give birth."

"I have never seen a whale before," Sarah said still standing staring out to sea."

"Well then, you will have to do a whale-watching boat tour during your stay. It is best to book a late in the day one. That way you will see spinner dolphins as well. But you better sit down before everyone thinks you're a tourist."

Sarah looked back at Alex with a sharp glare. He was laughing.

"Sorry," he said pulling in his grin. "It's sort of a local joke. Please don't take offense. I understand your excitement. I really do."

Sarah smiled and sat back down.

"You want to see something special?" asked Alex with a serious tone. "Come follow me. I do hope they are there."

Leaving their chairs and cooler behind, they headed for a pavilion just past the sandy part of the beach. The pavilion was located on the rocks right on the shore. Alex led Sarah to the wall that is closest to the water.

"Now watch in the waves located just out from the rocks," Alex instructed her.

They watched intensely. Alex suddenly pointed.

"There," Alex said while pointing into a wave.

Sarah gasped. "Oh my god," she responded, "It's a turtle! It's a wild sea turtle."

"Yes, and if you watch them, you can see that they are feeding. They are having lunch munching on the seaweed that grows on the rocks. Here in Hawaii, turtles are called honu. Keep watching and you will see them pop up their heads to get a breath of air.

Sarah was so excited. First, she saw the whale, and now a sea turtle. She took Alex's hand and looked straight into his green eyes.

"Thank you," she said with a voice that he knew came from deep in her heart.

She then leaned over and kissed him on the cheek. She did not immediately let go of Alex's hand as she continued to watch the waves for more turtles and whales. She only let go when she looked back at where the chairs and cooler were. They were gone!

Circles in Stone

"Someone stole our stuff! Sarah said with a nervous voice while looking at Alex.

"No, everything is still there," Alex said with a calm tone.

Sarah turned to look again and was shocked to see everything right where they had left it. She was sure it was gone when she looked a moment ago. Must drink more water, she thought to herself, has to be the heat getting to her.

Alex went over, collected all of their things, and moved them to the pavilion. They spent the rest of the afternoon watching the waves for whale spouts.

Sarah pulled out her notebook and began writing in it about what she had learned on the tour of the heiau. Alex just sat quietly watching her write and pointing out whale spouts to her. As he watched her, he thought how very nice it was to share a quiet time with someone else. He also felt, for the first time in his life, he wanted to share more of himself with another person. He wondered if he should allow his feelings toward her to grow. If he did, where would it lead? Was she allowing herself to feel the same towards him? Was the universe pulling them together? So many questions circled in his head. If they did fall in love with each other, how would he reveal to her who he actually is?

As he continued to ponder these questions and watch the waves, it accrued to him, that if they did fall in love, and the universe had arranged it, it would make a way for it to work. He did not know how but he was sure if love did happen, together they would find a way.

As it grew near evening, Alex suggested they stop at the Mauna Kea Resort for dinner at the Hau Tree. It is right next to the beach and they could watch the sunset from there. Sarah enthusiastically agreed. She did ask if maybe she needed to change. Alex told her not to worry. It was very casual and many people come straight in from a day of touring.

When they arrived at the restaurant, Sarah was thrilled at the setting. She ordered a Mai Tai and Alex his favorite lager. They each ordered their meal, Sarah, the Asian Chicken, and Alex the fish of the day, Seared Ahi (Tuna Steak).

Alex decided to ask a bit more about Sarah.

"So, I don't want to intrude in your personal life," Alex said in a humbled tone. "Tell me about your mother."

"There is not much to tell." She answered. "She died when I was born. My father is not my real father. No one has told me who my real father is. My mother asked my adopted father to take care of me. He knows who my real father is and said one day he would tell me. I know nothing of my mother's family for reasons that are said to be best for me, so I have been told. I have to admit it all seems a bit cloak and dagger to me. I trust my dad, so for now I will leave it to his judgment. In some ways, I have always felt a bit like an orphan. But, because of the thing with hearing thoughts I didn't mind being alone."

"Wow," Alex replied. "It must have been tough without a family to connect to. Even though I am alone now I had a family and many wonderful memories. My father and mother taught me so much about living and in some ways about dying. I am so grateful for all they taught me."

"I couldn't imagine what it would be like to lose my dad," Sarah said with a somber tone. "A group of sisters that ran the school I went to mostly raised me. But my dad always looked after me when he was home. I have never really felt alone or uncared for. The only thing I wish that I had was someone to teach me how to control or at least deal with the thought hearing condition. To be honest, until I met you, I thought I was alone with it. My dad is the only other person I was never able to hear. He told me I got the condition from my mother. All that still is confusing sometimes. I wonder if maybe some of her family had it too and maybe that's why knowing who they are has been kept from me."

"All the members of my family had the condition as you call it," Alex responded. "My father told me there might be others out in the world with it but, until you came along, I never had met any besides members of my family. My mother taught me the most about how to control it. She told me that some people were born deaf and others, like those in my family, had extra hearing. She taught me that we all have our special gifts to share. Some people will honor those gifts and some will want to take them from you. Some people will be afraid of them and some will love you for them. In the end, we are all the same inside."

"She sounds like she was a very wise woman," Sarah replied with a smile.

Their dinners arrived and they enjoyed them while watching the sun sink below the waves. Most of all, they enjoy the company of each other. Sarah realized that she had never felt so much peace in a long time the way she felt it now.

On the way back to their hotel, they chatted about the day like two friends that had known each other for years. Alex let Sarah off at the lobby entrance. Just before she got out of his Jeep, she leaned over to him. Kissed him on the cheek.

"Unless you're busy," Sarah asked. "Will I see you for breakfast?"

"It's a date," replied Alex. "See you in the morning. Have a good night."

Sarah waved to him as she walked into the hotel lobby and Alex drove off to park his Jeep.

Chapter 17

Where To From Here?

The next morning after their wonderful day out Alex and Sarah met for breakfast at the Ikena restaurant. Sarah had a continental breakfast that included yogurt, fruit, and cereals. Alex ordered the eggs and sausage which came with rice. Sarah found it strange that people in Hawaii ate so much rice.

As they enjoyed their meal, they talked about what places they could visit. Alex suggested a place called Lapakahi park about a 22-minute drive up the coast. It is the ruins of an ancient Hawaiian fishing village. From there they could drive to Hawi, the island's most northern village. They could get lunch there. Then to Kapauu, the birthplace of King Kamehameha. After that to the end of the road at Pololuu lookout.

"I am going to trust you about these places to go," Sarah said. "You know this island better than I do."

"I did grow up here," Alex said laughing. "It is an island, a bit hard to get lost."

"Do we need to take a packed lunch?"

"That won't be necessary," Alex replied. "Plenty of places along the way. I will pack water and some snacks though. Make sure you pack sunscreen. Looks to be another hot one. I need to go pack the water and get my jeep. I'll meet you out front in 20 minutes."

"Sounds good to me," Sarah answered as she drank the last of her coffee and got up to leave.

As Sarah walked off, Alex finished his coffee and asked to have one to go. After getting the coffee, he went to his room. Not only to pack the water and snack but to call Jack.

Jack informed him of the latest. That they knew where the ODR's man, Goddard, was staying. He also told him that their man, Ted Rowland, was due in and he would be picking him up at the airport.

Alex still did not tell Jack where he was nor did Jack ask. They both still believed this was the best strategy for the time being. Jack thanked Alex for checking in and wished him a great day. They ended the call.

Alex filled his backpack with bottles of water and snacks and headed for his jeep.

Sarah was waiting for him at the lobby entrance. She jumped in the jeep as if she did it every day, throwing her bag in the back.

"All ready to go find some past?" Alex asked Sarah as they pulled away.

As they drove onto the main road Sarah began to question Alex about what he knew about ancient Hawaiian practices.

"How did the ancient Hawaiians bury their dead?" she asked. "Did they have regular cemeteries, put them in coffins?"

"That's a complicated question," Alex replied "So I am going to give you the most uncomplicated answer I know. Part of the answer is, depends on who you were. The first thing you must know is that the flesh on the body had not much value. They believe that the bones contained the essence of the person. Their energy, who they were, and the knowledge or power they had in life, it was called their mana. In most cases, the flesh was first stripped from the bones. The bones were dried and sometimes wrapped in tapa cloth and buried. Other times just the bones were put in lava tubes. If you were a royal person or Ali, a special basket was woven, and the bones were put into it and hidden away so no one could steal the bones and use that person's mana. Mana is very important to Hawaiians. Not only can people have it, but places and objects. It all sounds a bit strange but it is not unlike catholic saint relics."

"I understand that," Sarah replied. "Most people, ancient and modern, have that same belief only express it in different ways."

"Yes," answered Alex. "The one thing that is different from a lot of people is, the Hawaiians have, a deep connection to the land, they call, the Aina. To bury a person is to plant them in the Ania. The Aina then uses their mana to nourish all the life that comes from it. The people and the Aina are one."

"I can see how that works. That was the way in many ancient cultures. In the old Arthur legend, King Arthur was connected to the land. If the king was distressed, so was the land. The idea that we are connected to the land has been lost. I think that way of thinking should be returned to the way people see the earth. So much disrespect for the earth is destroying our world."

"I could not agree more with you. If people only realized that the earth is a living thing. I fear like most living things if it is threatened too much, it will fight back."

They both were silent for a while as they each thought about the conversation that took place between them. They were just then passing through Kawaihae. One of the two shipping harbors on the island. Sarah noticed all the large containers piled up in the yard. It reminded her that almost everything on the islands has arrived by ship from someplace.

"Did you ever see the movie Waterworld?" asked Alex.

"Yes. Was fun to watch but was a bit silly."

"A lot of it was filmed in and around this harbor," Alex said. "Just a bit of trivia for you."

The landscape still looked dry along the drive but there seemed to be greener areas. There were more trees though sparsely scattered. The deep blue water of the sea was always insight on their left. Seeing all this open land Sarah asked,

"Why are there so few homes along here with such beautiful views of the ocean?"

"Water," Alex answered. "Or the lack of it I should say. The ground is very porous. It does not retain water very well. Very little rain falls on this side. What rain does fall quickly is absorbed by what little vegetation there is and any leftover just soaks into the rock and then out to sea. There are some deep wells in some places that tap the layer of fresh water. But that layer is very thin in many places. It is not enough to support a large number of homes."

"I noticed some houses have large storage tanks next to their houses. Are those for water?"

"Yes, they catch the rainwater from the roof of their house and save it in those tanks. For many, that is their only source of water."

"That is interesting. Such a contrast. Surrounded by beautiful blue water and it is so valuable on the land."

Just then they reached the entrance to their first stop. Lapakahi State Park. The ruins of an ancient Hawaiian fishing village. Putting on her sun hat and grabbing her bag, Sarah seemed focused on getting to the ruins. Alex locked the Jeep and followed behind. There were very few people about. This made Sarah relax as she began to wander around the site.

She took many photos and, in some places, pulled out her notebook and sketched what she was looking at. Alex did not say a word but just watched as she looked, seemingly, at every detail. A sign told her that the village was around 600 years old. Sarah took a special interest in the salt-making rocks once used by its residents.

There were also a few grass-covered structures in disrepair. Build not long ago to show how the Hawaiians had done it in the past. They gave the place a feeling of abandonment. As Sarah walked around the site, she tried to imagine what it must have looked like. The paths busy with people going about their daily work. Children running and playing. Men making nets and repairing canoes. She always did that at sites she visited or worked on. She thought at times she could hear those people of the past still living. To her, they were somehow still there.

For two hours they wandered around the site. Occasionally resting under a tree to get a break from the sun and for a drink of water and a snack. Hardly any words were exchanged between them.

Finally, Sarah looked at Alex.

"I hate to leave," she said. "But I think I have enough for now. Let's go find some lunch."

"If you're sure," Alex replied. "No rush."

"I'm sure. What I have will keep me busy for a while sorting and writing."

Back at the jeep, after they got in and were getting ready to leave, Sarah turned to Alex.

"I have been at a lot of digs and sites with a lot of different people over the years," she explained. "This is the first time I have ever been with a person that did not disturb me or try to show off their knowledge. Of course, no outside thoughts were intruding either. But I wanted you to know how special I found that. Thank You."

Alex looked at her and was so surprised by her comment he had no words. After a moment of awkward silence, he finally spoke.

"Thank You, it is an honor to see someone that truly focused on their work. But more so, I think it was even a greater honor to watch a person being in the moment. Simply doing what they were doing and being where they are."

Sarah smiled and reached over and squeezed his hand. They then set off for Hawi to find some lunch.

On the way there the landscape changed dramatically. It became very green and almost lush. Green grass, lots of trees, some of those with flowers. In Hawi, they found a charming little place called Bamboo restaurant. Sarah had the grilled fish sandwich with pineapple salsa and Alex had a BBQ pulled pork sandwich. Both cooled off with iced tea, Sarah's with sugar and Alex's without. After lunch, they did some window shopping in a few of the galleries in the town. Sarah found the old plantation-style buildings all along the main street, a step back in time from some storybook.

The next village was very small but is noted for being the birthplace of King Kamehameha. They only stopped so Sarah could snap a photo of the statue dedicated to him in front of the local civic center.

As they drove to their next stop Alex explained that a lot of Japanese lived in the area. They came to the islands to work the sugar cane that once covered the fields there. Sugar cane is no longer the king crop. Much of the land now is being planted with macadamia nuts and coffee.

After a short drive they arrived at the last stop, it was, literally the end of the road. Alex parked the jeep. Got out and put on his backpack. He then pulled two walking poles out of the back and gave one to Sarah.

"Let's go for a short hike," Alex said. "I want you to see something. Make sure you bring your camera."

"Okay, I'll follow you."

After locking the jeep, they set off. The trail was dirt and rocks and very uneven. It was well-worn and very steep in places. It took about 30 minutes to reach a point where Alex stopped.

"This is the spot," he said as he waited for Sarah.

When Sarah reached him, she stopped and stood spellbound. The views were beyond anything she could have imagined. There were some great views on the way down but this was perfect. Along the coast were four cliff-faced, tree-covered tongues of land facing the sea. Two small islands lay at the base of one of those cliff faces. To her right, she was looking straight up at a lush green valley that seemed to go on forever.

She took photos and would stop and just stare. Then take a few more and repeated this several times.

"Hope you like it," Alex said as he handed her a bottle of water. "I have always thought it was worth the hike. Well, at least when it's not raining."

"My god yes," Sarah said when she finally spoke. "What am I looking at?"

"Each one of those heads is the protruding ridges of four very steep narrow gulches. The whole area is the Kohala Forest Reserve. You can hike and camp but no one lives in the entire area. The islands you see are the Paokalani Sea Bird Sanctuary."

"I truly love it," Sarah said with eyes almost tearing up."

She reached over and took hold of Alex's hand. She stood there looking at the wonderful scenery holding his hand. This moved Alex in a way he never felt before. He then took the same hand she was holding and extended it to hold her by the waist. Sarah let go of his hand and put her arm around his waist as well. They looked into each other's eyes for a moment and smiled. They stood there listening to the waves below, the breeze blowing in the trees and the sound of birds singing as they fluttered from tree to tree.

Sarah looked at Alex again.

"We should have brought the chairs." She said with a grin.

Alex let out a laugh. Sarah heard a slight rustle behind her. She turned around to see two chairs unfolded behind them. Her face became flush for a moment. How could that be, she thought? She looked back at Alex. He just shrugged his shoulders and smiled. Sarah still a bit confused sat down and took a drink from her bottle of water. Alex sat next to her and pulled out some snacks from his backpack. They sat there until the afternoon shadows began to darken the valley before them. When they decided to leave Sarah watched Alex closely to see what he did with the chairs. The idea that they just appeared still hung in her mind.

Of course, Alex had used magic to get the chairs from the car. He did so without Sarah noticing. Knowing that Sarah was now watching him, he folded them up using magic to make it appear that they could be folded small enough to fit in his backpack,

"Wow," Sarah said with a puzzled glance. "I didn't know they made chairs that could do that. What will they think of next?"

"The magic of modern technology," Alex answered. "Phones once took up half a tabletop, now they fit in your pocket."

It was much more work going back up to the car than coming down. Sarah was not used to hiking like that. They stopped several times for a rest and some water. When they reached the car, Alex put the pack in the jeep and rested for a moment leaning against the back hatch door. Sarah came over to him. Facing him she placed both her arms on his shoulders. She looked directly into his eyes.

"Thank You," she said softly. "It was wonderful. The whole day has been wonderful. You are wonderful."

She took his head into her hands and pulled it toward her. First, there was a moment of hesitation, but then she put her lips to his. They kissed deeply. Alex responded by pulling her gently closer to him, but not too tight. He didn't want to make her feel he was taking. He wanted her to feel like she was giving and he was receiving. When the kiss ended Sarah kept looking into his eyes.

After a moment of silence, she asked, "Well, mister tour guide. Where do we go from here?"

Alex was at a loss for words for a moment. Once he regained his composure, he took her left hand and kissed it.

"Well," Lady Sarah," he said. "I shall drive you back to the hotel. We can shower and freshen up. After that, we shall find a place to have dinner. While we are dining on some wonderful cuisine, we can discuss the possibilities."

"Sounds like a plan to me Sir Alex," Sarah replied, still smiling at him.

They climbed into the jeep and headed back to the hotel. On the trip back they chatted about all that they experienced during the day. Each telling the other the way they saw things. Each listening to the other's view with deep attention. By the time they reached the hotel, they felt that a bond had formed between them. What they didn't know, was it was the first time either of them had ever felt such a bond in their lives.

After changing, they met at the Meridia Restaurant, located in the resort. Sarah ordered a Mai Tai and Alex his usual Long Board ale. For dinner, Sarah had Sea bass with herb Rice. Alex dined on Grilled Ahi covered in crushed Almonds.

Alex suggested that the next day they should go south. Take a change of clothes for an overnight stay at a BnB that a friend of his owns. During the day they could go snorkeling and in the evening after a change, they would attend a Luau in Kailua. It all sounded wonderful to Sarah.

After dinner, they spent the evening listening to a Hawaiian band in the Bar. After the music ended, they headed for their separate rooms. Sarah kissed him on the lips before they parted and thanked him again for a wonderful day. They agreed to meet for breakfast in the usual place. As they walked, each in their separate directions, Sarah was pleased that Alex had not pursued her for more. She felt safe with him. Something she had never felt with anyone except her father.

Alex, on the other hand, felt almost afraid. He had never felt such a deep pull toward a person, other than his parents. Was this how love felt when it is born? If so, it was something more powerful than any magic he had ever encountered. I shall go slowly, he thought, if love is magic, then one must not rush into it. Each has the power to enhance. Likewise, each also has the power to hurt. Like magic, he thought, love, should not be embraced lightly.

Chapter 18

Modern Magic

In England, the ODR's top teams were continuing at a breakneck speed making plans for the new base in Hawaii. Everyone was doing as much as possible to have everything arranged so once they all arrived in Hawaii, they could move fast.

Even though Goddard had not yet secured a location for the headquarters, each member worked via the internet and phone calls, using Scotland Yard phones, to obtain the things assigned to each of them.

Jason was buying communications equipment. One new piece that John Coke worked with Jason on is the voice recognition computer. Not only would this be used in Hawaii but would be installed in any meeting place. This would not only replace the tattoo ID mark for large meetings but weed out any potential enemies trying to infiltrate their ranks. Anyone now a member had to submit a voice recording. If a member were not available, past recordings of their voices is be used. The recorded voices of known enemies of the ODR would be entered also. For example, the voices of all the Morgans that attended the meeting in London were included in the software database. Every member that was engaging in a mission would now be required to carry a recording device on them. The tattoo mark would only be used in field missions.

Oliver Calvin was working on weapons detail. Instead of buying weapons in the US, he found it would be easier to take their own with them. Because all four members going to Hawaii were working members of the Scotland Yard anti-terrorist task force, it made it easy. The only request from the US and Hawaii governments was that the serial numbers of each gun be submitted along with the name of the person assigned to that weapon. Oliver decided to assign each member two G-17 9mm pistols. The reason for two was that if one broke down replacement parts might be hard to get. The weapons were to be used defensively only. They were all concerned about what the Morgans might do.

Circles in Stone

John Coke's mission was proving far less fruitful. He believed that by studying Hawaii's history he would be able to find clues or a trail of someone using magic. He was now spending a lot of time at the British library pouring over all manner of books and documents. Hawaii's history is filled with all manner of myths and legends. Stories of demigods holding back the sun, a fire goddess turning men into trees, and even one, of the islands being pulled up from the bottom of the sea with a fishhook. Separating anything that might prove to be useful was proving almost impossible. At times Coke felt he was not the right man for the job but continued to do his best anyway.

Pete Walker's mission was to arrange how and when the Morgans would be allowed to travel to Hawaii. Before he did that, he needed to know as much as possible about them. Since the Morgans were now on the terrorist watch list, he could use all Scotland Yard resources he wanted to track them. He took full advantage of this. The Morgans' every movement was tracked and reported directly back to him. Knowing how they acted and even what food they preferred could prove to be useful. Though he did his best to not be seen, he knew that the Morgans knew they were being watched.

The morale of these ODR members was at an all-time high. They were convinced, more than ever, that God's hand was upon them. Convinced the Merlin line descendant would be found along with the Jewel of Power and that the Jewel would soon be in their hands.

***

The Morgans were still frustrated by the fact that their magic could do nothing to help them break free of the travel restrictions placed on them by the ODR. Nevertheless, Rhyfel kept trying. Realizing that scrying was no longer working, he was convinced the ODR had discovered who it was that they had tagged. Rhyfel was also well aware that the ODR was using Scotland Yard to watch them. Knowing this, the Morgans' magic had once again become useful. The ODR did not know that many times the Morgans used magic to hide where they were. This use of magic is called cloaking. Making something appear to not be there or making something appear somewhere it was not. Using cloaking magic, the Morgans could travel freely over short distances in the country and not be detected. They could not travel too far for too long,

The magic did have limitations. They also would often create false information about what they were doing. The ODR would then receive this false information believing it was true.

Lord Ambrose used this magic to hide his many visits to the British Library in London. This had proved worth every moment he spent there. After many visits and a lot of time, Ambrose had finally found what he was looking for. He contacted Rhyfel to meet with him to discuss what he had discovered. Rhyfel agreed and arranged the meeting to take place at the Red Lion in Avebury. This beautiful thatched-roof pub is the only one in the world located inside a stone circle. The building dates to the 1600s and is said to be very much haunted.

Using magic to hide their travels, just the two of them arrived without the ODR being aware. Rhyfel even wore jeans and a checkered shirt to blend in. Each ordered a pint of ale and found a secluded table. Lord Ambrose unloaded a briefcase filled with pages of information he had collected.

"Master Rhyfel", Ambrose began. "I know who he is. I also know his name and, where he lives. Well, I say know. I am confident I know."

"What?" Rhyfel responded with disbelief. "How did you find out?"

"I started with our history," Ambrose continued. "Our history is well recorded. Our history is the most clouded during the time of James 1st. I figured the Merlin line had to be as well. For our line and anyone that wielded magic, it was a dark time. So, I began there with the Merlin line history. John Dee we well know was the direct line descendent of Merlin in Queen Elizabeth's court. While serving in her court we know he traveled all over the continent. He openly performed his magic while he was there. He married three times during his life. His first two wives died before having any children. His third wife, over time, bore him eight children. He named his first son Arthur of course.

"That was no coincidence", Rhyfel interjected.

"Of course not," continued Ambrose. "His third child was his second son they named Michael.

"I have never heard of him."

"No one has because this is where it gets interesting. There is a record only that this child was born in 1586, but died in Prague in 1594 on John Dee's birthday. I could find nothing else about his death. There is not even a record of where the child was buried. I don't believe his son Michael ever died. Actually, I am convinced he didn't."

"What do you mean he didn't die?"

"Follow me on this," replied Ambrose as he showed Rhyfel some papers from his pile.

John Dee dies in 1609 and his son Arthur takes over his father's practice. By now, James the 1st is on the throne of England. The king's first target is all those that were once in the former Queens court. As we know those that practiced magic were the first ones in his sights. Arthur Dee would have been one of James's targets. Somehow though, he befriended James. Not only that, but he managed to get James to free Walter Raleigh from the tower where the king had him locked up on charges of treason. He convinced the king to send Raleigh on a trip to South America to search for Eldorado."

"Why would he do that?"

"I am going to tell you why," continued Ambrose. "Right after Raleigh left on this wild trip Arthur goes to Russia where he lives most of his life. Everything becomes quiet in the Merlin line after that. No records of Arthur Dee's children as heirs, nothing. Why I asked myself?"

"Because the line and the Jewel were on Raleigh's ship," Rhyfel interjected. "Arthur had taken himself out of the mainline of decent and passed it on to his younger brother."

"Precisely," replied Ambrose. "So, I searched Hawaiian history for anything unusual around that time. That is where I found a historically unconfirmed account of a Spanish shipwreck on the Kona Coast of the Big Island of Hawaii in 1620. That would have made Michael Dee 34 years old and in his magical prime.

"He would have been in contact with his brother the whole time though scrying," Rhyfel said, surmising what may have taken place.

"It is what we would have done. So, following this idea, I then did land deed searches for the island of Hawaii. Once Hawaii became a Kingdom, they began writing down everything, this included putting into records every land transaction going back as far as they could. These transactions included ones passed down by way of oral tradition before Captain Cook arrived. Every transaction recorded before Cook arrived was to people with Hawaiian names except one. That last name was

Michaels. That piece of land is still owned by a person named Michaels. Alexander Michaels, which is located on the big island of Hawaii near the village of Volcano."

Ambrose leaned back, took a long drink of his ale, and watched for a reaction from Master Rhyfel.

Rhyfel sat there in silence still mulling over everything Ambrose just told him. It all made sense for the first time. He knew Lord Ambrose had to be right. He took a long drink of his ale and looked Ambrose directly in his eyes.

"You have done well Lord Ambrose," Rhyfel said with a grateful tone. "I don't know how you did it. But I am humbled and forever grateful that you did."

"I used magic," Ambrose said with a smile. "I used modern magic, the internet."

"I will inform the others. They will be so pleased. Now, all we need to do is get there.

"We will," Ambrose replied. "Just be patient Master. Once this is shared with our other members, it should not be spoken of again in any form. The ODR must not obtain this knowledge. I suggest we just lay low for now. Let the ODR make their plans. I am sure they will let us get to Hawaii in time. We now have a decisive advantage.

They finished their drinks and departed in high spirits.

**

Back in Hawaii Ted arrived on the Big Island landing at the Kona Airport. Colonel Jack met him just outside the terminal. Jack greeted Ted with the usual Hawaiian handshake and kukui nut lei.

"Aloha Colonel," Jack said as he placed the lei around his neck. "Welcome to the Big Island."

"Thank You, Colonel," Ted replied. "Feels like I am jumping from the frying pan and into the fire. And judging from this heat it is more literal than figurative."

Jack laughed as they walked toward his car.

"You won't need to rent a car," Jack said as they got into his car. "We have plenty of extras. I have one waiting for you at the office. Our office headquarters are in the King Kam hotel. That's what we locals call it. It's the King Kamehameha Hotel next to the pier in downtown Kailua.

We also have several suites we reserve for our visiting members. You need not look for a place to stay, your accommodations are taken care of."

"That sounds great," responded Ted. "Thank you very much. I am sure they will be great."

The office in the hotel is a 20-minute drive from the airport. The two men chatted about Ted's stay in Waikiki. Ted told him how much he enjoyed it having Sarah there. Jack tells him how different he would find the Big Island. Neither of them mentioned the mission during the drive to the hotel.

The parking area is behind the hotel. They entered the building just past the tennis courts. The office is located in the rear section of the hotel well away from the main entrance. There was a tourist information counter just inside the entrance of the office. One of the SGM members staffed the counter. The counter was a cover for clearing anyone entering the office. The inter-office doors only opened using a key pass chip located in the rings they wore, the same as in the main headquarters in England. Even though Jack and Ted knew each other, they each had to enter separately using their rings. This kind of vigilance is how the SGM operated so well.

Once through the first office, a hand scan let them into the next one. Once inside Ted was impressed with what he saw. Computers lined both walls. Ted counted 14 in all. Seven of them had someone working at them. In the center of the room, a table surrounded by chairs with notebooks piled in the middle. The next room was an eating area with a restroom located off one side. Ted followed Jack into the next room where Jack's office is located.

"Take a seat, Ted," Jack invited pointing to a chair in front of his desk. "How about a drink? I got Jack Daniels."

"Sure", Ted answered. "Never pass up a good whiskey."

Jack poured Ted and himself a drink. They raised their glass to each other without saying anything and took a good swallow. Jack sat down reached into a drawer in his desk and pulled out a pouch.

"I got something for you," Jack said as he handed it to Ted.

Ted opened the pouch and pulled out a gun with a holster. He took the pistol out of the holster and looked at Jack with surprise.

"This is a G17," Ted said as he looked over the weapon. "I was expecting a 357 or Beretta."

"They are too heavy for my taste," Jack replied. "I know you're already familiar with this weapon. It does everything we ever need to do. Scare the bad guys mostly and it's easier to carry."

"Thank you."

"Now that we got that taken care of," said Jack. "Let's get down to business. As you know, we have located where Goddard is staying. We have someone watching the place 24 7. He has not made any real moves yet. We think he is mostly working the phones looking for a place to set up a base."

"Why don't you tap his phone?"

"That could get us into big trouble here. Tapping phones is a big no-no unless you're invited to."

"There is your answer then," replied Ted. "Get him to invite you. You said this is a rented condominium. Let's put together a crew. Pay the property owner to have free safety cameras put in the place for the protection of the tenants. Goddard will think it will be for his protection. We will own the cameras therefore we will control them."

"Funny you should say that," answered Jack. "We already have a crew that does just that. We use them for monitoring drug dealers."

"Great. Let's do it then. We need to know what they are planning, if possible. General Wigmore still thinks they are going to set up bases on all the islands. I don't believe that is their plan. This Goddard fellow is smarter than that. His flying into Honolulu was a diversion."

"I have to agree with you," Jack replied. "They need somewhere to easily get supplies and not be noticed. The Big Island is the best choice. They could also bring in the Morgans here hoping to control them. We are not sure that is the plan, but if it is, it's a bad idea."

"To change the subject," Ted said. "Have you heard from Alexander?"

"Yes, but not today. In our last conversation, he told me he would be away on personal business. We still have no idea where he is. I have had people drive by his places to make sure they are all right. The one here in Kona is all-quiet. His main house outside Volcano appears to be gone. Which is weird, to say the least. The only thing I know is that because

151

his cloak is still in force, he is on the island somewhere. I know him well enough to know that."

"Wow. There are times I could have used that kind of trick or magic or whatever it is. Not looking after him does make our job a bit easier."

Jack reached into another drawer and retrieved a set of car keys. He gave them to Ted and told him they fit a white jeep in the parking lot where they came into. Jack then led Ted out of the office and showed him to the room that had been reserved for him on the floor above

They agreed to meet in the morning for breakfast in the hotel restaurant and begin the mission of getting the cameras installed in Goddard's condominium.

Chapter 19

The Dance of Life

After a restful night in the accommodations provided by the SGM at the King Kamehameha Hotel, Ted met with Jack for breakfast as he promised.

During breakfast, Ted asked Jack about the plans to put cameras in Goddard's Condo. Jack told him the plan was to have the cameras in place in one more day. Ted asked about the new base near Alex's place. Jack told him one had been secured at an old farmstead located just outside Volcano village. It was only a few miles from Alex's main house. Jack said the main problem was that supplies had to be brought up from Hilo some 40 miles away. The main SGM office on the Hilo side was located in the Wai Kea Villas, in the heart of Hilo. Ted suggested that he could go there to help with the setup. He could stay at the new site while the others gathered supplies and transported them to it. Jack thought that was an excellent idea.

"Come to the office after we finish eating," Jack said. "I will give you a map to find the place. Accommodations have already been set up for two people to stay there so far. At least two more rooms need to be made ready."

"Great," replied Ted. "I will pack my things. How far is it from here?"

"It's 98 miles from here. Takes about 2 ½ hours to make the drive. I will call the men there to let them know you are coming. Major Parker is in charge there, I will make sure he fills you in on all the details."

"Sounds like a good plan," Ted answered. "With the place being that close to Alex's house, I think I need to get the lay of the land. No matter how this plays out I feel that area will be the focus."

Ted went with Jack to the office following breakfast. Jack supplied Ted with everything he would need to find the new place. Ted thanked him, went to his room, and packed his belongings. He found the Jeep Jack gave him the keys to the day befor, and set off for the other side of the island.

Circles in Stone

At the Hapuna resort, Alex and Sarah were making their plans for the next 2 days over breakfast. Alex said the plan was for an overnight stay and then back to the hotel. He told Sarah there was a lot for her to see in those two days. He suggested she take an evening out dress for the Luau. He also suggested that she put on a bathing suit outfit for the drive down because the first stop is at the snorkeling beach.

"I don't know how to snorkel," Sarah said with an anxious tone. "We don't do much of that in England."

"No worry," responded Alex. "I will teach you. It is very simple really. The truth is most of the tourists that come here have never snorkeled either. I got a life jacket in the car if you want one, but after seeing you swim, I don't think you will need one. We will stop at Snorkel Bobs in Kailua and get a properly fitting mask for you."

Sarah laughed at the name Snorkel Bobs.

The direction they would be traveling would all be very new to her. She was getting excited about seeing more of the island.

"We will be passing through Kailua," Alex said. "Known to some locals as the Waikiki of the Big Island. Very much a tourist-centered town. Will have to give you the full tour one day soon."

Alex put their cases in the Jeep and they set off. It would take about an hour to reach Kahalu'u Beach. The beach was known for its snorkeling because of the large number of reef fish and turtles that frequent the place. Along the way, Alex pointed out all the places he thought would be interesting to Sarah. Once again Sarah was surprised by the sudden change in terrain and landscape. It became greener and she noticed a change in the air. Though it was hot it didn't seem so harsh.

When they were passing through Kailua Alex pointed out the Royal Palace. To her, it just looked like a big house. Alex explained to her that the name of the road they were on was called Ali Drive, which means the royal's roads in Hawaiian.

The shops mixed in with the trees gave it a very tropical feel.

Soon they were at Snorkel Bobs, where Alex and the shopkeeper helped find a mask that would be best suited for her. He also got her a pair of reef shoes. These are a must for walking on slippery and sometimes very sharp rocks.

Just before the beach where they were going to be snorkeling, Sarah looked suddenly with great attention out the window.

"Was that a Church next to ruins of a heiau?" Sarah asked as she turned to Alex.

"Yes. That is Kuemanu Heiau next to St. Peters Catholic church. The smallest church in Hawaii."

"Wow," Sarah replied. Just like England. When Christians came to England, they often build on the sacred sites of the Celts. It makes me sad when I see that. Overwriting one people's way of life with another. I have always felt there was something wrong with that."

By now Alex had pulled into the parking area. It was not too busy so it should be a good day to snorkel.

They both put on their reef shoes and headed for the shore. The waves were not very rough so getting in the water was easy. Alex put on his mask and snorkel showing Sarah how to put hers on. He took his time showing her how to adjust it and make it fit properly.

He slowly took her out to deeper water where she could put her face in the water with the mask on. He then instructed her to lay face down in the water and he held her by the waist until she got used to breathing through the snorkel. He slowly moved her along gently holding her and slowly letting her go. She gave him a thumbs up and soon she was snorkeling like a pro. Alex swam beside her pointing out all the different fish. It was not long before they were in the water at least 30 feet deep. Sarah would stay on top while Alex would dive deep from time to time.

At one point, Alex dove deep and settled on a rock holding his breath. He put out his hand and fish began swimming all around him. Soon he was surrounded by fish of all kinds. They all swam away when he came up for air. Shortly after that, he did the same thing again. This time he clapped his hands. Out of nowhere along with the hundreds of fish, came two sea turtles.

Sarah floated spellbound above him. The turtles swam around him several times. At no time did Alex attempt to touch them. As before, they swam away when he surfaced for air. He did this several more times. Sometimes the turtles would nudge him. The fish would also pick at his well-tanned skin.

One time Alex slowly swam up toward Sarah. The turtles followed him and began swimming right under her as if he had told them to do so. Sarah reached out to touch them until she saw Alex shaking his head no. Sarah had never seen anything like that. He had no food. They were wild fish and turtles. She was grateful though. It gave her a chance to see so many fish of so many blazing colors. She did not want to stop. But she could feel her back beginning to burn in the hot sun.

She signaled to Alex she wanted to go ashore so he followed her and helped her out of the water and take her snorkel gear off. Once she had dried off a bit and put her wrap on, she looked at Alex.

"What was going on with you and the fish and the turtles," she asked with a puzzled smile.

"They know me," he answered smiling back. "They just came over to say aloha. They know I am no threat. Just as the turtles knew you weren't."

"I don't know. It was all very wonderfully strange."

"I am glad you enjoyed it. I hope it will be something you will always treasure. That's what counts."

"Oh, I will for sure," Sarah replied with a large smile.

"What you say we go find some lunch," Alex said as they walked back to the Jeep. "I know just the place if you don't mind waiting for 20 minutes to get there."

"That will be fine. Give me a chance to dry off a bit."

***

They pulled out of the parking area and headed further south along the main road. Sarah rolled down the window and turned off the AC for the first time. She allowed the wind to blow through her hair to dry it. Alex looked over and thought how beautiful she looked doing it.

Sarah noticed the air was a bit cooler and could feel them climbing up away from the sea. The vegetation was lush and the air was filled with so many aromas. She began seeing what she knew to be coffee farms along the route. Once in a while, she could see the sea far below and coffee trees growing along the steep slopes toward the blue waters of the pacific.

Alex slowed and pulled into a parking area right along the road in front of a place called The Coffee Shack. It was a small wood-frame building. Sarah thought how special can this be? The only special thing she noticed was the under-sea mural painted on the front of the building.

As they entered the building a middle-aged woman behind the counter called out.

"Aloha Alika, good to see you again. Ben while since I see you. Hope you stayen ok?"

"Aloha sista," Alex replied in his pigeon English. "I be doin ok. Tryin stay out of trouble. I brought a friend to check out your place and have some those great grinds you make."

"Aloha and welcome," The woman said looking at Sarah. "I find you one good seat to check the view."

The woman came around and led them to a table along a railing as she handed Alex the menus.

"Let me know whens you ready for order," she said as she tapped both of them on the shoulders.

Sarah didn't even notice. She was standing next to the table with her eyes fixed on the view in front of her.

She had walked into the place at ground level. In a short distance, she was now at least 20 feet in the air. In front of her were rows of coffee trees flowing down a steep slope. Beyond that were houses that appeared to be toys they were so far away yet below her. In the distance were the deep blue waters of the sea. She could just make out the white string of waves coming ashore. Upon entering the place this was the furthest thing from what she could have imagined.

"You like it?" Alex asked with a big smile on his face.

"Very funny. I feel I have been set up," replied Sarah with a laugh.

"I call this place my shock and awe place."

"I can see why," Sarah said. "I wonder what other tricks you might have up your sleeve."

"Only time will tell," Alex replied. "Only time will tell."

They enjoyed both the views and the lunch. Sarah ate chicken salad and Alex had a Reuben sandwich. He told her it was his favorite sandwich even though she had never heard of it.

Leaving there it was only 3 miles to the place Alex had booked rooms for the two days.

He called it Rachel's place. It was her house that she rented out rooms as a B&B. As soon as they pulled in Rachel came out to welcome them. They were greeted with a kiss on the cheek and a warm Aloha. She told Alex it was good to see him again, and he followed up by asking where the cat was. Rachel gave them a tour which was for Sarah's benefit more than Alex's. When Sarah asked how they knew each other Rachel told her that Alex had helped with a lot of yard work after a storm. He also fixed her coffee huller. Sarah still wondered if there was maybe more to it. Sarah took a chance and listened to Rachel's thoughts. She felt bad when she heard nothing but friendship thoughts.

The place was wonderful. They each had separate rooms. Sarah's room had a view almost as wonderful as the coffee shack. The side of the house facing the sea had two-story glass windows from floor to ceiling. The wrap-around deck provided the same glorious views.

They were given full reign of the second story. Rachel lived in an apartment on the ground floor. There was also a swimming pool, which Rachel told them had underwater lights for night swimming. The refrigerator was filled with all sorts of things one would want for breakfast, and there were plenty of snacks for after that if they wished. The snorkeling, the coffee shack, and now this. Sarah was wondering if the magic would ever stop. Rachel offered them some cold drinks to enjoy after they showered. She wished them a most pleasant stay and left them to do as they wished. With it being only 2 pm now and having to leave at 4:15 to get to the Luau that started at 5 pm. They had plenty of time to get ready and even time to simply relax.

After each had showered, they met on the deck together to enjoy the views below them. Alex went inside and came back with a pair of binoculars that Rachel kept on the table for the guest. Alex gave them to

Sarah and pointed to a place far down on the shore along a point of land jetting out into the sea.

"Can you see a white obelisk monument?" asked Alex.

After some searching, she said, "Yes, I see it. What is it?"

"That is near where your famous Captain Cook died, he was killed after he shoved a chief in a skirmish over a supposed stolen longboat. That makes that spot part of English history."

"Thank You for pointing that out," she responded. "In so many ways these islands and ours are connected."

"In more ways than you know," Alex said. Knowing full well he was thinking of the connection he and his family has had for a very long time.

After a bit of sipping on wine and relaxing it was time to get ready for the Luau. Alex chose a blue aloha shirt with a white hibiscus print. Cream-colored slacks and a lei made of black kukui nuts finished off his outfit.

Sarah came from her room dressed in a long flowing aloha dress, violet in color with prints of plumeria on a background of white and green monstera leaves. It was cut just below the shoulders with short puffed sleeves. When Alex saw her, he held his breath at how beautiful she looked. Alex had asked Rachel to get him a plumeria lei to present to her. He placed the lei around her neck and kissed her cheek. She was perfect in his sight. The lei matched the flowers on her dress perfectly. Sarah swirled around showing off the dress.

"Do you like it?" she asked Alex

He pretended to think about it and then answered. "No, I don't like it at all. I love it"

Sarah took him by the arm and they went to the Jeep and headed for Kona.

It is a 30-minute drive from Rachels's place to the Royal Kona Resort. The resort hotel was on the seafront and the luau was outside near the water in the main courtyard next to the hotel.

When they arrived, they were greeted by a hostess and offered a Mai Tai, and told to feel free to look around. There were people demonstrating crafts. Sarah decided to join the group doing lei-making.

Circles in Stone

Alex decided to chat with the men attending the imu, Hawaiian in-ground oven.

Soon the sound of someone blowing on a conch was heard. This was to signal the beginning of the Luau. The first thing was the removal of the roasted pig and other items from the imu. The host then took the stage and directed people to take their seats. Alex had pre-arranged for them to be seated in the front row near the stage. Everyone was welcomed and then directed to help themselves to the buffet of food.

There was of course imu roasted pork, along with purple sweet potatoes, poi (baked and beaten taro root, a Hawaiian staple), baked fish, salads of all sorts, haupia (Hawaiian coconut pudding), and pineapple upside-down cake. Sarah enjoyed trying all the different foods and flavors.

While everyone was enjoying the meal a live band played Hawaiian music. With the sun setting over the water and the gentle ocean breeze flowing over them like a warm blanket. It truly gave everything a feeling of paradise.

Once the meal had ended the host opened the show. It was called, The Voyagers of the Pacific. A journey in song and dance across the Polynesian islands ending in Hawaii. Sarah had seen something similar on O'ahu at the Polynesian Cultural Center with her father. She enjoyed the show just the same. She loved all the costumes and music.

When they got to the Hawaiian Islands part of the show, the host invited people up to hula on stage. Some tourists did go up and it was all in good fun and laughs. When that part of the show ended the host stopped and paused for a moment. He looked straight down to where Sarah and Alex were sitting. Alex was shaking his head no, but the host kept making a gesture like an invite. Finally, it seemed that Alex agreed. Sarah was getting nervous, and even a bit afraid that it had something to do with her. Suddenly the host signaled to the musicians and announced,

"Ladies and gentlemen, we have a very special treat for you this evening. A very good friend of mine is sitting here in the front row and has agreed to perform for you tonight. I would like to introduce my friend for many years, Alika!"

Alex stood up leaned over to Sarah and whispered in her ear. It's ok just enjoy.

Alex went up on stage and hugged the host. Alex whispered in the host's ear who then went over to the musicians and said something to them. Alex took the mic and spoke in a very calm soft voice.

"On this island, there is a very special waterfall called Akaka falls. Some of you may have already seen it. If you have not, I invite you to take the time to look upon this wonder. We, on this island, know that water is life. We express this life in many ways. One of those ways is through the Hula. So, for me, Hula is the dance of life. I will perform a Hula dedicated to the life-giving waters of Akaka falls."

The music began and Alex began to dance a most beautiful hula. His movements were so graceful and seamless. Sarah found that she had tears welling up in her eyes as she watched him move. Who is this amazing person, she thought to herself? At the end of the dance. He took a bow and the audience stood and applauded. He stepped off the stage and handed the mic back to the host who thanked him and invited another round of applause. The host now announced the grand finale of the show. The Fire knife dancer. It was truly spectacular. Alex kept shouting at him to do more.

After the dance, the host thanked everyone for coming and wished them all a pleasant aloha. On the way back to the jeep Sarah hooked her arm into Alex's and looked up into his eyes.

"You truly are full of surprises," she said smiling

"You live in Hawaii you learn how to hula," he replied. "Not that big of a deal."

Sarah just smiled at him.

On the way back to Rachels's place Sarah leaned on his shoulder the whole way. Nothing was said, she even dozed off for a while. Once at the house they headed inside. Sarah kissed Alex again on the lips and told him how wonderful the day had been. So much excitement in one day had made her very tired.

Alex told her good night and said he was going to have a beer and sit on the deck for a while. He had a lot to think about. He knew for sure now he was falling in love.

Chapter 20

It Is Here

Ted's first night at the new headquarters in Volcano was very peaceful. The farmstead the SGM rented is well removed from other homes and set on a 20-acre lot well outside the village of Volcano. The house is a one-story wood-frame ranch with 4 bedrooms, and a den, which is being converted to an office. A large living room sporting a large wood-burning fireplace made of lava rock. There was a dining room and 2 full bathrooms. Also on the property is a bunkhouse that sleeps four.

As Ted stepped outside for his first cup of coffee of the day, he recalled the night before and how dark it was. He could not remember ever seeing the stars so bright in the night sky. The air on this first morning there was very crisp. The elevation was nearly 4,000 ft above sea level. It felt good to him, he was never one for the heat. The smell of breakfast cooking filled the air as the aromas flowed out the kitchen window where Joe Kimo, an SGM member, was cooking. He had been a cook for the US army before retiring after 20 years.

Soon the sound of a triangle dinner bell was ringing in Ted's ear. It was time to try out this cook's breakfast. There were only four of them at the breakfast table. Ted, Major Parker, Joe Kimo, and a woman. Her name was Major Susan Green. She was a computer and analysis expert. Her real talent was using computers to predict human behavior based on personality types. Jack had told Ted that this may prove useful in dealing with the members of the ODR. Once the computers were up and running General Wigmore suggested that Ted tell her everything that he knows about the head ODR members he had encountered while undercover as Lewis Hall.

Breakfast was wonderful in Ted's eyes. Fried eggs, bacon, Portuguese sausage, steamed rice, papaya, and fresh-squeezed orange juice all served with bottomless cups of Kona coffee.

After breakfast, Major Parker and Ted met in the still-being set-up office. Parker told Ted he would take him on a tour of the area around

Volcano with a drive-by where Alex's house was located. After that, they would visit The Hawaii Volcano's National Park. To Parker, that too needed to be included in the areas of possible conflict. As well as being the place where Alex worked.

***

On the other side of the island at Racheal's place, Sarah and Alex were also having breakfast. and talking about the luau they had attended the night before. Their discussion led to the plans for the day ahead. Alex would be taking Sarah to another historical site. This time it would be Pu'uhonua O' Honaunau. More commonly known as The City of Refuge. This place too is under the guidance and protection of the US National Park System. At the bequest of Alex, Racheal had prepared bagged lunches for them to take with them. Simple corned beef sandwiches and fresh fruit.

They decided that they would stop on the way back to the Hapuna resort to get their belonging. Rachel told them it would be fine. Her next guest was not expected to arrive until early evening. They would even have time to freshen up if they got back early enough. Alex assured her they would be and thanked her.

The drive to the park would be only 6 ½ miles. As they drove along the highway Sarah noticed that the tourist feel disappeared except for a few places advertising coffee farm tours. The highway was lined with lush tropical plants that grew right to the edge of the road. There was all manner of palm trees, banana trees, mango trees, and many others she didn't know. Many ordinary homes were built alongside small shops, schools, and churches. She thought this is what real Hawaii must look like. Somehow living in the world of being a tourist she had lost sight that to a lot of people these islands are home.

At that moment she thought of Alex from a different view. This was his home as well. She then thought about the feeling she had for him. She had already realized that she was falling in love with him. How would that play out she wondered. Her home was on the other side of the world. Should she hold back her feelings? Was she falling for him because he was the only person, besides her father, that she did not hear his thoughts? Was it perhaps he was so exotic and different from other

163

men she had met? Suddenly she felt a mess inside. She thought at that moment it was a good thing he could not hear her thoughts.

Suddenly, a new thought entered her mind. Maybe she was falling in love with him just because of who he was as a person. She had known men before for a lot longer than this and never felt this way, even though she liked them. She felt as if her heart and her head were in a tug of war. Her head kept telling her, you have only known him for a few days. But her heart was saying this is something special, don't mess it up. After a few miles of this battle, she decided on a compromise. She would hold her feelings where they were and get to know him more. Who he was, his history, and where and how he lived. Seeing where and how a person lives can tell a lot about them.

They had just turned onto the road that leads down to the park that is situated near the sea. Sarah could feel the descent in elevation was very fast. She could also feel the heat increase. The views were spectacular. The long sloping curve of the volcano was now clear. Soon the landscape began to change from a very lush green to a grassier look. The trees were fewer in number and much smaller. When they arrived at the park, she noticed a great number of coconut trees. The area was not as dry as the other Heiau Park. There were also far more visitors at this one. Once they had parked, Alex put on his backpack which always contained lots of water and snacks.

At the information counter, Alex got a map. Every ranger greeted him personally by his Hawaiian name, Alika. He always introduced Sarah as a friend he was showing around. He also made a point of telling the rangers of her qualifications. Once inside Sarah pulled out her notebook and sketchbook. Alex let her go off on her own, staying only within sight of her.

Sarah was impressed by the restored Heiau Temple and the carving of some of the many Hawaiian gods, which she not only took photos of but also sketched. As she toured the grounds, she understood why it was called "The City of Refuge." This was a place set aside for those fleeing from war and from prosecution of the death sentence for breaking a law. She was most impressed by the huge 10 ft high wall of dry-laid stone that separated the outside of the sanctuary from the inside. The idea of a place to be safe reminded her of how, in England and other countries, in the not-so-distant past, churches and cathedrals were used as places of protection in a very similar manner. She thought once more about how people all over the world, though different in many ways were, at heart, were so much the same.

They spent the entire morning exploring this most historic and fascinating place. When it came time for lunch. Alex made sure Sarah had seen all she wanted before moving on. When she said she had, he asked if it would be alright if they went to a place that was special to him to have their lunch. He assured her it was very close by.

Sarah agreed. To her, this might be a chance to see a side of him that she did not know.

When they left the park, instead of turning right to return the way they came, Alex turned left onto a very narrow paved road that went along the coast. Sarah was amazed at how straight the road was. The landscape was not barren, but it was not tropical. Mostly brush and grass grew along the road. Alex drove for about 3 miles to another very rough road on which he drove slowly. This mostly rock and dirt road went along and very close to the shore. After a short distance, there were houses. It was in a small local community. No signs announced the place. A little bit further along, the road ended. Alex parked the jeep and asked Sarah to follow him. Alex grabbed the lunches and they were headed to the beach. On the way, a couple of people saw them walking and called out to Alex.

"Aloha Alika. Good for see you again bro."

They would then give him the shaka sign A Hawaiian hand gesture meaning to "hang loose". This is done by holding down your three middle fingers and leaving only your thumb and little finger pointing up. You would then rotate your hand back and forth a few times. This sign is used all over the islands as a local form of waving.

After a short walk, they arrived at the water's edge. It was very rocky with a few places of sand and coral mixed leading into the water. Alex found a place on a small rock ledge near one of these sandy beaches to sit and spread out the lunch Rachel had prepared for them.

After offering Sarah a sandwich and a drink Alex sat quietly looking out at the waves as though he were far away. He ate his sandwich slowly as he continued to look at the waves washing onto the beach in front of them. Once Alex had finished eating Sarah finally broke the silence.

"So, may I ask? What is this place and why is it special to you?"

After a brief silence, Alex answered. "This is Ke'Ei beach. It is here, on this beach that it all began for my family here in Hawaii almost 400 years ago."

Sarah looked at him perplexed. How could that be? Perhaps he was talking about the Hawaiian part of his family She had already assumed he must be part Hawaiian. Going on this assumption, she asked.

"For your Hawaiian side of your family?"

He looked at her and smiled.

"No, this is where the Michaels started their life in Hawaii."

"How can that be? I thought white men did not arrive here until after Captain Cook came?"

"That's the official history," replied Alex. "It is said that he didn't find these islands by accident. That he had a 200-year-old Spanish map that showed these islands on it. I am sure it was the case. It was my family that arrived here on a Spanish ship that wrecked just out there on those rocks long before Cook arrived using the same map. They came ashore here and were taken in by the Hawaiian people. My family has been here on this island ever since that day. I come here often to honor them."

"Your family was Spanish?" asked Sarah probing further.

"No, they are English," Alex replied. "Before you ask, yes, they were English on a Spanish ship. The why, is a long story for another time. But I wanted to share this with you. I have never shared this with anyone else before. I feel close enough to you now to trust you with this. Please this is between us."

He looked at her with almost pleading eyes.

"Of course, I am honored that you shared it with me."

"Oh, and before I forget, Alex said. "This is for your notebook. Something else happened here. On this same beach, King Kamehameha had the first battle that set him on the path to becoming the ruler of all of Hawaii. It is called the Battle of Mokuohai. It is named after a plant that used to grow here, so I have been told."

Sarah reached over and took his hand in hers. They both sat for a while without saying a word. They quietly watched the waves.

After a while, Alex broke the moment.

"I think we should be heading back," Alex said as he got up. "We want to be back in time to have a shower and freshen up before heading back to the hotel."

Sarah agreed and helped him pack up what they had brought and went back to the Jeep. On the way back more people came out to wave at Alex. Some called to him, others just waved the shaka.

On the way back to Rachel's place not much was said. Sarah could tell Alex was still deep in thought. She too was thinking about how much it meant to her that he shared that place. She now was wanting to know the rest of the story. A wild thought then entered her mind. If he could hear thoughts like her, and he was from England, could it be possible that somehow in the distant past they are connected? Perhaps, this is why they were attracted to each other. She stopped that line of thinking before it got too far. She would make herself mad going down that path.

Soon they were back at Rachel's place and enjoying a refreshing shower. Each had a lot to think about. Each one was thinking if they could just know what the other was thinking. Alex knew he had the power to do that, but he cared too much for Sarah now to allow himself to violate that trust.

After they showered and thanked Rachel for a wonderful stay they headed back to the Hapuna Beach Resort. As they were traveling along, Alex came up with an idea.

"What you say we take a day off tomorrow?" asked Alex looking at Sarah. "Just relax on the beach, go for a swim, perhaps a bit of surfing, do whatever feels fun. The day after I must check on my house here on the Kona side. You are invited along if you like."

"I like that idea," Sarah answered. "I like that idea a lot. Yes, I would like to see your house. Thank you for the invitation."

Once this was settled, they both relaxed and enjoyed the trip back. Stopping for a pizza and shopping in Kailua.

***

In Volcano village, Major Parker was giving Ted a tour of the area. It didn't look like much of a village to Ted at first but, after Parker drove

167

him around the back roads, he realized that a lot of people lived in the area. It seemed the whole population had built their homes in the forest. Ted liked the feel of the place once he got a look around.

Parker then pulled onto a one-lane road that ended at a gate. Beyond the gate Ted saw nothing but trees and giant tree ferns, called hapu, growing over where a road should be. Parker stopped at the gate.

"This is Alex's place," Parker explained. "Any other time you would see a road and a glimpse of a house nestled among the trees. But now this is what you see."

"He cloaked the whole place with a magic spell?" asked Ted with a surprised tone.

"Yes," replied Parker. "I don't know how he does it. Not sure I want to know. But this tells me he is ok. It also tells me the kind of power we are protecting."

"How do you know he is ok by seeing this?"

"Colonel Fairway told me that these types of spells only hold if he is on the island and is ok. He could be in there right now and we would have no way of knowing."

"What would happen if we just walked up to the trees or illusion?"

"No one knows and no one wants to find out," Parker answered.

"I don't blame them," Ted said with a chuckle.

They turned around and headed next to the National Park. The SGM vehicles had a special sticker on them that allowed them to enter the park without paying. Most of the rangers knew many of the island's SGM members, so there were a lot of waves from them as they drove around. One of the stops was at the law enforcement office so Parker could introduce Ted.

After that, they stopped at the Kilauea Military Camp. This old military outpost was now converted into a place where the active and retired military and government workers could stay within the park when they were on holiday. It has all the facilities of a small resort, including places to get a good meal. This is what Ted and Parker were doing.

After lunch, it was on to the Jagger Museum located on a bluff overlooking the volcano's main caldera. The museum is named after Thomas Jagger, the first scientist to actively study the volcano. Next door to the Museum is the headquarters of the US Geological Survey or

USGS for short. There, a group of scientists carry on the work that Jagger started many years before. It was out of this office that Alex worked.

Slightly below the USGS was the very heart of the volcano. In the center of the massive caldera is the main crater known as Halema'uma'u. This was believed by many, to be the home of the fire goddess Pele.

Ted found it interesting, if not a bit unnerving, to be looking into the heart of an active volcano. He was also surprised that so many people lived so close to it. The view behind him impressed him the most. It was the cross-view of the volcano Mauna Loa. Its sheer size and raw beauty made him feel small yet privileged.

After a short tour of the facility there, Parker told Ted to settle in for a long drive along a road called, Chain of Craters Road. This road led from the tropical rainforest near the summit to the barren lava fields at sea level some 25 miles away.

The drive took them past many craters, cinder cones, and through lava fields, some recent and some old. The road ended at the sea coast which was lined with cliffs being crashed upon by waves. Here Ted stood on some of the youngest rocks on earth that now covered the road that once continued on further.

The one thought that Ted kept having, was that this is not at all how he pictured a volcano, active or otherwise. Parker explained to him that the volcanos of Hawaii were known as shield volcanos, because of their shape resembling that of an inverted Greek shield.

After a short break and they began the long drive back up to the summit. The views going back up gave Ted a real sense of the scale of the place. Ever in the military mindset, Ted made a mental map of everything he saw. Once back at the summit, they exited the Park and returned to the new ranch headquarters.

Inside, Ted was greeted with a message to contact Colonel Fairway which he did immediately.

Fairway informed him that the camera and sound surveillance of Goddard's place had paid off on the first day. Goddard had secured the use of an old resort hotel on Ali drive in Kona. Jack told him that the place is due to be demolished at some point but enough of the facility is still operational enough to be used. The ODR, through Goddard, managed to get a short-term lease of the whole first and second floors. It seemed this was to be the new HQ for the ODR.

Jack told Ted that they had the place under surveillance already and there was no need for him to return to Kona. Ted agreed that for now, he was the most useful where he was. They both agreed to keep each other up to date on any changes or needs.

Privately Ted was happy to stay in Volcano. The climate and atmosphere agreed with him, he also wanted time to talk to local people about Alex. He wanted to know more about this wizard they were doing so much to protect.

Chapter 21

Reaching for the Moon

Ted rose early the next morning as usual. He poured a cup of Kona coffee and outside to take in the alpine air of Volcano as Joe Kimo prepared breakfast. The previous evening, after he and Parker had returned from their trip out, Ted had sat down with Susan Green and filled her in on what he knew about members of the ODR. She now had her analysis computer up and running and was anxious to put it to work.

The bell rang for breakfast and Ted went in, joining the others already seated at the table. Today was steak and eggs day, Ted's favorite breakfast. As they ate, Susan began sharing what she had learned from the analysis she had already done on Jason Elliot.

"Based on what you told me, Ted," Susan explained. "Mr. Elliot is a self-absorbed person that likes to be in control. He believes he knows best even when others disagreed with him. Deep down though, he is insecure and very frightened of being wrong. He is also paranoid. Because of this, I predict that when he comes to the islands, and he will come here, he will have at least one if not two bodyguards accompany him."

"Well done, Susan," Parker replied. "What do you think Ted?"

"I have to trust her analysis," responded Ted. "I will forward this to Colonel Jack when I talk to him after breakfast. The airport team will need to keep a watch for others with him if or when Elliot arrives."

"I will let you know what I get on the others you mentioned as soon as I have that information," Susan told them.

When Ted finished eating, he got up from the table and headed for the office to call Jack. Just before he left the room he turned to Joe.

"Fantastic breakfast Mr. Kimo. Very good steak. Thank you."

"Mahalo," replied Joe. "Hawaii raised beef, da best!"

The first thing Ted always does before he goes about any business is to call Sarah. Even if it is just for a minute to find out how she is. She always answers and today, like most other days, just tells him where she visited last. But she is always careful not to mention anything about

Alex. She knows it would only bring on a rash of questions that she was not yet prepared to answer.

After the call to Sarah, Ted called Jack to pass on the information that Susan had given him. Jack informed Ted that after learning about where the new ODR headquarters were to be located. He was going to have a crew install a camera on a street light just opposite the entrance of the place. Ted thought it was a great idea.

***

Back in London, where it was now late evening, Charles Stewart was on the coded phone line to Goddard. Charles informed Goddard of how pleased he was that he had secured a place so quickly. He also informed Goddard that Jason Elliot should be arriving in the afternoon of that day. He should be traveling alone. He asked Goddard not to pick him up but instead to have a car waiting for him at the airport with instructions inside on how to find the place he would be lodging. Charles did not want to risk that he and Elliot would be seen together. Goddard told Charles that several cars had already been rented and would be waiting for each person when they arrived. Charles again told Goddard how pleased he was with the job he was doing. The conversation ended with Goddard looking forward to meeting up with Jason at the new headquarters.

***

After getting off the phone with her father, Sarah went down and met Alex for breakfast. He was already there having coffee dressed in his beach outfit. A bright blue aloha shirt with surfboards on it and green swimming trunks. Sarah was wearing her long beach wrap which concealed her bright green two-piece bathing suit laced with white flowers.

Sarah had her usual fruit-filled breakfast while Alex enjoyed an omelet filled with mushrooms.

After breakfast the two of them found a pair of beach lounges that had shade umbrellas. They staked out this as their territory for the day. Alex brought his own surfboard and suggested that Sarah rent one from the shop in the hotel. Sarah agreed and set off to find a board to rent that suited her. As soon as she returned, they headed for the water.

The waves were a bit higher today, which made for perfect surf conditions. Alex did have more experience but was by no means an expert. Soon they were both enjoying the thrill of wave riding. The sandy beach made for perfect landing conditions. No rocks to worry about. After about an hour of riding, they came out and retired to their lounges.

They both looked like the perfect couple on vacation. Each had water bottles and snacks nearby.

Some time had passed in this relaxed mode when Alex had an idea.

"How would you like to control your thought-reading?" asked Alex.

"What?" replied Sarah with a puzzled look. "You can teach me how?"

"My father and mother taught me. All I can do is try if you like?"

Sarah thought about it for a moment.

"Alright," she said, "But if it doesn't go well, we stop."

"Deal," Alex answered and then began to explain. "First thing you must learn is to unlearn the way you look at thought. There are two basic kinds of thought. Internal thought and projection thought. Internal thought is the kind you would use to do math in your head. There are no real pictures involved. Projection thought is the kind you feel with. Think of projection thought as talking with your mouth closed. It is speech confined to your mind."

"Wow," Sarah came back. "That makes sense."

"So," Alex continued. "If you can control what you're saying, then it makes sense you can also control what you're thinking. You know the saying "tell me what you're thinking," which proves that it is speech confined to your head. You follow me so far?"

"Yes," Sarah answered. "It almost sounds too simple."

"It is just that simple. You can control what you say by simply closing your mouth. You can control your projection thoughts by closing off that part of your mind. To do this you convert projection thought into internal thought. So instead of becoming speech confined it is thinking refined."

"How do you turn off the incoming thoughts of others?"

"By what my father called refocus. When you are concentrating on doing a task do you hear others' thoughts? I know I don't."

"No, I don't," Sarah answered. "I just recently discovered that when I was learning how to surf."

"That's the key," Alex replied. "It is good you learned that on your own. When you hear incoming thoughts, you don't want to hear, you refocus on something or someplace else. The refocus is like putting earmuffs on to block out sound. It takes practice but you get the hang of it after a while. It would be very hard to learn if you don't have someone that has, as you call it, the same condition."

"Can you show me how it works?"

"I can try," Alex replied. "If you're willing?"

"Okay, what do I have to do?"

"I will start it off."

Alex turned on his projection thought and began by thinking about how beautiful Sarah looked in her bathing suit. Sarah then replied in thought, "thank you."

"Now that we can hear each other in thought," Alex said in a plain voice. "You can now practice first to refocus. So now when I project thought to you, think of something else. It can be anything from the sand on your feet to the brightness of the sun. Ready?"

Alex thought of how white her legs were compared to his. He went on thinking the same thing over and over. Sarah could plainly hear it. She then focused on the color of the sea and how blue it was. The more she focused on that, the dimmer the sound of Alex's thought became until she could no longer hear him. She then turned to him and smiled. Alex knew it had worked and he blocked his projection.

'I can't believe how easy that was," Sarah said smiling widely.

"The hard part is the next one," Alex explained. "Converting projection into internal. Keep in mind this is only useful when you know the other person can hear your thoughts. For example, on a person like me. I found it liberating when I could block my parents from hearing me. Think of it as meditation. You are thinking to yourself. You are not speaking. It is more mindful. The direction is internal. One other thing, keep in mind that when you are listening you are not thinking, so there is no thought being projected or converted."

"What do I do now," Sarah asked.

"I want you to look at all the beach lounges and think of what they might cost and count them and figure out how much the hotel must have spent on them. I will see if I can hear you. Ready......., go."

Sarah did as Alex suggested. At first, she thought she hoped she would do it right. Alex heard that thought and came back to her by thinking "focus on the chairs." She turned to him and smiled and tried again. This time she did count them and tried to imagine their cost and then tried adding them up in her mind. Alex could hear nothing. When Sarah had come up with a number, she then thought the number toward Alex. Alex smiled and clapped his hands.

"Well done you," Alex said out loud still clapping. "Do you recall how you sensed the shift from when you were calculating to when you sent me the number?"

"Yes," Sarah said smiling. "It had a different feeling or sound to it."

"That's it. I am truly impressed you learned that so fast. After all that hard work let's get some lunch."

As they walked toward the Naupaka Beach grill for lunch, Sarah thought how proud she was of herself for what she had just learned. She didn't even care if Alex heard her or not. She now could even practice on her own. She understood for the first time it wasn't what she thought but it was how the thought felt. Right then she also realized that she would not have learned this if it were not for Alex. Also, for the first time she truly felt in control and free. It was wonderful. She thought that Alex was wonderful too for taking the time to teach her.

For lunch, Sarah enjoyed a club sandwich and Alex his standby, a burger.

After lunch, they returned to their lounges. Alex settled in and closed his eyes. Sarah watched him for a while and listened for any thoughts. She heard nothing. She then disrupted his resting with a question.

"Alex? Can I ask you a personal question?" inquired Sarah.

"Sure," Alex answered "Fire away."

"Just now when you are laying there in your internal thoughts, what are you thinking about?"

"I am not thinking," he replied. "I am meditating and listening."

"To what?"

"To everything and nothing," came his answer. "The sea, the waves, the birds, the sound of people's voices, and anything else the universe is saying. To most people, each sound is a separate thing. To me, they are combined to form a song. A song that will be played only once exactly as you hear it at this moment. If you come again on another day the song may sound the same but it will be different. The wind will be slightly different. The birds will be on different branches and sing slightly different tunes. It is the rule of the universe. The very pattern of it. Nothing ever is repeated, no moment, no sound, no grain of sand stays the same. Everything is in a constant state of change. Some see that as chaos. I see it as a pattern. The music of the universe, always playing a song but never the same tune twice."

Alex fell silent. He still had his eyes closed. Sarah stared at him as if she had seen him for the first time. Her heart raced, to think that a person she knew could have such profound insight. Sarah laid back in her seat and looked up at the clouds. She realized that one answer would now change the way she saw the world for the rest of her life. So profound, yet so simple.

"Can I ask you one now?" asked Alex still lying there with his eyes closed."

"Yes, I suppose it's only fair," Sarah answered.

"Do you believe in magic? I don't mean the kind you see in shows. I mean real magic. The spell casting, potion brewing, wand whipping, staff-wielding magic, like that of Merlin?"

"I suppose not," Sarah answered in a confused tone. "I have never seen any that I knew of. I know from my studies many ancient people believed in it. I think it was their way of explaining things they couldn't understand."

"Can you explain love? Like the kind, you feel for your father."

Sarah heard the spring on the trap snap shut. She already knew the question before he asked it without hearing any thoughts.

"I know where this is going," Sarah answered. "Is love magic? If not, then what is it?"

"You're wiser than you realize," Alex said with a smirk.

"I thought you were talking about the kind of magic that can change a person into a toad."

"Same thing really," Alex said as he sat up opening his eyes. "I believe each of us is limited by what we believe. And more so by what we are told to believe. Further still, by what we are told we cannot do or what is possible. Follow me on this. A father takes his child out one evening to look at the moon. While they are looking at it, the child reaches up to grab the moon. The father pulls her hand down and looks into her eyes and says, "You can't grasp the moon, it is too far away." So, for the rest of her life, she believes there is no way, no matter what she does, she cannot grasp the moon. In another place, another father does the same thing, except when his child reaches for the moon, he says, "keep reaching, if you want it bad enough you will find a way." Years later that child helps build rockets that carry men to the moon and brings back rocks that she can now hold in her hands. This is the real power of magic. Not so much what one believes is impossible but what one believes is possible."

Alex laid back down and closed his eyes again. Again, Sarah did not know what to say. She realized that she had achieved in her chosen field and, despite her condition, only because her father told her she could do anything she put her mind to. Now Alex had shown her the same thing. In a few hours, she felt as though she had gone from standing on a flat plain to standing on the edge of a high cliff wondering if she could fly.

Alex let her lay there thinking about what he had said. He knew what he was doing. He was feeling her out about how open she might be, if or when she was to know the truth about him. Finally, he broke the tension he could feel.

"I am not even going to ask what your feeling are about dragons," Alex said laughing out loud.

Sarah laughed too. They both got up and decided to go for a last swim before changing for dinner.

***

In Kona, Goddard had arranged the car for Jason to retrieve when he arrived. He had placed a local phone for him to use in the car with instructions on where to find it. Goddard figured that local phones would be the best to use between them in Hawaii and would be harder to track.

Goddard decided to wait at the airport parking area until Jason arrived to make sure he found the car. He would not make contact unless he could see there was a problem. He was not aware that the SGM was tracking his car and knew he was there. Jack was alerted because, if he was at the airport, they knew he was expecting someone to arrive. He had all the airport units put on high alert.

Around 3 pm one of the airport watchers called Jack. He was sure that Jason had just got off a plane from LA. It was based on a photo that all the SGM members had that were watching the airports statewide. Jack informed him to keep a tail on him but not too close.

In the parking area, Goddard was also watching. He knew what flight he was due in on because he had arranged it. After a while, he saw Jason headed straight for the car that was waiting for him. Goddard noticed two men following Jason very closely. He was not sure what to make of it.

Jason got in the car along with the two men. A short time later Goddard's local phone rang. It was Jason on the local phone he had left for him in the car.

"Yes Mr. Elliot," Goddard said answering.

"You did say the condominium was a two-bedroom?"

"Yes, replied Goddard. "Why?"

"I have two security guards with me," Jason told him. "We will need an extra bed in one of those rooms. Will also need another car for them."

"Mr. Stewart didn't tell me anything about two extra men," Goddard said, rather perturbed.

"Charles doesn't know and doesn't need to know," replied Jason in an ordering tone. "They are my men. They are also members so they fall under the coverage of the expense of the order. You have done a great job here so far. But I am in charge now. Do we understand each other?"

"Yes sir, Mr. Elliot," replied Goddard.

"Good," Jason snapped back. "I expect this to be taken care of before the end of the day. Will see you at the new HQ tomorrow."

Jason abruptly hung up the call. Goddard was tempted to call Charles and see what his reaction would be. He decided to wait for now to see how things went. He had heard about Jason doing things outside what was expected, but this is not what he thought they meant. He also thought that if Jason crossed him, he would not only inform Charles but he would walk away from this mission. Maybe take a holiday like he heard Lewis Hall had done.

Meanwhile, the SGM man at the airport reported to Jack about the two extra men he saw get into the car with Jason Elliot. Jack then called Ted and told him that it looked like Susan's prediction was correct. According to the airport units, these men carried themselves like a security detail. Ted suggested that Jack have a special recon unit sent to where Jason was staying and see if they could tag his car and any other cars the ODR was found to have. He also asked if it might be possible to find out who these two men are and do a background search on them.

Jack agreed with Ted and said he would call in a few local members that were good at that sort of thing. He would report back to Ted as soon as he found out anything new.

***

That evening after Alex and Sarah finished dinner, they retired to their rooms early. They were both tired from a day on the beach. When Alex returned to his room, he called Jack as usual. Jack filled him in on the latest. Alex told Jack he would be going to his Kona house the next day and would be bringing a tourist with him to show them the sights so the men he knew Jack assigned to watching the place were not to be alarmed. Jack told him not to worry he was calling in those men for the day for a special assignment. They each wished the other a pleasant evening and ended the call.

The arrival of one of ODR's top men gave Alex a bit of concern. He knew for sure now that things may well get heated. When or how bad he did not know nor could he see. For the first time, he was concerned about Sarah's safety. She might end up in the middle of something and have no idea why. At some point, he would have to choose to tell her who and what he is or slowly break it off to protect her. The love he was feeling for her was going to make this very difficult.

Chapter 22

Every Man A Price

Back in England, Rhyfel was increasingly getting impatient. Having the information that Lord Ambrose had given them he wanted to move. He was desperate to find a way to break free of the stranglehold the ODR had put on them. It not only made him frustrated it was beginning to make him angry.

One thing that Lord Ambrose had mentioned at their meeting in Avebury, was that while he was doing his research at the British Library in London, he recognized a man from the ODR meeting in London going there as much as he did. Good with names, he knew it was John Coke.

John Coke was one of the top ODR members. A middle-aged man, 5 foot 4 inches, balding, and wore thick glasses. Married with three children, he was very much a family man. John worked at Scotland Yard but was what some would call a desk jockey. He was not a fieldman. He specialized in information gathering and analysis.

Ambrose was correct. Coke was at the library a lot. Almost every day since after the meeting with the Morgans. He was trying to find a way through research to determine where in Hawaii the Merlin descendant was and even who he was, if possible. He focused on old stories from Hawaii hoping to track him through tales of magic told of the people in Hawaiian lore. This, of course, had been fruitless so far.

Another of Rhyfel's trusted members is Lord Remel. Remel is far more militant than any of the other Morgans. Rhyfel often referred to him as his General. One reason Rhyfel didn't invite him to the meetings with the ODR, was because Remel would have ended it far more violently. He was the one that killed the ODR member by the car after the chase with Ted. Now Rhyfel was thinking he may just have a use for his ways.

Rhyfel's plan was simple. Have Remel kidnap Coke and take him to a place and try to talk him away from the ODR.

***

Circles in Stone

The British Library is a short walk away from the King's Cross train station. Rhyfel already knew that Coke came to the library on a train in that station from what Ambrose had told him. Rhyfel told Remel to stake out the station and see if there was a pattern to Coke's comings and goings.

It did not take long before Coke's pattern revealed itself. After making sure the pattern held, Rhyfel gave Remel the order to proceed.

One afternoon as Coke was leaving the library and walking along the sidewalk next to Euston Road headed for the train station, two men approached him. One of them was Remel the other was Remel's driver and bodyguard. They approached Coke, Remel in front and his bodyguard from the rear. This stopped Coke in his tracks. Before Coke could speak, Remel did.

"You don't know me; my name is Lord Remel. But I believe you have met my master Rhyfel."

Coke froze. He remembered him well. He would never forget that encounter. He was about to answer but Remel didn't give him a chance.

"He wants to speak with you in private," said Remel with intimidation. "I suggest you make it easy on yourself and come with us."

Coke started to scramble to get away but suddenly felt frozen, unable to move. He saw Remel was holding what looked like a black pointed crystal of some sort. Remel took the crystal and whirled it around Coke's wrists. Coke felt the sensation of a rope pulling his wrist together as if they were being tied. It wasn't painful but he could not move his hands apart. He looked at his wrist, there was nothing there. He felt the rest of his body become free and able to move.

"Now," Remel said. "You will come with us. We mean you no harm. If you would just follow my friend here, we will take you to Master Rhyfel and soon you will be free to go."

Coke felt now he had no choice but to comply. He followed them a very short distance to a black car waiting in the car park in front of the St. Pancras station. Coke was put in the rear seat where Remel joined him. The bodyguard got in the driver's seat. Once they were all secure in the car and began to pull out Remel tapped the driver on the shoulder.

"To the Albert Memorial James," Remel told the driver with a laugh.

"Yes sir!"

Coke didn't know if the driver's name was James or if it was a joke. It didn't matter. Coke did know London well so he knew it would be only 15 minutes to get there in the current traffic. He was also thinking it was a strange place for a meeting.

Just as Coke had figured, they arrived at the memorial in about 15 minutes.

The driver pulled into the taxi stand in front of the memorial fence. He got out and opened the door for Coke. Remel was now out and directed Coke to the sidewalk that runs along the left side of the Monument. The two of them followed this until they arrived at a junction in front of a coffee shop.

On a bench, just before the café, Coke recognized the person sitting there. That is one face he will never forget. It was Master Rhyfel. This time he was wearing a long black trench coat. Under it, he could see the ruby-encrusted black orb. On the bench beside him was a rolled-up cloth and a small wooden box with a top handle. As Coke and Remel approached him Rhyfel spoke up.

"Come now Remel," he said. "This is a meeting, not a prisoner exchange. Release our friend from those restraints."

Lord Remel pulled the black crystal from his pocket and waved it around Coke's wrists. Coke felt whatever was binding them together disappear.

"Come, sit down," Rhyfel said as he pointed to the other end of the bench where he was sitting. "If you're thinking of running, Mr. Coke, you can see, if you look around, I have my trusted guards all around and I also have this."

Rhyfel unfolded the cloth beside him to reveal one of his magic-throwing daggers. He covered it back up and signaled Remel to get them some coffee from the café.

"How do you take yours," Rhyfel asked Coke.

"Black with one sugar," Coke answered nervously.

"Now," Rhyfel began. "Let us get down to business. I know all about you Mr. Coke. I know about your wonderful family, your beautiful home, and the nice mortgage that comes with it. I think you're a smart guy. In fact, I know you are. Scotland Yard couldn't run without your master of computers and sorting things out. As far as the ODR goes, I know you're a loyal member. But I am wondering if maybe your faith in them is a little flawed.

"My faith in them is not flawed," Coke snapped back.

"Oh, come now," Rhyfel continued. "Everything the ODR believes in is based on a book that was written by a church four hundred years after most of the events in it. My family goes back to a time before many of those events ever happened. You didn't even believe people like me were even real until this year. That same church only told you to believe what they wanted you to believe. And to fear anything else. Yet your ODR is now in a battle to obtain something that is supposed to be a myth. As a smart man, I would think you can see the flaw in that. We don't want the same thing. Your ODR wants to rule the world. We only want was has been rightfully ours, the throne of England."

Coke was silent, as he took the coffee Remel had brought him. Taking a sip of the coffee he knew that some of what Rhyfel was saying was true. The holy war the ODR was raging indeed seemed a bit much for him at times. They did want the Jewel of Power so they could rule the world. Charles had even said so at the meeting in Edinburgh. They wanted to use a jewel of magic to achieve this. That truly was flawed in some way. He wanted to say something but Rhyfel broke his line of thought.

"We will get the Jewel somehow," Rhyfel went on. "When we do, we will rule this country. The ODR will end and everyone, including you, will be our subjects. Some will be against us, some will not care, and others will be with us. The question is which of these groups will you belong to? I have here, in this box beside me something to help you decide. Would you like to see what it is?"

Coke did not answer, though he was curious. Then again it could be something terrible. He just remained silent. Rhyfel reached over and opened the box. What Coke saw almost made him gasp. He held back and tried not to look too surprised. It was filled with what appeared to be gold coins. Coke did not move.

"Don't worry," Rhyfel said. "They are real. Two hundred Victoria gold sovereigns. As coins, they are worth around £100,000 ($132,000 US). We Morgans have been around a long time, to us, this is pocket change. There is a lot more where this came from. As coins like this, it would be tax-free. No one needs to know but us. I know what your next question is. What do we want in exchange? We want you to use those great computer skills of yours to lift the travel restrictions that the ODR put on our family. That's all, nothing more. We get to leave the country. You get to keep the gold. I tell you what, I will let you walk away with this gold today in good faith. Once we get the Jewel a lot more of these coins will be yours."

Coke was speechless. He knew he could do it. As he thought about it, he could even make look like a computer glitch. Rhyfel broke the silence again.

"You want to know how sure we are that we will get the Jewel, Mr. Coke? I am going to tell you a secret just to show that I trust you. We not only know that this Merlin descendant is in Hawaii as does the ODR, we know both where he lives and his name."

Coke's eyes widened. This would explain why they wanted to get there in a hurry. Coke's head was in a whirl, his heart was pounding so hard he was sure it could be heard by others.

"What if you fail for some reason?" Coke asked.

"I will tell you what. If you make it possible for us to get off this island, and you don't betray us, and we still fail to get the Jewel, you get to keep the gold, no questions asked. Trust me we will know if you betray us."

Coke kept looking at the gold. He asked himself one question. What had the ODR ever offered him for all the work he did for them? He knew they had plenty of money. That was the tipping point but he did not let it show.

"Do we have a deal?"

Coke did not answer right away. He thought about how this much gold could help his family. He knew this decision would change his life.

Rhyfel closed the box containing the coins and began to pick it up.

"We have a deal," Coke said. "No tricks. I want my family safe no matter what happens. It will take a few days to make changes and the system to update. I will also find a way to get out of going to Hawaii myself."

"I understand completely," Rhyfel answered with a smile. "You have my word. We will need to know when the restrictions have been lifted. This is what you will do. You continue to come to the library as usual. After you have made the way clear you will check out a book about traveling to Hawaii. When you come out of the library. you will display the book in such a way that one of my men, who will be watching you, can see it. It's that simple."

"I understand," Coke answered.

Rhyfel signaled two of his guards over. He told them to take Coke home and make sure he got there safely. He did this to make sure Coke knew that he knew where he lived.

Coke picked up the box with the coins and followed the men to the waiting car. Remel came over to Rhyfel from where he had been listening from a distance.

"Do you trust him?" asked Remel.

"Yes, I do actually," answered Rhyfel. "Deep down he knows the truth, deeper still he is a family man. He did this for his family. That is his price, and every man has a price lord Remel. Every man has a price."

After Coke was dropped off at his home by Rhyfel's men, he went inside with the box of gold coins and put them directly in his safe. He went to his computer and began working on the plan to undo the restrictions the ODR had but on the Morgans. Whatever he did must not be tracked back to him. It had look like a system failure. The only way he could make sure this is what it looked like was that the Morgans would not be the only ones taken off the terrorist watch list. This was risky because he knew that there were very dangerous terrorists out there that should not be taken off. He would formulate a plan to have some taken off but no one would know for a while who they were. This would give the Morgans time to leave without other groups being alerted. He would build into the glitch a way for it to repair itself and the list would be reinstated after a short time. The other thing that concerned him was giving the Morgans too much of an advantage. He was very much aware of how dangerous they could be. He didn't know if the ODR should have the Jewel but he also did not want the Morgans to have it either. He thought if he could alert the ODR that the Morgans had found a way out of England, this would give the ODR enough time to at least be prepared for them.

When the new measures of security were put in place, code words were made up to alert the ODR systems if anyone found out the Morgans were on the move. The words were, "going fishing" and the other was "gone fishing." If anyone, regular Scotland yard personnel or ODR found out that the Morgans had found a way out of England they were to send a message into the system. "Going fishing," meaning that they were still in England but had found a way to leave. "Gone fishing," meant that the Morgans had already left the country. Coke decided that once he had made the way clear for the Morgans to leave and had given them enough time to make plans, he would find out where one of the teams that watched them were, go there in secret and send the message into the system from that location.

The next part of his plan was to get out of going to Hawaii. He knew he was not due to go for at least another week. He would get his doctor to submit a report showing that he would not be able to travel for at least a month. He had a good relationship with his doctor and knew he would be willing to do that for him.

As for the gold coins he already had a plan worked out for that too. He would take a few coins with him on his work travels and in different towns and cities sell them a few at a time to dealers. He would stash the cash in his safe, being careful not to spend any of it for anything other than an emergency. This would be his family's nest eggs. He knows Scotland Yard always tracked the finances of its members looking for any potential form of corruption.

John Coke truly is a family man at heart. Nothing meant more to him than that. Not politics, job, or anything else. The only reason he even joined the ODR in the first place was that he thought it would be good for his family overall. After seeing what lengths, they would go to for power, Rhyfel was right, he had lost faith in them.

All this planning seemed good to Coke but there was one thing that was not taken into account. The very thing that did happen. Ever since the meeting in Edinburgh that Ted attended disguised as Lewis Hall, each one of the members of the ODR that attended that meeting was being followed by the SGM. That included John Coke. The SGM now knew that a meeting between Coke and Rhyfel had taken place. What was said was not known to them. But experts in the field of analysis of such things would now come to bear on what they saw happen. A close watch on Coke, and what he does, could change the plans of many and, in the end the outcome of those plans.

Chapter 23

Kona House

After the day on the beach, Sarah was looking forward to getting to know more about the man she was falling in love with. To her, seeing where and how a person lived says a lot about them.

They met for breakfast, as usual. Alex told her not to pack any swimming gear. His place was not near the shore. He did suggest that she take a jacket or sweater because where they would be going it might be a bit chilly this time of year. Alex said the drive would take about 40 minutes.

Once on the main road heading south, they drove about 6 miles to an intersection Sarah had seen a few times before. To the west, the road went to the Waikoloa Resort. They turned east and headed up the Waikoloa Road.

At first, the landscape was the same as when they turned, mostly barren lava fields on either side of the road. But soon the landscape changed as she felt the increase in elevation. It became grasslands mostly. She even began to see wild goats grazing along the sides of the road. They then passed close to a large group of houses that looked like a village. Alex told her it was Waikoloa village. A complete planned community with shops, a school, and a golf course. Further along, were still more green grasslands. Sarah could feel the steady increase in the angle of going uphill. The road wound around a bit but it was a pleasant drive. After about 12 miles the road ended at an intersection at which they went right. They were now on Highway 190. As they continued, they were still increasing in elevation. Sarah noticed the change in temperature to the point that she turned off the AC and opened the window to take in the fresh cool air. Alex told her much of the land on either side of the road was used as ranch land for grazing cattle.

After 9 miles along this road, they entered another community. The homes were barely visible, hidden behind trees, vegetation, and sometimes well-built stone walls. Further along this road, Alex turned into a drive with signs on either side that said Puu Lani Ranch. Each side of the road was beautifully groomed and had a white wooden fence set back just off the road. Ahead they approached a gate crossing the road. Alex pulled down his visor and retrieved a remote control. Pressed a button and the gate swung open. They were on Puu Lani Drive. Soon Sarah began seeing very well-groomed front lawns in front of very large houses. She realized now that if this is where he lived it was in a gated community. As they rounded a curve Alex pointed out the clubhouse that was for use by the members of the community. Alex slowed the Jeep, pulled out another remote from under his seat and pressed a button. A large gate located in the middle of a perfectly laid up lava rock stone wall opened. Alex pulled into the drive and the gate closed behind them.

"Were here," he said as he pulled up in front of the house. "This is my Kona home. Welcome to Wahi Kaulike, Place of Balance."

The house was a light green, wood-framed, one-story ranch-style home with a white sheet metal roof. The house was raised slightly off the ground on posts and piers, (this is a common construction in Hawaii). A covered lanai wrapped all around the house. Lava stone steps led up to the front door.

Alex got out of his jeep and going up the steps, unlocked the door.

"Please come in," Alex invited Sarah. "Make yourself at home. Please, feel free to wander and look around. I'll open the house up and find us some cool drinks."

Sarah began to do just that. She didn't follow him directly into the house. She was looking at the perfectly groomed lawn that had several palm trees and other flowering bushes scattered around giving almost the sense of being in a small park. As she approached the front steps, she stopped to look at the two statues on either side. They were medieval dragons carved of stone in a laying position looking out across the lawn. What was unusual were their eyes. They were glass but very real-looking. Also, each dragon was looking in opposite directions as if to make sure, that together, they could view the whole lawn.

Going up the steps she entered the house through a set of glass French doors each with leaf and flower designs inlaid in the glass. Upon entering, she was now in a hallway of sorts that led directly to another set of French doors at the rear of the house that Alex had already opened. On the floor in front of the door, there is a round rug with the design of a compass rose woven into it. Each compass point was of a different color.

Circles in Stone

Looking at the rug made Sarah realize that the house was not set perfectly parallel to the road like the other homes she saw. She reached into her bag and took out her phone. She wanted to check something. She went to her compass app and opened it. Using the app, she could see the house was laid out perfectly to the points of the compass. The rug in front of her was in line with the compass on her phone. It was also in line with the layout of the house.

Further in, a doorway on her left led to a very large great room. In the center of the room was a grand lava stone wood-burning fireplace with a generous couch in front of it. Above the mantel of the fireplace was mounted a large flat-screen television. Two large windows on either side of the fireplace flooded the room with light and gave wonderful views of the outdoors. Further along, but in the same room was an extensive dining table with matching chairs. Based on what she had learned so far about Hawaiian wood, it appeared to be Koa, a native tree often used to make high-end furniture. Beyond the table was a wall with an opening to what she could see to be the kitchen. She could see Alex standing at a counter in front of a large window making drinks.

Sarah walked slowly toward the kitchen taking mental note of all the decorations in both the living and the dining room.

"Come in," Alex said. "I have made us some very nice fresh lime aid. Hope you like it."

Alex handed her the drink that was in a beautiful tall cobalt blue glass. Sarah took a sip and looked at Alex.

"Something wrong?" Alex asked in response to her look. "Too sweet maybe?"

Sarah then laughed.

"I was expecting a fizzy drink from a bottle. I forgot that what Americans call lemon or lime aid is not what we call it. It is lovely. I like it very much. Thank you."

"Would you like to see the backyard, sorry back garden as you would call it?" Alex asked inviting her along. "It is a beautiful day to enjoy it."

They walked out through the rear French doors and down another set of lava stone steps onto a walkway made of large slabs of lava laid perfectly level with the ground. Near the house, two circles were made of lava and white coral inlaid in concrete on either side of the walkway. The one on the right was the Ying and Yang symbol. The one on the left was a spiral. The black and white contrast made them striking to look at.

The views were spectacular, a clear view of Mauna Kea gave a feeling that the place you were standing was floating on a cloud.

In the center of the yard is a large circle planted with all manner of flowers and flowering shrubs. Again, Sarah felt as though she was strolling in a park.

"Do you do the gardening?" asked Sarah.

"No. I have someone do this; they are wonderful. I also have a housekeeper who takes care of the house when I am not here. She stocks up my frig when she knows I am coming. I phoned her yesterday and told her I would be here today. So, we have plenty for lunch when you are ready."

They went back to the house and sat on the lanai to finish their drinks and take in the view.

"Did you have this built?"

"Not really. This was my father's dream place. He designed it all and built much of it with his own hands. I helped a lot of course. He and my mother loved it here. They turned the volcano house over to me and settled here. So much of who they were is here. I feel their energy every time I come. It is not a sad thing for me. Their love is here and that brings me joy and peace."

"What a wonderful way to look at it," Sarah responded. "I have never lost anyone close to me. I have known people that have and they seem to never get out of the grief."

"Grief is for a short time and it is for you. It doesn't bring anyone back. To truly bring them back is to remember what was wonderful about them. Hear their laughter and rekindle their love in your heart. Then they are alive. The dead never live in grief. Life only dwells where life is. Grief is like lava rock. It is barren and remains so until it has water. Memories are like water. Once the water is put on, life will soon cover the rock and it will become alive."

Sarah was silent, like so many times after Alex spoke things so profound. This time it got the better of her.

"Where does all this wisdom come from? Your answers sometimes leave me speechless."

"The ancestors. They are always giving us knowledge and wisdom if we take the time to listen."

"You hear them talking to you?"

"Not in an audible voice. No need to call the men in white coats yet," Alex answered laughing. "Haven't you been puzzled about something and suddenly unexpectedly you have the answer? Perhaps you were doing research and the right book somehow ends up in your hands with the knowledge you were seeking. That is the ancestors."

"So, you're saying they speak to us in many forms?"

"Yes, of course. The problem is that today people don't take the time to listen. Every book you ever read was written by someone else. It is the voice of the person that wrote it. It remains their voice no matter if it is 2 months old or 5000 years old. When you are reading it, you are hearing their voice. That makes them an ancestor. A transmitter of knowledge, wisdom, joy, fear, laughter, and a host of so much more. Images in dreams can also be them speaking to you. Taking the time to listen to the wisdom they impart from the universe can help in so many ways. We need more of that these days."

Again, Sarah was silent. Pondering what he just told her. It all made sense to her in so many ways. She realized that Alex never pushed any of this on her. He only answered questions she had asked. He didn't keep following up to make his point. He let her think about it in her own way.

"How about a tour of the rest of the house," Alex asked as he got up from his chair.

Sarah got up and followed. Back inside on the opposite side of the house from the kitchen and dining room were two bedrooms. The first one nearest the rear of the house was large and had a vast window through which you could see the mountain. It contained an enormous four-poster bed made of tree trunks. Large wooden dressers were along one of the other walls. The room felt powerful, yet the pastel colors of the walls and curtains added a softness to it that seemed to bring it into balance. Off one side of this bedroom was a full bathroom exclusive to the bedroom.

Further toward the front of the house was another hall off to the left. There was another full bathroom along this hall followed by the door to the second bedroom that faced the front of the house. The bed in this room was simple as were all the features in the room. The window in it overlooked the front lawn.

At the end of the hall was a door to an office /den. The walls had shelves filled with books. A heavily engraved desk faced the window to the south. Off to one side of the desk sat a computer.

After the tour, Alex went back to the kitchen. The kitchen was like any other, but very modern. Sarah was surprised to see oak cabinets. The counters were a mosaic of tiles that resembled waves in the sea. Alex said he was going to prepare a nice lunch. Sarah offered to help. Alex showed her where things were and told her she could make a salad. He was preparing grilled fish to make into sandwiches.

During lunch at the Koa table, Sarah continued to take in all the decorations. Some of them seemed so in tune with Hawaii, and yet others seemed out of place in some way. Like the dragons out in the front of the house. Another was along the back wall of the living room behind the sofa that faced the fireplace. It was a table, on it is a large bowl made of one piece of lava rock. On either side of the bowl were large candle stands. Each had a candle in them but of a different color. One was blue and one was gold. The whole setup seemed out of place with the rest of the décor.

Her archaeology training gave her a very sharp sense of how things should be and how to see things out of context.

"May I ask?" Sarah said looking at Alex. "How much of the deco in these rooms are you and how much is from your parents?"

"The furniture is from my parents. The sofa, the chairs, this table, and some of the paintings. The rest is mine. I moved much of it from my house in Volcano. Why, do you find it in bad taste?"

"Not at all. I was just curious."

From what she had seen and what she was now seeing, this man Alex was a mystery yet to be solved. There was so much she loved about him. Yet something was missing.

"Is your volcano house much different than this one?"

"Yes, very much so," answered Alex. "It, you could say, is much more who I am and who my family was. A lot has changed from the first grass-covered house of hundreds of years ago until now."

Sarah laughed. "Sorry, but your family actually lived in a grass-covered house?"

Alex looked at her in a very serious way.

"So did yours. And from what I saw on my visits a lot of people in England still do," Alex replied with a smirk.

Sarah stopped smiling when she realized he was referring to people that still have thatched roof houses all over the UK. She had never seen it that way before. Alex just smiled at her.

"No matter what your roof is made of," he said, "As long as it is home and love resides there, that is all that matters."

The smile returned to Sarah's face. Alex took her hand and leaned over and gave her a lite kiss on the lips. Sarah's heart jumped as if it had been hit by a spark. She reached back and pulled him close to her and return the kiss with a deep one.

"Sometimes," Alex said as he looked into her eyes after the kiss "I feel so at home with you. As if I have known you forever."

"And the other times?"

"You're my best friend that has returned after being away a long time. And sometimes, both feelings are mixed into one. Both feel wonderful."

Sarah smiled and continued to look into his eyes thinking that maybe if she looked hard enough, she could see more of who this wonderful man was that had entered her life. She could not hold back the next question that was banging around in her head.

"When do I get to see this other house," she asked still staring into his eyes to see if the answer would pour out.

It took Alex by surprise. He knew he could not take her there without revealing who and what he is. He still wasn't sure she could handle it. He wanted so bad to tell her but didn't know how or what would happen. Would she run away? Would she become afraid? He knew they needed a bit more time together for him to decide.

At that moment an idea came into Alex's head.

"How about we tour as much of the island together as we can and if you still like me, we will conclude the tour there? I promise to respect you and take care of you as a gentleman if you trust me?"

"I am sitting here in your house alone and I feel safe," Sarah replied. "Yes, I trust you."

"Wonderful," Alex answered as he squeezed her hand.

They both got up and together cleaned up from lunch. Alex loaded a few things into his jeep while Sarah continued to wander around taking pictures. They then left his house and headed back to the hotel. On the way, Alex chatted about all the places he wanted to show her.

Sarah listened and watched him. He seemed so excited about what he was telling her. He was like a child wanting to show off his home to his friend. As complicated as he seemed at times, this side of him was simple. Sarah loved seeing him like this.

Chapter 24

Grand Tour

As Alex had promised Sarah at his house in Kona, he made plans for the grand tour of the rest of the island that would end at his house in Volcano. That evening, when they returned, Alex began making calls to arrange places for them to stay. Sarah, meanwhile, was packing for the trip. She would keep the room but take most of her belongings with her.

She called her father and told him she would be touring as much of the remaining parts of the island as possible over the next week. She told him not to worry but again failed to tell him anything about Alex. He in turn told her that what he was doing was very routine and told her to enjoy herself. She promised to call him when she could but if she didn't it might be she would be in an area without cell service. They ended the call on a positive note and Ted felt she was more than capable of taking care of herself as she had done in the past.

Sarah and Alex went to bed that evening excited about the upcoming trip.

***

That evening General Wigmore called Ted to inform him of information regarding John Coke having a meeting with Rhyfel. He told Ted a more detailed watch was now in place to track them both. Ted told Wigmore he was very concerned about this revelation. In the top leadership of the ODR, he considered Coke the weakest link. Ted told Wigmore he would run the details by Susan and see what she came up with regarding the Coke and Rhyfel meeting.

Following the call to Wigmore, Ted called Jack to see if any more details had been learned about Jason and the new ODR headquarters. Jack told him he had men on Jason and that the security detail at Jason's condo was so tight he dared not risk trying to put cameras in there. He reported that a lot of equipment was being transported to the new ODR headquarters. It appeared to be computers, generators, and external lighting. But nothing new had been learned from the cameras at Goddard's place. Jack figured that any ODR plans were now being discussed at the new headquarters. Ted told Jack that, since there had been no move by the ODR to set up anything on the Hilo side of the island, particularly near Volcano, that they must still not know where Alex's home is located. Jack agreed with that assessment so was making sure the SGM men on all islands be on high alert in case the ODR made a move somewhere else.

Both men agreed that the best thing for now, was to continue setting up their own new headquarters in Volcano.

***

The next morning, after breakfast, Alex loaded his jeep with their cases. Sarah jumped into the jeep like a child about to go to a toy store. Alex was also excited about sharing new island treasures with Sarah and soon they were off.

Their first stop would be Waimea, the cowboy town. At around 3000 ft above sea level, the cool climate is ideal for raising crops that flourish in the cool air, notably, strawberries. Surrounded by vast ranchlands, Waimea is most noted for the Parker Ranch. Founded in 1847 by John Parker, its spread includes some 130,000 acres and is one of the largest working cattle ranches in the US. Waimea has the air of a modern US western town. Everything seems themed around the "paniolo," Hawaiian cowboy.

Alex booked two nights in a place called Bella Vue B&B. located up high on one of the many hills around the town with sweeping views of the town below.

Their first day would be spent wandering the town's many art galleries and shops of all sorts and ended by having dinner at a local steak house that served only locally raised beef.

The following day Alex took Sarah to one of the island's most iconic landmarks, Waipio Valley. Just 20 miles from Waimea, it is a vast deep valley cut into the eastern side of the island. Much like the one Alex took Sarah to, where she first kissed him, only this valley is much larger. The valley has many homes and farms in it. People there raise traditional Hawaiian crops such as sweet potatoes and taro.

Alex arranged for them to have a horse-drawn wagon tour of the valley. Sarah was amazed to learn that the far end of the valley was only

4 miles from Waimea up and over the tall cliffs that enclosed the valley. A multitude of waterfalls cascaded into the valley over those cliffs.

On the return trip from the valley, they passed through the town of Honaka'a. There he stopped at the Tex Drive-in restaurant, famous for their malasadas, yeast-raised Portuguese donuts. They come filled with a variety of local flavors, and Sarah decided to try one of each.

From there it was back to Waimea and they packed for day three.

The next morning, after breakfast at the B&B, they headed back toward Honaka'a and began the trip down the eastern side of the island. Unlike the Kona side. This side of the island is green and lush, mile after mile.

For the first stop, Alex had arranged for a tour and lunch at the Hawaiian Vanilla Company. There, Sarah learned all about growing and harvesting vanilla beans. She had no idea so much work was involved in producing one of her favorite flavors.

Leaving there and traveling further down the coast Sarah saw field after field of planted trees. Alex explained that those fields used to be filled with sugar cane. Cane production is gone so they decided to plant many of them into trees for future timber and biomass.

The thick vegetation was such a contrast to what the other side of the island was.

Alex told Sarah to have her camera ready as the road curved sharply and dove into a deep ravine. The first of three of them he told her they would be passing through on the way to their next overnight location in the city of Hilo.

Hilo is known as the working city of the Big Island. It is here the government seats are located along with many industries, and supply stores. Not a lot of the city is dedicated to tourists.

The airport there brings in people from the other islands as well as some flights direct from the west coast of the mainland US. Produce from the surrounding fruit, flower, and Macadamia nut farms are some of the things brought into Hilo from outlying areas for export through that same airport. Hilo also has a deep-water port that docks shipping container barges and cruise ships. The city has the taste of both Hawaii and the mainland US, mixed for a home-like feeling.

Circles in Stone

Alex had booked three nights at the Hilo Hawaiian Hotel. One of the few tourist hotels located on Hilo Bay at one end of a group of hotels along a street known as Banyan Drive. The street gets its name from the many banyan trees growing on both sides of the road. They were planted by well-known celebrities that once visited the area. Among them was Babe Ruth and Amelia Earhart.

Alex booked ocean-view rooms from which they could watch the sunrise over Hilo harbor. That evening they dined in the hotel restaurant at an all-you-can-eat seafood buffet. Sarah had never seen such large crab legs in her life or so many ways shrimp can be prepared.

After a good night's sleep, they set out on what Alex called "a waterfall day." The first stop was right in Hilo at Rainbow Falls, named for the many rainbows that can be seen when the sun is just right on the falling water as it plunges into the pool below it.

Next, it was a short return up the coast to Akaka Falls. This is the waterfall that Alex did the hula about at the luau in Kona. A short walk on a path through the most intense rainforest Sarah had seen so far. The trail ended at an overlook of the 420-foot waterfall. To Sarah, this was the most postcard tropical waterfall one could envision.

Alex had packed a picnic lunch which made it even more perfect. They sat and had lunch listening to the sound of the water cascading over the cliff to the pool at the bottom.

On the way back from Akaka Falls Alex took a road off the main highway onto what is known as the scenic route, stopping at Hawaii

Botanical Gardens. There, they took the walk through the lush garden filled with tropical trees of all kinds and endless varieties of orchids and other exotic flowers. A stream on one part of the walk cascaded over old lava boulders that made a wonderful sound in the palm forest that it flowed through. The end of the trail gave way to spectacular views of Onomea Bay. Once a loading bay for sugar onto ships bound for faraway ports.

The day ended back at the hotel when, after dinner, Alex took Sarah on a walk across a bridge to Coconut Island to watch the lights of Hilo glimmering on the waters of Hilo Bay. There they chatted and kissed and chatted and kissed some more as the moon rose over the sea like a spotlight.

They both knew they were falling deeply in love. However, each night they returned to their separate rooms. Alex did not want to be an unwanted force in her life unless he was invited. Sarah was ever cautious not to get too involved until she knew more about this amazing man.

The next day, Alex led the way into Hilo town center for a morning of shopping, first at the Hilo's farmers market where they bought fresh tropical fruits and veggies. After that, it was exploring the many shops the waterfront has to offer. They had lunch at an open-air restaurant called Pineapples, after which they went back to the hotel to change into the beach and swimwear. Alex had planned an afternoon of swim and snorkeling at a local beach park named Richardson Ocean Park. There, Sarah was once again swimming among turtles on a black sand beach. This was the first time she had ever seen black sand. She kept picking it up and running it through her fingers.

That evening after a shower and a change of clothes they dined at the Hilo café. Just a short walk from the hotel through Liliuokalani Park, a Japanese garden park named after the last queen of Hawaii. The Hilo café is a fine restaurant that offers food for any local and nonlocal taste, from steak to sushi. They drank wine and chatted while again watching the lights of Hilo reflecting off the water of the bay. Alex told her the next day they would go to the last place to stay before heading to his home in Volcano.

Alex was beginning to feel very nervous about taking her to his home. He knew it would be the time he would have to reveal all. How would she react he wondered? Would it be a bit too much? Would it frighten her away? It was getting very close to the decisive moment.

Sarah was a bit nervous too. There were strange things about Alex. She could tell he was hiding something. She trusted him but she had noticed strange things happening around him. For example, the afternoon they were shopping in Hilo it began to rain just as they were about to cross the street. Neither of them had an umbrella. Alex teased her that if she ran fast enough, she could dodge between the raindrops and not get wet. She laughed, of course, and headed across the street in the pouring down rain. When she reached the other side undercover, she realized she had not a single drop of rain on her. She was perfectly dry. When Alex got to where she was, he was soaked. Alex looked at her and said "see I told you, you could dodge them" and laughed. The fact that when he was in the sea swimming, the fish and turtles would come up to him. Other times birds often would land on him when he was eating something. He would give them a piece of whatever it was and they would fly off. Whenever this would happen, he would laugh it off. Everywhere they went on the island people knew him. They always called him Alika, never Alex. It was an island of course but it was not that small and a lot of people lived there. Sometimes at cafes, people would offer them free meals. He always excepted, saying it would be rude and disrespectful not to do so. Sarah was hoping that when they finally got to his home he would open up and tell her all. Her feelings were so strong for him that it took everything she had inside to hold them back. But she wanted to be sure before she let them go.

The next morning, after packing up, they were off to the Puna district. Alex told her that up until then they had been either on the flanks of Mauna Kea or Mauna Loa. The Puna district was the flank of the most active volcano in the world, Kilauca.

The landscape looked no different than any other on the Hilo side with many different varieties of palm trees and other flowering trees. Alex explained that under all that vegetation was very little soil but nutrient-rich lava rock. The same rock that was on Kona's side. The difference was rain. The average rainfall in most parts of the Hilo side was over 200 inches a year. He explained to her that if Kona got the same amount of rain, it would look the same as the Hilo side.

Circles in Stone

The first stop on this day's travel was at the Macadamia nut factory. Sarah learned that Hawaii grew large amounts of this precious nut. The first trees were brought there from Australia. Learning about these nuts made Sarah understand why they cost so much to buy in the store.

Most of their travels so far were along or just off highway 19. This is the main highway that circles the entire island. Not long after leaving the Nut factory, Alex turned onto Highway 130. This is the main highway into the Puna district. This highway ends after 21 miles at the place where the lava crossed the road in the 1990s.

As they drove along the landscape looked almost flat. Alex explained that a large proportion of the population of the island lives in this district. The land was the least expensive here so many people moved in and built homes. He told her that just off both sides of the highway were large subdivisions. One of them contains nearly 9000 lots. The one they were headed to was called Leilani Estates, one of the smaller ones where they would spend three nights. He told Sarah that a friend of his was off-island and offered his home to stay in if he wanted. From there he could show her the heart of Puna.

After about thirty minutes they arrived in a town called Pahoa. There they found a small cafe /bar and had lunch. After lunch, Alex gave her a tour of the town. It was small but quaint with its wooden boardwalks and small shops. It was not a tourist town by any means.

Leaving Pahoa, they arrived at the home in Leilani Estates only a few minutes away from the town.

They decide to chill out the rest of the day. Alex took the smaller of the two bedrooms in the house. Sarah laid down and soon was asleep. Alex just relaxed on the porch of the house thinking about how he would break the news to Sarah about himself when the time came. The truth was that, even though many people knew his family went back many generations on the island, the only ones that knew he and his family were wizards were the SGM members.

Alex prepared a simple dinner that was ready when Sarah awoke. The evening was spent with Sarah writing in her notebook and Alex watching local tv. For a moment Alex tried to imagine what being married to Sarah would be like.

Circles in Stone

The next day, Alex drove Sarah to the end of highway 130 where the lava crossed the road. He drove a short way up the new gravel road that had been made on top of the flow; she was amazed to see people building new homes on the barren lava only a few years after it had cooled. Alex explained that the land it covered belonged to these people and still does. It is now only a bit higher than it was before. They are connected to that land the same as anyone else.

They then drove along a coastal road known locally as the red road, because it was once paved using a red cinder that gave it a red color.

Along the way, they stopped at Mackenzie state park. The park is covered in ironwood trees. It had a strange feel to it, Sarah thought, as they sat and ate their home-packed lunch listening to the waves crashing against the lava cliffs the park is noted for.

The next stop along the road was at Pokoiki Harbor with its small boat ramp for local fishermen and tour boats. They spent the rest of the day just relaxing and talking to local people about fishing, and surfing.

Back at the house they changed and went out to Pahoa for pizza. Sarah was beginning to feel what it was like to live in Hawaii. Not all glamor and pictures. But people just carving a place for themselves in paradise.

The next day would be the last before heading to Volcano to Alex's home. He decided one last special thing was in order. He left Sarah at the house to rest and went into town to collect things for a BBQ. When he came back, he told Sarah to pack her beach items for a day in the water.

The surprise, that Alex was taking Sarah to, is the Ahalanui Hot Pond. This is a large tidal pool that is volcanically heated. A small opening allowed seawater to mix with the heated freshwater that flows up through many springs forming the perfect swimming pond. The grounds also have BBQ stands and concrete tables

The pool is surrounded by coconut trees that drape over it like a nature-made roof. It is not well known by tourists so it is not crowded. Sarah dipped her feet in and was so surprised. It was like the perfect bath water temperature. The water was so clear she could see tropical fish swimming in it. She was very pleased that Alex had saved this for the last day of their tour.

Circles in Stone

As much as both were nervous about the next day. They decide to just relax and enjoy the one they were in. They played in the water like children. Alex made BBQ chicken that went well with the salad he had bought. They spent the whole day there. By the end of the day, Sarah's hands were wrinkled from being in the water so much. For them both, it was a day of just pure fun. Neither of them wanted it to end. That evening back at the house they sat on the lanai and enjoyed the stars while talking about all they had been to and seen in the last seven days. Neither one mentioned the upcoming day.

Chapter 25

Volcano House

It had been a quiet week for the SGM, both in Kona and Volcano. So far, the only thing to report was the continuing deliveries to the ODR headquarters in Kona. The same morning that Sarah and Alex were to leave Leilani Estates for his Volcano home, Ted received a call from General Wigmore. Oliver Calvin had been spotted boarding a plane out of England headed for the US. This could only mean he would be arriving in Hawaii in about 24 hours. Ted was not alarmed by this news and told the General that he would make sure all the SGM men watching the airports were also alerted. After the call, Ted alerted Jack who in turn did as Ted had told Wigmore would be done.

***

The sun rose bright over Leilani Estates as Alex and Sarah packed up to head for the final link in the trip. With all the magic and knowledge Alex knew, he had never known a feeling like he now had. His father had taught him to fear nothing but he now felt fear. Fear of losing a person he loved to the knowledge of who he is. The fear of hurting someone he cared for more than he had ever done before. What made him most afraid was that he could do nothing, by magic or other means to get rid of the fear.

Sarah on the other hand was excited. She hoped this part of the trip would bring how she felt about Alex into focus. If Alex had a dark side, she was sure she would have seen glimpses of it by now. She was confident that it all would be ok.

It was nearly an hour-long drive from where they were to his house so they set out early after a quick breakfast of fruit and cereal.

After about twenty-five minutes into the drive, Sarah noticed things begin to change. This time it was not the landscape as much as it was the vegetation. The palm trees disappeared. Large ferns and wild ginger appeared along the roadside and the air began to feel cooler too.

Further along, the very large trees that were everywhere before were now gone completely. The large ferns were now looking like trees themselves with vines of some sort woven on them and everything else like a blanket. The air was getting even cooler than she had felt anywhere in Hawaii so far.

Further along still, as she knew they must be getting close, the trees changed yet again. This time many were a kind she had not seen anywhere else. The ferns had now truly become the size of small trees.

Alex began to slow and looked at Sarah.

"You ready?" he asked with a stiffened smile.

"Yes of course I am," she answered.

Alex slowed to a stop and turned left into a drive that was lined with tall trees on either side that resembled the Breckland pines in England. A short distance down the drive, they came to a gate. Beyond the gate looked like trees covered in vines. It appeared to be a dead end.

Alex reached under his seat and pulled out a remote control. He pressed a few buttons and the gate swung open. He then drove straight ahead into the vines and trees. Sarah ducked ready to hear the branches hit the jeep. There was no sound. She looked up and saw that they were on a well-paved drive leading to a large house. She looked behind and saw the gate close behind them. She stared at Alex but didn't know what to say or ask. She just turned forward and focused on the house they were now approaching.

There was a carport off to one side of the house into which Alex pulled the Jeep.

"Would you like a tour before we unpack? asked Alex."

"Yes, that would be nice," Sarah replied as they exited the Jeep.

As they walked toward the house, Alex stretched out his arms and looking at Sarah proclaimed, "Welcome to the Michaels Estate. My home and the home of many generations of my family."

Sarah smiled and, looking back at the house, decided to take in as many details as she could.

The house was a long light blue wood frame building covered by a dark green sheet metal roof. The house was set up off the ground on a very well-laid lava stone foundation. She could already tell by the sun that this home also was oriented to the compass points just as the Kona house had been. The longest section was single-story going east to west. The North-south wings were two stories with a high gable end facing the drive. A lanai wrapped the entire house on the first floor and another one went across the front of the second floor. A set of French entrance doors were on the first story at the top of the steps that were flanked by two stone dragons, just like the ones she had seen at his Kona house. The second floor had two separate doors leading onto the lanai on that floor.

Alex walked up the front steps and unlocked the doors. Swinging them both open he invited Sarah in.

As she reached the top of the steps, Sarah turned to look across the yard that now stretched below her.

Large trees of different varieties were scattered around the yard. These were surrounded by large tree ferns and on the ferns, were growing orchids filled with blossoms. They looked like the ferns were dripping flowers. Sarah could hear birds singing from the tree tops as if to welcome them.

When Sarah finally walked inside, she realized that the house was much bigger than it looked from the outside. Wood was everywhere. Some light, some dark. Tree trunks held up anything that needed support and were all polished to a mirror shine. The front room looked like a sitting room with several grand chairs. Doors led off on either side to somewhere not yet explored. Straight ahead the room opened all the way to the roof of the second story. In the center of this room inlaid into the wood floor was a rose compass, similar to the one she had seen in the Kona house, only bigger. A railed balcony went all the way around the second floor to the doors of the rooms up there. Stairs on one side of the room led up to the balcony.

Sarah stopped there to take in the décor. Alex said nothing. He let her look it over the same way he let her explore ruins.

On the wood-paneled walls hung an assortment of paintings. Many of Hawaii and some were of medieval castles and others looked to be of English landscapes. What Sarah knew to be old Spanish swords and helmets also hung in various well-placed positions on the walls. This room had the feel of a grand hall of a medieval castle.

On the many small tables along the walls were highly decorated vases waiting for flowers. Other tables had large crystals of every shape and color. In the center of the main wall, one large table held what looked like a large jeweled egg. It glowed as if it were a lamp but Sarah could not see a cord coming from it. A large brass and glass chandelier hung from the center beam that ran along the peak of the room.

Alex had now opened the second set of double doors that opened out onto a backyard. Sarah slowly walked toward the doors but stopped for a moment to look back, realizing that this center section of the house was the same length as the east-west sections. That the house seemed to form a perfect cross with all four wings being the same length.

Sarah stopped dead in her tracks when she stepped through the door leading to the backyard. There in front of her was a scaled-down version of a restored Stonehenge. It was made of cut stone, not concrete. The only difference from the real thing, besides the size, from the real thing, was that in the center were two stone benches facing a stone table. The benches were on the north and south side of the table.

Sarah walked toward it but would look back at Alex every so often as if seeking his permission. He would nod and she would continue. As she entered the circle, she could see the remarkable detail that went into its creation. The lintels, though smaller, were still well over her head.

Alex had now joined her in the center of the circle sitting on one of the benches. Sarah sat on the other one opposite him.

Sarah began to speak, "Are these....?" Alex interrupted her question with the answer.

"Yes, they are made of the same stone as the real one," he said. "That includes the blue stones. Long before me, there was one made of lava rock. After Cook's arrival, my ancestors had this one shipped stone by stone from the UK."

Sarah noticed it was the only feature in the entire backyard. It did look as if it were sitting on a scaled-down Salisbury plain.

Looking directly at Alex, Sarah asked the obvious.

"Why did they go to all this trouble?"

"Will tell you later," Alex replied with a grin.

Alex got up and headed back toward the house.

"Shall we continue? asked Alex as he went up the steps.

Sarah got up and followed him back into the house. This time Alex led her into the east wing. Through a large sliding pocket door, she entered a dining room that was open to the main living room. The dining table was round and made of Koa wood. It was nearly seven-foot in diameter from what Sarah could tell. Around were placed six finely carved koa chairs with high backs. In the living room centered along the end wall stood a fireplace made with round beach-washed lava rock. A koa mantel dressed it out perfectly. An extensive curved sofa was centered and faced the fireplace. Various oriental tables, stands, and cabinets were located around the room. One of the larger cabinets was an entertainment center containing a television. Paintings of Hawaiian scenes dressed the walls. In one corner of the room was a tall glass-fronted cabinet. Sarah walked over to it for a closer look. The only thing in it was what looked like a walking staff. It was decorated with all manner of symbols and writing that Sarah recognized as ancient runes. On the top of it was a large clear crystal. A leather hand grip wrapped around it about a foot from the top. What wood it was made of she did not know. It rested against a velvet-lined backrest. Sarah looked at Alex with an expression of wonder.

"What is this," she asked.

"Will tell you that later too," replied Alex.

Sarah looked at him with a bit of a perturbed expression. How much later she wondered?

She circled back around to the dining area and into the kitchen which had a breakfast counter facing the dining room. The kitchen was modern with a large window over the sink looking onto the front yard.

"Let's have lunch," Alex blurted out. I called my caretaker yesterday and had him fill the fridge for us. Alex opened a bottle of white wine that he pointed out was bottled right there in Volcano at a local vineyard.

For lunch, they feasted on the local fair that his caretaker had put in the fridge. There was shrimp salad, sushi rolls, Hawaiian poke, (uncooked yellowfin tuna, sweet onions, soy sauce, sliced scallions, sesame seed oil and topped with crushed macadamia nuts), and Lomi Lomi salmon, (Salted salmon, tomatoes, sweet onions, all chopped and marinated under a layer of ice).

After lunch, Alex decided to show Sarah the four bedrooms. The first he showed her was on the second floor. It was the master bedroom located on the north end of the house overlooking the rear yard and the stone circle. This bedroom was very large. It took up the entire width of the house, some 40 feet wide. In one corner was a full bathroom private to this bedroom. A king-size bed was located against the east wall. It was a four-poster bed of light-colored wood. The headboard had a tree of life carved into it. The four posts each had elemental symbols carved into them. Each post had a different symbol. One had fire, another water, another earth, and the last one, wind. The rest of the furniture matched the bed in the type of wood and was also carved with animals, trees, and other images. A set of double glass doors opened onto the lanai overlooking the rear yard. The large round rug in the center of the room had a Celtic knot woven into it.

Sarah loved the room and asked if it could be hers for however long she stayed. Alex said of course and that he would stay in his childhood room on the other end of that house across from that one. This was the next room he showed Sarah.

This bedroom was also on the second floor but face south. It was half the size of the master bedroom and had a shared bathroom with the bedroom next to it. The bed in this room was made of tree branches and trunks. The other furniture was also rustic. Looked to have been handmade. On the walls were paintings of fish, turtles, birds, and other wildlife. This being Alex's childhood room made sense with his intimate connection to wildlife wherever he went that Sarah had seen.

The next bedroom over was the same size as Alex's and faced the same direction. The decor of this room was completely different. The room was bright, and cheerful with a different pastel color on each wall. Blue, green, yellow, and rose. Pictures of fairies without wings were all over the walls. Some looked like photographs. Even the simple post bed had images of little people carved on them. Sarah knew whose room this was. It was Alex's late sister's room. She turned to Alex.

"You never told me her name," Sarah said in an inquisitive voice.

"Kathleen," Alex answered with a sad tone. "I do still miss her. She was like a forest bird. Always singing and flitting around as if from tree to tree."

"How old was she when she passed?"

"Fifteen, filled with life, she now rests with the ancestors."

Sarah could tell the room was kept just as it must have been when she passed. She decided not to press him anymore and left the room. They then headed back down to the first floor.

Circles in Stone

Sarah asked where the loo, (bathroom) was, she needed to use it. Alex led her to a pocket door in the center of the west wall of the central hall. Behind it was the bathroom. It was a full bathroom but without a tub. Only a large walk-in shower all tiled very ornately with blue and white tile.

When Sarah exited the bathroom Alex led her to another pocket door that opened into the first-floor bedroom. It was long but not too wide. A large bed with a koa headboard was located at the far end. The other furniture was mostly wicker. A set of glass double doors opened onto the wrap-around lanai. Alex explained this was the guest room.

Out of the bedroom and again into the main hall Alex led her to another door on the same wall. This was the last door that had not been explored yet. This time it was not a pocket door. This was an oak door with a carved image of the green man on it. Alex took hold of the door handle and took a deep breath. Sarah could see the anxiety on his face as he opened the door for her.

Sarah stepped into what looked to be a library. The room was the same size as the bedroom she just left but it felt smaller because one wall was filled with books from floor to ceiling. Only a window looking out to the rear yard broke the bookshelves into two sections. In front of the window was a large high back leather chair with a reading lamp next to it. The opposite wall was covered in charts, maps, and more Spanish swords and armor. In the corner of this wall was another high-back leather chair matching the one on the other side of the room. Just behind the chair on the short wall hung a ship's wheel. A table, that looked like a converted shipping trunk, stood along this long interior wall. On the top of the trunk was a collection of crystals and a black stone bowl surrounded by black candles. This bowl had water in it. When Sarah looked into the bowl, she could see her reflection as in a mirror. On the right side of the bowl was a book covered in leather and the face of the green man embossed into it. She was about to open the book when she heard Alex cough. She knew that sort of cough meant please don't. She decided not to but continued to look around the room. At the very end of the room, facing south, was a window. In front of the window was a large office desk made of oak with a large high-back leather swivel chair behind it. On the wall behind the desk on either side of the window were mounted all manner of items. Ram horns, turtle shells, large seashells, stuffed crows, a fan, made entirely of large feathers, and other small metal and brass objects that Sarah had never seen before. At one end of the desk was a world globe. On the other end was a celestial globe. In the center of the desk was a computer monitor and keyboard. On the one corner of the desk was a human skull engraved with symbols and runic writing.

In front of the deck was a cabinet with a glass cover. It was about sixteen inches from front to back and about thirty inches long. Below the glass case, it had two small doors. Sarah walked up to it to see what was under the glass cover. This time she was pretty sure of what she was looking at. Wands, magic wands of all shapes and styles. Some with runic writing on the other with pointed crystals on the small end and others with crystals on the handle end. All were made of wood but each one seemed to be made of different woods. Each one in its own mount within the case, the way one might store surgical tools.

Sarah looked at Alex but this time said nothing. This is when she began to look very carefully at the books on the wall. Some of the books she could tell were very old. Hundreds of years old. No titles showed on the binders on these. But others did. There were a great number of history books about England. Other history books were about the English monarchy. Another section particularly caught her eye. She saw book after book about magic. There were books about spell casting, palm reading, astrology, shape-shifting, divination, history of the dark arts, potion-making, and much more.

At last, Sarah had had enough. No more waiting, she wanted answers. She looked at Alex in a yearning yet puzzled way. He could see the wanting look in her eyes. He knew the time had come.

He pulled the chair from in front of the window and moved it next to the other chair in the corner. He sat in the chair in the corner and invited Sarah to sit in the one he just moved in front of it.

Sarah sat down. Alex stared into her eyes and was thinking as calmly as possible about where to begin.

Chapter 26

Light in the Dark

Sarah sat in the chair near Alex wanting to hear what he was going to say. A part of her was not sure if wanted to hear it. Almost everything about Alex is what she had hoped for in a man. Kind, understanding, intelligent, fun to be with, and of course good-looking. Perhaps, she thought, finding a man was like being on a dig. Everything thing you find points to what you understand it to be and then something changes it completely.

Alex sat quietly for a moment considering carefully how to begin. He finally decided that the direct truth would be the best. He would let the words come from his heart as well as his mind.

"First I would like to tell you that I love you," Alex began. "If that were not true, you would not be here. No one has ever been where you are right now. I have never let anyone this far into my heart or my house before. My caretaker has never even been in this room. The last people to have been in this room besides me were my parents. This is how special you are to me."

Sarah was about to answer but Alex stopped her before she could speak.

"Please," Alex continued. "Let me tell you my story. As you know I told you my ancestors arrived here on a Spanish shipwreck centuries ago. My history goes back further than that and I know most of it. It goes back to England before it was England. The books you see on the part of the wall closest to the desk. The real old ones contain the history of my family back to the middle of the fifth century. A time just after the Romans had left the British Isles to the time just before King Arthur. I know people wonder if Arthur was real or if it was all just stories. Much of what is written today is just stories. But Arthur was real. He was a king and he ruled a large part of what became England."

Sarah's eyes became fixed on his face. This is not true she thought. No evidence had ever been found to conclusively prove he ever was real. There were many possible candidates for a possible person that the stories were based on. She wanted to ask questions but she decided to let Alex continue.

"Without going into detail," Alex went on. "Before you ask, no I am not related to Arthur. Not directly anyway. But I am related to another person in the stories. That person is Merlin. I, Alexander Michaels am a direct-line descendent of the wizard Merlin. No story ever tells that he had children. That is because he wanted it that way. Every descendent from him has always made sure that knowledge was hidden from all but a few select people sworn to protect, not only the knowledge but their existence. As you already know, I'm sure, that a legend says, that when a time comes that England needs a savior, Arthur will return to save it. Those that believe this think it means he will awaken from a deep sleep where he is hidden away someplace. That part is not true. But his return is true. There is no direct bloodline of Arthur remaining. As I am also sure you know from the stories, Arthur came into being when Uther Pendragon was disguised by Merlin to look like the Duke of Cornwall so he could sleep with the duke's wife after the duke had been lured away to a battle in which he was killed. Part of that story is true. The true story is that the duke's wife and Uther had been having an affair for a while. Merlin found out about the affair and asked the Uther to break it off. He refused to because he said they were in love. Merlin had no interest in their love or politics. He wanted Britain to have a king. One that would rule better than other kings that had come before. So, he told Uther that if he continued with the affair, he would use magic to cause a child to come out of the union and that child would be his, (Merlin's), to raise as he saw fit. If not, Merlin said he would call the dragons from the far corners of the realm and destroy him and his kingdom. Merlin also told Uther that this child would be the first of a line of monarchs that would never be broken. Uther believing it meant his line, agreed and Arthur was born. The part about a line of unbroken monarchs was true. Merlin never said it would be Uther's line. Just monarchs."

Sarah listened intently. She could tell by the way he was telling this, that he must have learned it. His demeanor was sincere. To her, this story seems a bit far out, but she could tell he was telling it as if it were true in every detail. Again, she decided to let him continue without interrupting.

Alex continued, "We all know that Arthur came to the throne after pulling the sword from the stone. It was Merlin, of course, that put the sword there and made sure that no one could pull it out except Arthur. Many people think the sword was Excalibur. If you just read the stories that are out there you can see that it was not. The sword Excalibur came from the Lady of the lake at the request of Merlin. What is not known, is the lady of the lake got the sword from a magic-wielding smith that had been taught his trade by a dragon. The sword was constructed at the request of Merlin shortly after Arthur was born. The sword had magical powers but those powers extended beyond the sword. Another part of the story that is missing is that, in the pommel of the sword, Merlin had the smith place a powerful Jewel. It was this Jewel that gave the sword its power and it was the Jewel that gave Arthur his authority to rule as king. When Arthur was dying on the battlefield, he requested that his Knight, Sir Bedivere, take the sword and returned it to the lady of the lake. He also cried out for Merlin. Merlin arrived to comfort his king as he passed. He asked where the sword was. Arthur told him what he had done. Merlin immediately cast a spell preventing Sir Bedivere from completing his task. When he returned with the sword Merlin removed the Jewel from the pommel and then sent Bedivere back to the lake to complete the request. Merlin told Arthur that he and his descendants would hold the Jewel and keep a place for him until he was called upon again to rule over Britain. That promise and our line of wizards has kept a monarch on the throne ever since that day. Now I am the wizard in that line. The Merlin line is the only one that knows how to cause another Arthur to be born. The power of our line holds the monarchy in place to ensure that, when the new Arthur is born, he will have a place to rule from."

Alex stopped talking to gauge Sarah's reaction. He knew it was a lot to take in.

Sarah took the pause as permission for her to speak.

"If I follow you," Sarah asked with a puzzled expression. "You are telling me that you are a sort of modern Merlin and, if you die without an heir the British monarchy would come to an end?"

"Yes and no," Alex answered. "There is another sorcerer's line just as old as ours. This would be the line of Morgan Le Fay, Arthurs's half-sister. They have always claimed that the throne of Britain belongs to them. It has been the existence of our line that has prevented them from taking it. They wield magic just as powerful as we do. They don't want to destroy the monarchy; they want to be the monarch. They have never understood that magic is here to assist the throne, not sit on it."

"When you say wield magic, what does that mean? asked Sarah.

"Not the kind you see on the stage. This is real deep earth elemental magic. I cast spells, use divination, do weather pushing, shapeshift the elements, and most other things considered part of the magic world. I consult with the fae, or fairies as some call them, and honor the ancestors."

Sarah thought that if this was real it would explain some of the things she has seen or thought she had seen. But another part of her did not believe any of it. She was beginning to feel like she had been drawn into a scam. She was beginning to feel hurt. She rubbed her eyes and pulled back her hair as it all began to sink in. What a fool she had been, she thought. Trick sleight of hand just so this man could find someone to have an heir to fulfill his fantasy.

"You know, I thought I was in love with you too," Sarah said as tears began to come to her eyes. "So, you see this nice English woman that can hear your thoughts and decided oh, this would make a great mother for an heir. I'll show her Hawaii and she will fall for my fantasy and I won't let my family down by letting it die out."

Alex was about to speak but Sarah put her hand up to stop him as she began to cry.

"I don't know who concocted the story you just told but it is a whopper," Sarah said through her tears. You told it with such conviction. You and your family have been on this island too long. You know, I think you believe some of what you said. I don't mean to be offensive but your parents did a good job telling them if that is where they came from."

Alex could not speak. It was obvious that he had not done it right or he just plain failed. He wished his father or mother were there. For the first time in his life, he truly felt lost. Worst yet, he had hurt the person he cared for more than anyone he ever had before.

Sarah got up from the chair and, with tears streaming down her face she looked at Alex.

"I know it's a long way back to my hotel," she said. "In the morning I want you to take me back to the hotel first thing. No more sightseeing. I do thank you for showing me around. But I can't deal with this. You seem like a nice guy but you have some serious issues. I can't live in your fantasy world. Can you do that for me please?"

"Yes of course. I'll bring your bags in and put them in your room. I'll make some dinner for you, just tell me what you want."

"Thanks, but I'll just have some fruit thank you," Sarah answered. "I'll have it in my room if that's ok?"

"Yes of course," Alex replied in a sad tone.

Alex went to the Jeep and retrieved Sarah's bags and took them to the master bedroom where she was already waiting. He put them down and looked at Sarah without saying a word. He left the room and Sarah closed and locked the door behind him. Alex went to the kitchen to prepare a light dinner. He didn't feel much like eating but he at least made chicken soup and a grilled cheese sandwich for Sarah along with the fruit she requested. He placed the food on a small table outside the door of the room. Knocked on the door and let her know it was there and left for the library. He could hear Sarah open the door and take the tray of food and again close the door.

In the library, he sat in his chair behind his desk. He thought hard and long about all the things he could do if he wanted to. He could use the scrying bowl to see what she was doing. He could cloak himself and listen by the door. He could have put a potion in her food to cause her to think in a controlled manner. He knew he could do all these things but, wouldn't. It was everything his parents had taught him not to do to anyone except an enemy. Doing nothing, even with all his powers, would be the right thing to do.

There was one thing he could do and decided would do when it got later. Call on his old dear friend, Queen Hollyberry.

Queen Hollyberry is the queen of the fairies on that side of the island. She lives in the fern forest near the summit of Kilauea. The fae has been in Hawaii even before humans first arrived. Even the Hawaiians knew about them. They called them the Menehune. No matter what people call them they are fairies.

Before he called her and her court, he had to prepare a feast for them. Cream, butter, fruit, and honey were always favorites. He had a recipe for sweet cakes that included strawberry jam that he would get busy preparing. Making them would help get his mind off the pain in his heart.

Alex spent about an hour making the cakes. He would take a nap while waiting for it to get dark. He would need the rest. The queen liked long visits.

Sarah meanwhile, was busy with her notebook to keep her mind off what Alex had told her. It didn't help much. She would try to work and then just burst into tears. She had never felt this much in love with a person before. Her tears would be followed by streams of anger that she had fallen for and a person that, in her mind, was just a scammer looking for a mother to have a child with. One thing did bother her. The house she was now in, the Kona house. The Jeep he drove, all these things must have cost plenty of money. How did he keep all that going on the salary of the part-time geologist? If he had that kind of money, why would he need to scam a woman into giving him an heir? Why would he need to resort to outrageous stories to explain himself? None of that made any sense. But perhaps it didn't need to. She would calm down and go back to her notes only to again remember how much fun they had together and start crying again. She couldn't wait to just get back to the hotel and hear her father's voice.

Alex's nap lasted for about 3 hours. When he awoke, he went down to the kitchen and prepared the food. He put it all on a large tray to take out to the stone circle. This is where they always met. Before he left the house he went into his library and in the cabinet, under the wands, he took out a special bell. This bell let out a tone that only fairies could hear. Putting the bell on the tray he quietly went outside. He took no light with him. Fairies don't like bright lights because they are bio luminous beings, creating their own light. He put the tray on the stone table in the center of the circle. He looked up at the room where Sarah was. He could see that she must be in bed because there were no lights on. He could also see that she had left the door to the balcony slightly ajar for fresh air.

Alex carefully laid out the food and taking the bell he swung it back and forth. Even though it made no sound to him, he was sure it was loud and clear to fairies nearby.

Soon he could see a dim light of one coming out of the forest. Then another and another. Then he could see a bright light descending from the treetops. He knew this was the Queen. Alex sat on a bench waiting for her arrival. She slowly settled onto the round table next to one of the sweet cakes he had made. She sat down next to it and tasted it. She waved the scepter she was carrying and all the other fairies began to feast on the food Alex had prepared.

Fairies can speak and have their own language, but they communicate with humans with telepathy. The queen let Alex know she was very pleased with the cake and how good it was to see him again. She also could sense he was very sad. Alex through thought, began to tell her all that had happened and why he was so sad.

Sarah had been sound asleep for several hours when she was suddenly awakened by something touching her face. She rolled over not paying too much attention when she felt it again. She opened her eyes and thought she saw a light dash across the room. She thought it must be Alex checking on her. And decided to sit up and confront him. When she looked to where the light was it darted to the other side of the room and stopped on top of one of the dressers. This was no flashlight. She thought it must be a large firefly. She got up and put on her bathrobe and headed towards it. It then became very bright and darted to the door she had left open. It stopped in the opening and hovered there. She again headed toward it. This time it went out the door and came to rest on the railing on the balcony. Sarah decided to follow it. She slowly crept toward the door, expecting it to dart away when she got close. But it stayed there. She could now see a glow coming from the rear yard below her as she slowly opened the door. She stepped out on the balcony and looked toward the glow. It was bright now and she could see it clearly. She looked at the light still on the railing and her knees began to shake. She looked again at the glow coming from the stone circle below. She now felt her hands trembling. She was becoming weak on her legs, as if blood were rushing from her head. She grabbed the railing firmly to keep herself from falling over. She could see now that the light that had to waken her was a very tiny human-looking being. It flew up and landed on her shoulder. She started to back off but then stopped. She could hear its thoughts. It let her know it meant her no harm. This she now realized must be a fairy. Like the ones in the painting in Alex's sister's room, it had no wings but it moved through the air like a fish in water. Below her, at the stone circle, she could now see hundreds of them. Flying and lighting around Alex. She rubbed her eyes, even pinched herself to make sure she was not dreaming. She looked at the one on her shoulder and smiled. Tears were again in her eyes. This time they were tears of joy and wonder. She now knew, not only with her mind but with her heart that Alex had been telling the truth.

Sarah put on her evening robe and headed down and out the door to the stone circle as fast as she could. She stopped just shy of the round table where the fairy queen was sitting. Alex rose to his feet to meet her. He took her by the hand and led her to the table.

"Sarah," Alex said with his hand stretched out toward the queen. "This is Queen Hollyberry, Queen of the fae on this side of the island. Madam Queen this is Sarah, the lady I've been telling you about."

"An honor to meet you, your majesty," Sarah said as she curtsied.

Sarah heard a hum of laughter come from all the fairies. Many fairies were now flying and hovering all around her. So many that she looked aglow with the light from them. The Queen replied to Sarah through thought that it was a pleasure to meet her. The queen got up from sitting and flew over to Sarah's hand. Sarah slowly raised her hand with her palm up. The queen landed on her hand. Sarah could feel a warm sensation go up her arm. Once again, she felt weak in the knees. The queen looked into Sarah's eyes and told her in thoughts that Alex loved her. The reason she knew this was because he told her so and that no one can be untruthful to a fairy without them knowing. The queen then flew up to Sarah's face and touched her on the cheek. Sarah thought she was going to pass out, but held firm. The queen then went over to Alex and also touched him on the cheek. Alex bowed and told the Queen it was good to see her again and thanked her for coming. The Queen waved her scepter and, in a flash, all the fairies vanished into the forest leaving Alex and Sarah alone in the dark.

Alex took Sarah by the hand to lead her back to the house. Sarah stopped him and pulled him toward her.

"I am so sorry," Sarah said with a tremble in her voice.

"It's ok," Alex replied. It is perfectly understandable. "It is my fault really. I was expecting too much in such a short time. My feelings got the better of me."

Sarah put her fingers on his lips to stop him from talking. She then took his head in her hands and kissed him in a deep passionate kiss. Alex in turn pulled her close and after the kiss just held her.

They walked to the house, stopped in the great hall, and kissed again.

"Would you do something for me?" asked Sarah.

"Yes, of course. Anything, what would you like?"

"Would you spend the night with me just sleeping? I just want you close to me the rest of the night. In the morning I want to know everything else there is to know."

Alex smiled

"Yes, of course. I would be honored."

Alex got dressed for bed and met Sarah in her room. They laid down together and fell asleep holding each other.

Chapter 27

Tarian Tan

Ted rose early, as usual, the morning after Sarah had the encounter with the fairies. Little did he know that Sarah was only a couple of miles from where he was in Volcano.

His phone rang early. It was Jack in Kona informing him that Oliver Calvin had arrived and had his own place not far from the others. He had arrived alone unlike Jason had done. Jack asked Ted if he thought they should put cameras in his place like they did Goddard. Ted said he thought it would be a waste of resources. He told Jack that he knows Oliver well enough to know he would do nothing without Jason. The best thing the SGM could do at this point was to continue to watch them and monitor all they could about what ODR was putting together in their headquarters. Jack told Ted that so far it looked like a lot of computer hardware. He thought perhaps they were setting up a data collecting center.

***

When Sarah awoke, Alex had already slipped out of bed and was preparing American pancakes and sausage for breakfast. Sarah could smell them all the way to her room. She got out of bed and putting her robe on went to the door at the balcony and looked down at the stone circle. What had happened the night before seemed like a dream but she knew it was not. She touched her cheek remembering where the fairy queen had touched it. The sound of Alex knocking on the door interrupted her memories.

"Breakfast is ready," Alex called as he slowly opened the door carrying a tray loaded with their breakfast.

He placed it on a small table near the door. And pulled up a chair for himself. He set the table for the two of them and waited for Sarah to join him.

Sarah sat down as Alex uncovered the food and poured fresh orange juice and coffee. She watched him smiling all the while. Neither of them said anything as they ate.

When they had finished eating Alex looked at Sarah and broke the silence.

"You still want to go back to Kona today?" he asked.

Sarah looked at him with a scolding look.

"No," she replied. "I want to know everything else there is to know and if there are more secrets you have not shown me, I want to see them."

"Ok then, I do have something in mind. How about a visit to where my parents and my sister are resting? If you're up to it?"

"Yes, that would be wonderful. Is it far?

"About a half-mile through the forest. There is a trail. It is not well defined but I know the way of course. You will have to dress for hiking. I'll pack a backpack and some lunch."

"If it is that close, why do we need lunch?

"There is someone there I want you to meet. Could say they are the caretaker of their resting place along with all my other ancestors. It would be rude not to spend time with him. I am sure he is looking forward to meeting you in person."

"In person?" Sarah asked with a surprised look.

"Yes, I am sure Queen Hollyberry has already informed him. They are very good friends. The whole forest knows about you by now," Alex said laughing.

Sarah was not sure what that meant but this was all new to her. After what she experienced the night before she knew that everything she believed before was now in question. There was so much she wanted to ask but felt that there would be time for that later. For now, she would just follow Alex's lead and see what that uncovered.

Sarah helped Alex clean up after breakfast and pack the lunch. Along with the lunch, she saw Alex pack flashlights, BBQ lighter fluid, and water. The water she understood but the other two items were a puzzle. She decided not to ask and accept that he knew what he was doing.

Before they left the house Alex went to the cabinet in the living room and took out the walking staff with the crystal on top. He went to another closet and took out a plain walking stick and gave it to Sarah. Throwing the backpack over his shoulder and turned to Sarah.

"Okay, we're all set," he said. "Let's go for a hike."

They set off across his rear yard toward the forest. Ducking under some low-growing tree ferns they began following a very narrow path into the forest. Sarah could feel the ground going downhill. The path led over fallen trees, around large boulders, and over some large cracks in the ground. When she passed over some of the cracks Sarah could feel heat and steam coming up from them. These reminded her that she was on an active volcano. The trail continued like this for the better part of an hour. Sarah learned that hiking in a forest such as these, even for a half-mile took a lot of time. Finally, they came to the end of the trail. In front of them was a sheer rock face. Trees and ferns grew out of it everywhere. Alex took off his backpack and took out some water for them both. Looking at the rock wall, Sarah wondered where the burial place was and who were they supposed to meet, and where were they.

After a short rest on a fallen log, Alex stood up and before he put his backpack on, he took out the flashlights and the lighter fluid. With his staff in hand looked at Sarah.

"Are you ready?" asked Alex.

Before Sarah could answer Alex continued.

"I ask that you follow me," he said. "There is a well-defined path. I ask that you please stay on it until I tell you that you can do otherwise."

Sarah nodded her head but still wondered what path he was talking about. There was nothing ahead of them except a rock wall covered in vines and other vegetation.

Alex turned toward the wall, took his staff, and raised it in the air. He said some unrecognized words and hit the ground with the staff. What Sarah saw next made the hair on the back of her neck stand up. The vines and vegetation in front of them parted like a great drape curtain on a theater stage. Behind it was the opening to a cave so large that Sarah imagined that a freight truck could have entered without touching at any point.

Alex went over to his backpack and took out the flashlight and lighter fluid. He then motioned Sarah to follow him as they entered the cave. A short distance in Alex shined the flashlight on a tall wooden box leaning against the cave wall. He opened the box and took out four large wood-handled torches. Pouring the lighter fluid on one of them he set it alight with a lighter he pulled from his pocket. He handed the torch to Sarah. He then did the same to another one. Again, signaling for Sarah to follow he went forward. Sarah could now see the path in front of them. What puzzled her was why would you need fire torches when he had an electric one.

After about 200 feet into the cave, Sarah began to see man-made shapes in front of her. Soon she could see that they were old wooden trunks and barrels lined against the wall of the cave. Some distance beyond the barrels Sarah noticed that the cave room had widened to double the size. She could also see that this great room led off in two different directions. She realized she was at some sort of junction. Alex took one of the other torches and lit it and placed it on a hanger on the wall. He took the other one and did the same with the other one on the opposite wall. He took the one from Sarah and placed it in a holder standing in the center of this great room. The whole room was now full of light. She could now see why this was better than a flashlight.

Sarah had been in caves before on digs. This cave, its walls, floor, and ceiling looked nothing like anything she had ever seen. For one thing, the floor was relatively flat for a cave and the walls were very smooth and, in some places, glistened like metal.

Alex came and stood next to her and told her she was standing in an ancient lava tube. This cave was made by lava flowing out from a vent some distance from where they were. The lava crusted over and the lava continued to flow through it like water in a pipe. When the supply of the lava stopped, in the tube drained out leaving the tube she was standing in. The floor of the tube was the solidified top of the last bit of lava that drained out. To Sarah, it was not only amazing but beautiful. Alex then led Sarah a little further into one of the branch tubes. and stopped. He pointed forward. There, lined up along the wall as far as the light would allow her to see were silver caskets.

"These are my ancestors," Alex said. Many generations. resting in this quiet place.

"Those look like silver caskets," Sarah said.

"They are. Wood on the inside and covered with silver on the outside.

Circles in Stone

Alex knew that Sarah must have wondered where so much silver could have come from, especially on an island in the middle of the Pacific. Alex knew the answer would soon reveal itself.

Alex turned and led Sarah back to the center of the junction in the large room. There they sat down on a rock in the center and had the lunch they prepared. After they ate and packed up the remains, Alex got up and went a short distance up the other tube that formed the junction. He stopped and signaled for Sarah to go in front of him. From there Sarah could see a strange formation lying directly in front of her on the floor of the cave. It was a very large formation but somehow looked out of place. She reached out her hand to feel it. Alex grabbed her hand and pulled it back.

"I wouldn't do that," he said with an anxious voice. "At least not yet."

"It's ok," came a deep voice from the formation.

Sarah fell back against Alex. He held her up as she witnessed a transformation. The formation changed form and texture. The front of it raised up and two very large eyes appeared. Sarah quickly moved behind Alex. In front of them, Sarah was looking at a living breathing dragon.

"Sarah, I would like you to meet Tarian Tan," Alex said with a bit of a chuckle in his voice. "I call him Tan for short."

Sarah was frozen with fear. Its head was larger than her and Alex put together. Its eyes were the size of dinner plates and glowed in the darkness of the cave.

"Seems she is a bit shy," Tarian said in his deep voice. "Or it could be that she has never seen a live dragon before."

"I think it's the latter," replied Alex. "How are you, my old friend? I suppose Queen Hollyberry paid you a visit this morning?"

"Yes, she did," Tarian answered. "Fairies can't hold news for more than a few hours without telling someone."

"This lovely creature is Sarah?" Tarian asked as he lifted his head more and looked behind Alex at her. "You need not fear me lady Sarah. If I wanted to hurt you, I would have done so when you entered my home."

Sarah slowly began to calm down. She thought the fairies were something. This more than topped that, even though it was a bit more frightening. She finally got up the courage to speak as she moved a little more forward but stayed tight to Alex.

"Glad to meet you, sir," she said with a tremble in her voice. "Before today I didn't think dragons were real."

Tarian laughed in a low rumble.

"I find that funny since England's patron saint is a man killing one of us," Tarian said with a snarl. "We have been around longer than man has."

Tarian turned sharply to face Sarah directly.

"It was our kind that taught man to speak," he said in a firm yet low voice. "I think sometimes that was a big mistake. We also taught man the ways of magic. But most have forgotten that along with us. They believe we disappeared, or never were, as well as magic. In both cases it is wrong."

He moved into the light more and Sarah could now see more of his size. His movements were very graceful for such a large beast. He was almost fluid. Sarah was now becoming more relaxed as a thousand questions raced through her head.

"May I ask how you made yourself look like a rock formation?" she asked.

"That's not hard to do," Tarian answered. "Octopus does it by just changing his color to match where he is resting. We dragons just added shape-shifting to the mix. We are all around the world. But since man's creation of modern weapons, we evolved. Many times, we are right next to them and they don't take the time to notice. That is a good thing otherwise we would have been hunted to extinction."

"When did you come to Hawaii," Sarah asked next.

"I followed the ship that brought Michael Dee and his family. It is my sworn duty to protect the family line. No one hunted me here. The Hawaiian people respected me and let me live in peace. They call me a great mo'o."

Tarian slipped around where Sarah and Alex were standing and looked down towards where the silver caskets were as if to check on them.

"I knew them all," Tarian said in a sad moan. "And all the ones before them as far back as Merlin the Great. I was much younger then.

Serving him and watching over Arthur at such a young age was an honor."

He moved back around to where he had been when Sarah had first seen him. He barely moved a pebble on the floor of the cave in his motions.

"Just one more question sir if you don't mind," Sarah asked. "What do you eat that and how can you live so long?"

Tarian laughed loud this time as he swung his head to a point that his nose almost touched Sarah's face. She became frighted once again and could smell his breath.

"My Lady," he answered as he slowly pulled his head back. "You have asked me two questions. But I shall answer them both since you asked them in the same breath. When I first came here, I lived on mostly fish from the sea. I do like fish and back then there were a lot more than today. I would take my fill while hunting Spanish gallons taking stolen silver from the peoples of South America. I would take it from them and bring what I could carry here. You saw some of that in those trunks and barrels you passed on your way in, did you not?

Now I hunt pigs and goats and wild sheep, thanks to the people that brought them here shortly after your Captain Cook arrived. As far as living long. Sleeping is the trick. When dragons sleep, we can slow our heartbeat to a single beat a day. We do sleep a lot. Now it's my turn to ask questions."

Tarian settled down just in front of Sarah and Alex. This time he directed his attention to Alex.

"Queen Hollyberry tells me you love this fine lady," he said looking directly at Alex. "Do you think she will have you? If she would, I give my permission for her to have you. I can sense her heart. She is good and honest. If she does have you and you break her heart, you will have to contend with me. Honest hearts are hard to find these days."

"I have not asked her," replied Alex. "I wanted her to know all about me first. There may be danger coming my way."

"What sort of danger?" asked Tarian.

"It seems that some group calling themselves the Order of the Divine Right and the Morgans are on the hunt for me. I am not sure why now."

"The Morgans have always hunted your line," answered Tarian. "They have always been trouble and always will be."

Sarah looked at Tarian and back at Alex. Those were almost the exact words that her father had used to describe her mother's family. Must be a coincidence but it just struck a nerve.

"Don't understand the rights order looking for you," continued Tarian. "Do they know about the silver or do they think you will help them achieve some demented plan of some sort? If the Morgans arrive here I will handle them. Rest assured Lady Sarah, you are safe here with us."

"Thank you, sir," Sarah replied.

"I must get some rest," Tarian said as he laid down his head. "It has been good to see you again my friend and to meet you, Lady Sarah."

"It has been an honor," Sarah answered.

"Rest well my friend," Alex said as Tarian once again took on the shape of a rock formation in the lava tube.

Alex handed Sarah a torch and he took the other three. He extinguished two of them out and led the way back out of the cave the way they had come in. As they passed by the trunks and the barrels, Sarah stopped to look at them.

"Are they really filled with silver?" she asked.

"Yes," answered Alex. "There is a lot more behind Tarian deeper in the cave. Now you know how my family was able to afford the houses. There is enough in there to last for many generations to come. I only take what I need. To flaunt wealth is to make yourself a target."

They continued out of the cave. Alex put out the last two torches and put them in the storage case. Once outside the opening, Alex took up his staff and again spoke some words while hitting the staff on the ground, the vegetation once again covered the entrance.

Sarah turned to Alex.

"How does Tarian get out when he wants to eat?" she asked.

"Lava tubes most often have more than one entrance. Sometimes there are several ways into them. This is my entrance because it is the closest to my home. I am not even sure where the other ones are."

Sarah smiled the entire way back through the forest to the house. In just under a day her new experiences had opened her mind in ways she could have never imagined. She was now glad that fate had seen fit for her to meet Alex.

That evening they fixed a dinner of grilled fish and salads. They sat out at the stone circle and ate dinner. Alex continued to fill her in on his family history and tell her about what it meant to be a wizard. Their conversation went on well into the night. That night they slept in separate rooms. Each dreaming of what the days ahead might bring. Sarah was now thinking of telling her father about Alex and how she would explain to him what she knew about him.

Alex hoped that somehow, Sarah loved him as much as he did her. At this point loving a woman as much as he did her was more than he could have hoped for, only a few weeks before.

Chapter 28

On The Move

The morning after the day Sarah met the dragon, a few miles away her father received a phone call from General Wigmore. It was evening in England but was first dawn in Hawaii.

"Good evening, General," Ted said as he answered his phone during his first coffee.

"Good morning to you Colonel," Wigmore responded. "I am calling you because there have been some major developments. As you know we have been keeping a close watch on the Morgans, especially after we learned that John Coke met with him. We have known all along that the ODR had used Scotland Yard to keep them on the terrorist watch group. This has been a good thing because it has kept them from traveling outside the country."

"Yes," Ted replied. "It has given us time to prepare our bases here in Hawaii."

"I am afraid you are going to have to speed them up." Wigmore continued. "We have just found the Morgans are on the move and have now left the country. We got the news in time to find out they are in Amsterdam. I called our people there and they found out that only three of them are traveling. Master Rhyfel of course. Traveling with him are Lord Ambrose and his wife Lady Selma."

Ted's blood ran cold when he heard the news. Rhyfel was bad enough but of all the other lords and ladies, Ambrose and Selma gave him concern. He, as well as all the of the SGM knew that Ambrose was Rhyfel's right-hand man.

"When are they due to arrive here?" Ted asked with concern.

"We are not sure. It could be anytime," answered Wigmore. "Our Amsterdam people informed us they have observed them searching for a flight out of there as soon as possible. The units there are keeping surveillance on them and will let us know of any moves they make."

"How did this happen?" asked Ted. "Did the ODR arrange this?"

"It appears from their communications; this took them completely by surprise. Using our contacts in MI5 we determined there was a glitch in the computer system that took them and some others, off the terrorist watch list. The Morgans somehow knew the minute it was clear for them to travel."

"John Coke," blurted Ted.

"Yes," said Wigmore. "I suspected the same as soon as I found out. I went to Coke's house and interviewed him about his meeting with Master Rhyfel. After some convincing that he would be safe, he told me that Rhyfel threatened his family. Not sure if that is the whole story but it is not important now. He did tell me his doctor said he is unable to travel for at least a month. We just found out this morning that ODR member Pete Walker is already on his way to Hawaii. You can be expecting him anytime. I can tell you that from the ODR phone traffic, they are in panic mode."

"That would be expected since they thought they had the Morgans under control. I have an idea sir if you care to hear it?"

"Of course," Wigmore replied with anticipation.

"When the Morgans arrive here, the ODR will be their first targets. I don't believe they are prepared for them. I suggest that we make contact with the ODR here and offer to help at least protect them. We don't want a bunch of Scotland Yard staff to die on American soil. The questions it would raise would not be good for them or us."

Wigmore didn't answer right away. Ted could hear talking going on in the background. After about a minute of waiting Wigmore answered.

"We concur with your assessment of the situation. Only you and Jack are to make contact. Use your best judgment on how to approach them. You must offer protection only, nothing more. Do not let any of our other units over there know what you are doing."

"Understood sir," Ted replied. "I will leave for Kona as soon as I have eaten breakfast. I suggest sir, that you call Jack. It is best if this comes directly from you so there is no misunderstanding."

"You are right Colonel. I will call him next. I will contact one of you if we find out anything new about the movements of the Morgans. Meanwhile, Good luck."

"Thank you, sir," Ted replied and ended the call.

As soon as Ted finished breakfast, he explained to the members in the Volcano headquarters that he was needed in Kona and left.

It took Ted just over two hours to reach the SGM headquarters in the King Kam hotel in Kailua Kona. He went straight into Jack's office. Jack offered him a drink and they sat down to discuss how to deal with the latest crisis.

"Well Jack," Ted said, "how do you think we should handle this? I know three of the guys were going to be dealing with. Oliver Calvin is not too bad. His main weakness is that he does whatever Jason Elliott tells him. Pete Walker is as straight as an arrow which makes him predictable. I don't know much about Goddard. I suspect he is a numbers and details man. It's Jason that is the wild card. Rules don't mean much to him. He is all about ego and power. This makes him the most dangerous."

"I have been thinking about it a lot since the General called," Jack responded. "I don't believe Walker will be there. There has been no report of his arrival yet. I think we need to try and take a passive approach. We should each take a vehicle. We should wear aloha shirts to give the impression of a peaceful motive. I should go and approach first. None of them know me. I know they knew you as Lewis Hall and hopefully, they don't see his features in you as you are. The fact that you are out of context will help."

"I agree. You should do most of the talking as my voice might be recognized. I will try to disguise if I need to speak. I also think we should be armed. Guns under our shirts and an extra clip in our pocket perhaps? I pray we won't need them."

"Let's make it happen then," Jack responded as he stood up.

Jack went into the closet in his office and pulled out two loose-fitting aloha shirts. The two men put them on and put their G-17 pistols in holsters under their shirts. They each took a jeep and headed for the ODR headquarters.

The drive only took 20 minutes to the gate in front of the building. They pulled into a drive on the opposite side of the road and parked their Jeeps there. Taking their guns out of their holsters they tucked them in the back of their trousers. They walk slowly across the road and through the open gate, which to their surprise was not guarded. Ted was sure cameras were watching them. They walked past the now abandoned tennis courts and onto the main drive. Ted stopped and let Jack continue. As Jack approached two men came out to meet him.

"May I help you?" one of the men called out to Jack.

"I would like to see the person in charge," Jack replied. "I believe his name is Mr. Elliott."

One of the men pulled his cell phone and spoke into it.

"He wants to know what this is about?" was the man's reply.

"I can only speak directly to him in person I'm afraid," Jack answered. "Tell him it is in regards to the safety of him and everyone else here."

The man spoke again on his phone. After a brief pause, he signaled for him to come inside. He then looked at Ted and signaled him too to come in as well.

They walked into what used to be the main lobby of the hotel. There were some office dividers up and lots of cables laying on the floor. The large hotel lobby counter was still in place. Next to the counter through a door that used to be the office, Jason appeared. Behind him was Oliver. There was a table with some chairs around it just beyond the counter in front of some large glass windows. Jason and Oliver walked toward the table with two men that must be Jason's bodyguards and signaled Ted and Jack to have a seat.

"What is this safety issue you wish to discuss," Jason asked as he and the other sat down.

Jack looked at Ted then back at Jason.

"Before I tell you, I want you to know we're here to help." Jack began. "We have information that could put you and your men in extreme danger."

"What kind of information?" asked Oliver.

Jack hesitated but then decided to just come out with it. Ted sensed what he was about to say and slowly move his hand close to his gun just in case.

"My name is Colonel Jack Fairway, I, and my partner Ted here, are from the SGM."

Oliver began to stand up along with the bodyguards but Jason signaled them to sit back down.

"The SGM you say?" Jason said smiling. "And what is your rank, Ted?"

"I am also a Colonel," replied Ted in a half-disguised foreign accent.

"My goodness," Jason answered. "Two colonels? This must be important. I must admit I underestimated your group. To be able to find us here and know my name. You have done your homework."

"That's not all we know," Ted interrupted still trying to disguise his voice.

"Please tell," Jason asked.

"We know that your organization has been trying to control the movements of the Morgans," Jack began. "By now you must know that they are out of England. Our information tells us they are in Amsterdam waiting for a flight out directly here to this island. The same source tells us that, somehow, they know you're here and are planning on making you their first target when they arrive. As a group, we are very aware of what they are capable of. We have come to offer our assistance in protecting you. That is all."

By now Oliver's eyes were larger than usual. Jason glanced over at him and shook his head to reassure him.

"We want you to know," Ted broke in. "We have no plans to interfere with whatever it is you're doing here. Our only mission is to offer protection. All we need is your permission and we can work out the details together to your liking."

Jason stared at Ted intensely as he spoke.

"Do I know you from someplace?" Jason asked Ted.

Ted was about to reply when the office door opened and another man stepped out and came toward them. Jack knew it was Goddard. Goddard went directly to Jason and whispered something in his ear. Jason responded by getting up and following Goddard. They went into the room that they had come out of and closed the door behind them.

In the office, Goddard directed Jason's attention to a computer screen. Jason stared at it intensely.

"Are you sure this is right?" Jason asked Goddard. "There is no way this can be a glitch or something?"

"No way," answered Goddard. "The computer can't lie."

What Jason was looking at was the new voice recognition software. It was showing a comparison of the voices of Jack and Ted to known voices in their database. Jack's voice had no matches. But Ted's voice was a perfect match to that of Lewis Hall. Jason's blood began to boil. It all made sense now. Lewis Hall was a spy. That spy was sitting right out there in their lobby.

Jason immediately went out and with a forced smile asked Oliver and the two bodyguards to join him in the office.

"Excuse me, gentlemen," Jason said to Ted and Jack. "We have a crisis we have to deal with at the moment."

Ted's instincts told him this was not good. He looked at Jack who also sensed something was not right. They both got up from their chairs and walked calmly toward a large pillar in the center of the lobby. Just as they reached the pillar the office door burst open.

Jack and Ted turned to see Oliver and the two bodyguards come out with Jason close behind. They all had guns drawn and pointed at Jack and Ted except Jason.

"You're not going anywhere!" shouted Jason.

Ted and Jason now had their guns drawn and pointing back at them.

"There is no need for this," Ted shouted back at them. "We came here to offer help. If you don't want it, fine, we will walk out of here and nothing more will be said."

"Just let us leave in peace," Jack followed, "We meant no disrespect. We will leave and leave you be. No one needs to get hurt."

"I don't give a shit about your help or respect," Jason said in response. "As far as you go Colonel Fairway, you can leave. Your friend Ted or Lewis or whatever you call him, he stays. He is a traitor and a murderer. He goes back to England and stands trial."

"You know damn well I did not kill anyone," Ted responded. "It was your greed for power that got that man killed by the hands of the Morgans."

Ted stepped out slightly from behind the pillar in hopes to reason with Jason. Suddenly one of the bodyguards fired his gun at Ted. Ted ducked back behind the pillar knowing the shot had missed him as he heard the bullet hit the pillar above his head. Ted and Jack both took the safeties off on their guns and loaded the chamber. Jack took a pocket knife from his pocket and tossed it just to the side of the pillar. A shot hit the floor coming from the other bodyguard's gun. Jack popped out quickly and fired back at him hitting the man in the leg. He let out a cry and hit the floor.

"You need to stop this shit now," shouted Ted. "You're going too far Jason. This is not your domain."

"Shut the hell up, you traitor!" Jason shouted as he grabbed the gun the bodyguard had dropped and fired back at the pillar to cover his movement.

Ted looked around the pillar to see how bad the man was that Jack shot. As he did a shot ran out from Oliver's gun with a bullet grazing the pillar next to his head. Ted rolled back out in a snap and fired back hitting Oliver in the hand and knocking the gun out of it. In the next instant, the other bodyguard fired at Ted again missing him by a hair, and the bullet went through a window on the far side of the room shattering it. Jack in turn fired at the bodyguard grazing his right shoulder and causing him to toss his gun out on the floor.

Jack looked at Ted and Ted at him and they both nodded. In one swift move, they both came out from behind the pillar pointing their guns at Jason.

"Time to give it up," Jack said to Jason with both his and Ted's guns pointing at him.

Jason dropped the gun he was holding. Ted went over and kicked the gun away from his reach. Jack slowly opened the door to the office and found Goddard trying to delete files from the computer.

"I would stop right there if I were you," Jack said to Goddard.

Goddard put both his hands in the air as Jack motioned for him to go out of the room.

Ted had taken a cell phone out of Jason's pocket after a search to make sure he didn't have a weapon hidden on him. He threw it back to Jason and ordered him to call 911 for an ambulance.

With Ted still holding his weapon over all of them, Jack checked the wounds of the others. Oliver had already wrapped his hand with the shirt he had removed. The one man that Jack grazed in the shoulder was leaning against the wall and didn't seem in any danger. Jack retrieved his pocket knife he had thrown as a diversion and cut the other man's trousers open to see a very bad wound. He completed cutting the leg of the trousers off the man and made a tourniquet to stop the bleeding. Ted then asked Goddard to remove his shirt. Jack made a makeshift pad, placed it directly on the man's wound, and told Goddard to hold pressure on it until the ambulance got there. Ted then searched each of them to make sure they had no other weapons. Once he was confident there were none, he put his gun away took out his phone, and called the police.

All this time Jason sat in a chair and said nothing. He now realized that the mission he was sent to Hawaii for was no longer possible. His bodyguards and his friend Oliver lay on the floor wounded because of his pride. Whatever he thought of Ted as a traitor was nothing compared to this. He also remembered he was in the US and a long way from home with no one to help him out of this. His only hope was that because he was employed in Scotland Yard might have some influence.

Soon the sound of sirens could be heard as the police cars entered the grounds. Several police entered the building with their guns out but not pointed at anyone. Both Ted and Jack were now attending to the other two wounded. Jack knew all the officers that had entered.

"That one over there is the worse," Jack told one of the officers as he pointed to the man with the leg wound.

The rescue team soon arrived and attended to each of the wounded. A second ambulance arrived and all three wounded were on their way to a hospital. Meanwhile, Ted and Jack gave reports to the police about what had gone down. Jason was arrested on a firearms charge. Goddard was let go based on the statements of Jack and Ted and with the condition, that he does not leave the country until he came in and filed an official statement. The police confiscated all firearms including Jacks and Teds to do ballistics on them to make sure everyone's story matched. Ted and Jack were let free to go on the same conditions they gave to Goddard.

Soon an FBI agent showed up when he heard Jack was involved. They spoke to the local police and got them to give permission for the SGM to remove the computers from the building. Ted and Jack both knew they would contain a lot of important information about what the ODR had been planning and who was involved. By the time everyone was taken away and all statements had been taken it was dark. Ted and

Jack returned to the SGM headquarters. They would each have to write a detailed report before calling General Wigmore and inform him of what happened before they could consider taking a much-deserved rest.

Chapter 29

Most Powerful Magic

The morning after their visit to Tarian the dragon, Alex suggested they go into the National Park and visit where he worked. Sarah asked if they should pack a lunch. Alex said no, that they would have lunch at the world-famous Volcano House, the hotel that is perched on the edge of the volcano caldera.

The entrance to the park is only a mile and a half from Alex's house. Alex has a sticker on his Jeep window that allows him to drive straight into the park past the entrance station. Once through the entrance, it is a short distance to the main office and visitors center.

Alex stopped there and gave Sarah a personal tour of the displays inside, from which she learned how the islands were formed, about the flora and fauna and how they got to the islands before man arrived. The wonderful displays made it all easy to understand. She even watched a movie about an eruption that occurred in 1959.

Alex took her on a VIP tour behind the scenes into the offices from where many of the rangers worked. Everyone there knew him and Alex, as always, introduced Sarah to everyone as his personal friend. Sarah found it nice that he made no assumptions about what their relationship was or might be.

After leaving the visitors center Alex took Sarah on a walk to the sulfur banks that was only a short distance from there. The sulfur banks are where sulfur-laden steam rises from the volcano and leaves deposits of sulfur on the rocks as it disperses into the air.

After leaving there and going back to the jeep and taking the road called Crater Rim Drive, they next stopped at the steam vents. In that place, plain steam from rainfall seeping into the rocks rises through cracks in the ground making the whole area appear to be on fire. Getting close to one of the vents, Sarah was amazed at how hot the steam was. In the same area, Alex led Sarah to the edge of the deep caldera at an area known as steaming bluffs. The view was something unexpected to Sarah.

This massive caldera with its high vertical cliffs was the very summit of the volcano.

Leaving there they drove further along still until they came to the location where Alex worked. This was the office of Hawaii Volcano's Observatory. Here scientists, such as Alex, monitor the volcano. They also conduct experiments and take samples of lava and gases. It is all to try to understand the workings of the volcano. The goal is to be able to better predict eruptions, not only here, but from volcanos around the world. This, they hoped, would help to save lives.

Alex's office was small but well-ordered like his house. There were shelves on the wall that contained rock samples of all sorts. There were also a get number of notebooks and regular books about volcanos.

Alex introduced Sarah to everyone and showed her some of the things other scientists were working on. It was all very fascinating to her.

He then took her outside to the main overlook in front of the Jagger Museum which is attached to the USGS and is named after the founder of the observatory, Thomas Jagger, whom some call the father of volcanology. This is one of the main viewing areas here park visitors come to gaze into the heart of the volcano. From there one can view the nine square mile caldera and the active crater within its center. This 4000-foot-plus-wide crater within the caldera is the very heart of the volcano. Within the crater is an 800-foot diameter hole that contains a lake of boiling lava. The name of this crater is Halema'uma'u which means House of ferns, or House of fire, depending on how you say it. Alex told Sarah the crater was the home of Pele, the Hawaiian goddess of fire. He explained that flowing lava is considered to be her body in motion. He spoke of her as if he knew her personally. After meeting the fairies and the dragon, Sarah had no doubt she may well be real.

Even though it was more than a mile away, she could see the lava splashing within the crater from where they were. For the first time, Sarah had the feeling the earth was more than just rocks. It felt more like something living.

Directly across the caldera from where they were and situated very close to the edge of the cliffs, Sarah saw a building. She asked Alex what it was. He told her it is the Volcano House hotel, where they were going to have lunch.

Circles in Stone

After a view of the many displays inside the Jagger Museum, Sarah was ready for the lunch Alex promised her. They drove back along Crater Rim Drive until they arrived at the hotel.

Inside the lobby, Sarah was immediately drawn to the wood-burning fireplace with its warm glowing fire. Sitting in one of the koa rocking chairs in front of the fireplace and smiling at Alex, she requested he should bring her slippers and some tea. He laughed and sat in the other rocking chair and asked who was going to bring his. Sitting there for a while they enjoyed the fire and each other's company until Sarah finally decided she wanted to eat.

The restaurant is next to the lobby where the fireplace was. Sitting next to one of the large windows that overlook the caldera, they enjoyed sandwiches and coffee as they watched the cloud of gas and ash rise out of the volcano's crater. Alex told Sarah he had hiked across that caldera many times to collect samples and other reasons. Sarah wanted to know what those reasons were.

"I often take offering to the Goddess at the crater," Alex said. "Sometimes it would go late at night to listen to the earth's heart beating. I know that caldera as well as I know my own backyard. Sometimes Tan would see me there on his return from hunting and sit next to me and tell me stories of times long ago. After my parents died I did it a lot. It helped me connect to my ancestors."

Sarah did not answer. She could see the deepness in his eyes that led straight to his heart.

After lunch, Alex took Sarah on the Chain of Craters Road, the same road that Major Parker had taken her father on not long ago. At the end of the road, they parked and walked out across old lava flows to watch the waves crash against the cliffs. Sarah felt overwhelmed by the landscapes. At times it didn't seem real. It all made her realize more deeply that the world was not as simple as it once seemed to her.

She would often find herself looking at Alex and her heart would jump with the love she now was letting flow freely within her. This man had not only changed the way she saw the world around her, but he had changed the way she felt about herself.

As the sun began to set, they drove the long road back to Alex's home. On the way back they stopped in the village of Volcano and Alex got a pizza to take back for them to eat at home.

Back at the house, Sarah put the pizza in the oven to keep it warm while Alex built a fire in the fireplace. When the fire was roaring well, he got a bottle of red wine from his collection He found two wine goblets and filled them as Sarah took the pizza from the oven and placed it, along with two plates, on the coffee table located between the fireplace and the sofa. Alex brought the glasses of wine and the bottle. They both sat down on the sofa and relaxed after the long day of touring.

"I want you to know something," Alex said looking at Sarah. "I have never invited a woman into this house before. The last woman to sit on this sofa with me was my mother."

Sarah smiled and served up slices of the pizza. Before they ate any they each took their glass of wine.

"What shall we toast to?" asked Sarah.

"To the most powerful magic in the world," Alex replied quickly.

"What would that be?" asked Sarah surprised.

"Love!"

"To 'love' then," Sarah replied raising her glass toward Alex.

Their glasses touched and lingered against each other for a moment before they each took a drink of wine.

As they were eating Sarah tossed her hair back over her shoulder to get a clear view of Alex's face.

"If love is magic," Sarah asked. "Have you used magic on me? I mean to get me to like you or love you?"

Alex looked at her surprised.

"No, of course not," answered Alex. "To use magic in such a way is not only unethical it creates a false love that fades as the spell wears off. The person is nothing more than a puppet. Everything about that type of love would be hollow. I was taught to never use magic for personal gain that deprives the other person of the will to choose what is right for them. That is where the line is between magic and sorcery. It is why I never showed you any magic when you didn't believe me about who I am. You had to make your own choice to believe or not, or at least, let the universe give you that choice. You being awakened by the fairy that night was the universe revealing it to you. It was not me. After saying all that, I must say also that we all cast spells no matter if you're a wizard or not."

"How is that possible?" Sarah asked with a puzzled tone.

"Spells are words arranged in such a way to change events or conditions that influence the way a person acts or thinks. For example, if you see a person on the street in the morning and tell them that they look terrible. They will think they do whether they do or not. The way they think about themselves is altered for the rest of the day. Now if you meet the same person and tell them how wonderful they look this will also alter the way they see and think about themselves. But each time you met them they looked the same. It was only your words directed at them that changed. This is a simple example but it shows how much power we have with our words."

Sarah had never thought of the idea of our words having that kind of power or considered them as spells.

She knew in her heart that Alex was telling the truth about never using magic on her. The look in his eyes told her that he was telling the truth. She thought back about their time together and she never felt as if she was being led into something she did not want. She also knew that those times that she could not understand what happened must have been him using magic but trying to keep it concealed. She felt it must be hard for him to keep what he is hidden from the world. She didn't know if she could have done it if she had that kind of power.

Alex was feeling lost again. The feelings he had for Sarah were so strong, yet he felt weakened by them. He wanted so to reach out and hold her close but feared it would make her afraid. He never realized that love could create so much fear. But he had to make clear one thing to her.

"I want to clear something up," Alex said. When I mentioned about an heir before. It is not now, or ever was, and shall never be, the goal of loving you. When I said I loved you I meant it from my heart with no goal in mind. My father told me that he married my mother not caring if there had children or not. He married her because he loved her. He told me, when the time came, to do the same. He said that the universe would take care of the rest. I have never been in love before so please forgive me if I made mistakes."

Sarah smiled; she already knew that was true. She was glad that he told her just the same. It revealed more of his heart to her.

When she finished eating, she took her glass of wine and moved close to him. Leaning her head on his chest, she sipped her wine and watched the fire. Alex put his glass down and slipped his arm around her and kissed her on the top of her head.

He suddenly realized his fear had vanished. How strange it seemed to him. He suddenly felt safe somehow. He always thought it was the man that was supposed to make the woman feel safe. He never knew, until that moment, that the love of a woman could make a man feel safe.

After sitting together watching the fire, they heard the rain pounding on the metal roof of the house. The sound was somehow very comforting.

Sarah reached her hand around to the back of Alex's head and pulled him to her. She kissed him slowly and deeply. At the same time, she took off the band that held his hair in a ponytail and pulled his hair around until it draped over his shoulder. For the first time, she realized his hair was the same length as hers. She ran her fingers through his hair as they continued to kiss.

Sarah pulling back, smiled at him.

"I am going to get ready for bed," she said as she got up. "Better put more wood on that fire. I think it will be a chilly night if the fire goes out."

Sarah went up the stairs to her room while Alex put more wood on the fire and secured it for the night. He went about turning off all the lights and locking the doors before he also headed up the stairs to go to bed. He stopped by the door of Sarah's room.

"I wish you a good night," he shouted outside her door.

The door opened and Sarah took him by the shirt and pulled him into the room closing the door behind him with her foot. She put her arms around him and slowly backed into the room. Alex responded to her every move.

Alex opened his eyes slightly to see that the only light in the room was from the candles that Sarah had lit on the bedside tables. Seeing the bed covers rolled to the foot of the bed Alex didn't need any magic to know what Sarah wanted from him. He has wanted the same from her for a while now, but held back. He decided it was time to let go.

Alex was going to say something but every time he tried to pull his lips away from hers, she pulled them back. He gave in and let go of his last bit of resistance. He lowered his hands from her shoulders to her waist and pulled her closer. They were now truly dancing to the rhythm of the rain on the roof locked in a kiss that neither had any desire to break.

He slowly began to run his hands up and down her back, each time going lower down on her body and then higher up.

Sarah slipped one hand down from his shoulder and began to unbutton his shirt. All the time still kissing, keeping his head close to hers with the other hand.

As they slowly moved closer toward the bed Alex slipped one hand up under her shirt and with one flick, unhooked her bra. He slowly pulled it loose from her breast and pushed his hand slowly up under it until he could feel their softness along with the firmness at the end of each one.

Sarah responded with a raise in her body moving closer to his. She now had his shirt unbuttoned and was caressing his hair-covered chest.

She broke their kiss and pushed off his shirt letting it drop to the floor. As she did that he pulled Sarah's arms out of her shirt one at a time and pulled it over her head letting it, along with her bra fall on the floor.

Alex then pulled Sarah close and began kissing her neck, first on one side then the other as they continued the slow dance closer to the bed. He slowly worked his way around the front of her neck as she tilted her head back in submission. He continued to kiss her soft skin slowly moving lower with each kiss. Lower and lower toward her breast at the same time running his hands slowly from her waist, up her back to her neck and back down barely touching her skin.

Sarah could feel what felt like sparks coming from his fingertips with each pass of his hands.

She responded to his caresses with her own along his back pulling him ever closer until she could feel his chest against hers.

Alex moved his hands around to her breast and swirled his thumbs on their tips. Sarah responded with a soft moan of satisfaction.

She moved her hands from his back to his front and unfastened Alex's belt and buttons that held his jeans on. In one slow action while still kissing him let his jeans fall to the floor.

Alex now did the same to her jeans. They each returned to slowly hardly ever breaking the kissing. Sarah stepped out of her jeans pushing them to one side with her foot.

She broke the kiss as she pulled him as close as possible and with her hand push down the last bit of clothing he was wearing. Alex responded with the same move and each stepped from them on the floor.

Both now naked, they again locked in deep passionate kissing, pulling each other as close as possible, feeling their bodies pressed against each other. They once again began to dance to the rhythm of the rain, moving ever closer toward the bed as the candlelight cast their shadows on the walls around the room.

When they reached the bed Sarah broke the kiss, and got into bed, tugging on Alex's hand to join her.

Both lying down they reunited their lips and entangled their bodies with their arms and legs for what seemed to be forever.

Sarah could feel an energy radiating from his body into hers. It aroused her every sense and sensation.

With Sarah laying on her back, Alex broke their kiss to only begin it again all along her neck, slowly moving down to her breast. Reaching them he caressed them with his hands and kissed each one in circles until he reached their tips where he switched to caressing them with his tongue.

As he did this to each of them, Sarah would respond by arching her back slightly and running her fingers firmly down his back.

While kneeling over her and continuing to kiss her breast, he moved his hand slowly down her sides and along her legs as far as he could reach. With each move, his hands moved ever closer to her thighs. Repeating this over and over until he slowly passed one of his hands over her womanhood. Sarah's legs opened to invite him in more.

Alex, after much slow teasing, entered her softness with his fingers. Sarah pulled Alex closer and moaned with pleasure at his touch and caresses.

Sarah was sure she could feel the energy coming from his fingertips each time. She wanted to have him so much but also enjoyed the ecstasy of his foreplay.

Sarah now reached down to feel Alex's hardness which made him raise up and gasp for air in response to her touch.

They each now could feel the magical pleasure flowing back and forth between them with every touch, caress, and kiss. They seemed in a dance of physical love and ecstasy that neither of them had ever known.

Suddenly Alex opened his mind so Sarah could hear his thoughts. She could feel what he felt. Not so much in words but in images of light and color. His thoughts penetrated her mind so deeply it enhanced her pleasure even more as he touched her.

She now decided to do the same by letting her thoughts flow freely. The moment she did her whole body responded with pleasure as if their minds were now wrapped together as their bodies were.

Each one now knew what the other wanted and liked without asking or hinting. They now flowed from pleasure to pleasure ever seeming to get closer and higher to some as yet unreached goal.

Suddenly Sarah got up and pushed Alex down on his back. She then climbed on top of his with her legs straddled over his. She bent over and kissed him. First his neck and then his chest. Repeating what he had done to her.

They both knew what the other wanted to happen next.

Sarah rocked slowly over his hardness until she let him slip inside her. Once inside she stopped and holding him deep within her, she bent over and kissed him deeply.

Alex pulled her closer and breaking the kiss whispered with his hot breath into her ear.

"I love you!!"

The feel of his breath in her ear sent hot sensations of pleasure down Sarah's spine.

Sarah slowly began to rock her body over Alex's which made his trust upward as much as he could with her on top.

This dance continued until Sarah was at a point when she almost climaxed. She had never felt like that before. It was as if there was energy touching her insides with each movement. With each motion the sensations became stronger.

Alex too was feeling his own energy flowing out and then return bringing him closer and closer to a point of no return.

Sarah suddenly felt his body arch upward at the same moment hers went into a convulsion of pleasure waves pulsing through her own.

They each responded with a pleasure expressing moan that only enhanced the sensations they were both feeling. Not only did their bodies feel the streams of ecstasy but their minds also seemed to explode into each other.

Even though they had stopped moving, the sensations seemed to last forever.

When the pleasure rush finally subsided Sarah, still on top, bent over again and kissed him deeply. Leaning back slightly she looked into his eyes.

"I love you," she said. "I want this moment to last forever. Can you use some magic to make it happen?"

"I love you too," Alex said. "And I wish I could, but I know now what real magic feels like."

Sarah sat up and savored the time that they were joined together. After a long while had passed and more touching and kissing Sarah laid down next to him and cradled in his arms fell asleep. Alex soon followed.

Chapter 30

I Love Him

The morning after the gunfight Jack called the FBI and informed them that another ODR member was scheduled to arrive in Kona that day. That person is Pete Walker. Jack gave them all the information he had about him. The agent in charge told Jack they would handle it and would most likely reject his visa and send him directly back to England.

A meeting was scheduled later that morning for Jack and Ted to meet with the Hawaii police to give a statement. Jack asked the FBI agent if they could have someone from their office accompany them at the interview. The FBI agent said they would be happy to. The SGM had often been of great assistance to the FBI as well as immigration and the local police with investigations of drug trafficking and illegal immigrants.

Ted arrived in Jack's office shortly after Jack had finished with his call to the FBI. He no sooner had got a cup of coffee and sat down when General Wigmore called.

The night before, Ted and Jack had talked to him on the phone about the confrontation at the ODR headquarters. When the call came in, Jack put it on speakerphone, as they did the night before so Ted could hear and participate.

"Good morning, Colonels," The General began. "I hope you got some rest. I know you have a full day ahead so I will get right to the point. Our units in Amsterdam have informed us that the Morgans have found a flight out and may arrive in Hawaii today. Our information we have has them arriving in Hilo, not Kona. I understand that is on the other side of the island from where you are now."

"That is correct General," Jack responded.

"After a discussion here, we have decided that they must not be confronted," Wigmore said. "All we must do is monitor them. We do not want a repeat of what happened with the ODR. I trust you have men at that airport that can handle this?"

"Yes, we have," replied Jack. "I will inform them as soon as we're finished here. They all have photos of them on their phones."

"That's good," Wigmore said. "We found out that Coke had contacted the Morgans as soon as the news broke in the ODR about what happened yesterday. I suspect this is why the Morgans shifted their flights to Hilo."

"I agree," replied Ted. "There is something more than fear for his family's safety going on between the Morgans and Coke. Susan in Volcano said that her analyst shows that the Morgans must have paid him off. Knowing him I would agree with her. This is of no importance now; the damage is done and we will have to deal with it. There is one concern I have General."

"What is that, Colonel?" asked Wigmore.

"You said he changed his flight to Hilo," Ted answered. "This is a sign that they know where Alexander is located. I know it could mean that they found some open seats that would get them here as soon as possible, but it could also mean the other. With the ODR out of the way, there would be no need to land in Kona."

"I understand your concern, Colonel," Wigmore replied. "The best we can do at this point is to inform Alexander and let him deal with it directly. If we get too involved, we could cause more damage than good. So, I cannot express this more urgently. We must not confront them directly. Do you understand me, gentlemen?"

"Yes sir," Ted and Jack answered him at the same time.

"Have a good day and good luck with everything," Wigmore said as he ended the call.

After the call, the next thing Jack did was to call a crew together to retrieve the computers from the ODR headquarters and bring them to their headquarters for analysis.

The phone again rang shortly after Jack had finished with the crew. It was the FBI agent telling Jack that he was on his way to the Hawaii county police headquarters in Kona to assist in the statements. Ted and Jack immediately set off for the police headquarters about 2 miles away.

Inside police headquarters, Jack and Ted were separated while each gave their statements. After each had done this, they were brought together in a room with the chief of police, along with the FBI agent.

Circles in Stone

All were seated and coffee was served to all in the room.

"I find no problems with your statements," the chief said. "My men at the site confirm the evidence is in line with what you have told us. After a sweep of the building, we also recovered security tapes that were running at the time of the shooting. The Group had cameras installed to record all comings and goings. Everything on those tapes shows you two acted in self-defense and the fight was provoked by them. Do either of you have anything else to add?"

"How are the wounded doing?" asked Ted.

"Two of them are ok and are being retained here until we complete our investigation. The other man is still in the hospital and is expected to make a full recovery."

"Our office has been in touch with Scotland Yard about this," the FBI agent cut in. "They would like this cleared up as soon as possible. We have agreed to permanently revoke their travel visas and bar them from ever returning to the US again. Their story is that they were here on some anti-terrorist mission. Our office believes it is a cover story for something else. We're just not sure what that is."

"We will clear this up as soon as we can," the chief said. "We don't want them here any longer than need be. The company they rented the place from has been warned not to rent it out to anyone else without first clearing it with the County Council. They told us it is set to be demolished soon, so that would not be a problem. The other thing I wanted to say is that your group, SGM, has often been a great help to us. I don't want this to diminish our working relationship in any way."

"There is no need to worry about that," Jack responded. "We will continue to work together for the well-being of all the peoples of these islands for as long as we can."

"Wonderful," the chief said as he stood up. "I guess that's all we need then. You are free to go and if there is anything else we need we will be in touch."

They all stood up and shook hands. Jack and Ted left there and returned to the SGM office to make plans for the next event; the arrival of the three Morgans. After some lunch, Ted returned to his room for a break and to call Sarah.

***

Sarah and Alex had slept in late after their night of passion. Sarah felt more full of life than anytime she could remember. By the time they got up and showered it was almost lunchtime. Alex prepared banana waffles and bacon for the late breakfast. As they were eating, they could not stop smiling at each other.

Alex thought about how much his life had changed and would now change if Sarah would accept the next thing he had in mind.

"How would you like to go on a little drive with me to a very special spot," Alex asked her. "I will make us a picnic and make a day of it. If you trust me that is?"

Sarah laughed, "Hmmm, should I trust you?" She said holding her hand under her chin as if she were truly thinking about it. "After some consideration, I have decided to trust you. But only this one time."

They both laughed like children playing a game.

Sarah went up to her room to change while Alex prepared the picnic. She had just finished changing when her special phone rang. The one she only uses to talk to her father.

"Hi Dad," Sarah said answering it with a happy tone. "I was going to call you later but am so glad you called now. How are you?"

"Been a rough couple of days, but I am all right," he answered. "It is good to hear your voice. Are you still on the Hilo side of the island?"

"Yes, I am in Volcano village, well just outside the village really, in a beautiful home of someone wonderful."

Ted was puzzled by that answer.

"Oh? Tell me about it."

"I have to tell you, something Dad," Sarah began, "I have not told you everything. I have been traveling with someone that I met at the hotel in Kona. Before you ask, yes, it is a man. He is the most wonderful and amazing man. He has two houses. One in Kona and one here in Volcano."

Ted felt a chill go up to his spine when she told him about having two homes. And had met him at the hotel. Please no, he thought to himself. But he decided to ask anyway.

"Please don't tell me his name is Alexander?" Ted asked her with his heart-pounding.

Sarah was silent for a moment.

"Yes," she answered in hesitation, "How did you know?

"How serious is it," Ted asked not wanting to sound alarmed.

"I love him, dad," she answered. "How did you know his name?"

"I don't want to tell you how to live your life," Ted responded still hoping it would not be who he now feared it was. "How much do you know about him?"

"A lot more than most know about him," Sarah answered. "Things you would not believe if I told you. You still did not tell me how you know his name?"

"Is his last name Michaels," Ted asked in one last hope.

"Yes, it is, how do you know that?"

Good thing Ted was sitting down otherwise he would have fallen over. His daughter was in love and in the house of the man he has spent years and is now in Hawaii to protect. The same man he knew the Morgans were on their way there to confront and would do anything to get the Jewel from him. He had tried so hard to keep her out of danger and now she was in the very center of it. He was silent on the phone as he thought of how this was his fault. How was he going to tell her? How much did she know?

"Dad? Are you there?" Sarah asked as she did not hear her father answer.

"Yes, I am here," answered her father with a tone of uncertainty. "I have never met him but I know who he is. All I can say is that if you stay there, you may be in great danger. You don't know what you are dealing with."

"With respect father, I know exactly what I am into," Sarah said with a determined voice. "I know everything about him things you can't imagine in your wildest dreams."

Ted thought for a second. Is it possible that Alexander had revealed himself to her? If so, how much did he tell her about the SGM? He decided to ask a few questions to see if she knew anything.

"Did Alexander ever mention anything about a group called Society of the Green Man? Or perhaps another group called the Morgans?"

"Never heard him speak about any Green Man group," She answered, "But he and a friend of his mentioned the Morgans. Said they were bad news and always will be or something to that effect."

254

Ted was surprised by her answer. He decided to press further.

"Don't think me weird Sarah," Ted pressed on. "Did he ever mention anything about magic or wizards or a Jewel of some kind?"

It was Sarah's time to be surprised by her father's questions. She decided to answer him honestly and frankly to see what that did.

"Okay Dad, he is a wizard," she answered with tears in her voice. "He told me he is a direct descent from Merlin, and I believe him. I have seen things Dad; you would not believe."

Ted knew at once Alex had revealed himself to his daughter. He suddenly thought that if he loved her also that perhaps Sarah was not in as much danger as he thought. That Alex would make sure she was protected. After all, Alex had ways of dealing with things that the SGM did not.

"Listen, Sarah," Ted answered. "I know more about him than you can imagine. Anything you would tell me about him would not surprise me. That's all I can say right now. I will be coming to Volcano tonight. I will being staying at a place there that I only left a couple of days ago. I had no idea you were there too. Just do me one favor. Ask Alexander to tell you everything he knows about the Society of the Green Man and the Morgans. And please stay close to him until I get there. I will call you in the morning so we can meet. I do look forward to meeting Alexander. If he tells you everything you will understand why. You must tell him that you are my daughter. You must tell him my full name. I am sure he will have heard it. Can you do that for me?"

"Yes Dad," Sarah replied with a calmness she now felt run through her being.

"Love you, Sarah. See you tomorrow."

They ended the call and Sarah was now full of questions. How was Alex connected to her father? Who or what is this society he mentioned? She loved Alex and was sure he loved her. She was confident he would tell her everything she wanted to know. And what about the Morgans? And a Jewel? Alex had a lot of jewels of sorts around. She was determined to get answers today. This outing she and Alex were going on would be the perfect time to get them.

Alex had packed up the picnic and loaded it in the Jeep by the time Sarah completed her call with her father. Sarah jumped in the passenger side of the Jeep and they set off. Once on the main road, Alex headed south toward the park entrance but passed it. They passed a road that went to a golf course and took the next right. This road is the Mauna Loa Road. The entire road is within the Hawaii Volcanos National Park. This road heads up the eastern side of Mauna Loa Volcano. Eleven and a half miles long it ends at an elevation of 6500 ft above sea level.

They drove first through the green forest of a mix of native and nonnative trees. Sarah could feel the grade of the road get steeper as they went along. After a mile or so they went through an area of many dead trees. Alex told her there had been a forest fire a few years before. The understory of this area was already green with tall grass and small trees. The road then became a single lane and was very winding. Around each curve Sarah was seeing more Koa trees. There were young trees mixed with many very large old ones. Soon the trees formed a complete canopy over the road. It was along this section of the road Sarah decided to seek the answers she wanted.

"Do you know a man by the name of Ted Rowland?" began Sarah.

Alex, who was driving slowly because of the many curves in the road stopped the Jeep suddenly and looked at Sarah as if he had seen a ghost.

"Yes, I know of him. I have never met him. How did you hear that name? Do you know him?"

"He is my father," Sarah responded with a grin. "I want to know how you know him. While you are at it, I want to know what you know about a group called Green Man Society."

Alex looked at her frozen. After a short moment of silence, he answered

"Circles of Stone," he said as he looked at Sarah and saw the wanting to know the reason for that answer. "I will tell you another time."

Alex decided to drive a bit further and stop at a pull off along the road within the forest. After shutting off the engine he leaned back in his seat and stared out the window. Then finally looking at Sarah he spoke.

"If Ted Rowland is your father and you know about the Green Man Society you know he works for them.

"No. He works for some secret military branch."

Alex laughed. "I suppose you could call The Green Man society that. Let's take out the chairs and sit in this lovely forest and I will tell you the story."

Sarah agreed and Alex set up two folding chairs and opened a thermos of coffee and poured them each a cup. He sat down and took a deep sigh.

As they drank their coffee, Alex told her the long story of the Green Man Society dating back to the time of Merlin when they were known then as the Knights of Merlin. He told her how they were sworn to protect his family line and to protect the Monarchy of Britain until the day when Arthur would again return. He went on to tell her of the family of Morgans. Of them being sorcerers and their desire to take the throne of England for themselves. Alex answered every question put to him by Sarah honestly and openly.

Sarah now knowing her father's part in everything, a lot of things fell into place. Why they were in Hawaii. How he must have wanted to include her in this trip, though on a mission wanting to be close to her.

"My father said something about a Jewel of some sort," Sarah inquired.

"There is a Jewel that they also protect, known as the Jewel of Power and Authority. It is the one I told you about the day I revealed myself to you. The Morgans have been looking for that Jewel since it left the pommel of Excalibur."

He did not mention where it was though which was all right for Sarah.

To Sarah, it was all as if someone had just proven to her that reindeer do fly. Sarah now felt she was a part of something much larger than herself and she was proud to know her father was part of that too. For the first time, she also felt she was truly part of her father's life. It made her feel special. Only one thing remained. Would she continue to be part of Alex's life?

"Shall we continue to the special place I wanted to show you before it gets too late," Alex asked.

"Yes please," Sarah answered filled with satisfaction.

They continued to drive the rest of the 11 ½ miles to the end of the road. Alex parked the jeep and opened the door for Sarah took out the picnic lunch. He told her to follow close to him on a path just off the parking area. A short distance up the path, Alex stopped revealing an amazing view of the Kilauea volcano far below them. He then took Sarah by the hand and led her to a spot where he showed her the most amazing plant. Around its base were shiny narrow velvet leaves and out of its center stood a tall stalk topped with short branches with small purplish flowers blooming. The whole plant was at tall as she was.

This was the very endangered silver sword plant, Alex told her. Found nowhere else but in Hawaii and at this high elevation. To see one in bloom Alex said, was a rare privilege. To Sarah, everything about the day had been rare.

They each found a rock to sit on in front of it and had their picnic while looking at it and each other.

After the meal, Alex packed up the remains and sat down next to her.

"I have something for you, if you will accept it," Alex said as he reached into his jacket pocket.

Alex got up and knelt in front of her. He opened a small box and showed it to Sarah as he looked into her eyes.

"This was my mothers," Alex said with tears welling up in his eyes. "I would be honored beyond words if you would accept this along with me, and be my wife."

Sarah sat there stunned. Tears started to well up in her eyes as well, as she looked down at a Peacock Sapphire surrounded by 6 diamonds mounted on a ring.

She reached down and scooped up Alex's hands holding the ring and pulled them to her face. She was shaking as badly as the night she first saw the fairies. Taking her time, she finally answered.

"Yes," she said "I would be honored. I do accept you and your love."

Alex took the ring from the box and placed it on her finger. It fit perfectly. They both stood up and kissed long and passionately. At the end of the kiss, they looked into each other's eyes and said at the same time.

"I love you"

Chapter 31

More Revelations

On the way back down the mountain, after the proposal, Sarah and Alex could not stop looking at each other and smiling. Sarah held on to Alex as tightly as she could and still allow him to drive. There was a lot to plan but for the moment they lived in the joy.

Shortly before they reached the main road Sarah spoke up.

"My father told me this morning that he was returning here to Volcano today. He should be here already. I think we should invite him to lunch tomorrow and tell him the news. What do you think?"

"Sound like a great idea. I think it's about time I met the man sent here to assure my protection not to mention the father of the woman I love."

"I will call him as soon as we get back. Perhaps around 1 pm would be good."

"That would be good," Alex responded as he turned onto the main road. "I will get the BBQ going. The farmer's market is open tomorrow in the village. Perhaps you could go early and get some fresh fruit and veggies."

"That is a good idea," Sarah said laughing. "Oh my god, listen to us. We are already talking like a married couple."

They both laughed out loud. It all sounded wonderful to them.

Sarah was so happy she could hardly keep from giggling from the joy. Alex was not only happy but was feeling a bit of sadness too. He wished his parents could have been alive for this moment. But he had no doubt that they were with him as well as all the ancestors before them. This thought always gave him comfort when he was confronted with major events in his life.

They were soon at the house again. Sarah raced into the house to call her father and have a shower, while Alex put the Jeep away and secured the house for the night. Each of them doing their task could barely wait to get into each other's arms for the night and celebrate the day with intimate love.

Circles in Stone

***

When Ted arrived in Volcano the afternoon after he and Sarah had spoken on the phone, he was greeted with news he was dreading. The Morgans had arrived that morning in Hilo and had been tracked to Volcano. Ted realized, because of the time differences, the information about their arrival in Hawaii had somehow gotten delayed. Ted was informed that Jack was already on his way to Volcano. He had left Kona as soon as he got the news. The new SGM headquarters in Volcano was abuzz with activity. Units from the Hilo side were all being informed and arrangements were being made for them to be on standby.

Shortly after Ted had been briefed with all this news, one of the SGM units called in to let them know that the Morgans had rented a vacation house on Fourth Street in the subdivision called Mauna Loa estates. This would put them less than 4 miles from the SGM headquarters and less than two miles from Alex's house. The news made the hairs on Ted's neck stand up. He was sure they now knew right where Alex was. All he could think about now was Sarah. Ted asked Susan what she thought the Morgan's next move would be. She told him that they would likely take some time to settle in and get a feel for the landscape before making any move. The information she had on Rhyfel told her he might be impatient but he was not rash. He would plan his move carefully to make sure he had the advantage. Ted thought it through and believed she was right. The one comfort Ted and all the SGM had was that the ODR was not a player anymore. Ted would for now focus on the mission at hand and wait for Sarah to call.

***

Ted had to wait until the evening for the call from Sarah. When he saw the call come in, he raced outside so he could talk in private.

"Good evening my dear Sarah," Ted answered with a tremor in his voice. "Are you alright?"

"Yes, of course I am," she answered. "I want you to know I asked Alex the questions you told me to. He told me everything. Who you work for, why we are here in Hawaii, and many other things. He has been completely open and honest about everything. There is no need for you to worry."

Ted felt a huge weight lift from his shoulders. He could tell from Sarah's voice that she was not angry with him. Strangely, she sounded happy.

"That is wonderful," Ted responded. "I am sorry I could not have been open with you about it all. I hope you forgive me."

"There is nothing to forgive Dad," Sarah answered wanting to tell him the news of her engagement, but she decided to wait until the next day.

"We, Alex, and I would like you to join us for a late lunch tomorrow here at this house. Say around 1 pm. Do you think you can come?"

"Yes, that would be wonderful," Ted answered with some relief. "I look forward to it. Tell me is Alexander there close by? I need to talk to him if you don't mind?"

"Hold on, he just came into the house," Sarah replied as she called Alex to come to the phone.

Alex took the phone from Sarah and with a bit of hesitation spoke.

"Aloha Colonel Rowland," Alex said with a nervous tone. "It is good to finally speak to you."

"And me also. Sarah has invited me to your place tomorrow but what I need to tell you can't wait until then. The Morgans arrived here in Hawaii this morning. They are staying less than 3 miles from your house. There are three of them. Rhyfel, Lord Ambrose, and Lady Selma. My main concern is the safety of my daughter. Do you understand?"

"I understand completely sir," Alex replied with some concern. "I can assure you that she is completely safe here. I give you my word on that Colonel. No harm or threat can come to her in my house. I have taken every step to make sure. I hope you trust me in that?"

There was a bit of silence from Ted. Ted knew what he was saying was true. He knew deep inside she would be safer with Alex than even with him.

"Yes, I trust you," Ted finally replied. "I guess I will see you tomorrow then."

"Great," Alex said, "Would you like Sarah again?"

"It's alright," Ted answered, "Tell her I love her and look forward to seeing her tomorrow."

"Will do," Alex replied as they ended the call.

Circles in Stone

The next morning Alex and Sarah rose early to prepare for the visit of Sarah's father. Alex set about preparing the food for BBQ, including steaks and fish. Sarah headed off to the farmers' market in the village to buy fresh fruits and veggies.

The market opens very early so she needed to be there early to get the best selection and quality. The market is located only a couple of miles from Alex's house in the Volcano community center.

It was a good thing it was not too far for Sarah to drive. She had not driven very much since arriving in Hawaii and still found it a challenge to drive on the other side of the road.

When she arrived at the market it was already very busy. As soon as she began looking at all the different vendors' goods, she could feel people watching her. With Alex's help, she had mastered the skill of turning off the incoming thoughts of others. She felt almost normal now in crowds.

There were many wonderful stalls selling all manner of fresh fruits and vegetables. There was also a large assortment of homemade jams and a variety of breads. She thought it would be nice to have some of those for lunch as well.

As she was making a selection from one of the vendors selling bread, she heard a thought come in to head loud and clear. She thought it was a real voice for a moment but then she realized it was not. She froze in mid-action to listen again and even tried to block it but she could not.

"That can't be," was the thought she heard.

"That looks like Helena's daughter," the voice continued. "What would she be doing here? If that is her? If it is, she is the spitting image of her mother. I must find out."

Sarah looked around and saw a tall middle-aged well-dressed woman staring at her. She wore a long colorful dress and a stylish sun hat with flowers all around it. Around her neck hung a long black pearl necklace with a black orb at the end. The necklace looked out of place Sarah thought, for the rest of the outfit.

The woman approached Sarah.

"Hi," the lady said to Sarah. "My name is Selma, forgive me for the intrusion, but you look like someone I once knew and wondered if you were somehow related to her."

Sarah was shocked to hear the woman speak with an English accent. She was not sure what to say. And how did she project her thoughts into her head so strongly that she couldn't block them? Before Sarah could answer her the woman continued.

"Your name wouldn't by any chance be Sarah?" asked Selma. "The person I knew had a daughter named Sarah."

Sarah's face froze in shock as if she had seen a ghost. She was not sure whether to be afraid or press for more information. Sarah chose the latter.

"Yes, my name is Sarah. I never knew my mother so I can't tell you much about whether she knew you or not. She died when I was born."

Selma put her hand to her mouth and gasped when she heard Sarah speak.

"Would your last name happen to be Harper?"

Sarah froze again. How could she know that? Did this strange woman know her mother? Reluctantly Sarah answered her.

"Yes, it is."

Sarah could see tears well up in the woman's eyes.

"My heavens," Selma replied. "You are her. Your Helena's daughter."

"You knew my mother? And my father?"

Sarah saw Selma's demeanor change when she mentioned her father. Selma suddenly took control of the situation.

"Listen," Selma said. "My husband and I and a family friend just arrived here yesterday. We're staying only about a mile from here. I came to the market to get some fresh food. Please don't think this forward but if you can spare a little time could you come to our place for tea when you finish your shopping. I have a million questions as I am sure you do too."

Sarah stood there thinking as Selma waited for her answer. If this woman knew her mother perhaps, she could shed some light on things that her father had not told her. There was plenty of time to have tea and make it back in time to prepare lunch. She did have questions.

"Alright," Sarah answered. "I must get back and prepare for a luncheon. I could spare an hour."

"Splendid," Selma responded. "I will wait for you in the carpark and you can follow me to where we are staying."

Selma walked away and continued shopping. Sarah watched her for a while and then continued with her shopping. When she had finished shopping Sarah met Selma in the parking area. Selma showed her which car was hers and pulling out waited for Sarah to follow. As Sarah followed, she made a choice not to call Alex and tell him where she was going. They might be engaged but they were not married yet, she thought laughing to herself.

Selma was right, it was only about a mile when she turned into a drive next to a reddish-brown one-story wood-frame house. Selma signaled Sarah to follow her down a wooden walkway that ran along the side of the house to a door. As Selma got near the door she shouted out.

"Lord Ambrose put the kettle on; we have a guest. You're not going to believe who I just met at the market," she said as she entered the house.

Sarah followed her into the house and found two men standing next to a large oval table waiting to meet her.

"Lord Ambrose," Selma began. "This is Sarah Harper, daughter of Helena Harper. Sarah this is my husband, Lord Ambrose."

"It is a pleasure," Ambrose said as he reached to shake Sarah's hand. "The last time I saw you was when you were an infant."

Selma was about to introduce Master Rhyfel but he shook his head. Selma knew that it meant not to use his title.

"Brother Rhyfel," Selma said, "I would like you to also meet Sarah Harper."

"Pleased to meet you," Rhyfel responded. "I have heard of your mother but I never had the pleasure of meeting her. Please sit down. We shall have some tea. Afraid we don't have much else to offer as we just arrived yesterday."

Selma set about making tea and putting donuts she had bought at the market on a large plate. Sarah was beginning to feel a bit out of place and had the feeling to run but the desire to get answers kept her in the chair.

"You knew my mother?" Sarah began with her questions. "How did you know her?"

Ambrose and Selma looked at each other and then at Rhyfel. Rhyfel gave a quick nod of yes to them.

"Your mother was my older sister," answered Selma. "I am your aunt. My maiden name was Selma Harper."

Sarah knew her mouth dropped open. She put her hand over it to cover her shock at what she was just told. How was this possible? But her next question seemed to come out without control.

"Then you must know who my real father is?" asked Sarah.

Selma looked at Ambrose and they looked at her puzzled.

"What do you mean by your real father? Ambrose inquired. "We don't understand."

Sarah was not sure how to respond to that. She was not sure if she should say who her adopted father was or not. She decided to reword the question.

"What was my real father's name?" she asked.

Not sure why Sarah had asked the question they gave the only answer they knew.

"Theodore Rowland of course," answered Selma as she poured the tea into each person's cup.

"No," Sarah snapped back. "He is my adopted father. I want to know who my biological father is. If my mother was your sister as you say, then you must know."

Again, Ambrose and Selma looked at each other puzzled. Meanwhile, Rhyfel was smiling. Selma seeing Rhyfel's smile stared at him and asked.

"What are you smiling at brother? Do you know something I don't?"

"You don't get it do you?" Rhyfel replied. "I have pieced together enough from what I know of your sister's story and the questions now to get the picture. Her real father Ted Rowland told her he had adopted her to protect her from us as well as you Selma. Because I am going to bet money that her father is a member of the Society of the Green Man. He was creating a wall between her and us and himself."

Sarah sat there stunned. How do they know about the Green Man Society? Was Rhyfel right? Was Selma right? Was the man she has always thought to be her adopted father her real father? Sarah gathered her strength. and decided to sort this out.

"Now let me get this correct," Sarah began. "Theodore, Ted Rowland, the man that has told me that he had adopted me at my mother's last request, is my real biological father?"

"Yes, that is correct," Selma said as she sat down next to Sarah. "My sister loved your father and wanted to marry him but our family would not allow them to get married. When your mother died, we got to see you once. After that your father took you and we had no idea where you or he went. We looked for you but could never find you so we decided your father must have left the country and taken you with him. You are part of a very special family. You are of the Morgan bloodline. Your mother denied it and chose to love someone outside of the line. Though you were born, I still believe it was a terrible mistake that cost her life."

"My father loved my mother," Sarah snapped back. "My father has looked after me all his life and still does. I know he loves me."

After her statement, she realized that these were the Morgans that Alex had warned about. She now knew she had better watch what she said. If they knew she was with Alex this could be dangerous for her as well as him. She decided to be bold and find out more.

"May I ask what you are doing here in Hawaii?"

"We're here on family business," Rhyfel answered. "Which makes it your business as well. You are part of our family whether you like it or not. Where is your father now?"

"What kind of family business could possibly bring you all the way to Hawaii?" Sarah inquired.

"Someone here has something that belongs to our family," Ambrose said picking up where Rhyfel left off. "It has taken us a lot of effort to find this person."

Sarah wanted to push them further but she needed to do so without revealing what she already knew.

"Is that person my father?" Sarah asked being coy. "We are here on holiday. He is showing me the islands while I study the ancient culture of Hawaiians. He is in the military and has been given leave. I don't know anything about any Green Man society or anything like that."

Sarah could feel Selma trying to probe her mind. She used everything thing Alex had taught her to block her. She could feel it working.

"No," answered Rhyfel. "It's not your father. If your father is in the military or not. If he is part of the Green Man society it won't matter. We will get what we came after. The family of the person we're seeking stole a jewel that rightfully belongs to us and we are not going to let anyone stop us from retrieving it. Being a part of this family, the Jewel belongs to you as much as anyone. You could join us and be a part of your true family once again."

"What happens if this person won't give you the Jewel?" Sarah asked knowing they meant Alex.

"That's up to him," Ambrose said. "We mean no harm to him but we are willing to do whatever it takes to get what is rightfully ours."

Sarah knew what that meant. It was time to get out of there. She had to warn both her father and Alex. She was a much bigger part of this than she ever could have realized before.

"I must be going," Sarah said as she stood up. "My father will be wondering where I am. I know how much he worries. I now have many questions for him thanks to you. Thank you for everything and I hope we can get together again. I would like to know more about my mother and, Mr. Rhyfel, I will consider your offer."

They all stood and saw her out to her car. Their goodbyes were cordial and kind but everyone could feel the tension. As she drove away the three Morgans looked at each other.

"I am not sure it was a good idea bringing her here," Rhyfel said as he headed back into the house. "I don't trust her."

"I don't either," Ambrose responded as he looked at his wife. I think she has too much of her mother in her."

Selma felt alone and confused. It was her only sister's daughter. She had tried to probe her thoughts and detected nothing. She found it hard to believe she could have learned to block her on her own. If she had then she was stronger than her mother had ever been.

They all returned to the house to mull over the encounter and what it might mean to the reason they were there. Rhyfel was determined that it would not interfere with his goal. Sarah may be of Morgan blood but that was not going to influence his determination to get the Jewel of Power. He had come too far to let anything interfere with that now.

Chapter 32

Not Here

As Sarah drove back to Alex's house she was in tears. What she had just learned was almost too much for her to bear. Her father had hidden the truth from her all this time about being her real biological father and that her mother was part of a family that Alex considered an enemy. Would this make her an enemy as well? Would he break off their engagement because of it? Just when she was feeling a part of something special, she now felt completely lost.

When she got back to the house, she noticed another Jeep in the drive. Was this her fathers? She dried her tears and decided to enter the house as if nothing had happened. She had just gathered the shopping when she saw her father come out of the house along with Alex. Her father raced over to take the shopping. He took the shopping from her and gave her a hug with his remaining arm.

"My dearest Sarah," Ted said with a broad smile. "It is so good to see you again. I missed you so much."

"And you too, Dad," Sarah replied, emphasizing the word, Dad. "We have a lot to talk about."

Alex walked over and kissed Sarah on the lips. He could tell that something was not right by her face and the way she reacted when he kissed her. Perhaps it was because her father was there. But something inside told him it was something else. He did not try to probe her mind even though he wanted to.

Sarah tried to cover her feeling with small talk as they walked to the house.

"You have finally met the man you're here to protect," Sarah said to her father. "Hope Alex has shown you around."

"Yes, he has," Ted answered. "It is an interesting place. Love the stone henge in the back garden."

They all went into the house and to the kitchen dining area. Alex was preparing the meat for the BBQ. Sarah began to cut up the fruit and vegetables she had bought at the market while Ted sat at the counter drinking a beer. There was silence among them except for that between Alex and Sarah about the food preparations. Ted felt the silence from Sarah. But he did not know what to make of it.

Sarah was mixing fruit in a bowl near her father when she suddenly slammed the spoon down on the counter. She looked straight into her father's eyes and burst into tears.

"Why didn't you tell me the truth?!" she asked him with a full weeping voice.

Alex stopped what he was doing and looked at Ted who was frozen in place by her question.

"I was not permitted to tell you about what I did," Ted finally responded. "I had no idea you would ever meet Alex."

"Not that!" Sarah cried back with a bit of anger in her voice. "Why didn't you tell me you are my real father and who my mother was?"

Ted put down his beer and a look of fear came over his face. How did she find out? Who here would have told her? He first looked at Alex who shrugged his shoulders and shook his head no, in a way that he knew Ted thought he might have found out somehow.

Suddenly Ted thought of the only other way she could have found out.

"My God," Ted said with a sense of dread. "You have met Selma."

"My aunt Selma," Sarah snapped back, still in tears. "My mother's sister. She recognized me at the market this morning. She invited me to tea so I went. I wanted to hear what she had to say. She told me everything."

Alex put the knife down he was cutting the meat with. He knew who Lady Selma was. He knew the names of all the Morgans. He moved closer to Sarah but didn't want to interfere with what going on between her and her father.

Sarah dried her tears and went back to mixing the fruit all the while staring at her father waiting for his answer.

"It was what your mother wanted," Ted finally answered. "Your mother's family wanted to take you away from me. She did not want them to raise you. She knew she was dying and made arrangements for me to adopt you. I loved her and you so much. She made me promise not to tell you until I thought the time was right. Her family hated me for loving her and causing her to be pregnant with you. We wanted to get married but they had so much influence that they prevented it from ever happening. That is when your mother came up with the plan to have me adopt you. Her family never suspected she did it. I joined the SGM and together they helped me fulfill your mother's wish to keep you hidden from them. It was all done because of our love for you and each other. I should have told you sooner. Trust me the last thing I wanted was for you to find out the way you did."

Sarah stood still and silent as her father explained. When he had finished, she saw tears in his eyes. She could not remember the last time she had seen that. She knew he was telling her the truth. The way her aunt had told her the things about him and her mother, Sarah had sensed bitterness. Selma might be her mother's sister but she felt no connection. In some ways, she remembered feeling contempt and fear. For the first time, she now felt closer to her father than ever. Finding out he was her real father explained a lot of things. She now knew why she could never hear his thoughts. A hundred emotions flooded her heart. She went around the counter and without saying a word hugged her father and kissed his cheek. It felt more real this time than ever before.

"I am sorry I snapped at you," she said to him. "I was just so shocked and didn't understand."

Ted hugged her back and they smiled at each other.

Alex stood stunned; this is not how he imagined the day would be going. There is no way he could think how Sarah must feel. He knew he had to approach this situation gently. But before he could say anything Sarah looked at him.

"You must hate me now?" Sarah said with new tears welling up. "I am a member of the family that wants to destroy you."

Alex looked back at her puzzled. He also walked around the kitchen counter and took her hand in his, not sparing anything even in front of her father.

"My love for you is not diminished in any way," Alex said. "I want to marry you more now than the day I asked you. You are the bravest woman I have ever known aside from my mother. If your mother was anything like you, I can see why your father loved her. Her heart was pure as is yours. Just as Tan had said. I am sure he knew your bloodline. They can smell your blood, you know."

Ted looked at Alex and then at Sarah. Sarah raised her hand to show him her ring.

"Was planning on telling you over lunch," she said. "But now you know."

Alex spoke up. "I wanted to ask your permission sir, and if you would give us your blessing."

Ted looked at Sarah who was now smiling.

"Yes, of course," Ted said. "As long as my Sarah is happy, that is all that matters."

"I am," Sarah answered without hesitation.

Sarah's demeanor suddenly changed

"They mean to destroy you," Sarah said looking at Alex still holding his hand. "If you don't give them what they want. They said it was something that rightfully belongs to them."

"The Jewel of Power and Authority," Ted broke in. "That's what the ODR wanted also. I heard them say so at the meeting in Edinburgh. They were trying to get it before the Morgans did. I don't mean to talk ill of your family line dear Sarah. But that's all they have ever been focused on."

"As Alex said, I might have their blood but you are my family," Sarah responded. "I am my mother's and my father's daughter."

"If I may ask?" Ted said looking at Alex. "Where is the Jewel now?"

Alex looked at both Ted and Sarah puzzled. Thought for a moment and then answered.

"I wish someone would have told me that it was the Jewel they were after. I could have saved a lot of people a lot of trouble. I don't have it. It is not here. I never had it. My family has never had it. I know about it because my father told me about it and taught me its value. But he told me he thought it had been lost a long time ago. He told me that it was our family line that was the value now. I thought they all wanted me gone to break the line and that somehow that power we hold would be theirs."

Ted looked at Alex perplexed. A concerned look soon replaced that.

"The Morgans are not going to believe you" Ted replied. "To think of all the energy wasted. Jack should have told you. The SGM has let you down by not telling you. I am sorry."

Alex smiled. "But then I would not have met your wonderful daughter. Circles in Stone. Circles in Stone."

Ted looked at Sarah and then Sarah at Alex.

"You said that once before," remarked Sarah. "What does that mean?"

"I think we should put these steaks and fish on the grill and have some lunch first," Alex replied. "I promise that after lunch I will tell you."

They all went about preparing lunch. The mode was now more joyful. Ted continued to ask Alex questions about his history and his house.

Alex made grilled steak and fish while Sarah made grilled vegetables and fruit salad for dessert. Lunch was served on the stone table in the center of the Stonehenge circle.

Once lunch had ended, they each sat with a drink in their hands. Sarah and Alex sat next to each other across from Ted. Alex and Ted each had a beer and Sarah a wine. Anticipation final got the best of Sarah.

"Tell us about the circles of stone," Sarah requested looking at Alex.

Alex leaned back took a long drink of his beer and began.

"What I am about to tell you is not in any history book except the one in my library. It is in a book that came here with my very first ancestor to this island. One of the later ancestors translated it into more modern English. My father read it to me and later I read it myself."

"Long before the time of Merlin," Alex continued. "At a time when villages were first turning into communities. People understood that when leaders of their community died, they did not disappear but went to what they called the "Other World" or the world of their ancestors. One of those communities, no one knows which one, began to erect stones to honor them. At first a single stone. Perhaps in the center of the village. As other leaders died, they erected more stones next to the others. As time passed these stone monuments took on the shape of their houses, circles. Other communities began doing the same. When people from other villages would come to visit, they would tell stories of the things these ancestors did while going from one stone to another. The circles began to be aligned with the setting of the sun and moon. Not just to mark the seasons but to make sure that when the sun or moon was in a certain place in the skies, those ancestors would be remembered and talked about. With no calendar, this was how you knew when to take the time to do so. It was not long before every village across Britain had circles of its own. Every village would celebrate the remembering on the same days of the year. Not as a time of sadness, but one of joy and thanksgiving for those ancestors continuing to watch over them. People would travel from village to village to hear the stories and then return to tell the people of their village what they had heard. They would also share ideas and bring knowledge of how-to farm better, or build a better house. Because these ideas came through the telling of the stories of those past leaders it was believed it was them, the ancestors, that were doing the sharing. Some people would travel great distances to hear these stories. Those travelers shared with each other and then took what was shared back to their own villages. Highways soon developed between the circles. Someone, no one knows who, came up with the idea of leaders of many communities meeting in one place. The place that was chosen was Salisbury plain. The story says that once that decided upon, the place moved their village's circle to that place as a mark of good faith. Those were the bluestones from Wales that are at the center of Stonehenge today. After that first meeting, every year members of each village from across the land were chosen to go to that location. They would bring animals, food, ideas, and even the bones of some recent dead to the celebration. The people of the land soon realized that they were all connected to one another. It was the ancestors that connected them. Once this connection was realized they set about building a monument to that connection. A place where they all were welcome. A place where ideas, food, healing, and differences could be shared. This is Stonehenge, the cathedral of the ancestors. The reason this henge has lintels and none of other ones do, is that, it is told, that all the people that would come to the celebration would form a great circle with their arms linked and heads bowed in respect. This action was built in stone to show the permanent link not only to each other, but to the ancestors they all honored, from wherever they came. It was understood, and still is by some of us, that we are all linked. All things return to a place of beginning. All things reveal their connectedness. It is the ancestors that assure that connection. What is to be, has already been, the universe may be ever-changing, but history repeats itself, what goes around comes around, sow to the wind reap the whirlwind, call it whatever you like. We are all connected by the past and into the future. That connection forms an endless spiral, knot, or circle. No matter how you envision it. The path may wander but the connection is set firmly in the stones of time."

When Alex had finished Ted and Sarah sat in silence looking at the stone circle, they were sitting in. Sarah was thinking of how she and Alex had met and how it was her father that worked to protect the man she now loved never knowing about the connection. How this morning's meeting had caused her to find out who she was. As an archaeologist, she could see how what he told them fit into the story of history. What he said made more sense than anything thing she had heard or read about the stone circles, and how and why Stonehenge was created.

Ted was thinking about how General Wigmore had asked him to bring Sarah along on this trip simply as a cover. How all the things had happened to bring him and her closer together than they had ever been.

For them, both what Alex had just told them seemed to make sense in a very personal way. For Alex, it was no surprise at all. To him, this is the way life was. To Alex, we each are one more stone in the vast circle of life.

"What about this stone circle?" asked Sarah.

"One of my great great great grandfathers decided that one needed to be built to remind our family of our ancestors," Alex explained. "This connects us to them as it will to those that will come after me until someday when Pele decides to bury it under lava."

They all sat enjoying their drinks and listening to the birds singing in the trees. Sarah was wondering to herself if the fairies, whom she had met in that very spot, were watching them. It all seemed so peaceful. Ted broke the quietness with a new subject.

"I need to ask," Ted inquired. "Will you confront the Morgans?"

Sarah turned and looked into Alex's eyes with worry. Alex sensed her concern.

"If they do not get what they came after I am sure they will not take no for an answer," Alex replied. "What I know about Rhyfel, he will take this personally. In his mind, he must prove he is the stronger and more powerful wizard. Don't worry. I have already thought about this. I will not confront him here or anywhere that puts anyone in danger. He has no chance of winning."

"How can you say that?" asked Ted. "I have seen his power. He got into the Tower of London as if it was a cakewalk."

"If he is more powerful or not is not the issue," Alex responded. "I have something that he does not."

"What?" asked Sarah concerned.

"Roots," Alex answered. "I have roots in this land. He does not."

Seeing the questions on both Sarah's face and Ted's, Alex continued.

Every wizard, witch, worker of magic, healer, or every person for that matter, draws their strength from roots, either from the land where they grew up, or from the family they are connected to. We are all connected to one or the other or both. They are our roots. All living things have roots. The very land that nourished us caused those roots to grow. Imagine that with every step you take you could see roots coming up and going down. When they go down the energy of the land flows up into you. The very term "Returning to your roots is far more literal than most people ever realize. For us wizards, it is very important. The very elements that give us power come from the land, the earth beneath us. If we have shallow or no roots, we can draw very little energy. We become uprooted. I suspect that Rhyfel, in his arrogance has forgotten this. With no roots in this land, he has little to draw on."

Ted looked at Sarah and smiled. She smiled back. Ted felt a sense of relief but not total comfort. As a military man, he knew that the best-made plans can go awry. But he had no choice but to trust Alex. All of this was out of his control. He could only do what he could to protect Sarah.

Sarah's concern did not vanish with Alex's words. The only thing she could do now was to give him all the support he needed.

Alex was more concerned than he let on. Not about being able to defeat Rhyfel, if it came to that, but about keeping those he cared about safe. Battles of magic could be nasty affairs. He had to find a way to make sure that if one did take place, no one would get hurt. He had to draw Rhyfel to place clear of any bystanders. As he pondered this it came to him. The volcano's caldera.

After a short while, they all agreed not to dwell on what might or might not happen in the days ahead. They decided instead to spend the rest of the day and evening talking about each of their shared memories of Hawaii and family stories.

Chapter 33

The Dragons Lair

Early in the morning following the visit from Sarah, Rhyfel had another mission. The one thing that still haunted him, even though he kept it to himself, was whether there was a dragon on the island. He knew that at the time that Alex's ancestor would have come to the island, dragons were still well known in the world of magic. Rhyfel had only told Ambrose that he had brought the magic tools that would tell him if there was one. Magic may not affect dragons, but it could be used to find them. It had been used very much in the past to search for them or to find if one might be hiding in a cave before entering it.

Rhyfel called Ambrose and the two of them set about making the spell to find out if one did exist on the island.

The spell was straightforward. Rhyfel had brought three things with him. A red and green polished Dragon Stone, the size and shape of a chicken's egg, a 10-inch diameter 8-inch-deep hand-beaten brass bowl with a handle arched over the top by which to carry it, and a hammer made of the antler of a red deer.

Rhyfel put the Dragon Stone egg in the brass bowl and then poured in rainwater filling it halfway. Holding the bowl by the handle he hit the top edge of the bowl with the hammer so it made a ringing sound.

What happened next would have been something no one had seen in hundreds of years.

The Dragon Stone spun around on the bottom of the bowl and then rose to the top of the water. The stone egg's narrow end then stopped and pointed in the general direction of the dragon's lair. The stone gently sank back to the bottom when the ringing sound faded.

Rhyfel looked and Ambrose with an expression of both surprise and concern.

"This is not good," Ambrose said to Rhyfel who had just hit the bowl again to make sure it was not a fluke.

The stone again spun around and rose to the top of the water just as before.

"We will have to deal with this first," responded Rhyfel.

"How?" asked Ambrose.

"We will use this to find the dragon's lair and seal the beast in," answered Rhyfel. "This bowl will lead us to where the dragon leaves and enters its lair. Once we find that, I will create a collapse that will seal it in. It will take months to dig or melt its way out. Underground a dragon's power is very limited. We need to find that lair entrance today. I need you to tell Lady Selma will be going on an exploratory tour for the day to get the lay of the land."

"Yes, of course, she was hoping to have a day of rest after traveling. She will be pleased with having a chance to relax," replied Ambrose.

"Just ask her if she could pack us some lunch to take with us," requested Rhyfel. "I have no idea how far we will have to walk or how long it will take to find. Better bring your shielding wand just in case we happen to catch the dragon outside of its cave. Chances are, it would only come out during the day if there is a heavy fog that would give it cover. Best if we find the lair entrance before nightfall."

While Selma was making the packed lunch, Rhyfel and Ambrose were packing backpacks and dressing for the possible conditions they might encounter. Ambrose made sure to pack bottles of rainwater for the bowl. Only rainwater can be used for the spell to work. Fortunately, the house they were staying in only used rainwater as its main water source, as did most houses in the area. The plan was to drive a few miles and then stop and repeat the spell. They would use this method until they could no longer use roads, then they would continue the search on foot, hopefully finding the lair entrance before dark.

***

Meanwhile, Alex, Ted, and Sarah were having breakfast. Ted informed Sarah and Alex he needed to return to the SGM Volcano headquarters. He needed to check in and call general Wigmore about the latest devolvement. Alex and Sarah had already decided that they needed to visit Tarian Tan. To Ted, they only said they needed to visit a friend. Alex felt it wise that the existence of a dragon should be kept only between himself and Sarah. Sarah agreed and felt special to know something this important that her father didn't.

Circles in Stone

After Ted left, Alex confided in Sarah that he was concerned about the fact that all those involved thought he had the Jewel of Power in his possession. Up until now he, like his father, believed the Jewel to be lost. But now he wondered what if it had not been lost. That it was still out there someplace and if so, was it in the care of another descendant? How could something this important be lost yet still hold power?

Alex asked Sarah to join him in the library and help him search through some old documents, to see if there were any clues or information that he and his father may have overlooked. Sarah was more than happy to be a part of this. She was trained to look for subtle clues and details others missed. She felt that she was now a part of Alex's deeper life, even though they were not yet married.

The search began with the records of Alex's ancestor Michael Dee's arrival on the island in 1620. The manuscripts from that time had been put into book form by Alex's great grandfather. While Alex searched through the records, Sarah pulled books randomly from a special section of the library. Many of these books had to do with the records of Alex's family history. Who they were, what royal court they served in, or where they lived. Some had a history of wars long ago, others were about how the Society of the Greenman, then called The Knights of Merlin, defended the royals, and protected the Merlin line.

Sarah then came across a very old book, that had been translated into modern English that told the stories from the time of Arthur and Merlin. Much of the stories didn't match the myth stories she had read in the past. It seemed to be more of a historical account. Stories of battles Arthur fought in, and of knights with names she had never heard of. Much of it was written in verse as was the custom at the time.

As she read through them one caught her attention. Sarah showed it to Alex. Alex told her it was a verse describing the promise of there always being a monarch on the throne of England following Arthur, after he was given the sword Excalibur, and the oath of Merlin's line to protect that promise. Sarah read it again. To her, there was something more in it. The verse she had found read as follows.

From the dragon's mouth, the spell was cast,
From the dragon's word that will ever last.

Raised the King Pendragon's son,
The land and thee, they are one.

The lady's hand from water risen,
To the king's side, the power was given.

House of thee shall forever stay,
From the land, it must not stray.

Blood in veins, it can change,
Crown of the sword, it must remain.

Magics hand kept in guard,
Magics seed keep thy charge.

Father to son and son to child,
Lord or Lady means not who keeps.

Father to son, that son to child when old,
Kept in the land, in line must hold.

Sarah sat down and went over the verse repeatedly slowly. Finally, she raised her concern to Alex.

"Didn't you tell me that the Jewel of power was once mounted in the pommel of Excalibur? And didn't you tell me the Jewel contained a dragon's tooth?"

"Yes, that's correct," Alex replied.

"Then why can't this verse contain a reference to the Jewel as well?" Sarah continued. "This verse refers to the spell being cast from the dragon's mouth. That is where you would get a dragon's tooth. You told me that the Arthurs' power came from The Jewel in the sword, not the sword. The second verse says the power given to the king from the ladies' hand from the water was now by his side. That refers to the sword but the power must refer to the Jewel in the sword."

By now Alex was by Sarah's side looking at the verse with her. Reading it as if the verse was referring to The Jewel also. Alex now saw what she saw. The verse took on a whole new meaning. One that Alex had never noticed before. He now could see that there were several references to staying in the land. He was taught that it meant the monarch remaining in England. But if it referred to the Jewel, this meant it was warning that it must never leave the land of which it was a part, for its power to remain intact. If this was true then the Jewel would still have to be in England. There is only one way to find out if this was true. Take the verse with them on their visit to Tan and ask him.

Alex kissed Sarah. He told her that she may have just unlocked the secret.

"You are a better Wizard than I am," Alex told her smiling. "We make a great team."

Sarah smiled. She was now feeling a real part of Alex's life. She felt for the first time that she belonged.

***

When Ted arrived at the SGM Volcano headquarters he went directly to his office. Jack, being still in Volcano, went in to meet with him.

"How was your day with your daughter," asked Jack.

"Good and different all at once," Ted answered. "More than I expected would be an understatement. My daughter is engaged to be married to Alexander."

Jack stood there stunned for a moment, then left the office without saying anything, and returned in a minute later carrying a bottle of Jack Daniels whiskey and two glasses.

"This calls for a drink," Jack said, as he put the glasses on the table and poured whiskey into each.

"That's not all," Ted continued. "Sarah also met with Selma and learned the truth about me and who her mother was."

"I will make it a double then," Jack responded as he poured more whisky into each glass. "That should be a weight off your shoulders. The part of her now knowing the truth. How do you feel about the engagement?"

"She is happy but I still have concerns about her safety," Ted said looking worried. "I also found out that he does not have the Jewel of Power. He says his family here has never had it. He says he has no idea where it might be or if it still exists."

Jack handed Ted the whiskey he poured for him.

"Wow, that is a revelation I did not expect," Jack responded. "I guess we all assumed he had it. That information could have saved a lot of people a lot of trouble."

"That's what I said," Ted replied as he took a large sip of his whiskey. "The bad news is the Morgans are here and are not going to believe it to be true. That is what worries me. Rhyfel will not stop until he has what he came after. I fear for Alexander and Sarah both. Alexander tried to assure me that Rhyfel can't win in a pitched magic battle with him. My concern is what if the Morgans resort to more conventual means, like guns."

"I see your concern," Jack said, as he sat down and sipped his whisky. "We better tell the general as soon as we can. But if I may? As far as the engagement goes, I am pleased for Alexander and your daughter. I have known, Alika as I call him, for a long time. You could not ask for a finer or more kind man. I knew his father and mother too. They were the best people and I considered them, as Alika, good friends. I can't speak for you and your concerns about Rhyfel. I can only do what the General recommends."

"Then we best get to that," Ted replied, as he swallowed the last bit of whisky in his glass.

Jack remained in the office when Ted called General Wigmore, putting the phone on speaker so Jack could hear. Ted told the General everything and voiced his concerns about Sarah's safety. The General told them that the official rule as far as the SGM was concerned was to stay out of the fight. Not to approach the Morgans or engage with them in any way unless they were to engage the SGM or its personnel directly. He reminded them that, after the ordeal with the ODR in Kona the US officials would not take likely to having another encounter on their soil. The General was also surprised that Alex told Ted that the Jewel was not or never had been in Hawaii. He understood that this knowledge could incite the Morgans to do something rash. His recommendation to Ted about Sarah was to see if he could get her away from the situation until things either come to a head or cool down. Both Jack and Ted agreed with the General's orders and ideas. They ended the call as always promising to keep him informed of any changes as they would occur.

Ted decided to return to Alex's place in the evening to try to convince Alex and Sarah to follow what the general recommended.

***

Alex and Sarah packed a light lunch and set off for the resting place of Alex's descendants and Tan's lava tube.

The hike was a bit easier for Sarah this time because she had been on it once before.

Alex had his staff and repeated what Sarah had seen him do the first time she went with him. Casting magic, he parted the vegetation revealing the opening to the cave. Lighting the torches as he did before, it was not long before they were both deep in the cave. Alex stopped a while and paid respect to his parents in their silver-lined coffins. Then he spent a few more minutes at his sister's coffin nearby.

Sarah followed Alex deeper into the cave than they did before. Tan was not where he was the last time. Sarah could tell because what she had the first time mistaken for a rock formation was now gone. A few hundred yards further in Alex stopped. He sat down on a rock and took out a bottle of water. Sarah sat next to him as he passed the bottle to her.

Alex next reached into his jacket pocket and took out a red candle. From his inside shirt pocket, he retrieved a folded piece of paper that he then handed to Sarah. Alex then lit the candle from the fire of the torch. Leaned over close to Sarah he said,

"I would like you to call him, I will hold the candle so you can see the words on the paper. All you need to do is read them slowly and loudly. Once you finish do not say anything. Just sit still and wait."

Sarah looked at him in astonishment. She felt a bit of fear and yet honored that he would trust her to do this.

"I will do my best," she replied.

"Just take your time," Alex said, reassuring her. "Take a deep breath, then breathe out and begin when you are ready."

Sarah read the words on the paper to herself several times. She then took in a deep breath and slowly exhaled and began;

"Tarian Tan, Shield of Fire, Awaken and come is our desire."

"Master of claw and of flame, whose name is and shall be endless fame."

"Humbly we to your realm do come, your wisdom seeks we, oh mighty one."

Sarah's voice echoed throughout the massive cavern. She slowly folded up the paper and handed it back to Alex who signaled for her to keep it. Alex put his finger to his lips to remind her to be silent.

They both sat in silence and watched the shadows dance off the walls of the lava tube that were created by the flames of their torches. Suddenly, the flame of their torches began to dance as they felt a breeze come from deep in the darkness beyond. The sound of tumbling pebbles could now be heard and they both strained their vision into the dark.

Without hardly any sound there appeared in front of them, two plate size eyes reflecting in the firelight.

Tarian settled down in front of them. Sarah could feel and smell his breath on her face he was so close.

"Good to see you two again," Tarian said in his usual low deep voice. "Queen Holly has informed me you have news to share."

Tarian grinned wide as he looked at them both. Alex and Sarah looked at each other and smiled.

"Yes," Alex replied. "We have come to ask your blessing."

"You have it then," Tarian said still grinning. "I gave it to you the last time you were here if you remember? But I am glad to give it again. You are blessed to have a woman of such a pure heart. Truly rare among those of Morgan blood."

Sarah looked at Alex surprised.

"I told you he knew," Alex responded with a smile.

"Now that is out of the way," Alex said as he reached his hand out and stroked Tarian's face. How are you, my old friend, I sense you are stressed?"

"I heard a sound I have not heard in many hundreds of years," answered Tarian. "The brass bell of someone searching for my lair. You need not tell me who. I already know. I could smell their blood hours ago. What I don't understand is why this one is so determined to destroy you."

"He is not after me," Alex replied. "He thinks I have the Jewel of Power and Authority."

"That's not possible," Tarian answered pulling back his head a bit. "Even if you did have it, it would be of no use. It has no power if it leaves the land of Britain's isles."

"That answers that question," Alex said looking at Sarah.

"What question?" Tarian asked.

Alex took out a copy of the page that Sarah had found and read it to Tarian.

"Sarah said she thought that much of this verse refers to the Jewel and not just about the monarchy."

"Of course, it refers to the Jewel," Tarian responded with a bit of a snarl. "I was there when it was written. Even the Morgans should have known that."

Just then the whole cave shook. A loud sound of collapsing rocks could be heard in the distance. Tarian raised his head and looked behind him as a few small rocks fell from the ceiling landing near Sarah and Alex. Another loud sound followed and shook the whole cave again.

Tan turned his whole body around and looked back into the darkness and sniffed the air.

It was the first time Sarah saw how big Tarian was and she could see his wings shimmer in the torchlight. Alex put his arms over Sarah's head and pulled her to the floor of the cave as more rocks fell.

"Fools!" Tarian roared, "They think they can seal me in this cave. There are more ways in and out of here than they will ever know about."

Tarian turned back to Sarah and Alex.

"No time for proper goodbyes," Tan said to them. "You need to get out of here as fast as you can. Falling rocks roll off me like water, but I fear that is not the case for you."

Tarian suddenly disappeared into the darkness of the cave from which he first came. Alex pulled out a wand from under his jacket and created a shield above himself and Sarah as they made a fast exit as rocks continued to fall. Alex did not bother with putting the torches away as he did before. They both made it out of the entrance safely. Alex did conceal the entrance as usual and they both headed back to the house as quickly as they could. They made it back in time to see Ted pulling into the drive. Ted jumped out of his jeep and ran toward Sarah.

"Are you alright?" Ted asked as he put his arm around Sarah. "Was that an earthquake?"

"Sort of," Alex replied. "Let's all get in the house and I will try to explain it."

Chapter 34

Prepare for Battle

Once back at Alex's house, Sarah went to her room to shower. Alex also showered in the bathroom in his old room. Ted was preparing the dinner of take-out from the local Tai restaurant he had picked up on the way from the SGM headquarters. Sarah and Alex were grateful for this as neither one felt much like cooking.

At dinner, they were all very quiet as they ate. Commenting only on how good the food was.

Once everyone had finished eating Ted turned to Alex.

"What can you tell me about that earthquake," Ted asked.

Alex looked at Sarah, she looked back and shrugged her shoulders.

"Ted," began Alex. "You will soon be a part of my family and its history. You have been a part of my protection for a long time so I am going to trust you. I can't order you to do or not do anything, but I need you to understand that there are things that must be kept out of the realm of general knowledge. Some secrets must, for my sake and the sake of the future, remain secrets. I have already shared many of those secrets with Sarah. As her father, I am going to trust you."

"I understand what you are saying," Ted interrupted. "Whatever you tell me I will keep to myself as long as it protects Sarah and of course you."

"Okay," Alex continued. "What you thought was an earthquake was actually a lava tube collapse caused by the Morgans. If I were to guess it was Rhyfel that caused it. They were trying to seal the entrance to the home of my dear friend and protector Tarian Tan who just happens to be a very old large fire-breathing earth dragon."

Ted looked at Alex in disbelief and then at Sarah.

"I have met him myself," Sarah said smiling. "He is a wonderful and magnificent creature."

"You took my daughter into a cave with a fire-breathing dragon?" Ted asked with alarm.

288

Sarah blurted out, "It's perfectly alright Dad. I like him. He treated me with great respect and assured me that he would protect both me and Alex if such a time should come."

"The dragon can talk?" asked Ted surprised.

"Yes," Alex interjected. "All dragons can speak. As Sarah now knows, it was dragons that taught man to speak. It was also dragons that taught men and women the ways of magic. Much of that has been forgotten of course. I want you to know that I would never put Sarah in any danger. Tarian has protected our family line since the time of Arthur and Merlin."

Ted sat quietly for a while as he took in what he had just been told. Finally, his military mind clicked in gear.

"Why would the Morgans want to seal the dragon in a cave?" Ted inquired. "Couldn't he use such a beast to his advantage?"

"No," Alex replied. "Once a dragon forms a bond it cannot break it. It will defend that bond to the death if necessary. Tarian's bond is with my family. Tarian already recognizes Sarah as being part of my family as well. She is now part of that bond. What Rhyfel doesn't know is that the geology of lava tubes is not like the caves of Britain. Lava tubes most often, and is likely so in the case of the one that Tarian lives in, have multiple entrances. As wise as Earth Dragons are their one weakness was to dwell in caves. Underground they have limited abilities. Unfortunately, it was this weakness that became the demise of so many of them. Gunpowder brought the end of many more as well. I know you have many questions still but that will have to wait for another time."

Ted at least for now felt some relief. But living dragons were almost more than he could believe. But his daughter was going to marry a Merlin line wizard so he would have to get used to strange things. Ted thought about Alex being concerned about him telling others secrets like that. It made him smile inside to think if he did, he would be locked away in a place where he would be attended by servants with lots of keys and wearing white coats.

"There is only one reason that Rhyfel tried to make sure the dragon was sealed in," Alex said snapping Ted's attention back into reality. "He means to challenge me. He wanted to make sure that a battle between us would be on equal footing. I have given a lot of thought to where I would battle with him if it came to that. The best place is in the caldera of the volcano. It is a wide-open space with limited outside resources like trees and such. It would also be the safest place to keep innocent people from being put at risk. It too is a place I know better than most people."

Sarah sat now with a worried look on her face. She heard Alex explain before that he would have an advantage but, nevertheless, she was worried. She now knew what many women felt when their men talked about going off to war. The fear of losing them and feeling powerless to stop it.

"Won't there be people in the National Park?" asked Ted with concern.

"I can take care of that," Alex replied. "The Morgans' attempt to seal Tarian in has made that an easy task. I will convince the staff at the USGS that I believe the earthquake is a precursor to an impending eruption here at the summit. They in turn will inform the Park officials who will clear the area of visitors."

Ted smiled at the tactical thinking of Alex. Sarah saw the smile and was unsure of why he did.

"You would have made a good soldier," Ted responded.

"There is more," continued Alex. "I would like you to take Sarah to the SGM headquarters for her safety."

Sarah was going to object but she could tell by the look on her father's face it would be unwise.

"I am sure that the Morgans will come here looking for me," Alex went on. "They don't know that Sarah has any association with me at this point. I want to keep it that way for as long as possible. But I do have one problem. I need to lure Rhyfel into the caldera. I can get there easy enough by saying I am going there to take samples, but how do I get him to meet me there?"

"I could come back here and tell them where you went if they show up," offered Ted.

"No," Alex replied. "They may know you and would sense a trap. I could use my housekeeper but I don't want her to be put in danger not knowing why. It would need to be someone that they would not know and not suspect but, would be aware of the danger."

"I think I know someone that would do it," Ted interjected. "There is a woman at the headquarters. She is our computer analyst, but I know she has been wanting to take a more active part in what's going on. She knows all the players better than most and could handle it with no problem. I will ask her in the morning. Because this is not an official mission, I cannot order her to do it. She would have to volunteer. But I am sure she would jump at the chance. If only we knew when Rhyfel was going to make his move."

"I may have the solution to that," Alex answered. "If Sarah is willing to help me. Nothing dangerous I assure you."

Alex looked at Sarah, she looked back and smiled.

"Of course, I will," she answered. "What do I have to do?"

"Help me cast a spell," Alex replied.

Sarah looked at him and smiled.

"Sounds like fun," she said laughing. "Can dad watch?"

"Please don't take offense," Alex said with a serious tone. "Casting spells is always serious, and yes, I insist that your father watches. If you both would follow me into my office we can get started."

Alex got up and Ted and Sarah followed him. When Ted entered the office, he stopped in his tracks and looked around. He thought to himself "if these walls could talk."

Alex went to his desk and took out a pair of scissors and handed them to Sarah. Without saying anything he went over to the large trunk with the black stone bowl on it. The bowl still had water in it as when Sarah first saw it. He took some matches from his pocket and lit the four black candles that surrounded it. Alex then flipped through the leather book on the right side of it until he found the page he was looking for and placed a feather as a bookmark in it. He then signaled Ted to join him and Sarah next to the bowl.

"What I am about to do is a form of scrying," Alex began. "Most times scrying is used to attempt to see into the future, which even us wizards know is not possible because it is always shifting. But the one thing we can do, is view a place either near or far as long as we have a connection to it. Call it a version of a magical spy camera. With your help Sarah, we can see what the Morgans are up to."

"What do I do?" she asked.

"You are the connection," Alex replied. "You have Morgan blood so all I need is a small lock of your hair. It is your choice of course."

Sarah did not hesitate to clip a bit of her hair and handed it to Alex.

"Before we begin, I must ask you to obey one thing," Alex told them. "Once I begin the spell you must not make a single sound. Once the window is open, not only can we see and hear them but they could hear us. The Morgans, being wizards in their own right, would know in an instant what would be going on. Absolute silence on our part is critical. We have no idea what they are going to say or when. Much of it may be boring so we must be patient."

Ted and Sarah nodded and Alex signaled to Ted to close the door to the office. Ted closed the door and returned to his place next to the bowl.

Alex picked up the feather from the book and taking the lock of Sarah's hair, he placed it in the water. He then stirred the water with the hair in it with the feather and read out loud from the book the following words.

"Candlelight,
Fire bright,
Give to us distant sight.

Bring us near,
Let us hear.

Let it be,
Let us see.

Hair in water in this bowl,
Join together, kindred soul.

So we have spoken, so be it done."

Alex stopped stirring the water and put the feather down beside the bowl. Looked at Sarah and Ted and nodded.

Sarah was watching the water with an intense glare. As the water became still, she began to see images and hear voices. When the water became perfectly still the images and voices were perfectly crisp and clear. Ted was also staring into the bowl with his eyes wide and full of amazement. This was Ted's first time seeing this kind of magic firsthand and up close.

After a short while of listening and watching, Sarah realized they were seeing and hearing through her aunt Selma.

The first images that came through were of Selma cleaning up after dinner. They could hear the tapping of someone on a computer keyboard in the background. No one seemed to be talking at the time.

After a short time of this, they heard the voice of Ambrose.

"That was some impressive work you did today, Master Rhyfel," they heard Ambrose say. "You moved a lot of rock, if I must say so myself."

"He is well sealed," Rhyfel replied. "Though I must admit it seemed to have drained me more than usual. Must be the altitude."

"You have not recovered from the long trip here," Selma said. "You both need to take a rest. The one I had today made me feel so much better even though I was not pleased when I learned what you two had been up to."

"She is right," replied Ambrose. "I know I feel tired."

"Perhaps your right Lady Selma," Rhyfel responded. "I need to be sharp when I confront this, Alexander. No room for mistakes. If he was wise, he would do the right thing and hand the Jewel over. But I am sure he won't. The reason I know this is because it is not what I would do."

The sound of all three of them laughing could be heard by Sarah. It made her have more contempt than ever before.

"We rest tomorrow." Rhyfel could be heard saying. "I will confront him the following day."

"I will come with you," Ambrose commented. "We will take him together."

"No!" Rhyfel could be heard snapping back loudly. "I will take him alone. You are the next in line to take my place at the head of this family line. I can't risk both of us. Not that I think I will fail, I know I won't, but you and Lady Selma must be there to take my place in case something goes wrong. If something does go wrong, you and Lady Selma must return to England and gather everyone together and continue the pursuit. Do I make myself clear?"

"Yes of course Master Rhyfel," Ambrose replied. "But I will not stay here. I will follow from a distance then, and on that, I will not debate."

"Agreed," Rhyfel was heard responding. "I will go to this Merlin's line wizards house day after tomorrow in the morning just after the sun rises. I will catch him off guard hopefully and we will see what he is made of."

Alex picked up the feather again very quietly and brushed it across the surface of the water in the bowl. The images and the sound vanished.

"It's safe to talk now," Alex said putting the feather down and blowing out the candles. "We now know we have a day to prepare."

"The timing of the scrying could not have been better," Ted commented.

"Gut feeling," Alex replied. "You, as a military man, know you should follow your gut feelings."

"Your right," responded Ted laughing.

"I need a glass of wine after all that," Sarah jumped in. "Anyone care to join me?"

"A beer for me," Ted said as he followed Sarah out of the room.

Alex joined them in the lounge with his beer. They sat in silence thinking about what they had just heard from the scrying bowl. Ted finally broke the quiet.

"Couldn't they do the same to us here?" he asked Alex.

"Only if they knew Sarah was here. Since they have not drawn that connection, it is not possible without something or someone to link with. Most wizards rely on an object to make the link. Jack told me about what happened to the ODR member being tagged. So, I would guess the Morgans rely on objects as well. Besides, I doubt they carried many spell books with them when they came. You must understand something about magic. Details matter. For example, Sarah's hair, the feather is that of a crow, the water is rainwater, and the black candles are made from beeswax and charcoal from local wood. If one of these is not in place the spell would not work."

Ted nodded with understanding. He was being introduced into a world he always knew was there but had never encountered in such a profound way.

After they each had finished their drinks, Ted decided he would leave and spend the night back at the SGM headquarters. He needed to talk to Susan in the morning and make arrangements for Sarah to stay there the following night.

Once Ted had left, Alex and Sarah decided to have an early night. They were sleeping together every night now. Sarah found that she now slept better with Alex next to her.

Once in bed, Alex would often read a story from one of his old books. Tales of knights of old, dragons, and battles to save the common people from an evil landlord. Sometimes he would read poetry. Each time Sarah would fall to sleep at the sound of his voice.

This night when he picked up a book Sarah took it from his hands and put it out of his reach. She rolled back and climbed half a top of him and kissed him deeply. From that point, they made love with the passion they did the first time. No words were spoken, just long slow passionate love.

After an hour of love-making, they lay in each other's arms listening to the rain that had begun falling hard. Something was soothing about the sound of the rain on the roof. For them both it seemed to make them feel safe.

Sarah turned and looked Alex in the eyes and said, "I want to get married as soon as possible. I don't want to wait until I get back to England. I want to get married here. I don't want one of those posh show-off weddings either. I would like simple but meaningful."

"It is possible here," Alex replied. It is very easy to marry in Hawaii. A few easy rules, all of which we would be able to fulfill."

"I would like it to be here, in your Stonehenge," Sarah said. "Would that be possible?"

"Yes, of course, there are very few restrictions on location for a wedding. All you need is a license and someone that is legally permitted to perform it."

"Do you know anyone?"

"Yes, now that you asked, I know someone that would be happy to perform a wedding. She is a priestess in the local pagan community. She loves her motorcycles," Alex replied smiling.

"Oh?" Sarah inquired. "Sounds like you know her very well."

"I do," he answered. "But not that kind of well. She was there for me when my parents died. A friend I trust and needed at the time. We never had any interest in each other. She has an instinct that is as sharp as a shark's tooth. She always knew that there was something different about our family but never said anything. That's why I trust her."

Sarah smiled knowing that Alex sensed her jealously.

"Sounds like the kind of person I want to perform our special ceremony," Sarah responded."

"You will understand why I smiled when you meet her," Alex said. "After this ordeal with the Morgans is over I promise to make the arrangements for our wedding."

"Thank you. I love you so much."

"I love you too Sarah," Alex replied. "More than I can ever express."

They kissed deeply and fell asleep in each other's arms to the sound of the rain continuing to fall.

Chapter 35

The House of Merlin

Early the next morning while Sarah and Alex still lay sleeping, Ted was on the phone with General Wigmore. At first, Ted was going to go ahead with his plan to ask Susan without the General's knowledge. But as he thought more about it, he decided it would be best to have everyone informed in case something went wrong.

On the phone, Ted told Wigmore his plan and why he thought it was the best idea. He informed the General, that in a way, it was Alex asking for their help. After a moment of thought, Wigmore agreed but only if Susan volunteered with no pressure and that she knew the risk.

As soon as the phone call was over Ted called Susan into his office along with Jack. He carefully laid out what they were thinking and what she would be doing if she were to accept the mission. Susan did not hesitate, just as Ted had predicted. She was excited to do something besides looking at computer screens. Jack informed Susan that she must play the part of a housekeeper with a convincing demeanor. Susan informed both men that it would not be difficult since she was a housekeeper at home much of the time. Jack and Ted laughed and told her that they were glad that she accepted and were confident she would be fine. Ted told her that he would take her to meet Alex later and that she would need an overnight bag.

***

Sarah and Alex stayed in bed late enjoying each other's company. Sarah tried to hide her worry but Alex could see it in her eyes, even without hearing her thoughts. He tried to reassure her that everything would be alright. His father had trained him well for just such a day, just as every generation before him had been trained. He told Sarah it was not so much his strength as a wizard that counted, but his knowledge of the land and knowing the weakness of his opponent. He reminded her that Rhyfel's first mistake was to think that Tarian the dragon would not be a threat.

"How will Tarian know you need his help?" Sarah asked.

297

"One of those ornaments you saw on the wall in my office is an Ancient Dragons Horn," Alex replied. "The horn was converted into one that can be blown in times of need. I will be taking it with me. All I need to do is blow it and Tarian will hear it from where ever he is and come."

Sarah smiled. Perhaps she did worry too much.

"I think we best get up," Alex said. "I have much to do today and your father will be around soon, I am sure. Better put the coffee on for him."

Sarah laughed as she jumped out of bed and raced to the bathroom to be the first one in.

"There are more of them in this house!" Alex shouted and laughed as he passed the door on his way out of the room.

No sooner had Alex and Sarah finished eating breakfast than Ted arrived. Ted walked straight into the house with Susan and into the kitchen.

"Good morning, everyone," Ted said to Sarah and Alex. "I would like you to meet Major Susan Green. Alex's new stand-in housekeeper."

"Aloha," Alex said. "Please help yourself to some coffee."

"Hi," Sarah followed up handing Susan and her father a cup of coffee. "I am Sarah. Glad to meet you."

"It's my honor," Susan answered. "Thank you both."

"Sarah will show you around," Alex said to Susan as he was packing a backpack. "I must get to the USGS and do what I suggested last night. But first I must stop on the way and cause an earthquake."

Sarah smiled but Ted looked at him concerned.

"Are you serious?" asked Ted.

"Yes, I am," replied Alex. "Don't worry it will be a small one but it will make my report more convincing."

"I don't want to know anymore," Ted replied. "I am sure you know what you're doing."

Alex completed loading his backpack, took his staff from the case in the lounge, kissed Sarah, and headed out the door.

Alex left his house, entered the park, and took the first left after the entrance station heading down Crater Rim Drive. Where the road turns into Chain of Craters Road, Alex got out and unlock a barricade that blocked the road. Passed through and locked the gate behind him.

This road had been closed some years back when a gas eruption in the main crater made it a danger to visitors. That same gas eruption had now become the lava lake within the same crater.

Alex continued to the next barricade and unlock that one. He was now on the main floor of the caldera not far from Halema'uma'u crater. Alex stopped his Jeep a short distance from the old parking area near the edge of the crater. He knew that his Jeep would have already been spotted by park rangers and they would have identified it as his. Knowing he worked for the USGS they would know he is permitted to be there. Alex exited his Jeep and retrieved from the back a case with instruments for collecting gas, and of course his staff. He always took his staff into the field with him. To everyone else, it was his fancy walking stick.

He walked several hundred yards from the road onto the caldera floor. Open his case, and if anyone had been watching, would appear to be taking samples from a fumarole venting gas.

He then took out a small book from his pocket. Taking his staff, he placed it into the fumarole. He read aloud a spell from the book and shook his staff. He quickly removed the staff from the hole and almost immediately the earth shook. It shook strongest where he was of course and almost knocked him off balance. This would be registered as a 3.0 on the Richter scale. Strong enough to be felt but not to do any real damage. To him, it wasn't how strong that mattered. It was the location. Being within the caldera to the scientist at USGS would mean changes were happening within the heart of the volcano. This is what he wanted.

After creating the quake, he immediately went back to his Jeep and continued driving until he reached the USGS headquarters next to the Jagger Museum.

He went straight into the office of the lead scientist, Matt Jefferson. Matt stood up and reached out his hand. Alex shook it.

"Hope you had a great vacation?" Matt said. "Good to have you back. Seems it was just in time. What do you think?"

"I have been monitoring this for a while via my computer," Alex replied. "And I was just out in the field when this latest one hit. Two in as many days right here on the summit and the increase in gas emissions could mean only one thing. A possible change in the eruption pattern."

They were both sitting down now and were joined by another scientist. Thomas Alan.

"What kind of change?" asked Thomas.

"My gut tells me that we could be looking at another summit outbreak," Alex said. "The problem is it could be anywhere here on the summit."

"I must admit you do have good instincts," Matt replied looking at Alex. "You did predict the one at the base of Puu O'O and the rise of the lava lake."

Of course, Alex, being who he was could always tell when the earth made changes within it. The fairies always knew along with Tarian ahead of an eruption when a new one would begin.

"What do you think Thomas?" asked Matt.

"All we can do is alert the park officials," replied Thomas. "Can't tell them to do anything. But I can make a good case. Perhaps we should recommend closing the summit area for a couple of days. Give us more time to assess the situation."

"I think that would be a good call," Alex responded. "Tell them to start tomorrow so as not to create a panic."

"As I said," Thomas replied. "All I can do is recommend it. The rest is up to them. I will call the Park super and meet with him today."

"Good," Matt said. "I will write up an official report for you to take with you."

"I will go back to my house and load the information into my computer," Alex interjected. "Will get back to you if I see anything else."

"Thanks," Matts said to Alex as he stood up. "Good to have you back. See you later then."

"Yes," Alex replied. "I will get back to you as soon as I have something new."

Alex left the office and got in his Jeep to return home. He had never created an earthquake before. He did not like the idea of deceiving his colleagues but he knew this was for the safety of people that had nothing to do with his life. Only one thing more he would have to do before the battle he knew was coming. He would do that early in the morning. That would be to call down a fog into the caldera. It was not uncommon for a fog to fill the caldera for days. The only thing he would do differently was to make the fog hover just above the caldera floor so he could see around him better.

***

It was late afternoon by the time Alex got back to his home. Ted, Sarah, and Susan were waiting for him.

"Was that quake you?" Ted asked as soon as he saw Alex.

"Yes, am afraid it was," Alex answered. "It was the first one I have ever done. It's not wise to mess with the forces of nature unless there is a good reason. The earth spirits become restless when you do. But I do believe it has done what I have hoped."

"What now?" asked Sarah.

"I must prepare myself," Alex replied. "Please, the rest of you make yourself at home. I must meditate, read some old text, and prepare some items. I will have to focus, so I must have a clear mind."

"Do you want dinner?" Sarah asked worriedly. "What can I do to help?"

"Dinner would be great. If you could see that Susan is settled into the guest room. Choose whatever dinner you like and maybe you could get the others to help you. I would be most grateful, Love. Call me when it's ready I will be in my study."

Alex hugged and kissed Sarah and departed for his library. Sarah took charge and got her father and Susan busy making dinner. She decided on grilled pork chops, baked potatoes, baked beans, and green salad. For dessert, she would make Alex's favorite pineapple upside-down cake.

In the library, Alex pulled down some old books. He wanted to brush up on what would be the best protection amulet to wear and what kind of spell he needs to cast onto it. After some study, he went to a small safe hidden behind some fake books on the wall near his desk and opened it. He took out a case that contained several different amulets. Most were different types of crystals. Others were gold or silver medallions with symbols on them. Alex chose one with an amethyst wired within a silver cage. It hung on a simple-looking cord. But if one examined it, they would find the cord was made of human hair. Alex did not know whose hair it was, but it could have been from several of his ancestors. Alex was aware this was the same type of crystal that Merlin had in his staff and is now in the royal scepter of England that started this whole ordeal.

Alex then took out a black velvet cloth from one of his desk drawers and placed it on the top of the desk. The cloth had a golden seven-pointed fairy star embroidered on it. Placing the amulet on the cloth, Alex took one of the books he had pulled down earlier and flipped to a page he had marked. Standing, he extended both his hands over the amulet and recited a spell of protection over it in Latin. Nothing visibly happened but Alex knew that it was now charged with the magic he wanted. He carefully wrapped it up in the cloth and placed it on the case containing his wands. He would choose which wand he would take in the morning just before he left.

Alex next knew he must make a Hookupu. This was a Hawaiian blessing gift to be offered to Pele, the fire goddess whose home is in the volcano. To make the offering, Alex made a dash outside before it got dark. There he gathered a bunch of Ti leaves from the edge of the forest. He then gathered a cluster of orchid blossoms from his garden. Next, he cut some Ohia blossoms from a tree that was blooming near his driveway.

He hurried back into the house and to his library to put the offering together. On his way back in he could hear Sarah, her father, and Susan chatting in the kitchen.

Once in the library Alex took out a small folding table from behind one of his chairs and set it up in the middle of the room. It was on this he would assemble his offering.

First, he placed several of the bright green Ti leaves in the middle of the table forming a multiple-pointed star shape. He then took the orchid blossoms that filled his cupped hands and raising them to his face he breathed on them. With this action, he breathed his mana, life force, into them. He then placed the blossoms in the center of the leaves. Carefully he gathered the leaves up into a bunch at the top enclosing the blossoms inside. He then tied these together with some cotton string, securing it well. He then took some more sting and tied the Ohia blossoms around the neck of the offering. It was now complete. He knew that what was in the offering was secondary to the intention. He knew that in Hawaii it was always important to bring such an offering upon entering a sacred place.

Once he had completed constructing the offering, he went to his computer to check the National Park website for any updates. Just as he had hoped, there was a notice that the area around the Caldara was closed to visitors the next day until further notice. The park would remain open but visitors would only be allowed in the visitor center and down the chain of craters road. The Volcano House Hotel house was to remain open but he knew it was far enough away from the main crater to not be in any danger.

His plan was to lure Rhyfel to an area just off the crater rim drive just west of the Halemaumau crater. This area was about two miles from the Volcano House Hotel. It was also about one and a half miles from the USGS building, located on the opposite side of the caldera.

He had just shut down his computer when Sarah knocked on the door of the library letting him know that dinner was ready.

Alex answered the door to find Sarah waiting for him When he saw her, he took her in his arms, hugged her tightly, and kissed her. He could smell the aroma of the cake baking in the oven.

"Thank you," he whispered in her ear. "Thank you for being here, thank you for being in my life but, most of all, thank you for loving me."

Sarah smiled at him and kissed him back. She took him by the hand and led him to the dining area.

They all enjoyed the meal that had been so wonderfully prepared. As they ate, they talked about all manner of things but avoided any conversation about the upcoming day. Sarah even took the moment to announce that they would be having the wedding very soon and it was going to take place right there at Alex's house. This began a conversation between Susan and Sarah about flowers and a separate conversation between Ted and Alex about what kind of food to prepare.

Alex was most pleased with the cake that Sarah had made and served along with some vanilla ice cream that was always kept in the freezer. It was the first time she had ever made such a cake and it turned out beautiful.

While Alex was enjoying his cake, he thought to himself, though he was confident, that if something went wrong this could be his last proper meal. He also wondered about Rhyfel. What must he be doing? He even wondered if Rhyfel even considered the real danger of what could happen. He hoped in his heart that Rhyfel would see reason and seek another way to sort things out.

After dinner, Sarah gathered her things together to go with her father to the SGM headquarters. Though she knew it was the best thing to do, she did not want to go. Ted shook Alex's hand and wished him the best. He then picked up Sarah's case and headed to his car. Susan made herself scarce into the guest room that had been made ready for her.

Alex and Sarah stood just inside the front door. They were embraced in a tight hug and kiss. Tears were now flowing down from Sarah's eyes. Alex reached up and dried them with his hands the best he could.

"Don't you worry," Alex said trying to reassure her. "Everything will be ok. I not only have all the teaching of my parents, and the countless ancestors looking over me, but I have the most powerful magic of all as my weapon. Your love for me and my love for you. With that, I am the most powerful wizard in the world."

Sarah smiled and laughed through her tears.

"I love you so much," Sarah said, as a new flood of tears came out.

She hugged him tightly as she could. Alex pushed her back a bit and looked into her eyes.

"Now remember," he said. "Do not come over here, do not go to the park, no matter what you hear. You stay with your father. When it is over, I will come for you there. Do you understand?"

Sarah nodded. She then kissed him one more time and headed for the car where her father was waiting. She did not look back. In her mind, she decided to go about this as if it were any other short trip. She thought if she looked back it would be a final look forever. If she didn't, it would cast a spell that would make sure he returned.

Alex watched as they drove out of the drive. He then went inside to put on a jacket. He left the house and went to the stone circle to meditate. His mind now shifted to the task ahead. He must now become what he was born into. The House of Merlin!

Chapter 36

Line of Fire

The next morning Alex rose well before sunrise. Perhaps sleeping in his childhood room made him feel rested and alert even though he had gone to bed late. His first thoughts were of Sarah and wondered how her night had been. Even though he had slept alone all his life it seemed strange now to be sleeping without someone next to him. It was far too early to call her, so he focused on getting dressed for the day ahead.

Susan heard him rustling about so she got up and went to the kitchen to prepare coffee.

Alex's next thing was to collect all he thought he would need for the day ahead and take them to his Jeep.

The first thing he did was to put on the amulet he prepared the night before and choose a wand. He chose an oak wand with a clear quartz crystal tip to take with him. This was one of his most powerful wands. He put a sheath on his belt to carry it. All his wands had sheaths so they could be worn like daggers fastened to his belt.

Next, he took down the dragon horn from the wall in his library and packed it in his backpack. After that, he went to his closet and took out a long black cloak with a dark blue lining. This would make him harder to see against the black lava rock. The cloak also held magical powers of protection. His great-great-grandmother had made the cloak for her husband many years ago.

One of the most important things he was taking was the offering to Pele he had prepared the night before. He knew without the protection of the ancestors and the Gods of nature he would be very much alone.

Finally, he went to the special case in the living room and got his staff. This was the most powerful tool he possessed. This staff had been passed down through countless generations from one wizard to the next. No one in his family even really knew how old the staff was.

He now had all he needed except his morning coffee.

Susan not only made him coffee but also made scrambled eggs and toast. For this Alex was very grateful.

As he sat eating, he reached into his pocket a pulled out a small slip of paper.

"I know you must have been wondering how you were going to direct Rhyfel to me when he arrives," Alex said to Susan while she drank her coffee. "This piece of paper tells where I will be. You will know what the numbers on it mean when you see them. But I would like you to play as if you don't know when Rhyfel asked where I am and hand it to him. Tell him I am working. I don't want him to smell a trap."

Alex handed the paper to Susan. She looked at it and knew, just as he said, what the numbers were.

The numbers on the paper read; 19° 24' N, 155° 16' W.

"You must not hand them directly to him when he asked where I am." Alex said. "He must be convinced that I am not waiting for him."

"I understand completely sir," answered Susan. "I will handle it."

"I am sure you will," Alex said smiling. "You can call me Alex. I want to say thank you for doing this. I am very grateful."

Alex got up from the table, handed the house keys to Susan, shook her hand, and headed out the door for his Jeep.

As Susan saw him drive away, she hoped deeply that he would be alright.

Alex left his house at around 4 am. It was a 15-minute drive from his house to where he was going to park his jeep at the devastation trailhead. From there it was a two-mile hike to where Alex planned to leave his offering to Pele. With sunrise at around 6 am this would give him enough time to be where he planned well before Rhyfel would find him.

The one thing Alex did not have to do was call down a fog into the crater. There was a heavy fog already in the crater when he arrived.

As he hiked closer to the Halemaumau crater from where he had parked, he could see the fog being lit up by a red glow from the lava lake within it. This site was one Alex had seen many times and never tired of it.

When he reached the edge of the crater, he peered over the cliff to watch the lava lake below. The sound of the lake crackling and hissing echoed off the crater walls was filling the air. The huge lava lake moved from one edge to the other with the grace of a hula dancer. The surface looked like a patchwork of shifting floating scales. To the wizard side of him, it reminded Alex of dragon scales. The scientist side of him saw it as a mini-scale of the earth's great tectonic plates.

After watching the lake for a while, he took the offering from his backpack and placed it at the edge of the crater. Sitting down in the lotus position, he stretched his hands out toward the lava lake.

"Pele-honua-mea," Alex called out. "I bring this offering to you as I have entered your sacred place. I respect you and ask permission to be here. I am humbled at the work you are doing before me. I thank you for your power in this place. Please accept this offering as my gratitude."

Alex sat silent for many minutes with his arms remaining outstretched. He could now see the light of the day penetrating the fog. Alex finally stood and walked about 500 yards north from the edge of the crater and found a large rock to sit on. Here he would wait for Rhyfel.

***

At 6 am sharp at Alex's house Susan heard a knock at the door from the kitchen where she had just finished eating her breakfast. She looked at her watch and knew who it would be. She took in a deep breath and headed for the front door.

When she opened the door, the man before her looked more terrifying than she imagined. Rhyfel stood close to the door dressed the same way he had appeared on New Year's Eve at the Tower of London. Susan did not have a chance to speak before he did.

"Who might you be?" asked Rhyfel in a growling voice.

"I am the housekeeper," Susan managed to answer quickly. "May I ask who is calling?"

"Where is your master?" Rhyfel growled again.

"He is not my master, sir," Susan snapped back. "He is my employer and he is not here, he is working."

"Where can I find him?" Rhyfel asked again, in a more subdued voice this time. "I need to speak to him. It is very important I do so. It is a personal matter."

Susan saw this as her chance to give the information Alex had left her.

"If you could just wait here, sir," Susan said. "Mr. Michaels did leave a note in case someone needed to reach him."

Susan gently closed the door and walked to the middle of the main hall making sure her steps could be heard. She reached into her pocket and took out a copy of the note Alex had given her. She returned to the door and opened it.

"I wrote this down," Susan said as she handed the note to Rhyfel. "They are just numbers to me but he told me if someone needed him urgently, they would understand them and be able to find him. I would call him but he told me that where he would be there is no cell service. It is all I have sir; I hope it is enough otherwise you will have to come back another time."

Rhyfel looked at the note and read the numbers on it. He knew at once what they were. He smiled and thought to himself, that this would be what a true geologist would do.

"Yes, this will do perfectly," Rhyfel answered in a more pleasant tone. "Thank you."

Rhyfel turned and headed to his car. Susan watched as he drove out of the drive. She felt relieved when the car was out of sight.

Closing the door and said to herself out loud, "I need more coffee."

***

Once Rhyfel had pulled out of the drive to Alex's house, he pulled over to the side of the road. Ambrose was close by in a separate car and pulled up close to behind him when he stopped.

Rhyfel was putting the coordinates into his GPS device when Ambrose knocked on his window.

"Everything alright Master Rhyfel," asked Ambrose once Rhyfel rolled down the window.

"Everything is fine," replied Rhyfel. "He is not at his house but I did get his location from his housekeeper. It appears that he is in the crater someplace not far from where we were when we were tracking the Dragon."

"Are you sure you want to continue this now?" asked Ambrose concerned. "The fog is very thick. This is his home turf and, if you can't see, how will you challenge him."

"I will handle this just fine," Rhyfel retorted back. "It may give me an advantage. He will not see me coming. You just stay out of sight and danger. Maybe you can find a spell that can lift this fog once I get there. Call Lady Selma, she might know one."

"Yes of course Master," Ambrose answered. "I will do my best. Be safe and may the Gods protect you."

Rhyfel closed his window and headed off to the nearest place he could park to get to Alex's location. According to the map, it would be the same parking area as the one Alex was parked in.

When he arrived at the parking area, he noticed the locked barrier on the old Crater Rim Drive. Rhyfel checked the map on his GPS carefully. He realized that that road led to almost the location of the coordinates. If he took that road, he could avoid hiking almost 2 miles.

Rhyfel got out of his car and went to the barricade. Taking out one of his daggers and pointed it at the lock. It opened instantly. He opened the gate and drove through. He didn't even bother to close it behind him.

After about a mile he came to a second barrier. He got out of his car to do the same to that one when he saw Ambrose's car approach from behind. He unlocked the barrier and went to Ambrose's car, which had now stopped and he had gotten out.

"Go back," Rhyfel snapped, "This is far too close. I want you to go back to the parking area where I came through the barrier. Use your GPS map and find a place to watch from there. Do you understand? You can cast a spell from back there. I don't want two cars down here. He will surely become spooked. And close the gates behind you when you go out. I don't want anyone else following."

Ambrose did not respond. He waited for Rhyfel to go through the barrier and closed it behind him. He then turned his car around and head back out as he had been instructed.

Rhyfel continued for about another half a mile to a pullover on the road. His GPS said it put him about 500 yards from the location he had been given. He knew Alex must be close by. The fog was still heavy and he couldn't see more than 100 yards in any direction. He decided to stay with his car and hope Ambrose would cast a spell to lift this fog.

***

Ambrose returned to the parking area Rhyfel had told him to. There was a Jeep already parked there. He did not know who it belonged to but decided to park on the opposite side of the parking lot from it. He was checking the maps when his phone rang. It was Selma. He had phoned her earlier asking if she knew a fog-lifting spell.

"What did you find?" Ambrose asked when he answered.

"I'm sorry but nothing really," Selma answered. "I found a couple in the books I brought to cause fog but not any to banish it. I would say reverse it but you don't have what is needed to do even that. You would need some candles, some ashes from a local tree, and rainwater. I would say no, I have nothing you can use, sorry."

"It's ok dear," he replied. "You did your best. Sad thing is that I can't even call Master Rhyfel because where he is there is no cell service."

"He is always rushing into things."

"I know, I know. All I can do is wait it out. Don't worry I am safe. I will see you later no matter what. Bye for now."

Ambrose ended the call and went back to looking at his maps. He did see a place he would get a good vantage point if the fog did lift. It was less than a half-mile hike from his car. It was on top of a massive cinder cone called Pu'upua'i. It was in a restricted area but that made no difference to him. He got out, locked the car, and headed off.

***

Alex sat resting on a rock meditating. In his state of meditation, he could sense that Rhyfel was nearby. He just sat still waiting for Rhyfel to make the first move.

After a short while of sensing that Rhyfel was not moving, he realized he must be waiting for the fog to lift.

Alex reached into his backpack and took out two small jars and a white candle. Lighting the candle, he stood up. One of the jars was full of ashes from his fireplace. Moving in a counterclockwise direction, he poured the ashes out around him in a circle. He did the same with the other jar that contained rainwater. Reciting from memory he spoke.

"Mist of earth, clouds from the sky, ascend above me is my cry. Gently lift above the ground so that I may see what is around. Rise not too high into the air, make the weather in that space most fair. Grant this oh winds at my command, to be here now above this land. As I have spoken, let it be so."

Alex extended his staff and made a sweeping circular motion in a counterclockwise circle.

He sat back down and waited. Within moments, the fog began to lift. The area of about 20 feet above the ground became completely clear. At about that height the fog stopped moving upward. Where he was now would be like walking under a low-hanging cloud.

From his position, he could now clearly see Rhyfel's car. He remained seated and took out a bottle of water from his backpack. He then slowly reached again into his backpack and removed the dragon horn and laid it on the ground next to him.

Looking back at Rhyfel's car he could see he was now getting out and looking around.

Once Rhyfel saw the fog lift above the ground he got out of his car and looked in the direction the GPS said Alex should be. He was not sure if the fog had lifted on its own or if Ambrose had done it. At this point, it didn't matter.

After a moment next to his car scanning the landscape, he saw a person whom he believed to be his target. Gathering himself together he headed in their direction.

After walking about 150 yards toward his subject, who was now standing, he could now see it was a man about the height of himself and wearing a black cloak. And holding a staff with a large clear crystal on top. He was now sure it was Alexander. He moved another 200 yards closer and stopped. If this Alex was working, Rhyfel thought, he was dressed strangely for it. It was at that moment he realized that perhaps he had been set up. It was too late to back down now.

"Wizard Alexander I assume!" Rhyfel shouted.

"There is no need to assume," replied Alex. "I am he."

Rhyfel now moved closer and slowly took out one of his daggers as he walked. Soon he was close enough to see his face and would no longer need to shout.

"You know why I am here?" Rhyfel said knowing full well that he must.

"What you seek is not here," Alex replied. "I don't mean here with me. I mean on this island. It never has been."

"Do you expect me to believe that?" responded Rhyfel. "And do what? Just say sorry to bother you and walk away?"

"What you do is your choice," Alex said. "I speak the truth. What you believe is also your choice. Whatever injustice you believe my family has caused yours, you will not find the answer to that here. I wish you no harm or any of your family. But it is your choice to believe my words or not."

"I choose to believe that you would do and say anything to protect what you believe is rightfully yours," replied Rhyfel with a deep growl. "This leaves the choice to you to hand over the Jewel to me and avoid any further confrontation. If not, you shall be in my line of fire. I am sure we can come to an arrangement to hand it over."

"I have told you the truth already," Alex repeated. "I do not have the Jewel. I, nor any of my family on this island, have ever had it. I cannot give you what I do not have."

Alex sensed Rhyfel's anger rising so he slowly bent down and picked up the dragon horn and hung it around his waist behind his cloak, all the while keeping his staff in his other hand and his eyes on the sorcerer in front of him.

"I did not come all this way to walk away from this based on your lies," Rhyfel responded with a tone of anger. "I swear by the Gods that protect me, if necessary, I will destroy you and then will dismantle your house one stick at a time until I find it."

Alex knew, just as he had predicted, that Rhyfel would not back down. Though Alex could have struck first he had decided during his meditation he would not. He would defend himself. He knew that because Rhyfel had no roots in the land there, he would grow weaker the more he fought. Alex only needed to hold his defense, so he remained quiet.

Rhyfel's rage was now getting the better of him. He reached back and took out his second dagger and, in a flash, a stream of red magical energy flowed out the ends of both his daggers directly at Alex.

The fire from Rhyfel's daggers struck a ball shield that surrounded Alex and lit it up.

The battle had now begun.

Chapter 37

Battle on the Edge

After the first blast from Rhyfel's daggers, Alex knew he must maintain the defensive shield around himself. He slowly shifted position but did not strike back.

Rhyfel swirled his daggers and sent a second blast toward Alex. It too was deflected by Alex's energy shield. Rhyfel fired a third and forth with the same results.

Alex could feel the energy in each blast. He expected it to feel weaker, but to his surprise, he did not.

Rhyfel swirled his daggers again but this time Alex noticed it was different. One dagger went in one direction and the other in the opposite. Suddenly a whirlwind of rocks lifted into the air above Alex and then stopped. The rocks came crashing down toward him.

Alex pulled out his wand and deflected them away just before they rained down upon him. Just as he was distracted deflecting the rocks, Rhyfel sent a blast of wind across the ground hitting his legs and knocking Alex off balance. Alex just missed being crushed under the rain of rocks.

Alex jumped back to his feet still holding his staff in one hand and his wand in the other. This gave Alex a rude awakening. He now realized that Rhyfel's magic was far more powerful than he imagined. Alex's father had taught him to be defensive, never offensive. He knew he was going to need help.

Putting his wand away, he reached to his back under his cloak and pulled out the dragon horn. Taking his staff, he created a wall of fire between himself and Rhyfel. He then blew long and hard on the horn. The sound it made was something between an elephant's call and a deep loud roar. The sound echoed off the walls of the caldera all around. Alex repeated the call with the horn a second time. He could hear Rhyfel laughing on the other side of the flaming wall that was now dying down. Using his staff, Alex kept the wall of fire going to buy time as he thought through how to deal with the powerful sorcerer he now faced.

***

Ambrose was on top of the red cinder hill of Pu'upua'i when he heard the dragon horn. He had never heard one before but his instincts told him what it was. Within a couple of minutes of hearing the horn, he heard a rushing sound behind him. Looking around he saw the huge dark shadow of a dragon flying directly over his head. One of his wingtips nearly clipped him as he flew over. He now knew that Rhyfel had not been as successful as he had hoped in sealing the dragon in his lair.

***

Below, on the caldera floor, Alex was continuing to maintain the wall of fire as he slowly moved from where he had been to a position closer to the edge of Halemaumau crater.

Through the flames, Alex could see Rhyfel now crouching down swinging his daggers in a circle to dance around him. He suddenly stood up and swung his arms across each other holding his daggers straight out.

A massive rush of air followed. It was so powerful it nearly blew Alex to the ground. It also blew out Alex's wall of fire as it swept further afield. The force was so strong it blew the fog completely out of the crater.

Just as the fog cleared, Rhyfel saw the dragon descending directly toward him.

Tarian released a torrent of flames from his mouth as he passed just above Rhyfel's head. Rhyfel had seen him just in time to shield himself with a ball of energy.

Tarian swung around and landed near where Alex was standing relieved to see his old friend.

"You should have taken a geology course before you tried to seal my friend in his cave," Alex shouted to Rhyfel with a chuckle.

Rhyfel was not amused by the comment.

"You should have been better prepared to take me on," Rhyfel shouted in reply.

Tarian breathed in and released another round of flames at Rhyfel, which he again deflected away. Rhyfel reached around under his cloak and pulled out something no one could have imagined. It was a handheld grenade launcher. He pointed it directly at Tarian.

"Fly Tarian, fly!" Alex shouted when he saw it.

Rhyfel fired it at the same moment Tarian began to lift off. The grenade went off just above Tartan's left-wing filling it full of small holes. But his wing had shielded Alex from any shrapnel that might have hit him.

Tarian headed off toward Pu'upua'i where Ambrose was now able to see everything that was going on below him. Tarian had smelled Ambrose's Morgan blood when he flew over him the first time. He now made a beeline straight for him. Charging his throat with fire he blasted directly at Ambrose on top of the hill. Ambrose saw him coming. Just as the flames shot out, he dove to the ground and rolled down the hill. When he finally stopped rolling, he got up and ran faster than he ever had back to where his car was parked.

Tarian whirled around and came to rest on the top of the same hill letting out a loud roar as he touched down.

Rhyfel now began another tactic. He started forming balls of intense energy, forcing them into the ground causing shallow but intense earthquakes. Cracks began to open on the caldera floor. Rocks also began breaking off from the cliffs around the edge of the crater with some hitting the lava lake creating gas release explosions. Seeing this, Alex knew he must do something.

"Rhyfel!" shouted Alex. "Please stop this and listen to me!"

Rhyfel stopped to listen hoping Alex was going to tell him he would be turning over the Jewel.

"What I told you before was the truth," Alex continued. "Hear me out. I only found out a few days ago that you and the Order of Divine Right were even looking for the Jewel. I thought everyone was looking for me as a person. That did confuse me because I did not know how finding me would benefit the ODR. Knowing my family here never had the Jewel, I did some research to find out where it might be. What I discovered was a manuscript dating back to Merlin that made it clear that the Jewel could never leave Britain or it would lose its power. The dragon confirmed this the same day you tried to seal him in his lair. You know as well as I that dragons cannot lie. My ancestors must have known this as well and hid the Jewel someplace in Britain. I have no idea where it was hidden or who hid it. That is all the truth as I know it. That's all I can tell you because it is all I know."

Rhyfel stood silent, thinking about what Alex just told him. As he thought about it, it made sense. That meant all he would have to do is go back to England and resume the search there. If he could find Alex here in Hawaii, then how hard could it be to pick up the trail of his ancestors back in England?

"What you said makes sense and I believe you," yelled Rhyfel back. "There is still one problem."

Alex felt hope that this battle would end.

"What is that?" Alex called back in reply.

"You," Rhyfel said with a determined tone. "You are the problem. Your family has always been the problem. From what I have learned, you are the last of Merlin's cursed line. If what you say is true then you will make it your mission not to allow me to find it as will your precious SGM. The way I see it I can end this right here and now. I can, at last, do what should have been done long ago. Wipe your line from the earth once and for all. The curse of Arthur's return will finally be over. I will finish this here. I will bring the revenge of every Morgan down on your head and bury Merlin's blood here on this island. I will be able to walk into the Jewel house in London and take what is rightfully ours and no one will be able to stop us. You will not be able to defeat me. I do not need roots in the land to draw power from like you do. I have generation after generation of Morgans living within me. We have kept our line pure. Unlike you, whose blood is contaminated by outsiders.

I met one of our own impure just the other day. Her mother bred with an outsider and produced offspring a fraction of what she could be. It's a shame, really, but those like her should be banned from the family and be destroyed just as you are about to be."

Alex was shocked by what he was hearing. He was sure it was Sarah he was talking about. As Rhyfel spoke he could hear the determination rise in his voice. Alex knew he believed and meant every word. He now realized his life, and Sarah's, were in real danger. For the first time in a long-time anger swelled inside him. He was angry when his parents died but this anger exceeded that by far.

"Noooo!!" Alex cried with a loud voice as he slammed his staff on the ground and shot a stream of blue energy from its crystal at Rhyfel.

The blast was so powerful it knocked Rhyfel backward onto the ground. As Rhyfel sprang back to his feet Alex hit him with another blast pushing him back even further. He now had a plan. He would keep driving him backward until he pushed him over the edge of the crater and into the lava lake.

Alex got off two more blasts before Rhyfel made it securely to his feet and returned a blast from his daggers knocking Alex back a short distance. Alex again returned a blast again and again. Each time it was more powerful than the last. Rhyfel remained on his feet but kept retreating backward before he returned a blast of his own.

Rhyfel was now only a few feet from the edge of the crater. Alex grabbed the dragon horn and gave a blow. He hoped with Tarian's help he could push him over.

Alex fired another blast which was met this time by one at the same moment from Rhyfel. Rhyfel tried to push it back toward Alex as Alex did the same to his. They pushed against each other with all their energy. Neither one moved nor gave way. Where the two beams of energy met the glow was so intense neither of them could look directly at it. The rocks on the ground under the meeting point were turning red with the heat.

Rhyfel saw the dragon heading across the crater toward him. He stopped his attack on Alex and rolled to the ground causing Alex's energy blast to pass over him. Alex fell back at the release.

Rhyfel stayed on the ground as the dragon headed toward him. He reached under his cloak again and this time pulled out a flash grenade. Just as Tarian was about to breathe out his fire, Rhyfel threw the grenade at his mouth and covered his own head with his cloak. When Tarian's fire hit the grenade, a huge blast went off hurling Tarian backward in the sky. Tarian wailed out in pain, and whirled back but maintained his flight. The blast had blinded him. It would not be permanent but he would not be able to strike again for a while so he flew up high to glide until his sight cleared.

"You bastard!!" Alex called out when he heard Tarian wail in pain.

Alex fired off another blast but this time Rhyfel, now on his feet, deflected it back knocking Alex backward.

Rhyfel was looking into the lava lake below when Alex regained his footing.

Rhyfel shot a single dagger blast back at Alex and at the same time he pointed the other one into the lava lake making a swirling motion. At the same moment Alex deflected the blast, Rhyfel engaged his second dagger in the action toward the lava.

What Alex saw next brought a burst of terror into his heart. Rhyfel rose a tornado of lava from the lava lake below, and before Alex had a chance to send another blast to stop him, the lava came directly at him. Alex moved out of its path and put up the strongest shield he had ever created to deflect it. The whole torrent of lava landed on the ground like a great tree falling just feet from him. The lava splashed in every direction. Fortunately, Alex's shield held.

As Rhyfel stood admiring his work Alex took out his wand and shot a small but focused beam at Rhyfel's left hand knocking the dagger from it, and sending it careening over the edge of the crater into the lava lake below.

Rhyfel quickly reach into his boot and retrieved a spare. He then looked up at the sky where Tarian was still circling. He began swirling both daggers in his direction as if he was going to try to knock him out of the sky. Alex focused his attention on Tarian when Rhyfel suddenly swirled his daggers at the ground and in an instant created a whirlwind filled with rocks and boulders that sent them high into the air above Alex.

It was too late when Alex realized that Rhyfel's focus on Tarian had been a diversion. The rocks began to fall like rain. As Alex was creating a shield, Rhyfel hit him with a blast of energy that knocked him to the ground. Alex managed to get a shield up but not before a large rock landed on his left leg crushing his ankle. He let out a cry of pain as he reached for his foot letting go of his staff. Rhyfel send another small blast and knocked Alex's staff out of his reach.

"You and your line end now!" snarled Rhyfel as he walked along the edge of the crater toward Alex to finish him off.

Circles in Stone

As he passed by the offering that Alex had left to Pele, he kicked it into the crater like a football, and watched until it hit the lava lake below.

He began to walk again toward Alex when a huge earthquake shook the whole mountain almost knocking Rhyfel to the ground. Alex knew this was not something they had done. This was someplace much further away. When the ground had stopped shaking Alex and Rhyfel both heard a loud rushing sound. Rhyfel turned to look at the lava lake below only to see it draining away like water in a bathtub. He watched in amazement for a while and then continued toward Alex who was starting to crawl toward his staff.

"Oh no!" snarled Rhyfel. "It seems the lava is draining away and now your family line is going to do the same."

Rhyfel had both of his daggers pointed at Alex when a sudden flash of white light shot out of the crater where the lava lake had been. It blinded them both for a moment as it ascended high into the sky. It then stopped and descended just as fast.

Alex had heard about this from old Hawaiian stories. It only occurred just before a large eruption. Most scientists brushed it off as a myth. The Hawaiians said it was the goddess Pele on the move.

When the ball of light vanished below the rim of the crater Alex knew what was coming next. He began to crawl in earnest toward his staff.

Rhyfel stood transfixed for a moment trying to decide what he should do. He then decided he must not allow Alex to escape and headed toward him again.

Just as he took his second step, he heard a roar like nothing he had ever heard before coming from the crater. The earth under him began to shake violently. The roar behind him now was combined with a rushing sound so loud that he covered his ears. The ground shook again knocking him down. He quickly got to his feet only to notice that a 6-foot-wide crack had opened in front of him. He ran to jump over the crack but another violent shake and huge roar knocked him down before he could reach it. He turned to look behind him to see a massive column of ash, smoke, and rock rushing high into the sky. He managed to scramble to the crack only to discover it was now more than 10 feet wide. He looked back toward the crater to see the ever-growing column rising even higher. Looking around he realized he was on a large piece of the crater wall that was now separated from the main caldera floor on all sides.

Alex had now reached his staff and struggled to his feet using it as a crutch. His main goal now was to try to put as much distance between himself and the erupting crater. He could now see the situation that Rhyfel was in. Though a part of him wanted to try to rescue him he knew it would not be possible.

Every time Rhyfel tried to get to his feet the ground beneath him would shake or move knocking him off balance.

Suddenly the roaring died down. Rhyfel rolled over to see the column of ash and rock coming almost to a standstill. As he looked up at it his blood ran cold. In the giant cloud, he saw the image of a woman with long black hair holding a staff or stick towering over him. Her red glowing eyes were staring straight down at him.

Alex saw the same image from where he was and covered his head with his cloak.

The image held form for what seemed a lifetime to Rhyfel and then dissipated. When it did, the column of rock and ash began to collapse. The ledge of rock that Rhyfel was on began to sink into the crater. He knew his end had come and not as he had expected.

Alex looked up just in time to see Rhyfel sink out of sight into the crater and hear him cry out as the ledge fell.

Alex now continued to move further away, limping along on one foot and his staff. Rocks began falling all around him. He fell to the ground and used what strength he could to create a shield with his staff. He could feel the earth shifting below him. His science told him the caldera was collapsing. All he could do was keep his shield in place and hope for the best.

He suddenly felt something grasp him and lift him into the air. It was Tarian. Somehow, he managed to find him and was carrying him to safety in one of his huge taloned feet.

Alex could hear rocks crashing into the ground below him. The sky had become dark with smoke and ash. His thoughts turned to Sarah hoping the eruption would not put her or her family and friends in danger.

That worry ended when Tarian set him down in the parking area near where he had parked his car and could see that the eruption, for now, was limited to the caldera.

Tarian set himself down there also, and shook hard to clear all the rocks, dust, and ash from his wings.

Ambrose was inside his car when Tarian landed with Alex. He got out and went over to see if perhaps his Master was with them.

Tarian turned to Ambrose, lowered his head, and looked straight into his eyes.

"Your master is gone," Tarian said. "If you were wise enough to listen to this old dragon, I would suggest you leave this island and never return."

Tarian continued to stare at Ambrose until he turned and got into his car and drove away.

Alex managed to get into his Jeep but waited for Tarian to come to him.

"Thank you, my friend," Alex said with tears in his eyes. "How can I ever repay you?"

"You don't have to," replied Tarian. "And you never will. It was a pleasure to finally be of real service after being on this island for so long. It did my soul good to be a part of this day. But now I think I will return to my lair and see if there is anything left of it. Go to Sarah, she will be worried."

"I will," Alex responded as Tarian turned and mounted the air.

Fine ash was falling all around his Jeep as Alex drove out of the parking lot, being careful not to hurt his ankle any more than was necessary to drive.

For a moment, he looked back in his mirror at the still ongoing eruption and his thoughts turned to Rhyfel. Alex had to admit it to himself. Rhyfel had been a powerful sorcerer. If only he had used it for good. How much he could have achieved.

His thoughts quickly shifted to Sarah as he drove up the road that led out of the park.

Chapter 38

The Promise

Because it was Alex's left ankle that had been injured, he could drive without much problem. He was glad the Jeep was an automatic. He managed to call Jack on his private phone to inform him of his condition and that he was on his way to the SGM headquarters. Jack in turn said he would call the National Park Rescue Team to meet him there.

When Alex arrived at the SGM headquarters the rescue team was waiting there. He had seen them pass him on his way back. Also waiting were Sarah, Ted, Jack, and the rest of the staff.

Sarah rushed over to him and as soon as he opened the door of the Jeep, she threw her arms around him and kissed him hitting his ankle in the process. Alex let out a cry of pain while kissing her.

Stepping back, she said sorry and bent down to look at his leg while the rescue team rolled the stretcher over and lifted him on it. One of the team cut his trouser leg open to his knee to get a better look to see if the skin was broken anywhere. No open wounds were visible so they rolled him over to the ambulance to load him in. Sarah followed along his side.

"I'll be alright," Alex told Sarah as they loaded him in.

"We will follow you to the hospital," Ted called out. "Will meet you there."

"Someone needs to check on Susan," Alex called back.

I'll go get her." Jack answered.

Alex gave the thumbs up as they closed the door and the driver began to pull out. Ted and Sarah got into Ted's Jeep and followed close behind.

***

When Ambrose returned to their rented house, Selma ran out to meet him. Looking behind him she was expecting to see Rhyfel's car close behind. Once out of the car, Ambrose reached up with his hands and turned her head so he could look her in the eyes.

"He's gone," Ambrose said with a saddened tone. "Our master is no more."

"Nooo!" Selma cried raising her hand to her face. "How? Where?"

"I don't know. I couldn't see from where I was. The dragon told me."

"The dragon? But I thought...."

"So did I," Ambrose responded knowing what she was about to ask. "I am not sure if Alexander had beaten him, the dragon got him, or if the eruption did. What I do know is that dragons can't lie, so what he told me must be true. The dragon was carrying an injured Alexander when he landed near me. Personally, I think it was the eruption but we will never know. The dragon also said we had better leave and go back to England."

"Then that is what we should do," Selma said through her tears, "You are the head of the family now Lord Ambrose. What you say is what we must do."

"You are my Queen Lady Selma," he replied. "I love you and am so glad you are by my side."

They both went into the house locked arm in arm to prepare to go home.

***

Alex was taken to Hilo hospital and rushed into X-ray as soon as he arrived. By the time he arrived, news of the eruption was everywhere. Reports were now coming in that lava had broken out 24 miles down from the summit in the residential subdivision of Leilani Estates, threatening many homes. This was the same subdivision Alex and Sarah had spent the last days of their tour before going to Alex's home.

When Alex heard this, he now knew the battle between himself and Rhyfel had not caused it. This was much bigger than anything they, even collectively, could have made happen. His thoughts went out to all the people whose homes were now under threat.

The x-rays showed that Alex would need surgery to repair the damage. He would be spending the night in the hospital.

Sarah stayed with him for as long as she could before he went in. She would wait until the surgery was over before she and her father would get rooms for the night in the Hilo Hawaiian hotel.

***

Circles in Stone

The next morning, Sarah and Ted were at the hospital early to check on Alex. His surgery went well and he was awake and wanting breakfast. The doctors had to put a small metal plate and screws in his ankle and told him he should be fully recovered in about 6 to 8 weeks. Meanwhile, he would have to wear a cast boot.

The doctors released Alex to go home just after breakfast. Ted drove his jeep with himself and Alex and Sarah to Alex's house arriving around noon. When they arrived, there were already cars parked in his drive filled with people. As soon as they saw Ted's Jeep pull in with Alex inside the cars began to empty. Jack was there with Susan. Two cars had USGS people in them. And one car was from the National Park.

Ted went over to Jack.

"Who's running the office?" Ted asked Jack.

"Major Parker," answered Jack

Ted gave him the thumbs up as they headed toward the house.

Alex turned to Sarah. "I am going to need your help with this crowd," he said.

"Don't worry," Sarah replied. "I'll get Susan to help as soon as I get you settled in your parlor."

"Thank you, love," Alex responded with a smile. "I love you and am so glad you're here."

Everyone followed Sarah, Ted, and Alex into the house. Once inside Alex invited everyone into the dining area to have a seat around the table. Alex asked everyone to introduce themselves to each other to save time. Sarah and Susan dispatched themselves to the kitchen to make coffee.

Once everyone was seated Alex began by thanking everyone for all the attention he had received after his accident. He then asked if the USGS could update everyone on the eruption.

Matt Jefferson began by telling everyone that this was an unprecedented new eruption. That new lava had already taken a couple of homes and there was no way of knowing how bad it was going to get. He suggested that the National Park remain closed as it already was, until more information was available. Thomas Alan spoke next saying that the Jagger Museum and the USGS had suffered major damage and the USGS would be moving its control center to the University of Hawaii in Hilo until further notice.

Sally Jones, the PR person for the USGS, wanted to know about what Alex had experienced and what he knew about the missing person whose car was found near the crater.

Ted, Jack, and Sarah anxiously waited for Alex's reply.

"I only talked to him briefly before the eruption started. His name, from what I recall, was Rhyfel. He was here visiting from the UK. He arrived at my location just after dawn to view the lava lake. I had no authority to tell him to leave but made him aware of the dangers. He chose to stay and when the eruption began, he lost his footing. I had already been injured and could not reach him before I saw a large section of the crater wall where he was standing fall into the crater. I managed to find my way back to my car and escape without further injury. That's all I can tell you. I am sad that anyone should lose their life in such a way. I am grateful I did not also lose mine. Volcanos are not a respecter of persons."

The park superintendent John Morris spoke up saying that their law enforcement people managed to recover the car and determine the owner's name. It matched the one Alex just gave. He reported that his full name was Rhyfel Morgan and the situation was now being handled by the proper authorities.

Sarah and Susan served coffee and cookies all around as everyone continued to talk about the current eruption and what it could mean. Everyone suddenly stopped still as the house shook from an earthquake.

"I'd say about a 5.0," Matt said when the shaking stopped. "I suspect we shall feel a lot more of the same for a while."

Everyone looked at him with concern.

"I believe you may be right," Alex said. "I want to thank you all for coming but I do have something to attend to and a promise to keep. I will be in touch and you all have my email to do the same. I am sure you will all be busy for a while. Again, thank you for coming."

Everyone got up and went one by one to Alex wishing him the best. When Jack came to him, he whispered that he wanted him and Susan to stay.

After the others left, Alex moved to his favorite position on the couch and put his leg up. Sarah sat next to him snuggling in close. Ted, Jack, and Susan found the rest of the comfortable chairs.

"You handled the question about Rhyfel well enough," Jack said looking at Alex.

"Thanks," he replied. "I would like to let it rest now. What happened down there is between him and me. I would like to keep it that way for now if you don't mind."

"Of course," Jack responded feeling bad.

"Listen," Alex began. "I want to thank each of you personally for what you have all done. I cannot express my gratitude enough. Not only you, but please pass on my thanks to everyone behind the scenes that I have never had the pleasure to meet. To you, Jack, I would like to offer a special thanks. You have always been a good friend. I know you would never accept money, however; I would like to donate funds in your name to the SGM to be used to help with any needs this eruption might bring. I would like you to oversee those funds and anything the SGM can do if necessary."

"I would be honored," Jack replied with a smile.

"One more favor, if you wouldn't mind," Alex said speaking to Jack. "I would like you to be the best man at my wedding to this wonderful woman next to me."

Jack smiled, "Would be most honored and happy to do so."

"Susan," Alex continued. "I want to thank you also for stepping in on such short notice. You are a gift from the Gods."

Alex squeezed Sarah tightly to himself.

"You are my angel," Alex said looking at Sarah. "I can say no more. Except, maybe someone should call and order pizza for dinner and we should have a party."

"Sounds good to me," Ted responded. "I volunteer for that mission."

Everyone laughed. Alex was so grateful for being alive. For being in love. He now understood something his mother had told him many times. "True magic is found in the people around you."

***

In the morning, Alex announced at breakfast he wanted Sarah to go with him to start the fulfillment of the promise he made before the encounter with Rhyfel. That was to make arrangements for their wedding.

Sarah was excited to hear that and asked where they were going. Alex told her to meet the person that would perform the wedding, Mara Mayo, the pagan priestess. Alex said he had called the night before to make sure she would be home.

Alex asked Ted if he could make travel arrangements for the three of them after the wedding. Alex and Sarah had already decided that they wanted to spend their honeymoon back in England. Ted asked him why he wanted him to go along. He told him that the honeymoon was going to be combined with a mission to find, if possible, the location of the Jewel everyone was so determined to have. Alex would need the help of Ted's connections and knowledge to help with the search.

Ted looked at Sarah to see if she agreed with the idea. Knowing what her father was thinking, she told him that it was her idea, not Alex's. Ted smiled and agreed to get right on it.

Ted, Jack, and Susan all left for the SGM headquarters at the same time Sarah and Alex left on their mission.

Sarah insisted that she would drive, under Alex's direction of course. He conceded and found it a pleasure to just ride along. He had not been a passenger since his parents died.

Mara's home was about 30 minutes away, located in a large but remote subdivision called Hawaiian Acres. Some of the roads Alex directed Sarah over were not much more than lava rock cleared of trees.

Along one of those roads, Sarah was directed to enter a drive that was blocked by a bright blue gate with flowers painted on it. There was a sign on the gate that read; "Kapuu to All Except Those That Have Been Invited."

Alex reached under his jacket and pulled out a small wooden wand. He pointed it at the gate, which then swung open. Sarah looked at him and smiled shaking her head. Once through the gate, he did the same to close it behind them.

After a short drive up along a curved road that was bordered on both sides by thick vegetation, they arrived in front of a two-story dome-shaped house. Sarah pulled the Jeep in behind a blue pickup truck with flowers painted on the tailgate, the same as she had seen on the gate.

Circles in Stone

As Sarah and Alex got out of the Jeep, they heard a voice call out. "Come on in Alika, you know the way."

Sarah followed Alex along a path made of homemade paving stones. She could hear birds calling all around. Not just forest birds but what she recognized as being peacocks, and macaws. When she looked up in the trees, she was astounded to see a good number of peacocks roosting high above her head.

Alex opened the door to the house to the cry of a cockatiel sitting on a perch just inside.

A tall middle-aged woman appeared at the door in front of them. She had a long blond braid of hair that reach down to her waist and clear blue eyes. Wearing blue jeans and a tie-dyed tee shirt, she was not what Sarah expected. The woman reached out to Alex and hugged his neck. Stepping back, she looked at him and then at Sarah.

"Aloha and welcome. I am Mara," she said reaching out a hand and then hugging Sarah's neck.

Looking back at Alex and his leg in the cast she asked,

"What happened to you?" she asked "And who is this gorgeous creature you brought with you? Let me guess the first part. Pele hit you with a rock while you were playing in her house."

Alex laughed out loud.

"You got that right on," Alex replied. "And this is Sarah, my bride-to-be."

"Well come in," Mara said just as the cockatiel let out another call. "It's ok Fortune, they are my friends."

"That's Fortune," Mara said looking at Sarah. "He's harmless unless you poke a finger at him."

Sarah followed Alex and Mara into a sitting room. All around the walls on shelves were more crystals than Sarah had ever seen in one place. In the middle of the room, in front of a circular couch, was a glass table with a truly massive but beautiful amethyst geode that had been cut in half as its base.

"Have a seat and make yourselves comfortable, I have made tea and have some homemade cookies," Mara said as she went off into another part of the house.

Just before Sarah sat down, she looked out the large window that overlooked a yard. In the yard, she saw two large tortoises grazing on greens of some kind. Just beyond them, there was a large wired cage that contained a pair of bright blue macaws.

When Mara returned with a tray of tea and cookies, she found Sarah staring at a homemade broom above the doorway.

"I don't use it for transport," Mara said with a smile and a wink, "I much prefer my two-wheeled blue one parked in my carport."

Mara sat in a chair opposite them and poured the tea. They all sat and drank tea and ate cookies exchanging small talk, which included an introduction to her one-eyed black cat named Blackbeard. Mara asked Alex about his injury and Sarah about her life in England. It wasn't long before Sarah felt completely relaxed and comfortable. Sarah was captivated by Mara's storytelling and wisdom. She very much liked hearing about Alex's parents and how they had been great friends and how she missed them.

As Sarah listened to her and took in her home and surroundings, the image of a good witch kept coming into her mind. A forest witch perhaps. Mara had peace about her that made you relax and feel at home. Sarah understood why Alex connected to her. After more conversation, Mara showed Sarah around the house while Alex sat petting Blackbeard. Sarah was very much interested in the jewelry Mara made from semi-precious stone and bird feathers. In Mara's craft room, Sarah was amazed by the tile mosaic on the floor of a dragon wrapped around the world. She was even more amazed to learn that Mara had done it herself. It made Sarah wonder if Mara knew about Tarian and perhaps she did know about Alex and his family but never let them know.

After a while, Sarah returned to the sitting room where Alex was still petting the cat. She showed Alex the necklaces she was going to buy that Mara had made.

Finally, getting down to the business of why they were there Alex spoke up.

"As you already know I would like you to preside over our wedding. We would like it to be held in the Stonehenge in my yard. We would also like it to be as soon as possible if you are not too busy. I know it's asking a lot. What do you think?"

Mara smiled and answered, "I would love to. Yes, I can make all the arrangements if you like with the paperwork. I have the forms here. You can fill them out and I will submit them for you. That part should be ready in a couple of days after I submit them. I know your yard well from the many visits with your parents. I don't see any problems with having the wedding there. I'll give you some ideas for vows you can look over if you like. You won't find much convention in them. Just enough to make it legal."

"That would be wonderful," Sarah replied. "I feel honored to have you perform our wedding. I can tell that you are a truly wonderful person just from the little time I have spent with you today."

"Thank you," responded Mara. "It's just me being me."

After another round of tea and more conversation, Alex and Sarah left for home in Volcano. Sarah felt comfortable now thinking of Alex's house as being her home. Her hope was that, when they finally got to England, Alex would feel the same about hers.

Chapter 39

We Choose

Several days after Sarah and Alex had visited Mara, plans were well underway for the wedding. Jack had recruited the SGM cook Joe Kimo to put on a luau feast for the wedding reception. Joe was thrilled to have been asked. Susan and Sarah were putting their collective taste into planning the decorations and flowers. Alex told Sarah she was welcome to wear his mother's wedding dress with any alterations she wished to make to it. Sarah was overjoyed at the idea.

Invitations were sent to many personal friends of Alex's from around the island. He felt terrible that Sarah had only her father as a member of her family. Alex made his feeling known to Ted who then began arrangements for several of the sisters of St Gwen to fly in as a surprise.

With all this activity one thing weighed heavy on Alex's mind. The condition of his friend Tarian who had saved his life. The path to the cave entrance was too much for Alex to traverse in his condition.

One evening Alex called Sarah into his library and told her of his concern.

"I can go check on him," Sarah told Alex. "I know the way I just can't open the entrance."

"I trust that you know the way with no problem," he replied. "And I think I know a way that I can open the entrance from here. You can go but under one condition. That you do not go alone. I would insist your father go with you to the entrance at least."

Alex went to the stand that held his wands. With a key, he unlocked the bottom and took out a wooden box. Opening the box, he showed Sarah the contents. Inside were two shiny crystal orbs laying on a velvet cloth. They were each about 3 inches in diameter.

"These are scrying orbs made of angel aura quartz," Alex told her. "If you take one with you and I have one here we can communicate with each other. The same way we did when we spied on the Morgans. I can cast the spell to open the entrance and guide you in once you are there.

Your father must remain outside the cave. There is magic in the cave which could cause harm to him if he enters without me there in person."

"I understand," Sarah replied.

"I will instruct you what you need to do once inside. Your father is going to have to trust me on this. I will tell him myself as well. But this is important to me. I need to know Tarian is alright."

Sarah took Alex by the hand and turned him toward her. She then kissed him softly.

"You can trust me," she whispered in his ear. "I am so happy you love me enough to trust me to do this for you."

Alex smiled and kissed her back. They left the room hand in hand.

That same evening Alex took Ted into his office when he came over for dinner. With Sarah there also, he explained what he wanted him and Sarah to do the next day. Ted understood and agreed but felt a little disappointed that he would not be able to see the dragon in person.

***

The next morning, Sarah and her father set out on the hike to check on Tarian. Sarah led the way while Alex, having seen them off, sat in the center of the stone circle with his scrying orb waiting for Sarah to contact him with the one he gave her.

After an hour of hiking, Sarah and her father arrived at where the entrance of Tarian's lair was located. Sarah and her father sat down on a rock to take a break.

"How much further?" Ted asked his daughter.

"We're here," Sarah replied looking at him with a sly smile.

"I don't see anything but more jungle ahead on our left and a sheer rock face covered in vine and ferns," Ted responded puzzled.

"I know," Sarah replied again with a wide smile while sipping on her bottle of water.

Ted sat there still puzzled while Sarah was feeling very special in front of him. He always had been the one to guide her and protect her. She felt for the first time the roles had been switched.

After the break, Sarah opened her backpack and took out the Orb that Alex had given her. After whispering some words to it that her father did not understand she spoke out.

"Can you hear me?" She said out loud.

"Yes, I can, and see you too," Came the voice of Alex loud and clear as if he was right there.

Ted just shook his head as Sarah continued to smile at him.

"You are loving this aren't you?" Ted said to her.

"Kind of."

"I need you to stand in front of the entrance," Alex's voice came back. "Hold the Orb high above your head."

Sarah did as she was instructed. She heard Alex utter the strange words that he did the other times and could see him in the orb slam his staff onto the ground. A beam of light shot out from the orb. The vegetation parted revealing the entrance, just as Sarah had seen happen when she had visited before.

Ted got up and picked up his backpack as if he was going to follow Sarah.

"No Dad," Sarah said looking at him. "You can't follow me any further. You must wait here as Alex instructed."

"I am sorry sir," Alex's voice came back through the Orb. "I can't change that so please wait outside the cave. It is for your safety."

Ted did not respond as he watched his daughter enter the cave alone.

Sarah didn't need to follow all the protocols that she had learned from Alex regarding the torches. Using a powerful flashlight, she followed the path with Alex guiding her through the cave. She noticed the pathway was covered with rocks that weren't there on her last visit.

She soon found herself in front of the barrels of silver and further along she could see the coffins of Alex's parents and ancestors. They appeared to be in good condition except for some small rocks on top of them. She ventured further still and saw a familiar shape in front of her. It was the formation she had seen on her first visit that turned out to be Tarian.

Showing it to Alex through the orb in a whisper she asked what she should do.

"Nothing," Alex replied. "He is sleeping. He is aware you are there but knows you are no threat so he remains in his slumber. This means he is fine, thank goodness. Just head back."

Sarah stayed for a moment looking at Tarian disguised as a rock.

"Thank you, she said in a low voice.

She saw an eye open and wink and then closed again. She knew he had heard her.

Sarah headed back toward the entrance of the cave. Always holding the orb in front of her so Alex could guide her if she got confused. When she got to the barrels of silver Alex asked her to stop.

"I need you to go over to the first barrel and take a couple of dozen coins from it," Alex instructed her. "I want to give them as gifts to some of our friends at the wedding."

Sarah did as she was asked and headed out of the cave.

She found her father standing near the entrance looking with impatience as she appeared. He hugged her when she came out.

"I am glad you are safe," Ted said checking her over as if he were looking for damage.

Sarah smiled and she moved away from the entrance. Repeating what she had done to open it Alex closed it up through the orb. Telling Alex, they would see him soon, she put the orb back into her backpack. She and her father headed back into the forest following the way they came.

Alex waited patiently for their return with relief, knowing that his friend Tarian was fine. He could now look forward to the wedding with peace and joy.

***

The following ten days were filled with a flurry of activity and preparations for the wedding. The crew from SGM helped erect a large tent in Alex's yard not far from the stone circle. Joe Kimo was busy getting food ordered and the imu prepared for the pig roast that would be served at the luau. Sarah was busy altering her wedding dress and helping Susan arrange flowers.

Alex had assigned Ted to take charge of setting up a bar for drinks. Along with that, he was making arrangements for Sarah, Alex, and himself to travel back to England after the wedding.

Jack became the go-to person for anyone needing something. With his knowledge of the island, he knew where to find anything. Alex was so pleased he had taken control.

Along with all of that he and Ted kept in contact with General Wigmore and informed him of what had happened to Rhyfel. The

General told him that it had been on the news in England. It had reported him as being a tourist who was in the wrong place at the wrong time. Another story had already broken on how Rhyfel had been a person of good standing in his community and would be missed. Neither Jack, Ted, or Wigmore commented on that.

Sarah was so excited to see Sister Rose and Sister Clara arrive. It was a wonderful gift to her from Alex and her father to have flown them there for her wedding. Sarah made them comfortable by putting Sister Clara in Alex's old room and Sister Rose in his sister's room. It pleased Alex to have someone use his sister's room at last. He knew it would have been what his sister would have wanted.

Alex busied himself monitoring the eruption of the volcano. The lava was continuing to overrun homes and cover roads. At the summit, the crater continued to subside. Nothing like this had been witnessed in many generations. It was both sad and exciting. Alex wished he could be in the field to help study it but knew that would not be possible, so he monitored it from his home via computer. Perhaps it was a good thing he couldn't walk much. It kept him home to focus on his wedding. He kept reminding himself how fortunate he was to even be there.

After Sister Clara arrived, Alex took her aside and told her about not having the Jewel and showed her what Sarah had spotted. How the Jewel must be in England somewhere. They both agreed that the last person they knew that must have had it was his ancestor, Arthur Dee, Michael's older brother. She told Alex that would be the best place to pick up the trail. The archives contained many of his books and papers.

***

Three days before the wedding Mara showed up to go over the final bits of paperwork and fine-tune the details of the ceremony. Everything was in order and would be completed in time. The one thing she wanted to know was what name Sarah wanted to use after she was married. Some women like to retain their maiden name. Her father and Alex were sitting at the table when Sarah was asked the question. Alex told her it was her choice. After a moment of thought, she answered with confidence.

"I would like to be known as Mrs. Sarah Rowland Michaels."
Her father smiled.

"I mean no disrespect for my mother," Sarah said. "But it is time everyone knows who my father is."

Everyone smiled. Ted was proud of her beyond words. She didn't need to have her mother's name to honor her. She had her spirit.

***

The big day finally arrived. Smoke was rising early from the emu where the pig was being placed under Joe Kimo's supervision.

The two sisters and Susan helped Sarah into her dress, while Jack made sure Alex's outfit was all in order.

Mara had arrived and was greeting all the guests while showing them to the seating area that had been set up within the stone circle.

Ted was all dressed and waited with nervous anticipation to see his daughter. He did not have long to wait as she, guided by the sisters, emerged from the upstairs bedroom and onto the balcony overlooking the main hall. She glided down the stairs as if she was floating on air. She stopped in front of him so he could look at her. She saw tears well up in his eyes.

"You are the most beautiful thing I have ever seen," Ted exclaimed trying to hide his emotions.

She was wearing a full-length blue satin dress with silver fern leaf patterns sewed into it with silver thread. Over the dress flowed a white satin cloak. Both the dress and the cloak flared at the bottom. The cloak was laced in the front with white and silver cords leaving the blue dress exposed in the front to the floor. The sleeves draped down and ended with the same blue as the dress, giving it a medieval look. The collar was a plain white square cut bordered all around by gold braiding that went up around her neck. Around her neck was a gold chain necklace, and at the end, hung a large blue round sapphire surrounded by diamonds, which once belonged to her mother and given to her by her father. Her hair flowed down over her shoulders and her head was crowned with fresh flowers from the local forest.

To Ted, she looked every bit the princess he had always envisioned.

Ted was dressed in his military best and when he stood next to her to have their picture taken, they looked to be royalty. Ted guided her with her arm in his to the sitting room to await the start.

Just after that Alex emerged from his office with Jack, who was also dressed in his military best.

Not believing in the tradition of not seeing each other before the ceremony, Alex appeared in the doorway of the sitting room to see his bride and for her to see him.

Sarah looked at him and smiled broadly. He was the most handsome she had ever seen him.

Alex wore a satin silver and black vest that was part of a long white shirt with long draping sleeves trimmed in the same pattern as the vest. Over his shoulders was a light blue frock bordered all around by silver and gold stitching. The frock was open at the front showing off his wide brown leather belt inlaid with blue topaz crystals. His one black knee-high riding boot was laced with white cords, setting it off in a spectacular way. The other leg, still in a cast, was wrapped in black cloth and had laces to make it blend with the other one. His hair was pulled back and held in place by a gold ponytail clip encrusted with small amethyst crystals. Around his neck, he wore a silver chain with bearing a dragon emblem at the end.

When Alex saw Sarah, it took his breath away, and could not speak while walking toward her. When he reached her, he finally was able to say what he was thinking.

"I have never seen a more beautiful sight in all my life. There are no words in any language that I know that can come close to doing you justice. You are truly dazzling," Alex said as he kissed her hand and knelt before her despite his injured leg.

Just then cameras were flashing and clicking all around. They all lined up for a proper photo in front of the fireplace. From left to right it was Jack next to Alex who was next to Sarah and her father next to her.

After the photo session, Mara came through the door to signal it was time to begin. Alex went out first with Jack, to wait in front of the stone table in the center of the henge circle.

Recorded bridal march music played as Ted led his daughter out through the back door and down the steps to Alex's side in the center of the circle.

When the music stopped, Priestess Mara, wearing a green and white full-length hooded dress came and stood before them.

"Please join your right hands," Mara instructed them.

When they had done so, Mara took a four-colored braided cord and wrapped it around their wrist symbolically tying them together.

"The colors of this cord," Mara began. "Represent the colors of the four elements that bind all of us together. Gold, the Air, the breath of life, Red the Fire that cooks our food and warms our homes, Blue, the Water that sustains life, and Green, the Earth, from which we come and one day will return. This cord now binds you as you are bound by them. Braided together they represent love and life, the greatest of all forces. We have gathered here before friends and family. Along with all the gods and ancestors, to bear witness to the seal of love between this man and this woman. Now before them all, I ask you to declare this love."

Looking at Alex, Mara asked, "Do you Alexander choose to love honor, and protect this woman, Sarah, with all that is within you as long as you shall live?"

"I so choose," Alex answered.

Turning then to Sarah, Mara asked, "Do you Sarah choose to love honor, and protect this man, Alexander, with all that is within you as long as you shall live?"

"I so choose," Sarah answered.

The ring of stones in which we stand is the testimony to that love, they shall now exchange rings to symbolize that testimony.

Jack took two plain silver rings with rune engravings on them and handed each of them one.

Mara continued, "as you place these rings on each other's fingers, make a pledge from your heart with your own words.

Alex began, "With this ring, I bind myself to your heart and spirit with my love that is as endless as this ring."

Alex slipped the ring onto Sarah's finger.

Sarah spoke next, "May this ring I give you, be a reminder of my love for you that stands as solid as these stones in which we stand."

Sarah slipped the ring onto Alex's finger.

They both looked back to Mara, who then continued, "So, therefore, by the power invested in me by the state of Hawaii and the Gods that watch over us, I hereby pronounce you bound in marriage by your love. Join now in the kiss of love to seal your choice."

Sarah and Alex pulled each other together and kissed a long and passionate kiss to the cheers of all in attendance. They took the cord from around their wrist and hung it around Mara's neck. She in turn hung a flower lei around each of theirs.

The live band that Jack had found began to play music. Each of the guests in turn came forward congratulating them and placing a lei around their neck. Soon the flowers had almost covered their faces.

Once all the guests had made the round and, despite his injured ankle, Alex stood up on the stone bench in the circle and called out in a loud voice.

"Thank you all for coming and you must stay for the feast. So let the party begin!"

Just then everyone heard a conch shell being blown meaning that the feast was about to start. Major Parker, and others from the SGM headquarters in Volcano, helped Joe Kimo uncover and retrieve the roast pig from the imu. Ted manned the bar he had set up, serving drinks. Everyone else pitched in where ever help was needed. As the music played people ate, drank, and danced. The celebration went on long into the night.

By the time everyone left and all had calmed down, Sarah and Alex were happy to just get into bed and fall asleep in each other's arms. This time was different. They were husband and wife.

Chapter 40

Going Home

After the wedding, many people returned to help clean up and put things in order. Alex had already turned the running of the house over to Sarah. They needed to get ready for their journey to England for their honeymoon which would be in just a few days. Alex did what he could but Sarah insisted he stay off his leg as much as possible.

Jack had taken the two visiting sisters on a tour of the island while Ted, who had now moved into the house with Sarah and Alex to help where ever he could, canceled the room and car that he had arranged for Sarah when she first arrived on the island.

To Alex, it felt like he had a family again. The house was full of sound and activity. The way he remembered it when his parents were alive. He thought of them a lot now. Hoping they would be pleased with him and the choices he had made.

One thing that concerned Alex was that now that Rhyfel was gone, Ambrose's wife Selma would try to reconnect with Sarah using scrying. He had to protect Sarah from this. Looking through the collection of magical amulets his father had left him, Alex found what he needed.

One morning while Alex and Sarah were alone having coffee together, Alex presented Sarah with what he had found. Handing Sarah, a small box, she opened it. Inside was a fine braided silver chain. On the end was a small silver cage containing a round pale blue cloudy ball of glass. To Sarah, it was simple but beautiful.

"What is this?" Sarah asked smiling.

"It is a gift of protection," he answered. "It was made by my father. I was concerned that your Aunt Selma might try and find you using scrying. My father made this amulet for my mother in case someone tried to find her. He charmed it to block any attempt of outside scrying. It is sea glass, from what, only the gods know. It only works if the person it is meant for puts it on themselves. It is yours if you want it. The choice to block anyone from finding you is yours."

"Whether it is magical or not I love it. I will wear it to honor your father and mother and as a reminder of how much you care for me. Thank you."

Sarah placed it around her neck and kissed Alex.

***

Back in England chaos seemed to be the word of the times.

After the expulsion of the ODR members from Hawaii and the US following the gunfight with the SGM, the organization was completely thrown into disarray. Charles Stewart blamed Jason Elliot for his impulsive nature and desire for power. Jason blamed Charles for putting his trust in the traitor Lewis Hall, aka Ted Rowland. John Coke's betrayal was discovered and he was expelled from the Order.

At a leadership meeting in Edinburgh a row broke out, and a vote was called for among the members. After the vote, Charles and Jason were knocked out of any leadership roles and Oliver Calvin was elected the new leader and immediately made Goddard his right-hand man. The only good news was that those that held jobs in Scotland yard did not lose their positions. Among non-ODR members within Scotland Yard, the story was that Jason had been involved in a drug bust gone bad.

***

With the news of the loss of Rhyfel, the Morgans were not so much in disarray as they were in mourning. Ambrose and Selma were now the new leaders. Following a memorial service, they moved from their London home into Rhyfel's home in Tintagel. After what he experienced in Hawaii, Ambrose decided he would think long and hard about the next move of the Morgans.

One thing was sure, the quest was not to be given up. It was after all the very cause for their existence. With the loss of Rhyfel in such a dramatic way, their determination must be more focused than ever before. But Ambrose and Selma, both knew it was going to take more than determination to move forward. Times had changed and they would all have to change with them.

***

At last, the day arrived for Sarah, Alex, and Ted to leave Hawaii. Sarah and Alex asked Jack and Susan to watch over their home in

Volcano. Jack was given keys to the Kona house as well, to make sure the caretakers did their job while they were gone.

Jack drove all three to Hilo where they would fly out to Honolulu and then would fly from there to Gatwick via Vancouver. Sarah and Ted were glad to be heading home. Alex was happy to be going back to England, which he considered in many ways, to be his home by way of his roots of long ago. Alex was also happy to be traveling with his new wife and her father by his side.

Alex began to see more of the independence of Sarah's spirit. It made him love her even more if that were possible. He was always aware that being married to him was going to take a special kind of person. He saw more of that specialness each day in Sarah.

The travel time to England was a twenty-four-hour endurance for Alex with his leg. Traveling first class did make it more bearable. For Sarah and her father, it was just another trip. It had not been that long since they had made the same trip in the opposite direction.

General Wigmore had been alerted to when they would be arriving and agreed to pick them up at the airport. Using his SGM connections within the Home Office, he arranged VIP treatment going through customs and immigration upon their arrival.

It was early morning when they arrived. Wigmore drove them all to Sarah's house where Ted could pick up his Range Rover. After thanking the General for everything and saying good-by to Sarah and Alex, Ted headed for his home in Salisbury for some much-needed rest. The General headed back to Marlborough and the SGM headquarters. Alex and Sarah were left alone at last, in her home in England.

***

Ted spent the next few days just resting and adjusting to the time change. After checking the video footage from the other house, he saw when the ODR had come looking for him. There was a long break but he noticed the house was being checked again more recently. He was sure it was the ODR still trying to track him. He made sure he left no indications in that house that he was back.

***

Sarah and Alex spent days enjoying each other's company as husband and wife. Went out only to get food and supplies while Sarah's

344

housekeeper helped prepare meals. The time change was hardest on Alex. It had been a long time since he had traveled that far from Hawaii.

Sarah had called from time to time to talk to those on the dig she oversaw before she left. She did not give them any details of the things going on in her life while she was in Hawaii. After almost a week home she decided it was time to check in with them. She asked Alex to join her. Secretly she wanted to show him off. She would be doing all the driving now. Her car was a manual so, Alex in his condition, could not drive which he didn't mind. Everything had come full circle. Circles in Stone he would say.

When they arrived at the dig everyone was happy to see her and even more surprised to meet her new husband.

A lot had been discovered since she had left. The site was truly Roman, and a villa had been found including the remains of a beautiful mosaic floor. Alex seemed more excited than Sarah at the finds. The history of Roman Britain had always fascinated him. He knew his family's history as far back as Merlin but he knew nothing of it before then. He often wondered if he may have been related to the Romans from back then. From his studies, he knew the Romans believed in and practiced magic of all kinds. He often wondered what it would have been like to live in a world where you didn't have to hide your gifts.

They spent the whole day at the dig. On the way back home, Alex told Sarah that it had been a wonderful day. He had not felt so relaxed in a long time. He also told her he loved her home, to him, it felt almost normal. No magic, no hiding, no Jewel, just him and Sarah living and loving.

The next day Sarah received a call from her father inviting them to his house to stay for a few days. His house was only ten miles from Stonehenge, and thought Alex would like to spend some time there. Sarah said yes to the invitation knowing Alex would be thrilled.

When she told Alex of the idea, as predicted, he was thrilled. He had visited the Henge once when he was at college and always wanted to go back. That evening they packed up for the trip.

The following day, Alex and Sarah set off for Ted's house. The drive took about an hour and a half. Ted greeted them with excitement.

Circles in Stone

He had a catered lunch by a local vendor waiting for them when they arrived.

There was plenty of room for all of them in his two-story house. Except for when Sarah came to visit from time to time, he never had any guests. Ted gave Alex a tour of the house but never mentioned the other house behind his or the passageway connecting them.

That evening, they all sat around in the parlor talking about the trip to Hawaii and the wedding. Ted could not help but share stories with Alex about Sarah when she was young.

Alex truly felt like a part of a family again.

***

They all rose early the next day because Sarah had arranged for a sunrise visit and private tour of Stonehenge.

They arrived while it was still mostly dark with just a hint of daylight in the eastern sky. A friend of Sarah's from her work and research met them at the visitor center. She was thrilled to see Sarah again and most impressed that she was now married. Asking if Alex would be alright walking in his condition, she was assured that he had gotten used to walking with his cast on by now. Traveling part of the way by golf cart they stopped just outside the path that led to the world-famous monument.

Once out of the cart, Alex stood still and bowed his head, while leaning on the cane he now used to help him walk. The others did the same once they saw him. Sarah knew that he knew the true meaning of the place.

After a moment of silence, they slowly walked toward the stones. The sun was just beginning to peek over the horizon when they arrived in the center. Alex stood in still reverence as the sun slowly rose casting its light upon the ancient stones that surrounded him.

Ted and Sarah also stood transfixed at the site. Sarah reflected on her recent wedding day that took place in the smaller version in Alex's yard. She also reflected on the night she met the queen of the fairies sitting on the center stone table. As Sarah watched the sunrise and the shadows slowly move across the ground, she finally realized what Alex meant when he would say "Circles of Stone." Everything coming back around. Every moment was a link that joins to another that would come together and form a circle in the never-ending cycle of life and living. Each of us is just one of those links. The past is linked to the future, which is linked to the past. She truly felt a part of something much bigger than herself. She moved close to Alex, took his arm, and held him close.

Even Ted was moved by it all. He thought back to his younger days when he was in love with Sarah's mother. How proud she would be of her daughter. He also realized if it were not for his work with the SGM, Sarah would not have gone to Hawaii and met Alex. He did not believe that things were meant to be. But he now believed our choice was guided by those that had gone before, all we need to do is take the time and listen to them with our hearts.

Though no one is permitted to touch the stones, Sarah had gotten permission for Alex to lay his hand on one of the blue stones. These were the oldest of the stones in the monument. When he placed his hand on it, Sarah was sure she felt the earth shake. When she looked at her father and the guide, they looked at each other puzzled. They each had felt it also. It was not like an earthquake it was like a small gentle tremor. Sarah looked at Alex, who stood with his eyes closed and smiling. She knew he had made a connection with the ancestors.

After the sun had risen high enough that the public was beginning to arrive, they all left the monument. Alex gave a final bow before getting back into the golf cart that took them back to the visitors' center.

Once they left Stonehenge, they decided to make the 40-minute drive to Avebury, stopping at the ancient burial mound known as West Kennet Long Barrow. This burial chamber was constructed some 1000 years before Stonehenge was begun. Alex again showed great respect for the place. To him, this was not a tourist attraction. It was the burial site of the ancestors. People that were separated from him by over 5000 years but to Alex, it was as if they had been buried there only yesterday.

Sarah had always seen the place as an archaeological site. But she now saw it differently.

Ted did not connect to it in any way special but respected the way Sarah and Alex did.

Alex spent much time in meditation at the site. Sarah was sure he was listening for the voices of those that had once been buried there. She hadn't yet seen this deep side of her new husband. It did not trouble her. It was part of the man she loved and was still learning about.

From the Long barrow, they headed to Avebury only a couple of miles away. Avebury is the largest stone circle in England. Its beginnings date to just before Stonehenge.

While there they decide to have lunch at the Red Lion pub, which of course, is within the circle itself.

When Alex entered the pub, he froze in his tracks as if he had hit a glass wall.

"What's wrong?" Sarah asked him looking concerned.

Alex was staring straight ahead as if he was looking at something no one else could see.

"What's wrong?" Sarah asked again, this time with a bit of fear in her tone. "Are you alright? Please tell me."

Ted was now watching too with a bit of concern.

Finally, Alex snapped back into the moment.

"Let's get a table," Alex said as he headed inside.

Alex headed for a table on the far side of the room and sat down still in a bit of a daze. Sarah sat next to him and Ted opposite her.

Looking into Alex's eyes she asked again, "What's going on?"

"I saw a vision of the past, Alex answered looking back at her. Rhyfel was here with Ambrose."

"What? When? What did you see? Sarah asked.

"Just before they left for Hawaii. This is where Ambrose told Rhyfel who and where I was. In this very place. It was like watching a tape of the whole thing. I could see and hear them."

"How is that possible?" Ted inquired.

Alex relaxed and took Sarah's hand; it made him feel safe.

"It's the circle," Alex responded "We are inside the circle. Events that happen within them that are connected to another person that enters it are linked to them. The energy of those events continues to circulate until enough time passes for it to dissipate. Because he is now in the realm of the ancestors' part of his energy is now here and stronger than if he were still alive. Does that make any sense?"

Ted looked puzzled trying to take it in.

"I think I get it," answered Sarah. "These places are like hard drives. They record everything that happens within them and with the right trigger or keystroke, they retrieve it and play it back."

"Well said," Alex said smiling. "You put that into modern terms I could have never dreamed up. These circles are the strongest place for that to happen. It happens at other locations too depending on their history. Places where dramatic history happened, like battlefields, castles, churches, and ancient villages. The more recent the event the clearer it is to the person connected to it. I have experienced this before but never like I did here today."

"Are you alright now?" Sarah asked still concerned and holding his hand tightly.

"Yes, I am fine now. You being here helped a lot." Alex said as he pulled Sarah closer to him.

Ted looked at the two of them and shook his head.

"There are times I am really glad I don't live in your world," Ted said while grabbing a menu. "I think I need a beer."

Sarah and Alex both laughed out loud.

"I think we could all use a drink," Sarah responded.

They all ordered a drink and then lunch, after which they all walked the giant circle. Alex made it a point to touch every stone and stand for a moment of reflection before each of them.

After a final visit to the pub for a cup of coffee and a piece of cake, they headed back to Ted's home in Salisbury.

Once back at his house Ted checked his private phone for any messages. There was one from General Wigmore. He played it so Alex and Sarah could hear it as well. The General was inviting them all to the SGM headquarters in Marlborough the next day for lunch if they had time.

Ted looked at Sarah and Alex to see their reaction. Sarah shook her head in agreement as she looked at Alex who also agreed.

Sarah was thrilled. She felt as if for the first time she would truly be a part of her father's world.

Ted called the General back and told him they would be there in the late morning in time for lunch.

Ted then called for Chinese takeaway for dinner and they spent the evening chatting about the day's outing.

Chapter 41

The Search Begins

The next morning, after the trip out to Stonehenge and Avebury, Ted, Alex, and Sarah headed off to the SGM headquarters in Marlborough at Wigmore's invitation. Ted did the driving this time from his house to Merlin's Mound. He had made the near one-hour trip many times over the years. Alex had been to the headquarters a few times in the past. Each time he found it interesting.

Ted made a quick call to the General when they arrived so he could meet them at the secure entrance area. Though Ted's and Alex's prints were already in the system, Sarah's was not. The General was there to give clearance for Sarah to enter. Once inside, greetings were all around.

"General, I would like you to meet my daughter, Sarah," Ted said. "You of course know Alexander."

Finally, I meet you in person Sarah," Wigmore responded as he shook her hand. "I've heard so much about you, I feel I know you. I understand now why your father says you are the sun in his sky."

"Thank you," General, Sarah answered. "I can't say I know anything about you other than you're my dad's boss. I should thank you for many things but don't know where I should start."

"No need to thank me, it's a team effort here," Wigmore said. "We all just try our best to do our jobs which includes watching out for your husband. It pleases me to meet him again."

Wigmore shook Alex's hand and placed his arm around his shoulder.

"Hope you are healing up alright after your nasty encounter," Wigmore said to Alex. "Let's all go to my office where we can relax."

All three of them followed Wigmore to his office on the other side of the complex. Sarah walked slowly as she looked around and was amazed that all of this was inside the mound and no one outside of the SGM members knew it was there.

When they entered Wigmore's office and went inside, Ted was surprised to see six new very comfortable chairs around a new well-polished table.

"Please take a seat," Wigmore said inviting them with an outstretched hand. "Make yourself comfortable. I'll tell the kitchen you're here."

"New furnishing sir," Ted said leaning toward the General.

"Thought it was about time" the General answered with a smile.

After everyone was seated there was a knock at the door. Wigmore opened it and a man wheeled in a cart with coffee and tea and immediately began serving everyone. As soon as everyone had been served the man looked at the General.

"Lunch will be arriving shortly sir," the man said.

The general nodded and the man left.

"It is good to see you all here safe," Wigmore said. "It's been a rough ride these past months."

"It certainly has," Ted answered sipping on his coffee.

"After lunch, I will give Sarah a full tour," the General commented. "Speaking of you Sarah, we, here at the society, have decided to invite you as a full member. That is the real reason I invited you all here. Your education and experience are impressive enough but from what has been reported to me from Hawaii, we could use a person like yourself. Of course, it will be your choice. If you accept, we will get you registered as a full member, put your prints in our system and get you a ring."

"Would I get a tattoo like my dad's?" asked Sarah.

"Yes, of course," Wigmore answered.

"I always wanted one like his," Sarah said smiling and looking at her father. "Then I except.

"Then I hereby declare you a full member," the General answered. "Here at the SGM, we give nonmilitary personnel the title Ranger. You will be known as Ranger Sarah Michaels. You now have as much voice as anyone else of any rank."

Sarah was smiling widely as she looked at her father who was also smiling. Alex squeezed her hand and kissed her cheek.

"I am proud of you," Ted said holding back his tears. "As would be your mother."

Wigmore got up from his seat went to his desk and took out a bottle of brandy and four glasses. He placed one in front of each of them and one for himself and poured brandy into each.

Standing he raised his glass.

"To Ranger Sarah Michaels," he said.

Alex and Ted stood and did the same and together they all downed the brandy in one gulp.

Sarah sipped at hers and tried her best to hold back her tears, but one managed to get out and roll down her cheek.

At that moment a knock came at the door.

"I believe our lunch is here," Wigmore said as he opened the door.

Lunch was a choice of grilled steak or fish with a side of roasted potatoes and asparagus. Dessert was strawberry and rhubarb crumble with vanilla ice cream. The men all had a pint of ale and Sarah a glass of white wine.

After lunch was finished and the small talk had died down Wigmore spoke up.

"Before we go and get Sarah sorted, perhaps we should have a meeting. I understand there is some unfinished business you wish to address while here in England Alexander?"

Just as Alex was about to answer Sarah broke in.

"As I am a full member, I would like to address that General."

"Of course," responded Wigmore smiling and looking at Ted.

"As you must have been informed," Sarah began. "This Jewel that everyone has been searching for, and that almost cost my husband's life, was never in Hawaii with him or his family. From what we can make out it is here someplace in England. Always has been and must remain. It was my idea that we not only come to England for our honeymoon but also to take up this search ourselves. If we, I mean the SGM and Alex were to know where it was then I think his life and many others would be safer. If it should be discovered that it is lost forever, then let that be known so those that search for it will stop this dangerous pursuit. I suggest we should begin this search as soon as possible. The sooner we find it, or prove there is nothing to find, the better off we will all be. That's all I have to say."

The General sat stunned as did Alex and her father.

"You are your father's daughter," Wigmore said snapping out of his daze. "Well, Colonel Rowland, what do you think?"

"I can't argue with her logic sir," Ted replied. "I would suggest we start at the archives."

"I agree," Alex jumped in. "I spoke to Sister Clara before we left Hawaii. I explained to her the situation. She told me that there are many books and manuscripts left by one of my ancestors that may well give us the start we need."

"Then that's where to begin," Wigmore responded. "I had word that Sister Clara returned from Hawaii just the other day. Ever since the incident with the ODR, we keep the place under guard. Going there should not be a problem. The ODR still thinks you're all still in Hawaii so we have leaked information to them to keep them thinking that. Since it was your idea to do this search and with your training in archaeology and ancient history, I put, you, Ranger Michaels in charge of this mission. You will have to take orders from your daughter Colonel Rowland. Will that be a problem?"

"I been taking orders from her all my life sir," Ted answered. "So, this will be no different."

Alex and Wigmore both laughed.

"Thank you General," Sarah replied. "Just one thing sir. If you don't mind and mean no offense to my husband, I would like to be called Ranger Sarah."

"Of course," replied Wigmore. "Let's get you signed up then, Ranger Sarah, and give you the full tour I promised."

The rest of the afternoon was spent giving Sarah a tour of the headquarters and making her membership official on paper. She was fitted with a ring with the chip that allowed her entrance to the facility. An appointment was left open for when she would get her tattoo. She was also introduced to all the members that were currently in the place.

Sarah was impressed with all the work they did with other agencies to help protect the crown and the country. Sarah saw them as a modern version of knights of the realm. She was proud to now be a part of it all. After everything was complete, the three of them headed back to Ted's home.

***

The next morning at breakfast, Sarah, Alex, and Ted made plans for their trip to the archives. The night before, it was decided that Sarah and Alex would continue to stay at her father's house for the duration of the mission. If the news had gotten out about Sarah and Alex getting married, it would be a sure thing that the ODR, as well as the Morgans, would be watching Sarah's house. Now that Sarah was a member of the SGM, Ted told her and Alex about the secret house behind his and explained to them that would be the house the ODR would watch.

***

They arrived at the sisters of St Gwen's Place around 10 am. Ted had called ahead to let them know they were coming. Sister Rose and Sister Helen met them at the door. Asking where Sister Clara was, they told them she was already working in the archives.

"Then we better join her," ordered Sarah.

"Follow me Mrs. Michaels," Sister Rose said to Sarah.

"She is now Ranger Sarah," Ted instructed Sister Rose following her to the archives vault.

"Oh my," Sister Rose exclaimed. "How wonderful. I knew she was a special girl when she was in school here. Sister Helen and I will bring tea and cake shortly to celebrate."

Ted led the way down the stairs and into the vault where Sister Clara already had books and manuscript rolls laid out on the table. She dropped what she was doing and greeted them all.

"So good to see you all again," Sister Clara said as she hugged each of them.

Ted explained to her about Sarah's new position and that she would be overseeing the mission.

Alex immediately went to the table to look at the material laid out on it. After Ted and Sarah joined him is when Alex spoke up.

"What have you found so far Sister Clara?" he asked.

"I began with what we already knew," Sister Clara began. "That your ancestor, John Dee, had hid the death of Michael Dee, your name's sake, and was making plans to hide him when King James took the throne. He died and passed the mission on to his eldest son, Arthur Dee. We know that Arthur must have had the Jewel then. We all assumed that he put it on the ship with Michael headed for Hawaii. The trail here in

England ran cold based on that assumption. I checked the verse that Sarah thought indicated that the Jewel could never leave England. After looking at it myself I too believe Sarah is right. Based on that we must relook at the life of Arthur Dee and see what it reveals."

Sister Clara picked up a book and showed it to Alex and Sarah.

"This is just one of many books Arthur Dee left behind," Sister Clara continued to explain. "Everything you see on this table is from him. He seemed to like to write. Some of this is in his own hand and some are copies of his work. I believe the answer to where to pick up the trail of the Jewel must be in this someplace. It will take some time to find it."

"The sooner we get started the sooner we find it," Sarah declared. "In college, I took courses in reading the old script. I know my dear Alex knows how to read it as well. Along with you Sister Clara, there are three of us. I know Dad doesn't but he can be our food and coffee person."

"I can do that," Ted replied smiling.

Sarah, Alex, and Clara sat down at the table to begin the search. Clara had already sorted things by age. She took the oldest material, Sarah took the middle, and Alex took later writings and notes. Ted went up the stairs to assist the other sisters in preparing drinks and food.

The three of them poured over the documents in front of them. Very little conversation was exchanged between them until lunch. After lunch, they continued the same reading and making notes of anything they thought might be relevant.

Just before dinner time, they decided to take a break and share anything each of them had learned.

Alex began, "Everything so far is about the "Fasciculus Chemicus" (file of the chemist) That he first published in 1631, which he wrote while serving in the court of Tsar Mikhail 1st as his doctor. It is all about his search for the recipe for the Philosophers Stone and by his accounts he found it. Though the recipe is hidden in some sort of codex within the writings. My father told me about it but was not sure if it was real or not."

Sarah then told what she had found.

"There seems to have been a lot going on before he went to Russia," she said. "A lot of turmoil about his practices and this was just after

James came to the throne. This is when he made some sort of deal with the King to send Sir Walter Raleigh in search of El Dorado. Of course, this was when he put his brother Michael on those ships that took him to Hawaii. The problem is that the information is sketchy at best. Not much detail in what kind of deals were made or why was written down and for good reason I suppose."

Sister Clara had very little to declare either.

"The early stuff is all about his father John Dee," Clara reported. "Arthur's education is mentioned but even that is somewhat foggy. His marriage is mentioned and some of his children are also listed including, his oldest son, Rowland."

Sarah looked up at Clara when she mentioned Rowland. She then looked at Alex.

"Don't even say it," Sarah said to Alex. "I know, "Circles in Stone."

Alex smiled and said nothing.

"I think we should break for the day," Sarah said. "Come back in the morning with clear heads. Things often look better after a good night's sleep."

Everyone agreed. They ate dinner at the Sisters' house, that they and Ted had prepared. The short trip to Ted's home was followed by a well-deserved night's rest.

***

The next morning, they all returned to the Sister's place for breakfast at their invitation the night before. As breakfast concluded Sister Clara made an announcement.

"After you all left last night, I went back down to have a look for anything I might have missed. Not in what I had read but if I had found all the manuscripts that we had. I found one that I think might be of interest."

Alex and Sarah rose quickly from the table and followed Clara to the archives. When they arrived, Clara held up a small, very old poorly bound book. There was no title or markings on the cover. Clara laid the book on the table as Sarah and Alex moved in close to have a look as Clara opened it.

"This book is written in his hand," Clara began. "The title he gave it is "Immortalis Essential" or immortal essence. I read as much as I could last night until I fell asleep. It reads like a book of spells, incantations, prayers, and formulas all linked together. I found it among books that he willed to his friend, Sir Thomas Brown. Brown's family then gave the book to us as it seemed, I am sure to them, of no value. What I can make of it, so far, is that he was searching for, and seems to have found a way to preserve magical power in a body after death to last forever. It makes no sense to me why he would do, or want to do that."

"Mana," Alex broke in. "He was searching for mana."

"Mana?" asked Clara. "You mean manna?"

"No," Alex replied. "Mana, it's a Hawaiian word. It means the energy or power that resides in the objects or the bones of a person that has died. Chiefs, kings, and priest remains were thought to have a lot of energy. It was even believed that if another person were to possess their bones, they could inherit the energy from them. Sort of like relics of saints the church keeps. What I don't understand is why he would search for it? Was it for knowledge or for himself? My ancestors believed in it but they knew it became distorted over time and would eventually dissipate. To contain its effects, the body had to be buried in a silver coffin."

Sarah looked at Alex as if a light had come on. Alex saw her expression and knew what she was thinking.

"Yes, to your question," Alex said to Sarah, who then nodded.

Sarah had wondered why all the coffins of Alex's ancestors she saw in the dragon's cave were made of silver. She thought it was just for aesthetic reasons, but now she knew it was for a higher purpose.

"I am not sure if this has a bearing on where the Jewel is or went but I thought it interesting," Clara said. What I found most interesting was the last entry in the book. It seems to be a riddle or poem."

Clara handed the book to Alex for him to read it.

"What does it say?" Sarah asked. "Read it out loud."

Alex read it over a couple of times so he could read it out loud in modern English.

"The Ivy Grows" seems to be the title," Alex began. "The poem follows:

The ivy grows endless still,

From times past by our will.

Bloodline saved across two seas,

The throne be firm was laid to me.

Carry thee did not, to court not thine,

The fruit did stay upon the vine.

There I sought the holy stone of fame,

When did find, to home I came.

Return I did thee by my side,

My oath from youth I did abide.

When my time is here to end,

For thee do I now send.

A friend I trust the healer be,

The answer therefore send with me."

Alex stood in silence as did the others when he had finished reading. Sarah then took the book and read it herself.

"This is about the Jewel," Sarah said looking up from the book. "I am sure of it. Not only the Jewel but him fulfilling his duty to make sure the family line would continue. He is saying in this that the Jewel never left England even when he left for Russia. That he kept it safe. I also believe it tells where to look for the clues to lead to it or where it went."

"I agree with Sarah," Clara said. "In the last two lines, it refers to his friend Dr. Sir Thomas Brown, whom he gave this and many of his other books. It sounds like he is instructing his friend Brown to send something with him to his grave. If this is true then the clue to where the Jewel is could be with Arthur in his grave. I am not sure this is what it all means but it's the best lead we have so far."

"It makes sense to me," Alex injected. "It is just the sort of thing members of our family is noted for. It is connecting ourselves after death to both our ancestors and future generations. What we need to do then is find his grave or tomb and see if a clue is there. If it is not then we come back here and start again."

"Sounds like fun, no disrespect intended, Sarah replied smiling. "Let's get started."

Chapter 42

Norwich

Once Sarah, Alex, and Sister Clara agreed the best clue they had was the poem left behind in Arthurs Dee's handwritten book, Sarah decided that the next move was to look for his tomb. The hope was that a clue would be found in or on his tomb that would set them on the trail of the Jewel that everyone was so desperate to possess. Finding the location of Arthur Dee's tomb was the easiest part of the search so far. There were clear records of where and when he was buried from multiple sources. Clara had even discovered printed copies of his obituary and his last will and testament. They showed that he died in the city he last resided in; Norwich in county of Norfolk, England.

Norwich, as we know it now began just after the Norman invasion. The Saxon town was cleared and the construction of Norwich castle began. Later, the city was surrounded by a wall of which parts can still be seen around the city.

At the time Arthur Dee lived and died there, Norwich was known as the second city of England. The city boasted (and still does) one of the largest Norman cathedrals in England. In the city center, the large Norman castle can still be visited today.

With the river Wensun running through the city, it was at that time, a prosperous trading city with links to many of the cities on the European continent and beyond. Wool and textiles had made the city rich. If you wanted to be at the center of learning and trade but weren't in London from the 13th to 16th centuries, then Norwich was the place to be. It was told that medieval Norwich had 52 churches and 365 pubs. A church for every week of the year and a pub for every day. Norwich Cathedral, at the time, was said to have been one of the largest Norman Cathedrals in Europe. That cathedral is still there to this day. Its spire is second only to that of Salisbury.

Some 31 of the 52 churches, of Arthur Dee's time, can still be found in the city. Some have been converted to other uses, but some still function as living churches.

Circles in Stone

One of those living churches is St George church of Tombland, not far from Norwich's city center. Just a stone's throw, or as is noted in its history, an arrow shot from Norwich Cathedral. It is in this church that Arthur Dee is recorded to have been buried.

***

A decision had to be made whether a trip to Norwich would be worth it. There was very little to go on except the poem. Sarah decided to call for a break and consult with her father, Alex, and Sister Clara.

"What do you think are chances are?" asked Sarah. "With so little to go on would it be worth the time. We could stay here and continue to search the records until we have something more substantial."

"What does your gut tell you?" asked her father.

"My gut?" Sarah replied puzzled. "I am an archaeologist. I deal in facts and evidence Dad."

"What are the facts that we have?" Alex interjected. "None that I can see. The only evidence is the poem, which is subject to our interpretation."

"I trust the interpretation," Clara declared. "In my experience, it can sometimes be only one word that redefines the way we see things from the way they are."

"I agree with Sister Clara," Alex said, "In spell casting, one word can shift the outcome of the spell from negative to positive. Though the evidence we have is small it may be the key to the whole puzzle."

"I see your point," Sarah came back. "Sometimes we would choose to dig a site based on only one coin or piece of pottery. Sometimes we would find nothing and at others what we find far exceeds our expectations. Each time it was a risk."

"Ahh, there is the key word," Ted said smiling. "Risk, chance, and possibility. None of those is a fact word. When you take a chance, risk, and the time, anything can be possible. The fear of failure is the greatest barrier."

Sarah sat quietly as she thought about it. General Wigmore had put great confidence in her. She secretly also was trying to prove herself to her father. Deep down, even further within herself, she needed to prove to herself that she was more than a lost woman and outcast from a family she never knew. After thinking about it she decided what she needed to do was to be herself and let the chips fall where they may. She knew the one thing she could count on was the love of her father and her husband.

"I have decided that we should go," Sarah finally said with confidence. "I put you, Dad, in charge of making the arrangements. You're very good at that sort of stuff."

"I will get right on it," her father answered.

Sarah called an end to the meeting and they all went upstairs to the dining room where the other sisters had prepared tea and cake.

Following the tea break, Ted made contact with General Wigmore to tell them of the plan. The general approved and said he would make the arrangements for a place for them to stay.

As much as Sister Clara wanted to go, she decided it would be best to stay at the archives and continue to do research and see if any new information could be found.

***

Knowing that the trip to Norwich from Ted's House would take at least four hours Sarah, Alex and Ted decided to go back to the house and prepare for the trip while Clara would continue with her search.

Back at the house, while Ted and Sarah prepared dinner, Alex rested his leg and continued to read and reread the handwritten book that Clara had found. He was puzzled about what his ancestor had been trying to achieve, or did perhaps, in searching for Immortal Essence. As he read through the spells and incantations, it seemed to Alex that Arthur Dee was looking for a way to, not only preserve the magic within but to preserve the body to last forever, without either diminishing. But why? And did he find a way to do it? Perhaps the answer would be in his tomb if they found it.

While the three of them were having dinner and discussing what they might find, Sarah received a phone call from Sister Clara. Sarah put her phone on speaker so everyone could hear before she answered.

"Hello Sister," Sarah said answering. "Have you found something more?"

"Not really," Clara replied. "Some bad news I am afraid. Though the records are clear that Dee is buried at St George's church, my search into the church records does not show where in the church the tomb is located. I called the churchwarden and he told me the church seems to have no record of where his grave might be located. Also, according to him, they were not even aware that he was buried there. I sent a copy of the record to him via the internet to assure him that records did show he is there someplace. He told me anyone was welcome to come and look around but he was not aware of any grave or tomb with that name, so he would not be of much help."

Alex looked and Ted and then at Sarah for a reaction.

"What do you think?" Sarah asked looking back at her father and Alex.

"I think we should go anyway," Alex answered without hesitation. "Things often change when you are on the ground looking at it with your own eyes."

"I agree," Ted replied. "But it's your call Sarah, this is your mission."

Sarah thought for a moment relishing silently the idea that it was her choice.

"We're going anyway," Sarah answered back to Clara and the others. "Keep searching Sister Clara. You're good at what you do. I am sure you will find something more."

"Thank you and I will," Clara replied. "I will contact you if I find anything else. Have a safe trip and a good night."

After Sarah ended the call Alex and her father looked at her and smiled.

"Good call, I have faith that you made the right decision," Alex said as he stood and hobbled over to his wife to kiss her. "You make me glad I married you more each day."

Ted did the washing up while Alex and Sarah headed to their room to finish packing for the trip to Norwich.

After they finished packing, Sarah and Alex got ready for bed. Alex climbed into bed next to Sarah as he always did to hold her and kiss her goodnight. Sarah stopped him. Putting her finger on his lips she looked into his eyes in a way Alex had never seen before.

"There is something I have to tell you," Sarah began. "The thing is, I would like what I am going to tell you to remain between you and me for now. I would like it to remain between us until after we complete this mission or until I tell you it's ok to let it out."

Alex was feeling nervous. He had promised in the past to never try to read her thoughts, so he felt unsure of what was coming.

"Yes, Love," Alex answered. "What is it? Is something wrong? Are you alright?

"We are just fine," Sarah replied smiling.

It took a moment for Alex to pick up on the answer.

"We?" Alex asked with his eyes wide. "Are you?"

"Yes, I am," Sarah said still smiling. "You're going to be a father."

Alex sat up in the bed and looked at Sarah with a huge smile. Sarah sat up with him.

Alex grabbed Sarah and hugged and kissed her. Pulling back, he looked at Sarah with tears in his eyes.

"It is wonderful," he said wiping away the tears that had welded up in his eyes. "I love you so much."

Sarah pulled him back to her and held him tight.

"I am a bit afraid," She whispered in his ear.

"Why?" Alex asked pushing her back to look in her eyes. "Afraid of what?"

"My mother died after giving birth to me," Sarah answered. "What if it happens to me?"

"Nothing is going to happen to you. You are not your mother and this is your life, not hers. I will make sure you have the best care. Perhaps she didn't die from giving you birth but of a broken heart from not being able to marry your father. You are loved and married to me and you have your father too. With that much love, I am sure nothing will happen to you."

Alex's words brought some comfort to Sarah, but the fear still lingered. Though the idea of her mother dying of a broken heart had never entered her mind. She had seen her side of the family. Perhaps Alex was right.

Sarah again pulled Alex close to her and held him tight. They held each other for a long time kissing and smiling eventually falling asleep holding each other close.

***

The following morning, everyone was up by 6 am to get ready to leave for the trip ahead.

Circles in Stone

At breakfast, Ted noticed a change in both Sarah and Alex. They each kept looking at the other and smiling. He decided not to ask and focus on the day ahead. He had been awakened early by a call from General Wigmore. The General informed him that rooms had been booked for the three of them at Norwich's oldest hotel. The Maids Head on Palace Street. It is just across the street from Norwich Cathedral and only 125 yards from the Church of St George where Arthur Dee is buried. The General said he knew the hotel manager and was assured that special accommodations would be reserved for them when they arrived.

Sarah cleared up from breakfast while her father loaded his Land Rover with their bags. Alex made sure he did not forget his case containing special amulets and wands that he always carried with him when he traveled.

Soon they began the four-hour, 220-mile trip to Norwich. The trip would take them through nine of England's counties including the one they were leaving from.

Ted drove while Sarah and Alex, sitting in the rear seat, were discussing and going over and over Dee's handwritten book looking for anything that they might have missed that could help them find the tomb. The book and notes still puzzled Alex. Alex had now concluded that it was a very elaborate magic spell. It also contained recipes for potions that were also part of the spell. The more he studied it and discussed it with Sarah, he came to the conclusion that it was the longest and most complex incantation he had ever seen. Yet its true overall purpose remained a mystery.

The time seemed to have flown past fast. They were soon on the streets of Norwich. None of them had ever been to the city before. They were surprised at how beautiful it was with so many tree-lined streets. New buildings mixed smoothly with the old ones. Flint and stone churches seemed to be around every corner. Some were only a block from others.

Following the stat map, they soon arrived at the Maids Head Hotel in the heart of the city. Stepping out of the car they could all see the 315-foot spire of the Norwich Cathedral just across the road

Circles in Stone

The Maid's Head had the look of a Tudor building. Even though the exterior was made to look old, the heart of the building itself was very old, with parts of it dating back to its beginning in the 11th century. It had hosted some very historical people in the past. The first Bishop of Norwich made his palace there in 1094. Catherine of Aragon, King Henry the 8th first wife, stayed there in 1520, and later his daughter Queen Elizabeth 1st, visited in 1587.

At check-in, Alex and Sarah learned that they had been booked in the Queen Elizabeth 1st suite, which was said to be the very room she stayed in on her visit. Knowing that Elizabeth had visited made Alex wonder if his ancestor, Arthur Dee's father, John Dee, had also visited. John Dee was after all part of the Queen's court.

Parts of Alex and Sarah's room was like stepping back in time, while others were modern. The blend of past and present seemed to flow together seamlessly. Sarah was very pleased to see the medieval fireplace. The sitting area in front of it would make the perfect spot to gather and discuss the mission and share information.

Alex decided to lay on the bed, which looked like it came from a royal palace, and rest while Sarah changed and freshened up after the long trip.

Ted's room was the Filby Junior Suite, high in the gables. With its exposed oak beams that had seen much history themselves. It looked small but there was plenty of room. The décor of the room had Ted written all over it.

By the time they were all settled into their rooms, it was lunchtime. They found the dining at the restaurant was as grand as the hotel itself.

After lunch, they all wasted no time following Ted's phone map to the church of St George.

Out of the hotel entrance, across the road, and past the Grand Gate of the Cathedral on Tombland Street. Across that street and up Princes Street a very short distance stood the church they were looking for.

The church is a flint-constructed building sporting a tower with a blue clock on it and nestled tight among the buildings all around it. A church was recorded on the site as early as the 11th century, however, the core of the current church is from the 15th century.

Circles in Stone

They passed through an iron gate and into a small graveyard that extended out along the length of the church. Trying the church doors Ted discovered it was locked and a sign saying it would not be open until after 2 pm. It was now 1 pm so they had an hour to kill. Alex decided they should search the graveyard and the gravestones. Perhaps one would have a clue on it. Sarah knew from her experience that finding a gravestone from the 17th century outside a church was very rare. Most people from that period that could not afford to be buried inside the church were buried with no grave markers. Outside grave markers were more of an 18th-century invention.

As they were looking at the gravestones, they noticed a man unlocking the church. All three of them made a becline for the church. Once inside the churchwarden greeted them. Sarah told him they were visitors interested in old churches and wanted to look around and take pictures. He handed them all guides and said they were welcome to do so and could take as many pictures as they wanted to.

The warden disappeared into a side room near the rear of the church leaving them alone in the main church. The church was well beautifully decorated. With banners, statutes of St George and the dragon, and carved angels looking down from each roof's rafters, it was filled with color and life.

The layout was typical of churches of the period. There is a 13th-century marble font at the rear of the nave, topped with a magnificent carved wooden cover.

A central aisle with two side aisles. The north aisle contained a beautiful Victorian organ. All along the floor were a great number of tomb markers. These became the immediate focus of Sarah and Ted.

Alex, meanwhile, sat down in a pew near the rear to read the guidebook from which he learned that there were more than 4000 graves located in the churchyard. Alex thought to himself that this may be harder than he had hoped. The fact was that Alex had never really visited the inside of many England's medieval churches before. He would have to depend on Ted and Sarah to guide him if he had any chance of finding his ancestor's grave.

Chapter 43

The Jewel

While Sarah and Ted went about reading all the stone grave slabs on the floor. Alex sat in the pew continuing to read the guide and studying the layout of the building, when he suddenly felt a warm sensation come over him. He had felt that same feeling only once before in his life. It was when his father took him to the dragon's cave for the first time in Hawaii to show him the graves of his ancestors. His father opened the coffin of his grandfather to show him his remains. He remembered he stepped back when the feeling came over him. His father told him it was the magic energy from his grandfather flooding over him as it escaped the silver coffin. His father had explained to him that it was harmless and that only family members of the Merlin line could feel it.

Alex stood up and slowly walked toward the front of the church along the main aisle. Sarah and Ted were both watching him now. They both could see that something was happening to him.

"Are you alright?" Sarah asked him as she went to be next to him.

"I am alright," Alex answered as he continued to walk slowly up the aisle. "There is something here. I need quiet for a moment so I can concentrate."

Sarah stood to one side and signaled her father to stay where he was. Alex continued to walk slowly. The sensation was getting stronger with each step. He crossed over the transept and moved toward the main altar. Before he reached the altar, he stopped. Standing still for a moment he then turned left and walked toward the door of the sacristy. Reaching the door, he stopped again. He leaned his hand against the wall as if to steady himself. The sensation was so strong there that he found it hard to breathe. Alex signaled Sarah and Ted to join him.

When Sarah reached him, he looked at her. She could see his eyes seemed to be glowing.

"He, at least I think it is him," Alex said in a low strained voice. "Is here. Right here below my feet."

Looking down at the floor, Sarah saw that the threshold under the door was a grave marker. It had been painted red. She could make out that once there had been writing on the stone but had been worn off by the foot traffic over the years.

"I need to sit down," Alex said and he made his way to the first pew. Sarah sat next to him. The glow had gone from his eyes.

"I'm sure he must be here," Alex repeated. "He must have had powerful magical energy. But it's still so strong. I would have thought that it would have dispersed by now. Even my father's, coffin when I last opened it, did not have that kind of energy coming from it."

"If it is him, how are we going to get to him?" asked Sarah. "We can't just smash up the floor."

"You may not have to," Ted said as he stood next to them listening to the conversation. "Look there."

Ted was pointing to a slab on the floor in the center of the transept. Sarah got up to take a closer look. She could not believe her eyes. There, on the corner of the stone and carved into it in plain English were the words, "The Entrance of the Vault."

Alex now saw it too. They all looked at each other.

"There has to be a way to open it," Ted said.

"Maybe we should ask the churchwarden," Sarah suggested.

"I don't think that would be a good idea," Ted answered. "We don't want to tip him off of what we're doing here."

"Your right," Alex said. "Look around some more. Take pictures of everything."

"What if it's in one of the side rooms or the sacristy?" asked Sarah.

"We come back at night, like after midnight," Alex answered. "We carefully go over the pictures you take and contact Sister Clara and see if she can find anything."

"How do we get in?" asked Ted.

Sarah and Alex both looked at him and smiled.

"He's a wizard," Sarah said laughing quietly. "I don't think getting in is a problem."

Ted laughed, realizing how silly the question was.

After Sarah and Ted completed taking pictures, they all left for the hotel to go over what they had.

Circles in Stone

Alex called Sister Clara and explained to her what they had found so far.

"Can you shed any light on any of this? Alex asked Clara.

"Strange you should ask," Clara replied. "I was going over old notes from Sir Thomas Brown. He, for a brief time, was the Mayor of Norwich. I found a reference to that same church in his notes. The strange thing is, it is a poem that made no sense until now. I'll send you a copy via messenger. I have a feeling it is what you're looking for."

Alex ended the call and waited for the message. When it came through and he read it he smiled. Calling Sarah and Ted over he showed it to them. He then read it out loud.

"Anguish Am I

Anguish is the way to go, Anguish is the way below.

Her guild crown would fall down, when she is turned around.

Revealed now can be seen, the place forthwith to put the key.

First press the lady's gold above you find, Then his family crest press in line.

Pull right the column from the top and down, Reveals the way below the ground."

"It's instructions on how to open the vault," Sarah said with excitement in her voice.

"What kind of anguish does it mean," asked Ted.

"Anguish is not a kind," Sarah replied. "It's a name. It's the name of a family buried in the vault. Look."

Sarah pulled up one of the pictures she had taken from inside the church. It was a photo of a very ornate wall memorial to the Anguish family with deeply carved reliefs of all the family members.

"This family died before Dee did," Sarah continued. "But according to Dee's will, one of his daughters married an Anguish. So, there is a family connection. It fits perfectly. Dee, not having a vault of his own was allowed to be put in theirs. If you look at the detail in this picture you can see every detail described in the instructions on this plaque. And this plaque is located on the main wall just to the side of the vault entrance. The mechanism that operates the vault door must be in and just below that wall."

"What we need to do is go back there tonight and have a closer look," Alex said staring at the photo of the memorial plaque.

"There is a reference to a key," Ted responded.

Alex and Sarah looked at him and smiled. Ted realized too late that anything that needed a key was not an obstacle for Alex.

"What about the energy you felt?" Sarah asked Alex with concern.

Alex went to the nightstand to get his special case. Opening it he took out a beautiful amulet, one that Sarah had never seen before. It was made with a heavy silver chain. At the end of the chain hung a 3-inch diameter silver ring, at the center of the ring was a clear crystal in a silver cage. From the cage to the ring a seven-pointed star, also made of silver, held it all together.

"This will take care of it, Alex replied. "This will deflect and absorb any excess energy that might be omitted. The silver will gather the energy and focus it on the crystal, which is the highest-grade clear quartz. Commonly known as a Herkimer diamond. The crystal will store the energy until it can be dispersed in the light of a full moon."

"I'll trust you on that one," Sarah replied grinning.

Sarah called Clara back and thanked her for the information and would let her know how it all turned out.

Since it was still early in the evening, they all decided to walk over and visit the Cathedral.

Sarah took her notebook with her. Because it was a Norman Cathedral and not so much a Medieval one, she wanted to record anything that might be useful at some later date in her research.

They were all impressed with its grand interior. They spend the better part of two hours just walking around taking it all in. As they left it had just begun to get dark. They hung around outside to watch as the spire slowly began to glow from the floodlights cast upon it as the sun went down. They all agreed it was truly an inspiring sight.

From there they decided to go back to the Maid's Head for dinner and to have a rest before it was time to return to St George's for their midnight visit.

Ted met with Sarah and Alex in their room around 11:30 pm. He had three small high-powered flashlights, which he always carried several in his Land Rover. They all dressed in dark clothing to break up their profile in the dim lights of the street.

Alex put on his amulet and placed one of his wands in a holster under his jacket and put a small pouch of something in his pocket.

All three set out for the church at midnight sharp. When they left the hotel, they noticed how quiet the streets were. Barely any traffic and only a few pedestrians off in the distance.

Ted and Sarah stayed back as Alex went ahead so he could open the gate.

When Alex arrived at the iron gate outside the church, he pulled out his wand and touched it to the padlock which immediately opened. Using his phone, he signaled Sarah to let her know that she and Ted could now join him.

By the time they arrived, Alex was already inside the church and using his magic had shut down the alarm system.

Once inside the church, Ted indicated that perhaps he should remain outside in the church porch as a lookout. Sarah thought it was a good idea and agreed to it.

Alex stopped Sarah just inside the church. He took out the small pouch from his pocket and poured a black powder from it into his hand. He threw the powder in the air and waved his wand at the same time. In an instant, the powder grew in mass, divided up, and went to every window in the building covering them with a black film.

"We can now use our lights without being seen," Alex said as he turned on his flashlight. "That will last for hours or until I recall it. It should give us enough time to do what we came for."

Wasting no time, Sarah headed to where she remembered the plaque being. Alex followed her. When he got to her, he looked at his amulet. It was already lightly glowing.

Sarah set to work following the instructions from the poem that Clara had sent.

She found the image of a woman wearing a crown and turned it until her image was upside down. It then swung out revealing a keyhole.

"Time to do your thing," Sarah said to Alex pointing at the keyhole.

Alex placed the point of his wand at the keyhole and heard something in the wall make a loud click. Sarah then pressed the gold egg above Lady Anguish's image which caused another click to come from the wall. She then pressed the one above her husband's image upon which was the family crest. A clanking noise followed, also coming from inside the wall. Sarah then reached up and took hold of the top of the decorative column on the right side of the plaque and pulled it down. It pulled hard at first then gave way suddenly. The sound of metal chains and stones sliding was heard coming from the center of the church floor. Alex shone his light toward the sound and saw the floor open. He and Sarah both hurried over and shone their lights down the now open hole. In front of them was a staircase leading down into the darkness below.

Sarah and Alex looked at each other and smiled.

"Normally I would say ladies first," remarked Alex. "But perhaps I should go."

Sarah nodded shining her light on the stairs as Alex descended taking his time because of his leg. When he reached the bottom, he signaled to Sarah to join him. It was now his turn to shine the light as Sarah carefully climbed down.

When she reached the bottom, they stood together and shined their lights to get a look around. They were at least 10 feet below the church floor. A wall ran across the entire room behind the stairs. The room extended toward the front of the church at least fifty feet and was as wide as both the nave and the north aisle. All around the room were coffins of all sizes and shapes. Some ornate, some simple.

"Which one is it?" Sarah asked. "How are we going to find it in all this."

"With this," Alex said, holding the amulet on his chest. "Turn off your light."

She did as he asked. Once her eyes adjusted to the darkness, she could see faint streams of light flowing to the amulet coming from someplace in front of them.

"Follow me," Alex instructed her.

She followed him as he slowly walked forward, covering his flashlight with his hand, allowing just enough light for him to see the floor. He followed the stream of light entering his amulet toward the front of the church about 20 feet and stopped. He then turned left, just like he did during the day on the floor above.

In about 10 feet he stopped. The amulet on his chest was glowing enough to emit light.

Alex took his hand off his flashlight and shone it on a coffin in front of him. He waited for Sarah to join him at his side.

"This is it," Alex said in a whisper as he removed the dust from the top of the coffin.

"How can you be sure it's him?"

"You see this strange symbol here on the top of the coffin? The stick-like figure that sort of looks like a person wearing a crescent moon on its head. That is the astrological sign that his father created. It represents the sun, the moon, and all the elements. It's him alright."

Alex looked around the coffin with his light to see if there was a way to open it. Seeing none he took out his wand and tapped on the lid three times.

It slowly raised and Alex floated it to the side and set it on the floor.

They both now shined their light into the coffin. They could see that the coffin was lead-lined. And the body was covered in a blue shroud.

"We need to look for a clue," Sarah said looking intently at Alex. "He's your descendant, I will leave the searching to you. I will hold the light."

Alex slowly pulled back the shroud and they both got the shock of their life. There before them was a man that looked like he had been buried yesterday. His body and his clothes were in perfect condition.

"How is that possible?" Sarah asked with a tremble in her voice. "And where is the clue?"

Alex looked the body over more closely. He noticed that one of his hands was over his chest covered in a green velvet cloth while the other was down along his side.

"Maybe he is holding it," Alex replied as he reached to move the cloth from over his hand.

When he pulled it back, he gasped, and stepped back from the coffin.

Sarah saw what he saw, not understanding, reached for it.

Alex grabbed her hand and pulled it back.

"NO! don't touch it," he almost shouted.

"What is it?" Sarah asked annoyed.

"It's the Jewel!" Alex answered breathing heavily. "The Jewel of Power and Authority. The one everyone has been looking for."

Alex stepped back to the coffin and shone his light closely on his hand. There clasped between his thumb and forefinger was the amber orb containing the dragon's tooth. Sarah looked at it closer. She had never seen a picture of it so she didn't know what it looked like.

"All the fuss has been over that?" Sarah inquired as if annoyed.

"Yes. That was once in the pommel of the sword Excalibur that King Arthur had. And now here it is in the hand of my ancestor, Arthur Dee. It all makes sense now with the handwritten book. Immortal Essence. He found a way to preserve his magical essence along with his body so he could protect the Jewel forever. The power of the Jewel would remain intact without passing it on to any more descendants. He knew what a burden it was to protect it and he didn't want that for future generations. Even if the Merlin line died out the Jewel would still hold its power. His body continues to generate magical energy just as it did when he was alive. He perfected eternal mana."

"What do we do now?" Sarah asked with wonder in her eyes.

"Nothing. We leave it where it is. It could not be safer or in better hands than where it is."

Alex used his phone to take a picture of it. He then put the velvet cloth back as he had found it. Taking one last look, he covered Arthur's body once again with the shroud and replaced the lid on the coffin, while Sarah held the light in silence.

They both climbed the stairs without saying a word, and flipped the column lever back on the Anguish plaque, which closed the vault.

Once the vault was closed Alex went to Sarah took her in his arms and held her close.

"Thank you" Alex whispered in her ear. "For everything."

Sarah kissed him and smiled.

"Thank you," she said. "I personally think that what we learned here tonight will make us and our family safer than ever. But what will we report back to the General?"

"I think," Alex said. "You should tell the truth. Say in your report that Arthur Dee left a message in his coffin that the Jewel is safe and will be forever, and that where it is, he took with him to his grave."

Chapter 44

New Beginnings

Sarah and Alex sat in the church after finding the Jewel and decided that what they had seen and found must remain between them, at least for now. They both agreed that if news leaked out that the Jewel was there it would put a lot of people in danger. Alex knew the Morgans well enough to know they would raise the church to the ground if necessary to find it. What the ODR would do was anyone's guess.

Sarah agreed with that and added that finding it would raise a lot of other questions and problems. Such as who owned it, where should it be stored, and how did it affect written history? They agreed that the official story from them would be that there was a message in Arthur Dee's coffin that said the Jewel was safe and protected and that only he knew where it was.

They continued to sit in the church a while longer enjoying the peace and quiet, while contemplating the discovery that only they now knew existed. Sarah finally broke the silence.

"I think my father is still outside keeping watch," she said smiling. "I am sure he is worried about us, so perhaps we should let him know we're alright."

"I think your right," Alex replied. But before we do, I just want to say that your father is a very good man. I would say he is one of the best I have ever met. I am not saying that because he is your father. I would say the same thing even if he wasn't."

"Thank you. I will tell him you said that."

As they stood up to leave, Alex asked Sarah to turn off her flashlight. Once she did, Alex took out the pouch again from his pocket. Waving his wand, the black powder came off the windows, formed a dense cloud, and flowed, as if it were alive, back into the pouch.

They took one last look around the church now in the dark and opened the door to find Ted waiting for them. Alex told him and Sarah to head back toward the hotel while he used his magic to reset the alarms and lock the doors and gate.

They all met once again in Alex and Sarah's room. Since it was Sarah's mission, Alex let her explain to her father what they had found according to what she and Alex agreed on.

"That pretty much settles it then," Ted responded to what she told him. "We know it's out there somewhere and it's safe, that's all that counts. Mission complete, well-done Sarah."

"Yes, it is," Sarah answered. "I will write up an official report to give to General Wigmore and let him handle it from there."

"I think we should celebrate," Ted said as he got up and found some wine and some glasses.

Ted poured a small amount wine in each of the glasses and handed one each to Alex and Sarah.

"To my daughter, Ranger Sarah," Ted said raising his glass. "A father couldn't be prouder."

"Here, here," Alex responded as they all drank the wine down in one go.

Since it was near dawn, they all found themselves wanting to sleep and headed for bed.

***

They all slept in late the next day. Even Ted found himself being awakened by a call from General Wigmore at about 11 am. He explained to the General why he was late calling him and what Sarah had told him was found, and she would write a full report once they returned to the headquarters. The General was pleased and told him that they need not hurry back. Ted was sure Alex and Sarah would be glad to hear that.

Sarah and Alex got up around noon and ordered room service for breakfast. Sarah called her father after breakfast and learned about his call from Wigmore. She then called Sister Clara and told her she could keep looking if she liked but as far as she was concerned the mission was over.

With no hurry to get back they all decided to get together later and drive around the City of Norwich the rest of the day. They would leave for SGM headquarters the following morning.

During breakfast, Alex wondered what they would do after concluding the mission at SGM.

"We can do our proper honeymoon now," Alex said. "I was wondering where you would like to go?"

"To the lake district in Cumbria," Sarah answered without hesitation. "I love that area. I used to go there when I was younger and miss it."

"The lake district it is then," he replied. "I know very little about the area but I will make it my responsibility to learn about it and to find a place to stay."

"Wonderful. I look forward to what you find. You are welcome to use my computer if you like. I have also decided to tell my father about our future child once we are back at his house."

"That is a good idea. He deserves to be kept in the loop."

Alex hobbled over and kissed Sarah on the forehead as she got ready for the day.

Once Alex and Sarah joined with her father, Ted wondered if it might be better to walk around Norwich than drive if Alex was up to it. Alex said he could do it if they took breaks now and then. It was agreed and they set off.

They found the city wonderful to walk. The blend of the old and new buildings. The many shops, cafes, and pubs that seemed to be around every corner. Sarah found the marketplace wonderful.

As the day came to a close, they found a wonderful place to have dinner, called The Lamb. A restaurant pub tucked away among other buildings just off the marketplace with only a sign giving away its location.

After dinner, they all enjoyed a leisurely walk back to the Maids' Head to pack for the long trip the next day. The plan was to leave by 8 am and be at SGM headquarters by noon just in time for lunch.

***

The next morning everything went as planned. They began their 4-hour trip to Marlborough at just before 8 am. Sarah decided she would drive the first part of the trip with her father taking over halfway and completing the journey. Alex felt bad he could not help with the driving but because of his leg couldn't drive a manual transmission vehicle.

They arrived in Marlborough just before noon and headed straight to SGM headquarters where Sarah used her new ring for the first time to enter. Her hand was scanned and she walked straight in feeling proud that she was truly a full member.

Once inside, they all headed straight to Wigmore's office where they found he had lunch waiting for them.

After a lunch of choice sandwiches and cold drinks, they went right to work.

"I have finished my report of our finding and loaded it onto a flash drive for you," Sarah said handing the General the drive. "In my opinion, it would be a waste of resources to pursue this any further."

Putting the flash drive into his computer the General read over her report while the others waited for his response.

"This is a very fine report," the General finally said. "I agree with your assessment. I also believe it would be a good idea to leak a report to the public, that the pursuit of an ancient artifact that might have proved or disproved the existence of King Arthur was followed up and proved to be a fruitless endeavor. This would be picked up by the ODR and the Morgans. They would understand the true meaning of it and hopefully stop, or at least, slow any further pursuit."

"That sounds like a good idea," Ted replied. "Perhaps we can get back to things that are more important right now. I am not saying that the search for the Jewel was not important but with the drug and immigration problems the country has, I think, resources could be better spent."

"This is true," replied Wigmore, "However I would still like you as our point man on tracking the actions of the ODR and Morgans. These people still present a real threat and to ignore them would be fool hearty."

"I understand General," Ted replied. "Will be happy to continue that work, Sir."

"I believe my work is done for now," Sarah broke in. "Myself and Alex have not had a proper honeymoon and would like to take time for one. When I return, I would like to follow up on my other work, if you don't mind."

"Of course," Ranger Sarah," The General answered. "Please do go but keep in touch when you get back. You are a great asset and I am sure your father is very proud of you."

Ted looked at Sarah and smiled. She knew what that smile meant. "And what will you be doing Alex?" asked the General.

"I was thinking of getting a work visa and doing some research on the volcanos both ancient and active here in Europe. I'll return to Hawaii from time to time and take my beautiful wife with me and do some surfing together."

They all laughed as they prepared to leave. Wigmore said his goodbyes and wished them all luck and safe travels.

***

Leaving Marlborough, they headed for Ted's home in Salisbury. It was only an hour's drive and it felt good to relax once they arrived. The plan was for Alex and Sarah to spend the night and head for her home in the morning.

That evening at dinner Sarah told her father she had something to tell him.

"Dad," Sarah said smiling. "You're going to be a grandfather."

Ted stopped midway of putting a piece of steak into his mouth. He put his fork down and looked at both her and Alex, not knowing what to say. Finally, after a long pause, he stood up.

"That calls for a drink," he said going to his bar and taking out a bottle of Jack Daniels whiskey.

Pouring some into two glasses and handing one to Alex.

"To my special daughter," he said, as he raised his glass. "That has made the two men in this room the happiest on earth."

Alex and Ted drank the glasses empty in one go and they each took a turn kissing Sarah. Ted on her cheek and Alex on her lips.

***

The next morning, as Alex and Sarah had breakfast and packed for their trip to her house, they could hear Ted busy talking on the phone. When Sarah asked him what it was all about, he simply answered,

"You'll find out later."

Ted helped load the car and said his goodbyes and wished them a wonderful trip.

The drive to Sarah's house was 1 1/2 hours but went by quickly. Along the way, Alex completed the plans for their honeymoon to the Lake District. Keeping it a secret, he did wish he could help with the

383

driving. Where they would be going was at least a 5 ½ hour drive. He even wondered if perhaps he should rent a car with an automatic transmission so he could share the driving.

Just as Sarah was entering her drive, she notices two men unloading a car from a truck. She looked at Alex. He shrugged his shoulders and shook his head to indicate he had no clue what was going on.

Sarah got out of the car and went immediately to them with Alex not far behind.

"Sarah Rowland Michaels?" One of the men asked looking down at some paperwork.

"Yes, that would be me," Sarah answered.

"This is for you," The man said handing her an envelope.

Opening it she read the contents. With tears coming to her eyes, she read it to Alex.

"To my dearest Sarah and your husband and dear friend Alex. I never got you a proper wedding present. Because of the pride you two have brought to my heart and the joy of knowing you are with child; I hope you'll receive my humble gift to take on your honeymoon. Alex let me know how much he wished he could drive so I made sure it is and automatic. Your loving father, Ted."

The car they were unloading was a Silver Range Rover Velar. Sarah hugged and kissed Alex as they finished unloading it. She now knew what all the phone calls were just before they left her father's house. One of the men handed her the keys as Alex and she looked it over. She thought to herself, "She truly did have the best father in the world".

The rest of the day was spent packing and getting ready for their trip north. During dinner, Alex revealed that it was very hard to find a place to stay on such short notice, but did book a long-term stay at the Armathwaite Hall Hotel and Spa. He managed to get the Deluxe Lake view room with its view down the length of Bassenthwaite Lake. He had also arranged for Sarah to have all the spa had to offer. He thought it would be good for her in her condition.

Sarah was more than pleased with his choice and told him he had done very well. She had never been to a place with a spa, so she was looking forward to it.

***

Circles in Stone

The next morning, Sarah couldn't wait to get going and try out their new vehicle. After getting used to where everything was, they were off on the long drive. Sarah loved the new car and didn't want to stop driving it. Being an automatic it was so easy to drive. She remembered how much fun it was when she first drove one in Hawaii.

After 2 hours she let Alex drive for a while. It took him a while to get used to driving on the left side of the road but soon he had the hang of it as they headed up the M6 to their destination. When they reached the A66 Sarah took back over and completed the trip to the hotel.

They found the hotel grand and wonderful. The rest of the day Sarah spent unpacking and finished with a dip in the spa pool. Meanwhile, Alex was preparing for a special trip out for the following day.

***

After a wonderful night in the hotel, they had breakfast the next morning in the hotel's restaurant, where Alex told Sarah about his planned outing. He had the hotel arrange a packed lunch for them to take with them to the special location 12 miles away just outside Keswick. The Castlerigg stone circle.

This stone circle was said to be older than Stonehenge. Alex's plan was to have a picnic in the center of the circle.

Following the car's GPS, Sarah found the place easy enough. When they arrived, Sarah commented on the wonderful views of the mountains on all sides. Such a short distance from Keswick, you would never know a town was close by.

Alex, even with his leg still in a cast, helped carry the lunch and two folding chairs to the circle's center. He then went back to the car and brought his special bag containing his magic items.

Alex arranged the chairs so they were facing each other as close as possible. Sarah was wondering what he was doing but did not ask. She had learned to trust him in such things.

Once seated and each had a cool drink, Alex opened his bag and took out a stone pendulum on the end of a gold chain.

Finally, getting the best of her, Sarah had to ask, "What is that for?"

"This is to tell what sex the child you are carrying is," he answered. "But I will only do it with your permission."

"Yes," Sarah replied smiling widely. "Does it always work?"

"Yes, my mother taught me this; it has never failed to be right.

Alex took the pendulum and held it still over Sarah's belly. After a short pause, the pendulum began to swing in a straight line back and forth. Sarah noticed that Alex's hand did not move. The longer he held it the stronger the swing became.

"It's a boy," Alex said after a while of them both watching it swing. "If it had swung in a circle, it would mean it was a girl."

Sarah just smiled as he put the pendulum back in his bag and took out a case that Sarah had never seen before.

"Again, I need your permission for this," he said as he opened the case. This is most important. Every member of my family has been named using this magic."

He took out a small square board from the case and opened it in four directions that locked together to form a larger board. The board was covered with all sorts of symbols. Out of the same case, he took a small bag. He put his hand inside the bag and took out a hand full of round polished amethyst crystals, each having what Sarah knew to be runic letters carved into them.

"It's up to you now," Alex said looking at Sarah. "Whatever name is shown on the runes will be the child's name."

Sarah thought long and hard. Looking around her at where she was, she knew that the magic would be true and real. After a long pause, in which Alex did not push her in any way, she decided to go ahead.

Alex placed the board on her lap and made sure it was level. He then took out a wand and tapped the board three times. Putting the wand away he held the bag open to Sarah.

"You must draw the letters," Alex told her. "There are two of each letter in the bag. You can draw as many as you like at a time but can be no more than 12 total. Count them unseen in the bag. Once you have drawn them keep them in your other hand unseen until you have a number you are satisfied with.

Sarah reached into the bag and Alex could see she was counting. She took out a total of seven letters in one draw.

"Do you have all you want?"

Sarah nodded yes, so he put the bag away in his case.

"Now, start on your right and put down one rune at a time in a straight row to your left until they are all laid out.

As Sarah began to lay them out, a breeze began to blow. With each letter, the breeze got stronger. When she placed the last letter, the breeze turned into a gush of wind that nearly pushed the board off of her lap. She held the board firm until the wind suddenly stopped.

Alex had seen the letters as she laid them out. He felt a chill and then a warm sensation come over him when the last letter was laid down. Sarah knew some runes but couldn't read them the way Alex could.

"What do they say?" She asked anxiously.

Alex hesitated for a moment and then told her.

"In English, they spelled out the letters M -Y- R- D- D- I -N," Alex told her watching close for her reaction.

"That's the old word for Merlin," Sarah replied surprised. "What does it mean?"

"It means," Alex said. "You are carrying the next Merlin. The one that will bring back Arthur Pendragon. It means our child in your womb will bring about new beginnings in the Circles of Stone.

As they sat together in the center of the stone circle each thinking about the future. Alex wondered if finding the Jewel was the will of the ancestors and a new thought entered his mind. All those generations before were to bring this one into being. Perhaps it wasn't them, the Merlin line, that protected the Jewel but the Jewel that had protected them instead. Looking at Sarah he could see she had a question.

"What is it my dearest wife," he asked.

"I was just wondering, after I felt the wind, if the first Merlin had once been here too?"

"I can't say for sure but I suspect he was. But one thing I know for sure now.

"What's that?" she asked.

"He is here now," Alex answered with a smile as he kissed Sarah.

END

Printed in Great Britain
by Amazon